EDISON BEAKER

CREATURE SEEKER

THE LOST CITY

BY FRANK CAMMUSO

VIKING

For AiVy, Khai, and Van,
the original Creature Seekers
— F.C.

VIKING
An imprint of Penguin Random House LLC, New York

First published in the United States of America by Viking,
an imprint of Penguin Random House LLC, 2019

Copyright © 2019 by Frank Cammuso
Color assist by Peter Sieburg

Visit us online at penguinrandomhouse.com

LIBRARY OF CONGRESS CATALOGING-IN-PUBLICATION DATA IS AVAILABLE.
ISBN 9780425291955 (hardcover); ISBN 9780425291962 (paperback)

Manufactured in China

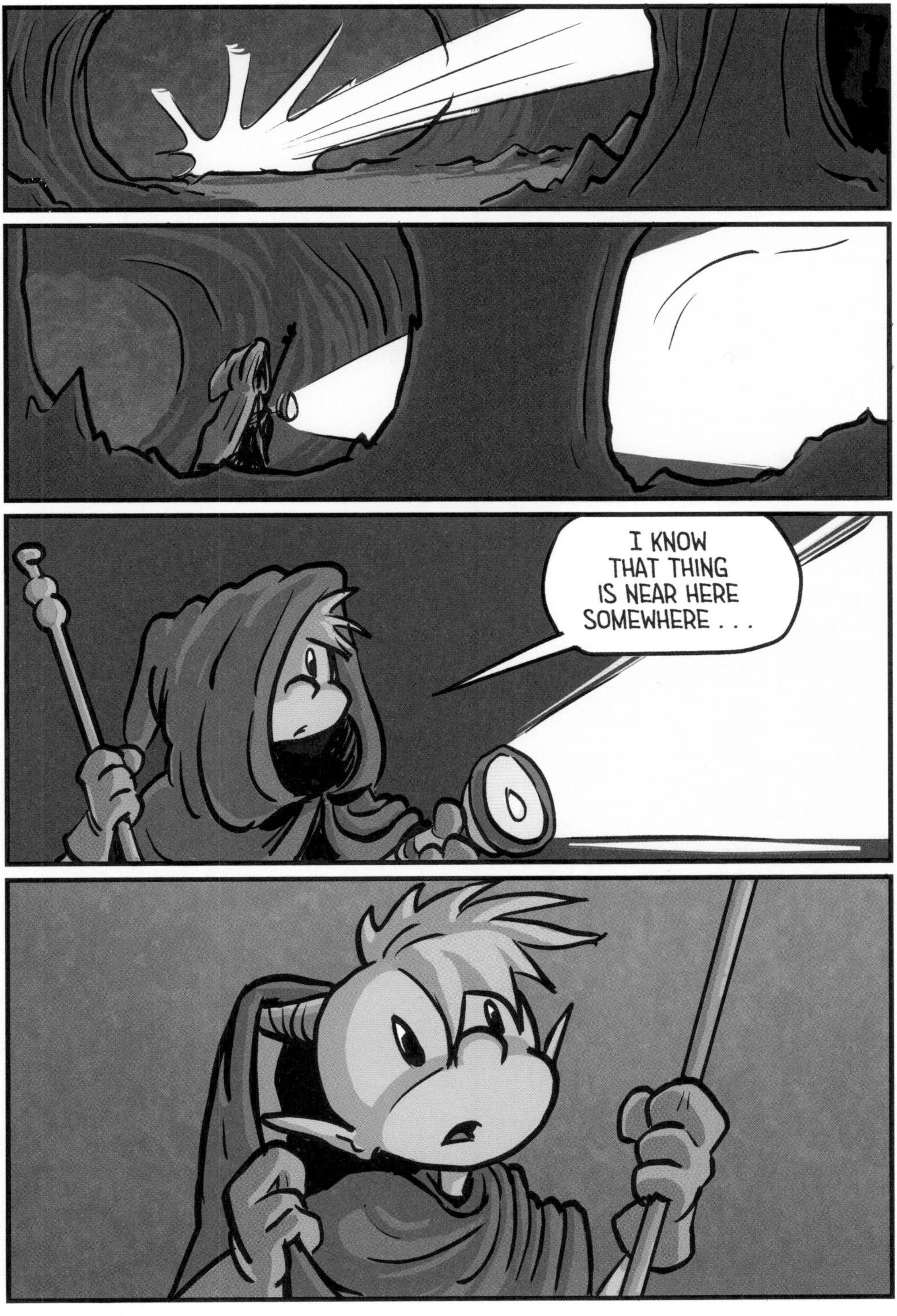
I KNOW THAT THING IS NEAR HERE SOMEWHERE . . .

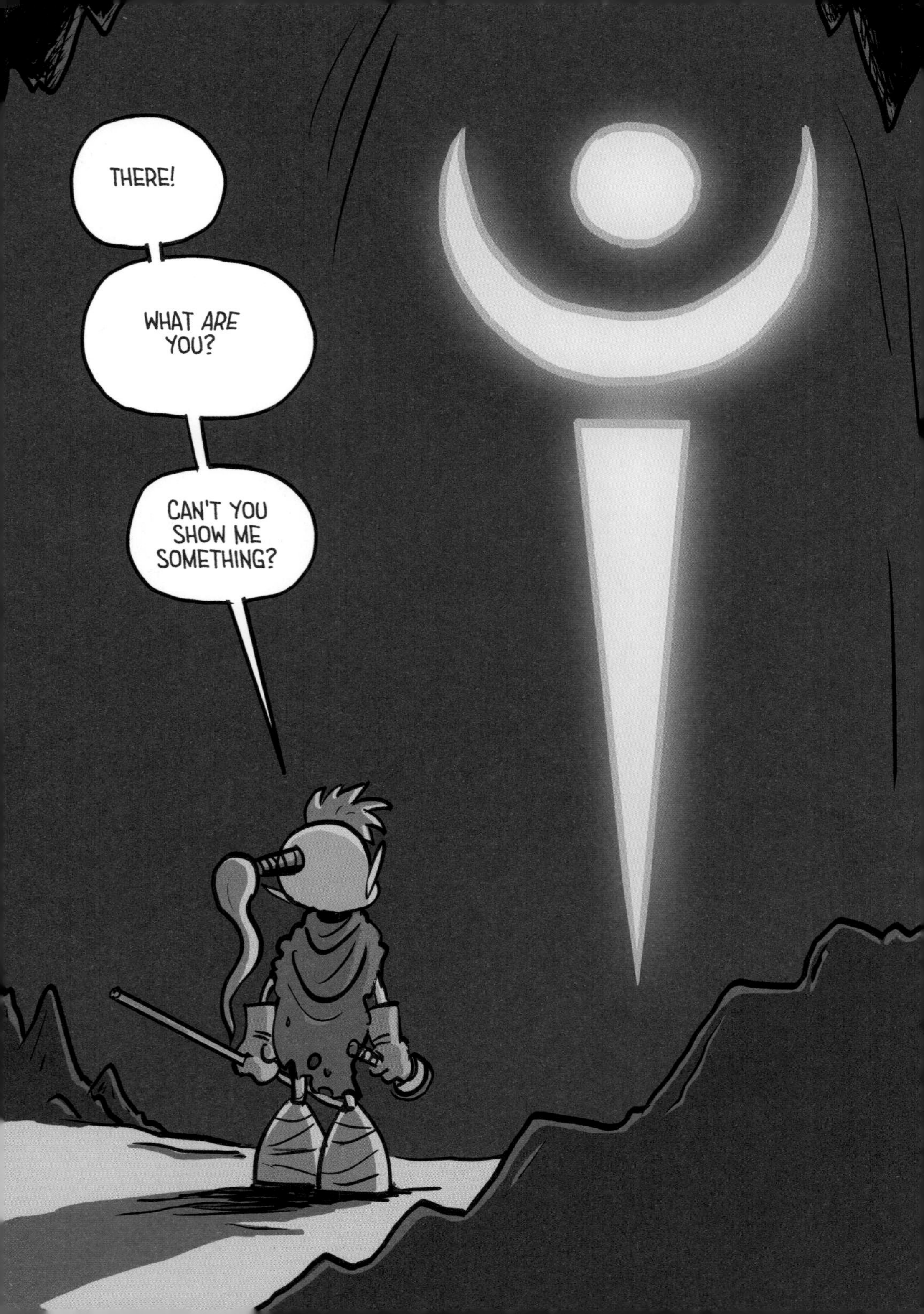
THERE!
WHAT *ARE* YOU?
CAN'T YOU SHOW ME SOMETHING?

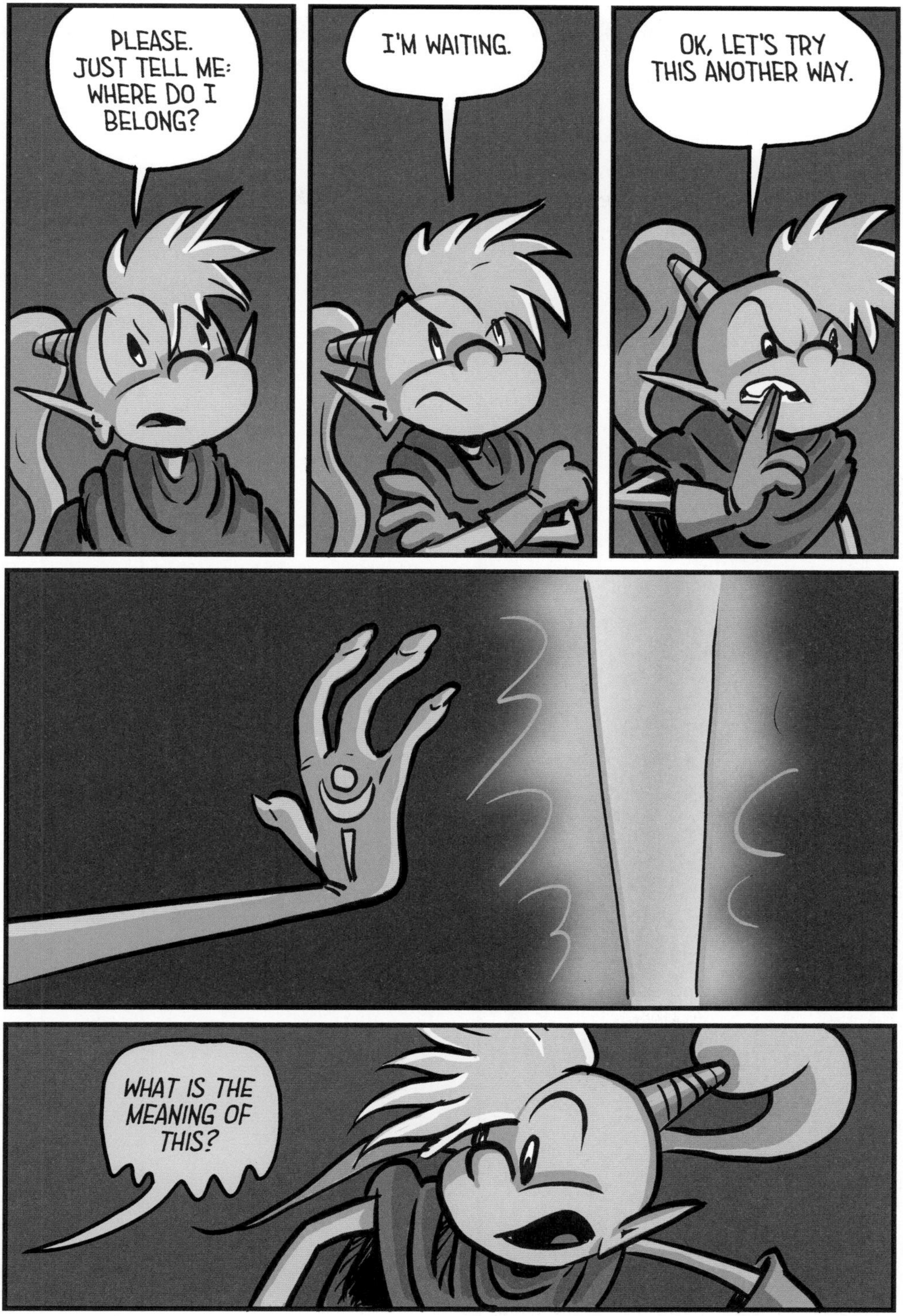
PLEASE. JUST TELL ME: WHERE DO I BELONG?
I'M WAITING.
OK, LET'S TRY THIS ANOTHER WAY.
WHAT IS THE MEANING OF THIS?

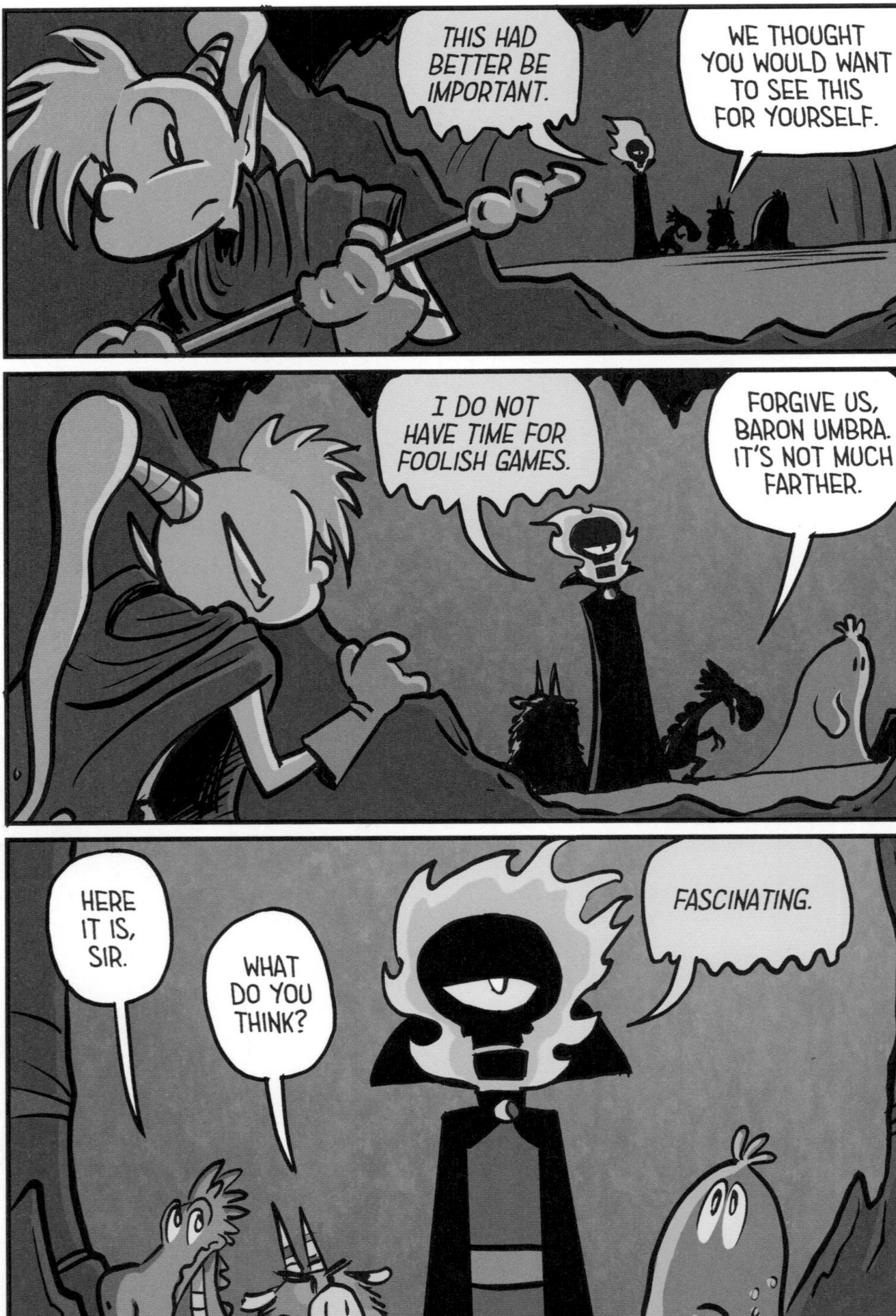
THIS HAD BETTER BE IMPORTANT.
WE THOUGHT YOU WOULD WANT TO SEE THIS FOR YOURSELF.
I DO NOT HAVE TIME FOR FOOLISH GAMES.
FORGIVE US, BARON UMBRA. IT'S NOT MUCH FARTHER.
HERE IT IS, SIR.
WHAT DO YOU THINK?
FASCINATING.

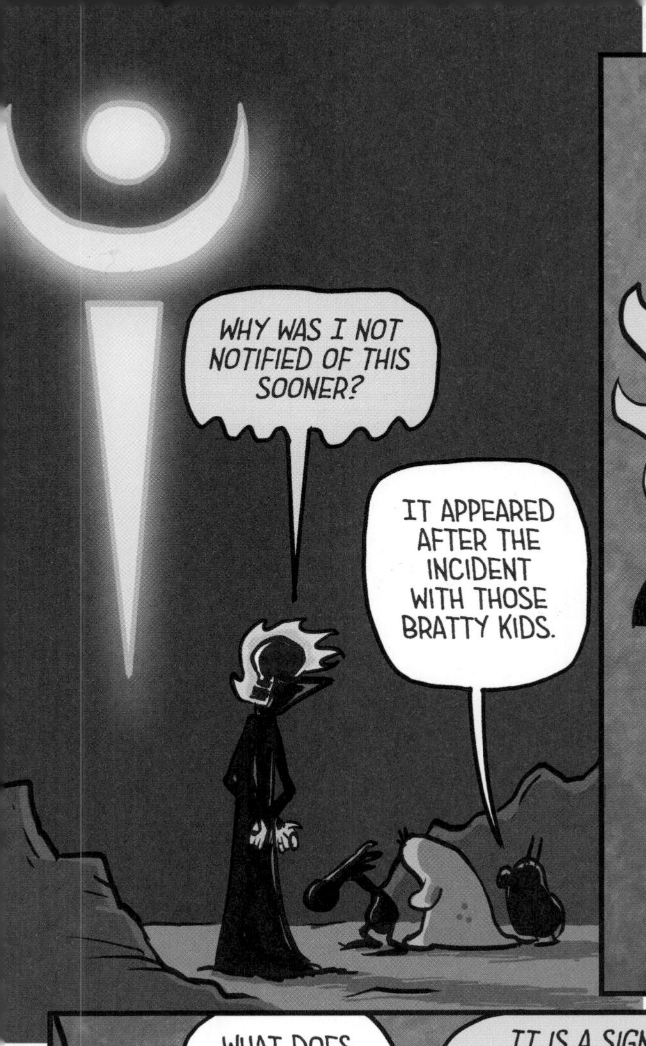
WHY WAS I NOT NOTIFIED OF THIS SOONER?
IT APPEARED AFTER THE INCIDENT WITH THOSE BRATTY KIDS.

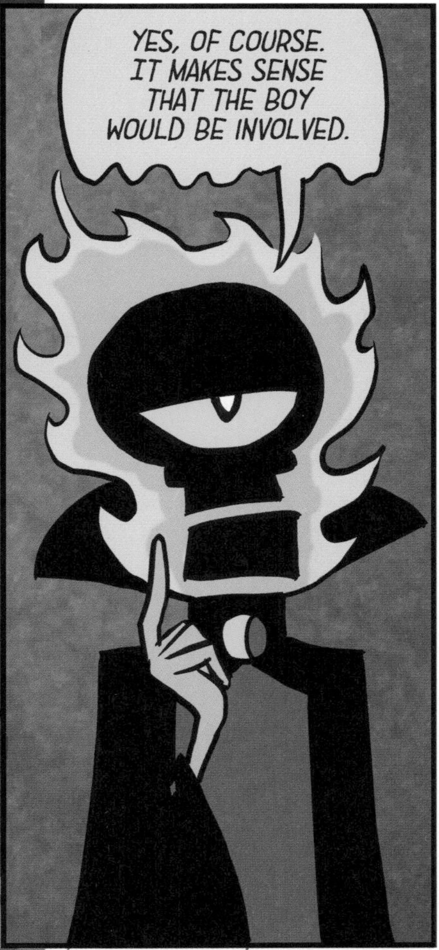
YES, OF COURSE. IT MAKES SENSE THAT THE BOY WOULD BE INVOLVED.

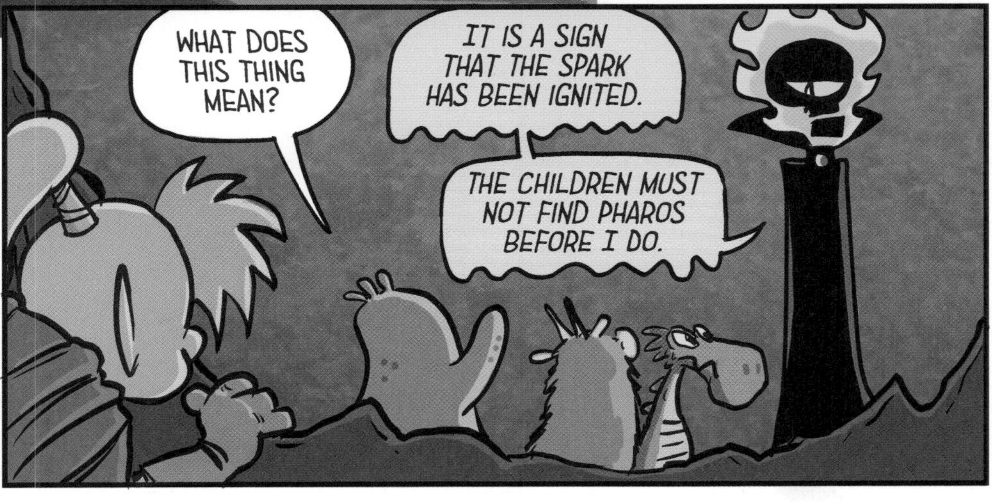
WHAT DOES THIS THING MEAN?
IT IS A SIGN THAT THE SPARK HAS BEEN IGNITED.
THE CHILDREN MUST NOT FIND PHAROS BEFORE I DO.

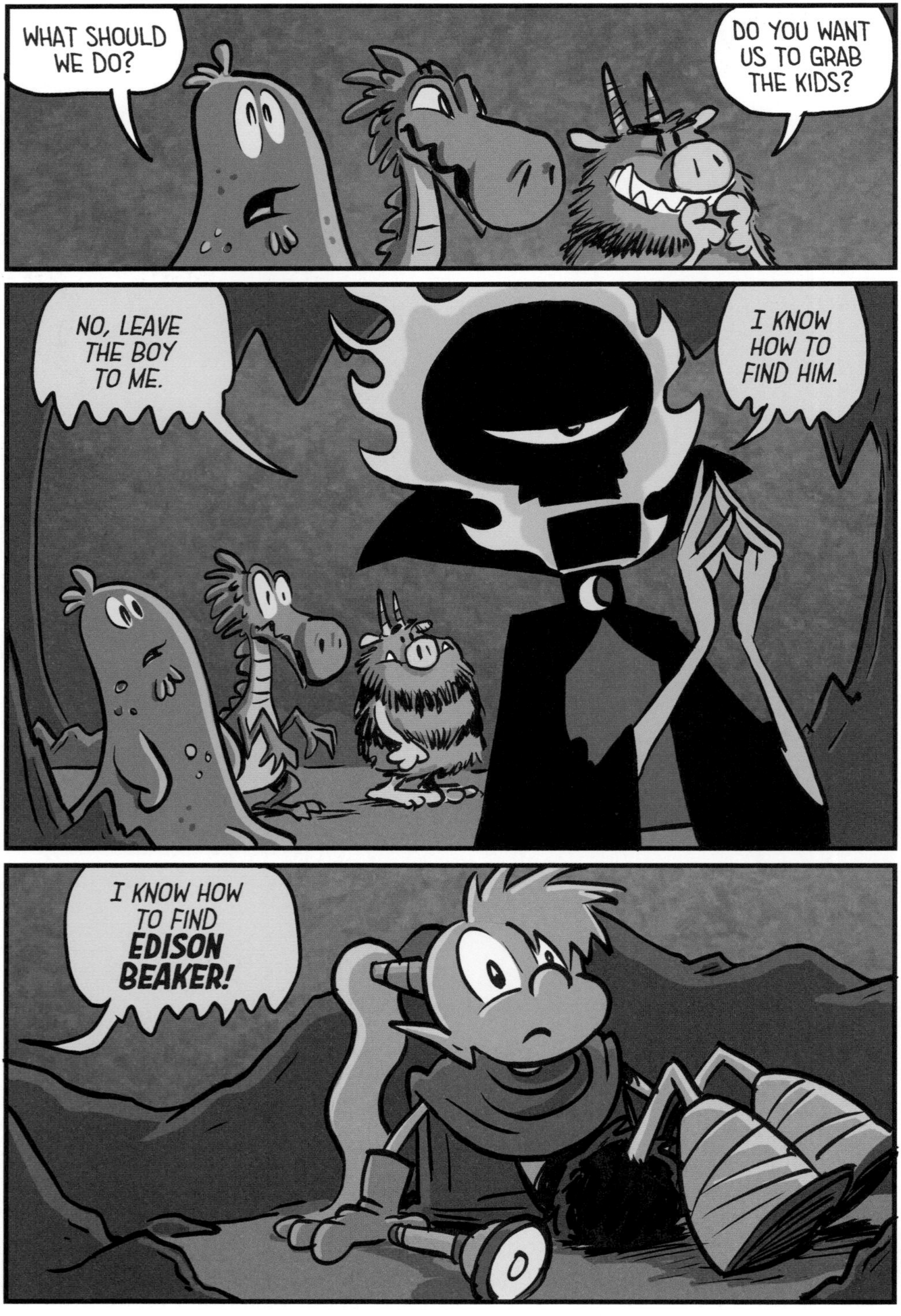
WHAT SHOULD WE DO?
DO YOU WANT US TO GRAB THE KIDS?
NO, LEAVE THE BOY TO ME.
I KNOW HOW TO FIND HIM.
I KNOW HOW TO FIND **EDISON BEAKER!**

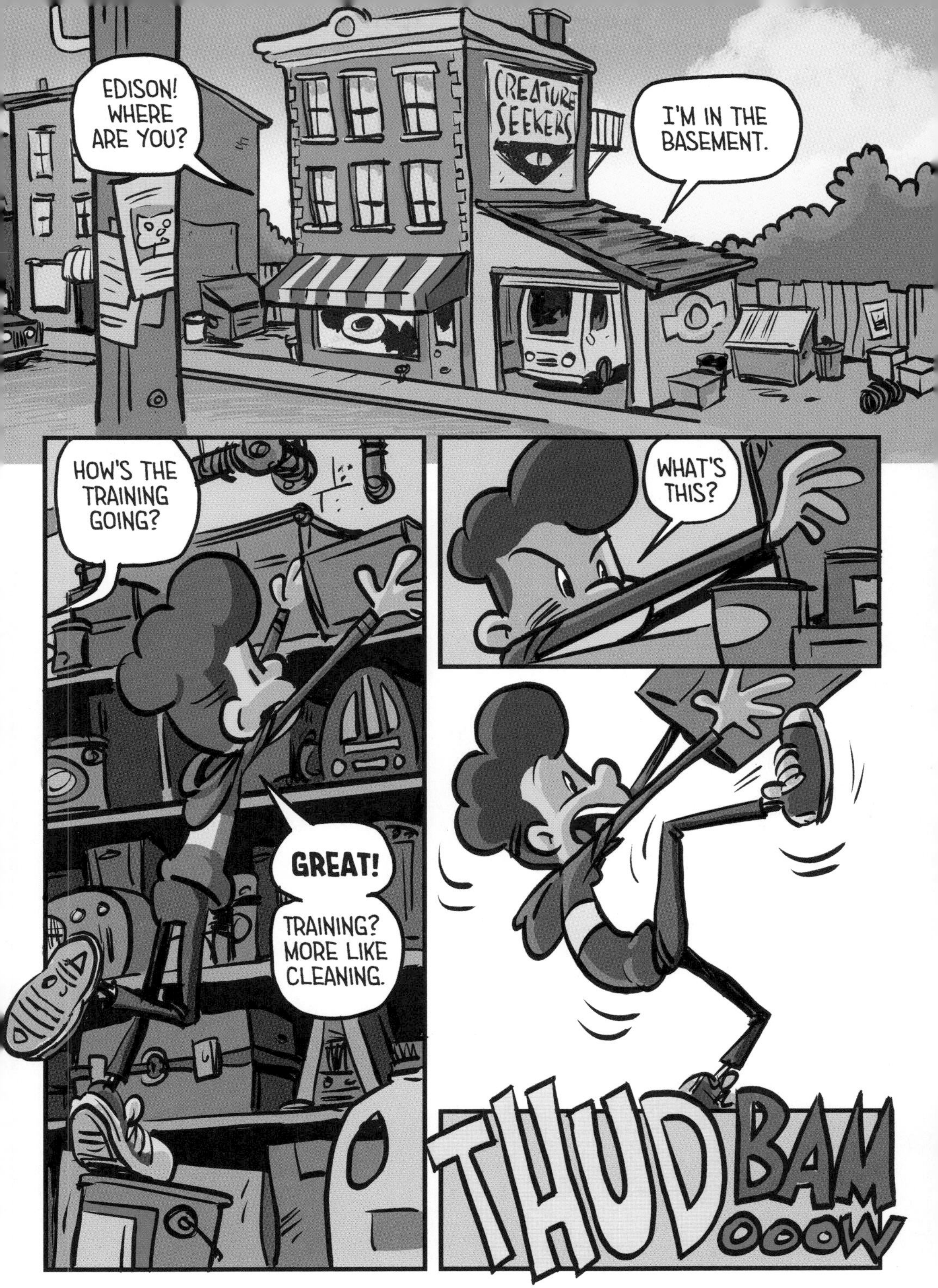

CREATURE SEEKERS
EDISON! WHERE ARE YOU?
I'M IN THE BASEMENT.
HOW'S THE TRAINING GOING?
GREAT!
TRAINING? MORE LIKE CLEANING.
WHAT'S THIS?
THUD
BAM
OOOW

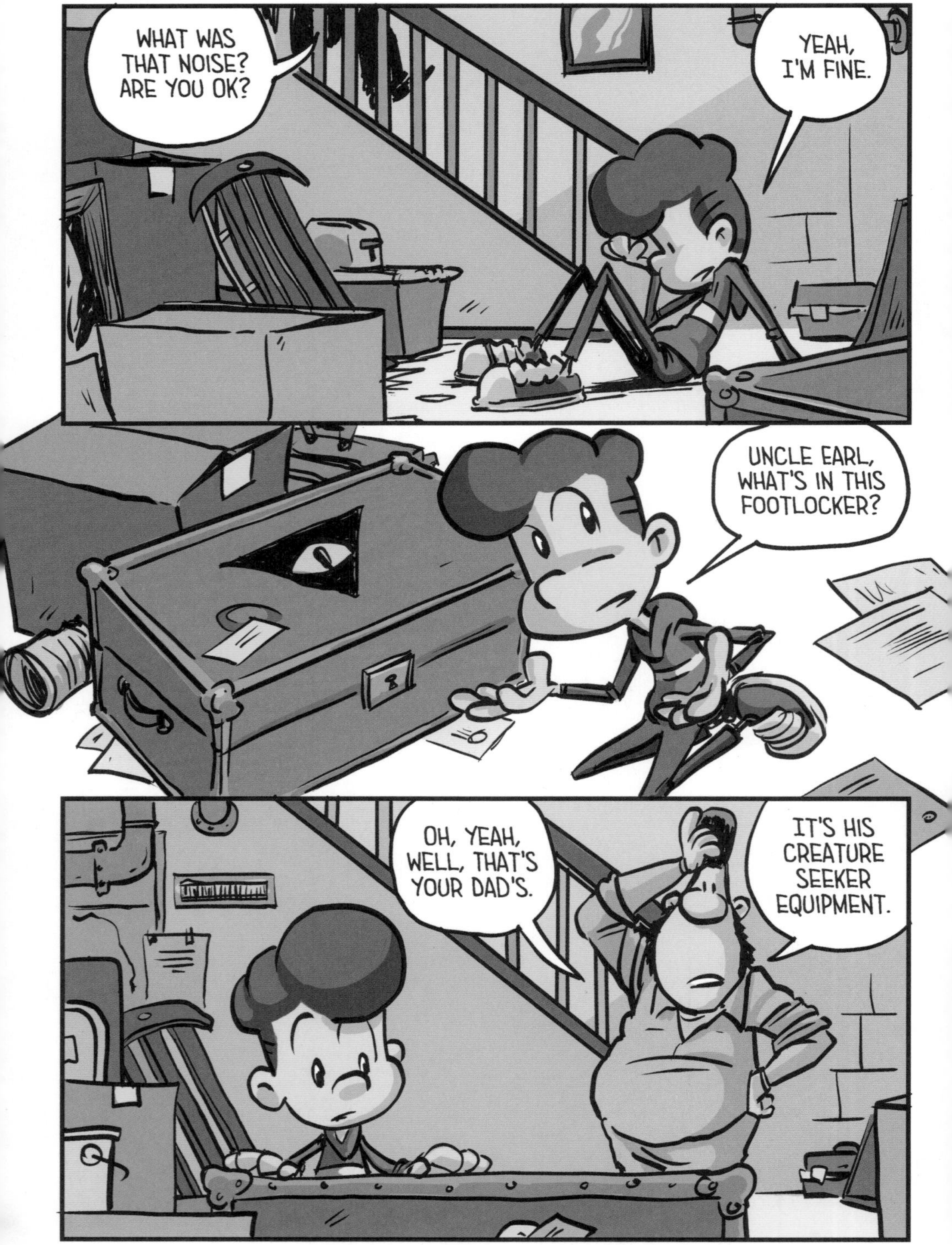
WHAT WAS THAT NOISE? ARE YOU OK?
YEAH, I'M FINE.
UNCLE EARL, WHAT'S IN THIS FOOTLOCKER?
OH, YEAH, WELL, THAT'S YOUR DAD'S.
IT'S HIS CREATURE SEEKER EQUIPMENT.

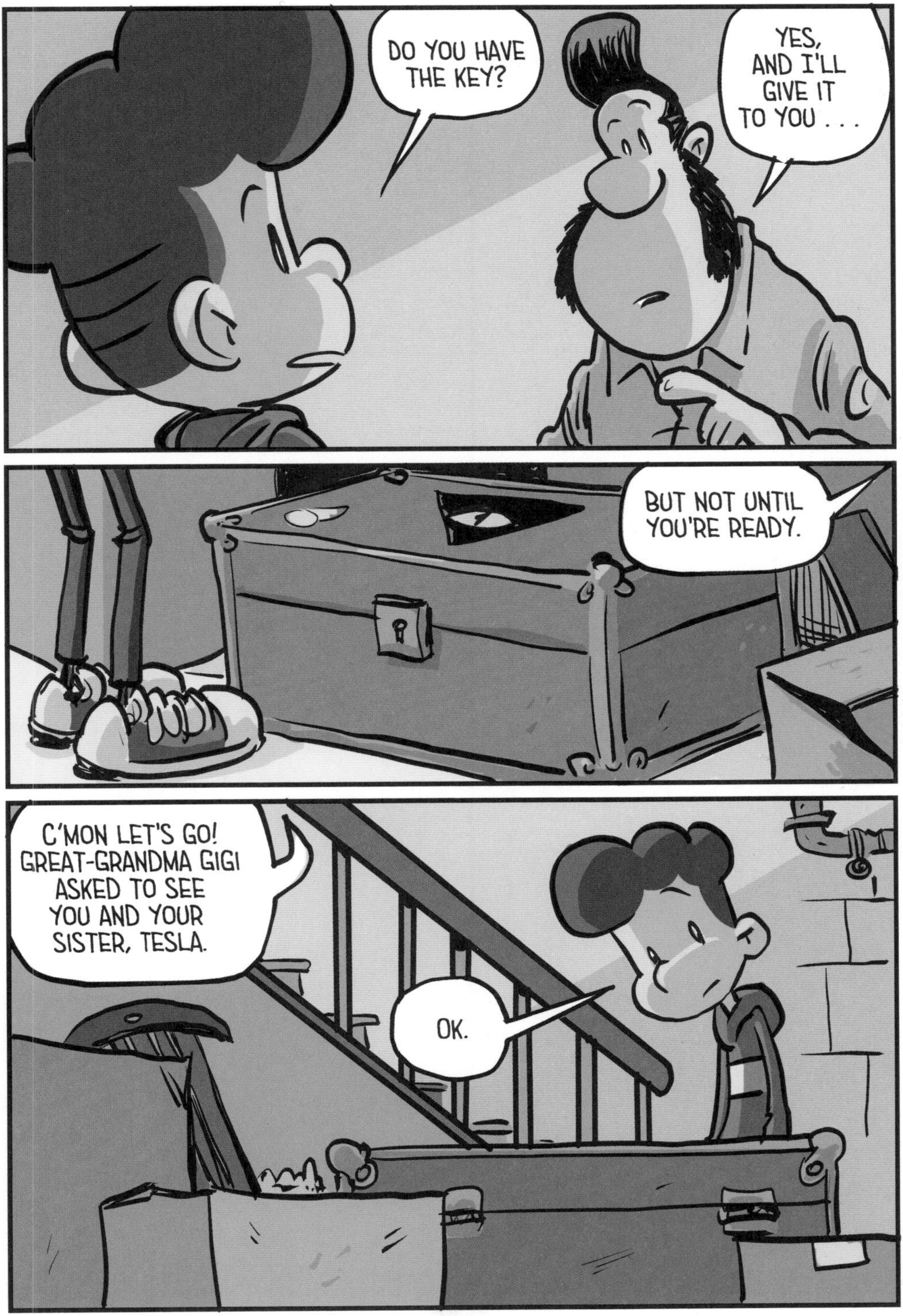
DO YOU HAVE THE KEY?
YES, AND I'LL GIVE IT TO YOU . . .
BUT NOT UNTIL YOU'RE READY.
C'MON LET'S GO! GREAT-GRANDMA GIGI ASKED TO SEE YOU AND YOUR SISTER, TESLA.
OK.

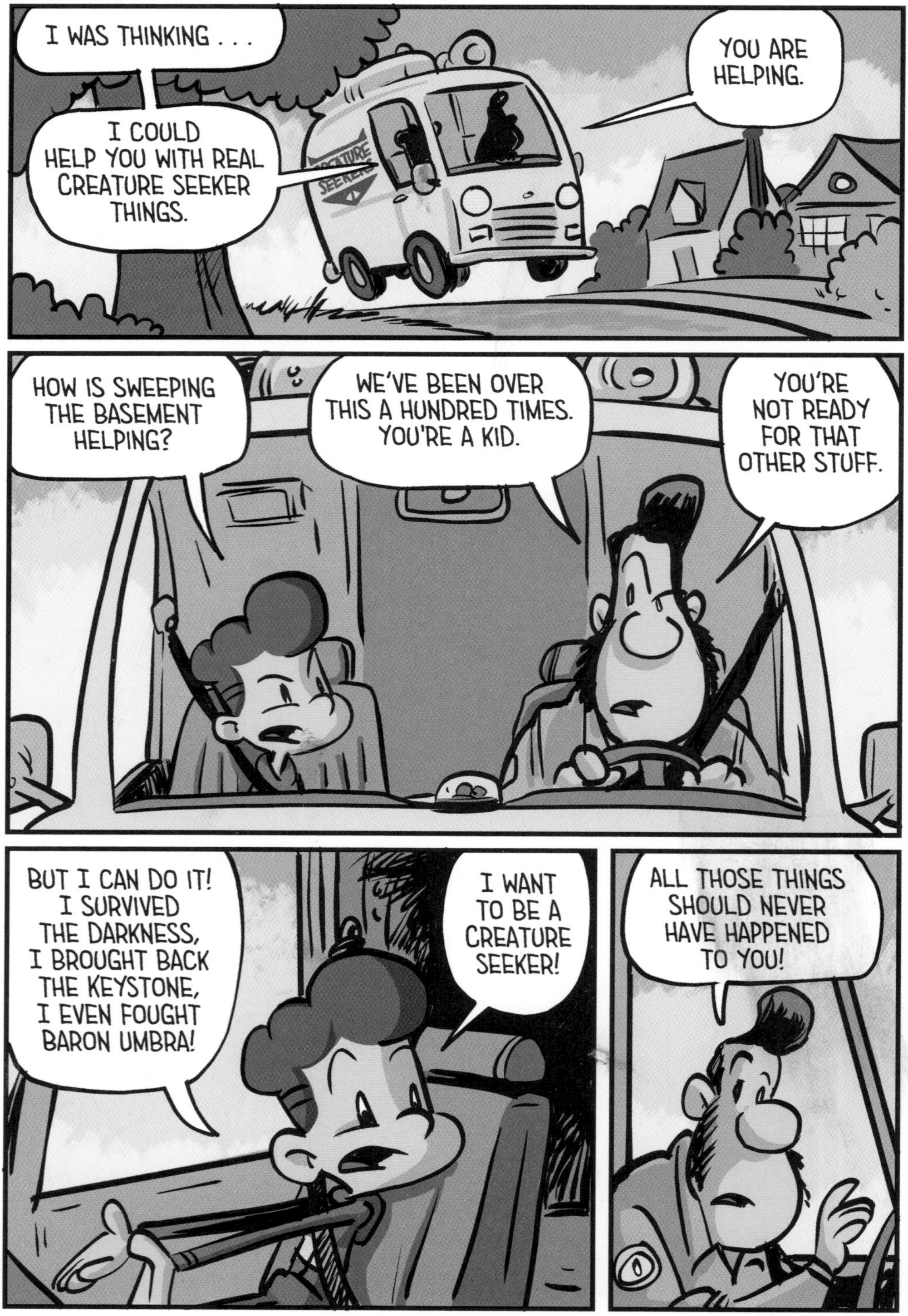
I WAS THINKING . . .
I COULD HELP YOU WITH REAL CREATURE SEEKER THINGS.
YOU ARE HELPING.
HOW IS SWEEPING THE BASEMENT HELPING?
WE'VE BEEN OVER THIS A HUNDRED TIMES. YOU'RE A KID.
YOU'RE NOT READY FOR THAT OTHER STUFF.
BUT I CAN DO IT! I SURVIVED THE DARKNESS, I BROUGHT BACK THE KEYSTONE, I EVEN FOUGHT BARON UMBRA!
I WANT TO BE A CREATURE SEEKER!
ALL THOSE THINGS SHOULD NEVER HAVE HAPPENED TO YOU!

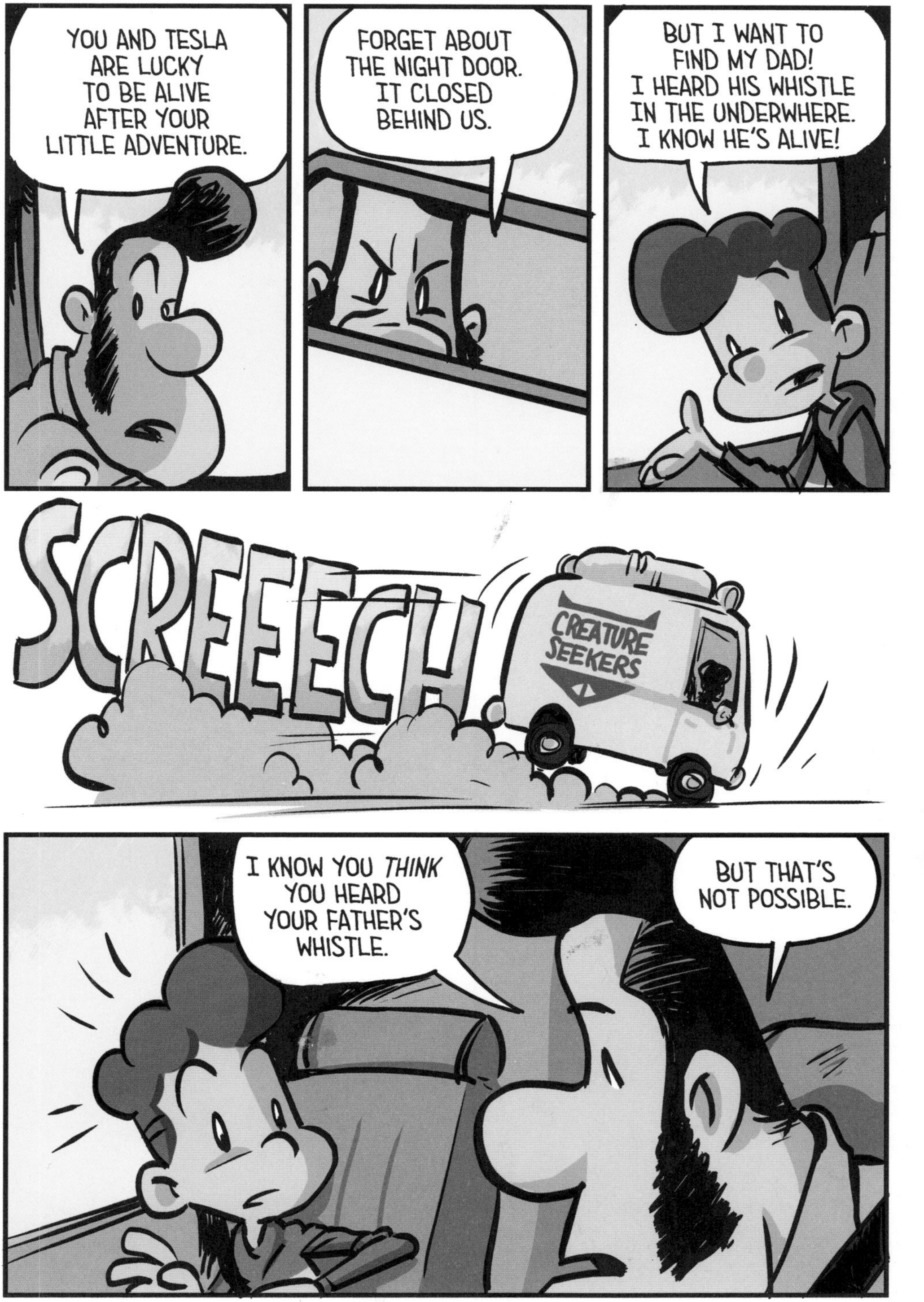
YOU AND TESLA ARE LUCKY TO BE ALIVE AFTER YOUR LITTLE ADVENTURE.
FORGET ABOUT THE NIGHT DOOR. IT CLOSED BEHIND US.
BUT I WANT TO FIND MY DAD! I HEARD HIS WHISTLE IN THE UNDERWHERE. I KNOW HE'S ALIVE!
SCREEECH
CREATURE SEEKERS
I KNOW YOU *THINK* YOU HEARD YOUR FATHER'S WHISTLE.
BUT THAT'S NOT POSSIBLE.

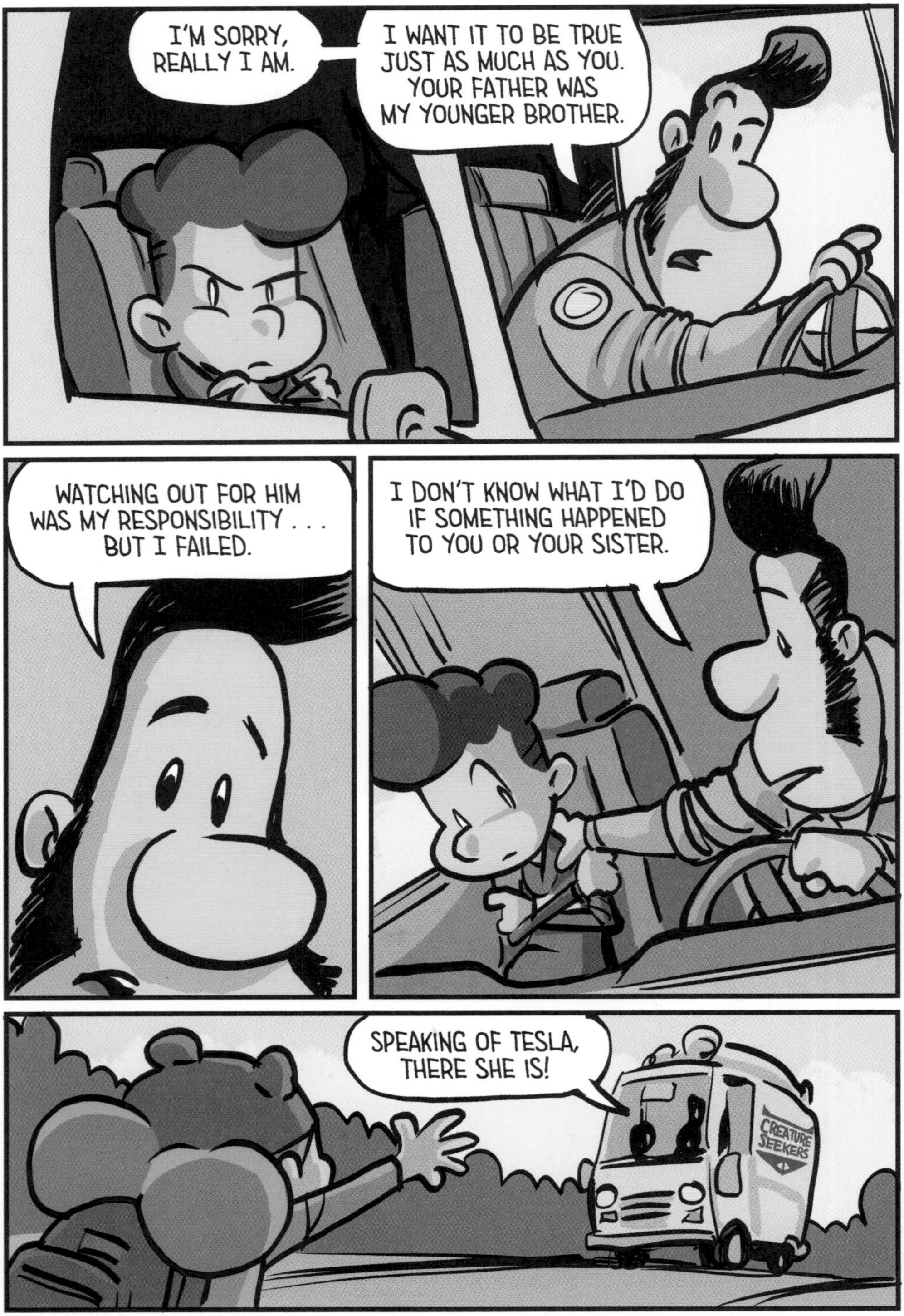
I'M SORRY, REALLY I AM.
I WANT IT TO BE TRUE JUST AS MUCH AS YOU. YOUR FATHER WAS MY YOUNGER BROTHER.
WATCHING OUT FOR HIM WAS MY RESPONSIBILITY . . . BUT I FAILED.
I DON'T KNOW WHAT I'D DO IF SOMETHING HAPPENED TO YOU OR YOUR SISTER.
SPEAKING OF TESLA, THERE SHE IS!
CREATURE SEEKERS

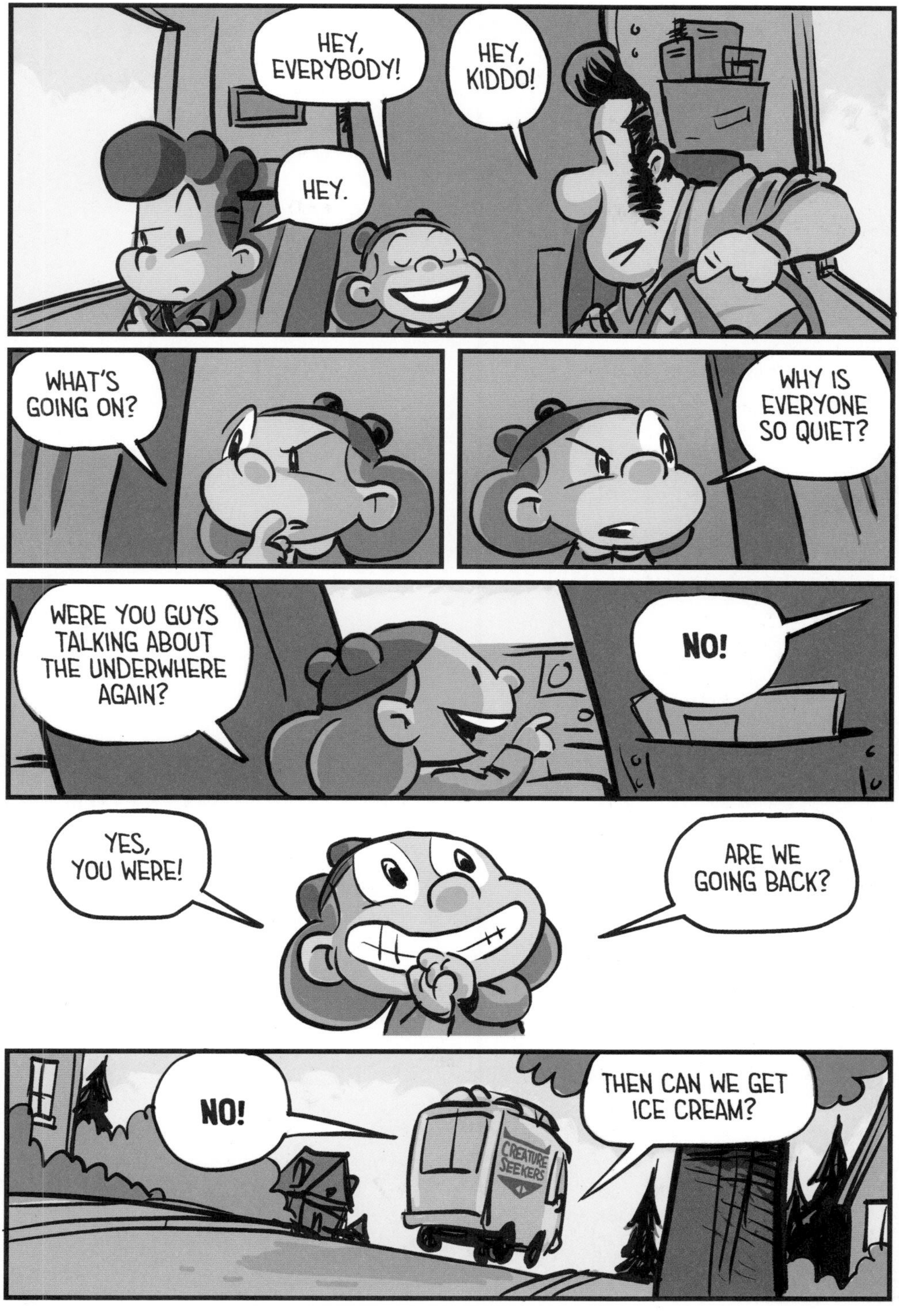
HEY, EVERYBODY!
HEY, KIDDO!
HEY.
WHAT'S GOING ON?
WHY IS EVERYONE SO QUIET?
WERE YOU GUYS TALKING ABOUT THE UNDERWHERE AGAIN?
NO!
YES, YOU WERE!
ARE WE GOING BACK?
NO!
THEN CAN WE GET ICE CREAM?
CREATURE SEEKERS

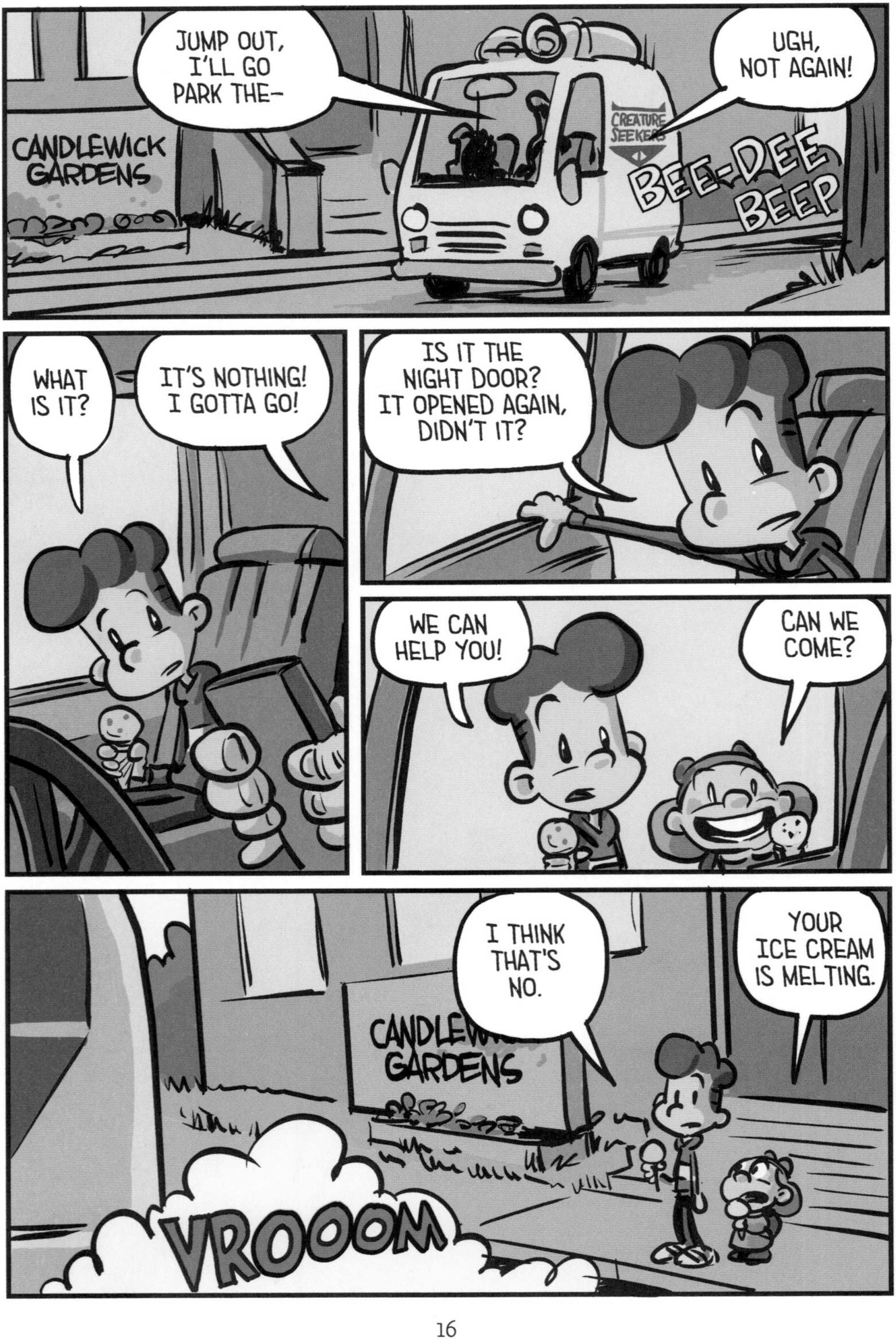
JUMP OUT, I'LL GO PARK THE–
UGH, NOT AGAIN!
CANDLEWICK GARDENS
CREATURE SEEKERS
BEE-DEE BEEP
WHAT IS IT?
IT'S NOTHING! I GOTTA GO!
IS IT THE NIGHT DOOR? IT OPENED AGAIN, DIDN'T IT?
WE CAN HELP YOU!
CAN WE COME?
I THINK THAT'S NO.
YOUR ICE CREAM IS MELTING.
VROOOM

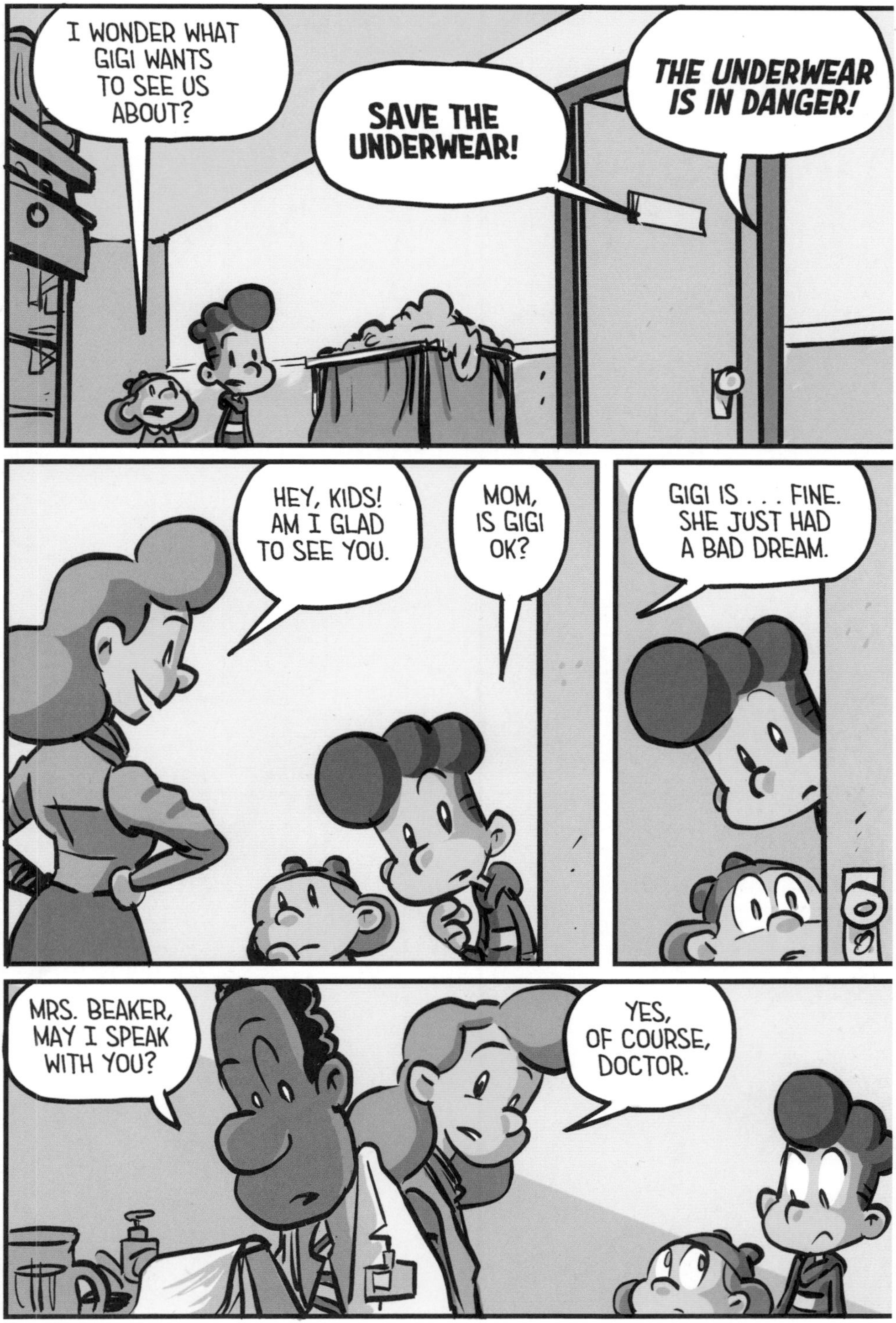
I WONDER WHAT GIGI WANTS TO SEE US ABOUT?
SAVE THE UNDERWEAR!
THE UNDERWEAR IS IN DANGER!
HEY, KIDS! AM I GLAD TO SEE YOU.
MOM, IS GIGI OK?
GIGI IS . . . FINE. SHE JUST HAD A BAD DREAM.
MRS. BEAKER, MAY I SPEAK WITH YOU?
YES, OF COURSE, DOCTOR.

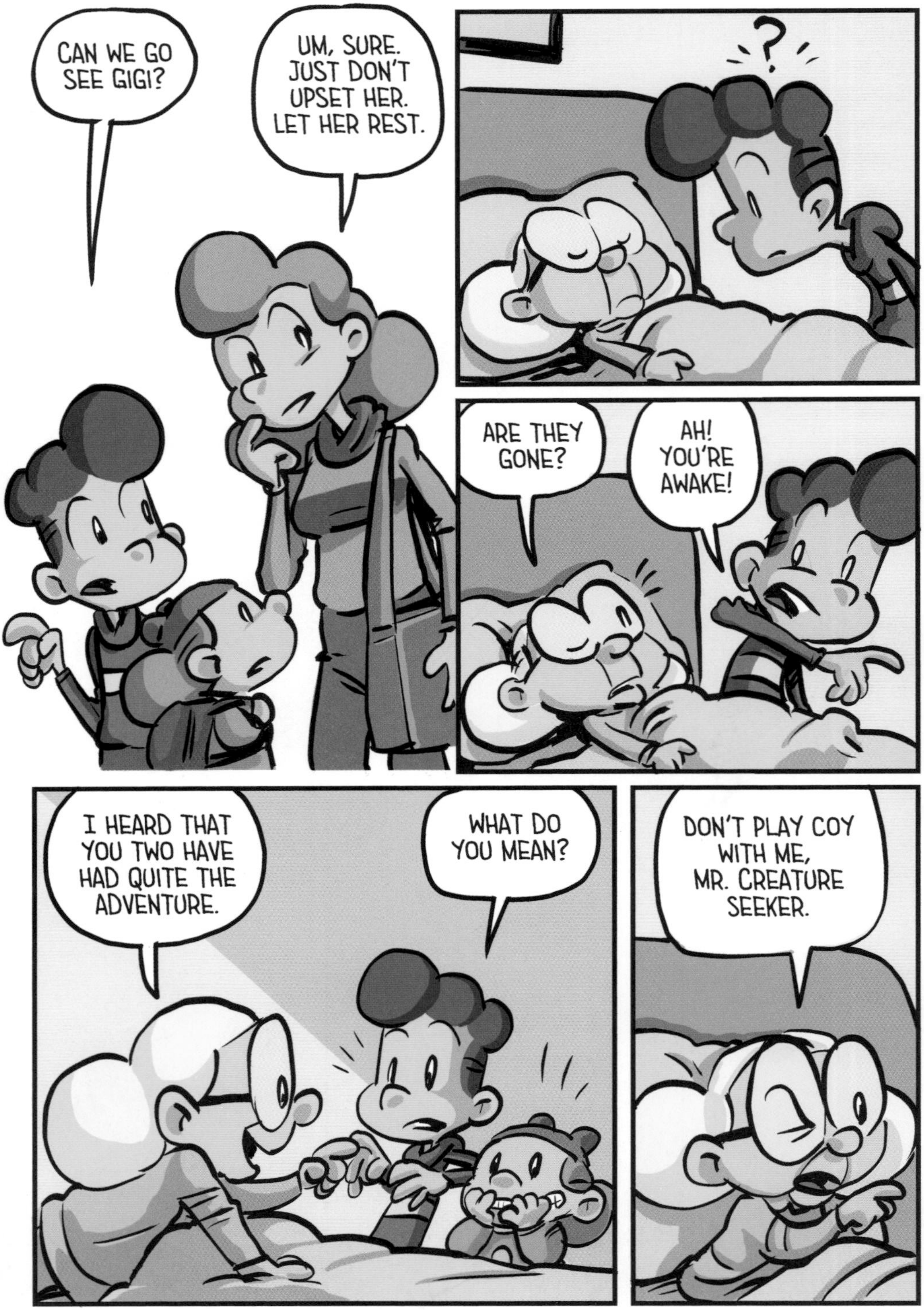
CAN WE GO SEE GIGI?
UM, SURE. JUST DON'T UPSET HER. LET HER REST.
?
ARE THEY GONE?
AH! YOU'RE AWAKE!
I HEARD THAT YOU TWO HAVE HAD QUITE THE ADVENTURE.
WHAT DO YOU MEAN?
DON'T PLAY COY WITH ME, MR. CREATURE SEEKER.

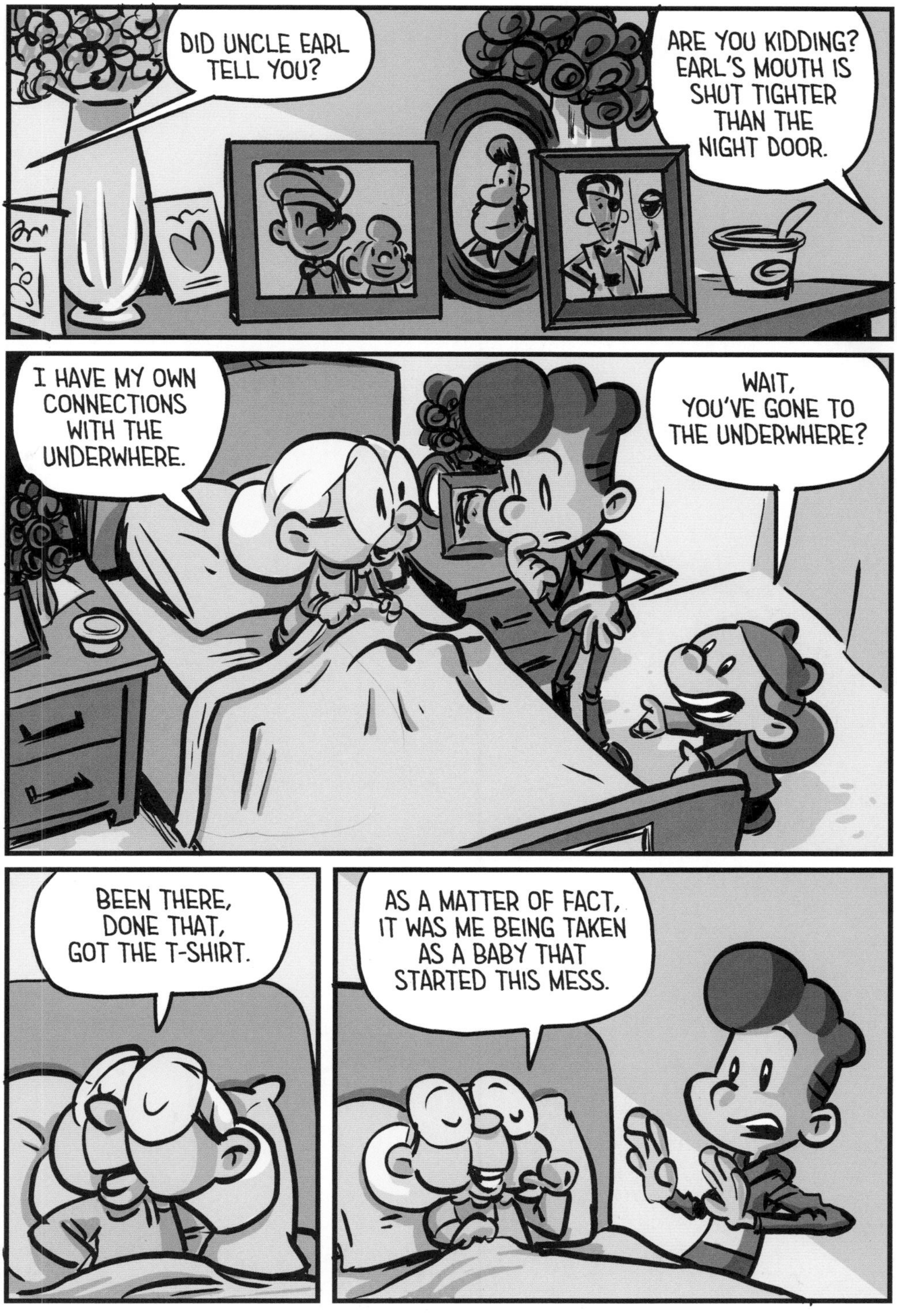
DID UNCLE EARL TELL YOU?
ARE YOU KIDDING? EARL'S MOUTH IS SHUT TIGHTER THAN THE NIGHT DOOR.
I HAVE MY OWN CONNECTIONS WITH THE UNDERWHERE.
WAIT, YOU'VE GONE TO THE UNDERWHERE?
BEEN THERE, DONE THAT, GOT THE T-SHIRT.
AS A MATTER OF FACT, IT WAS ME BEING TAKEN AS A BABY THAT STARTED THIS MESS.

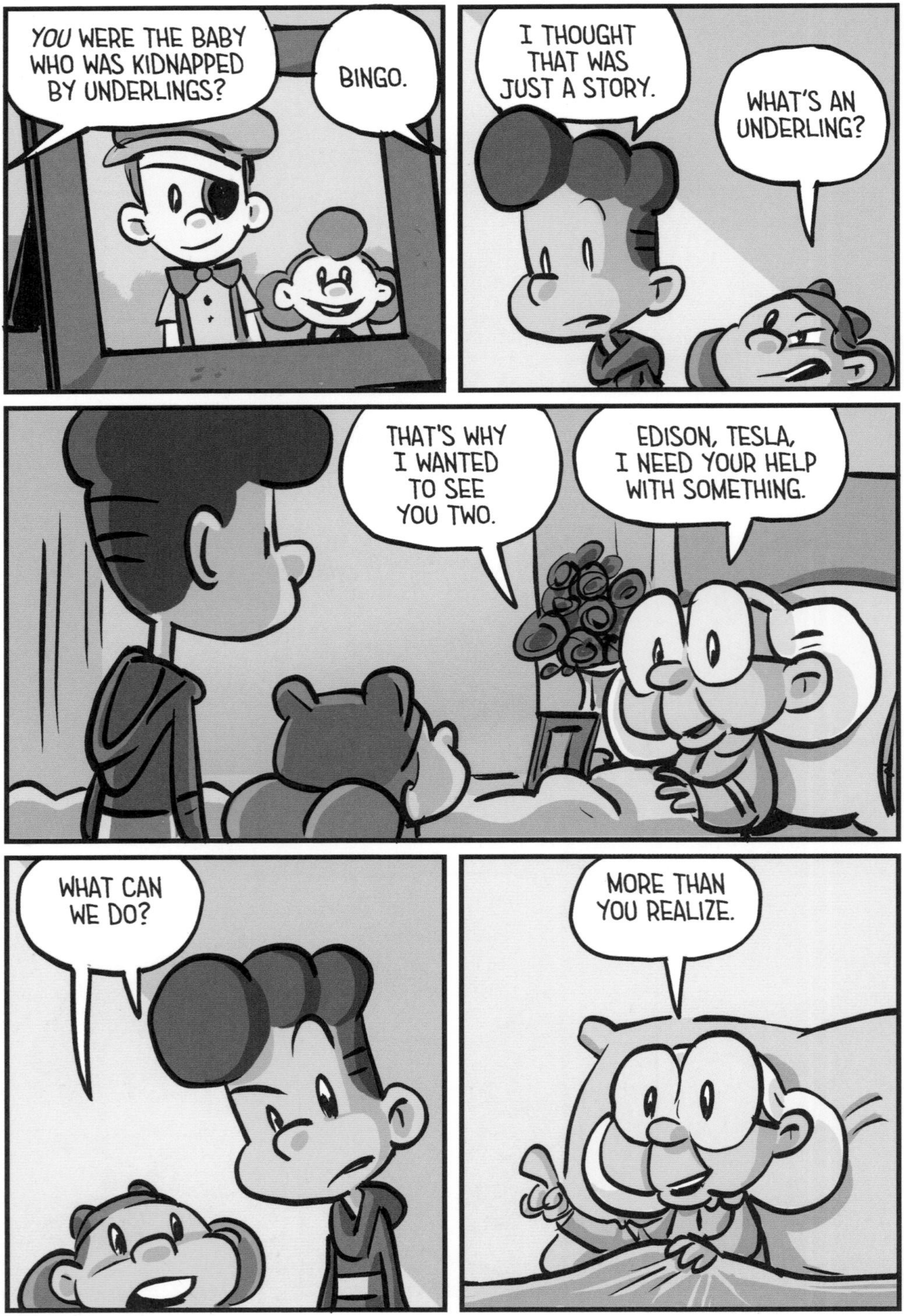
YOU WERE THE BABY WHO WAS KIDNAPPED BY UNDERLINGS?
BINGO.
I THOUGHT THAT WAS JUST A STORY.
WHAT'S AN UNDERLING?
THAT'S WHY I WANTED TO SEE YOU TWO.
EDISON, TESLA, I NEED YOUR HELP WITH SOMETHING.
WHAT CAN WE DO?
MORE THAN YOU REALIZE.

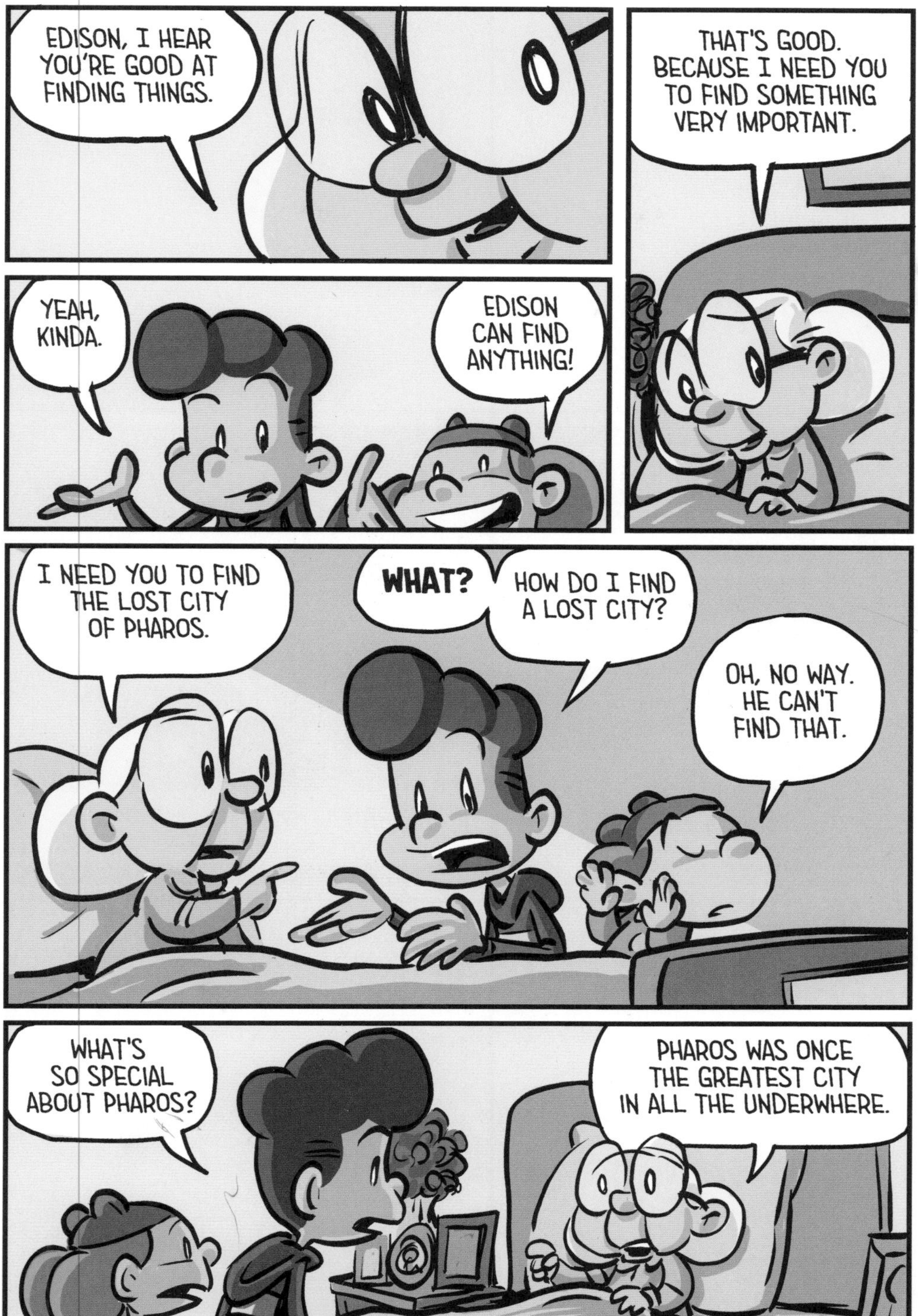
EDISON, I HEAR YOU'RE GOOD AT FINDING THINGS.
YEAH, KINDA.
EDISON CAN FIND ANYTHING!
THAT'S GOOD. BECAUSE I NEED YOU TO FIND SOMETHING VERY IMPORTANT.
I NEED YOU TO FIND THE LOST CITY OF PHAROS.
WHAT?
HOW DO I FIND A LOST CITY?
OH, NO WAY. HE CAN'T FIND THAT.
WHAT'S SO SPECIAL ABOUT PHAROS?
PHAROS WAS ONCE THE GREATEST CITY IN ALL THE UNDERWHERE.

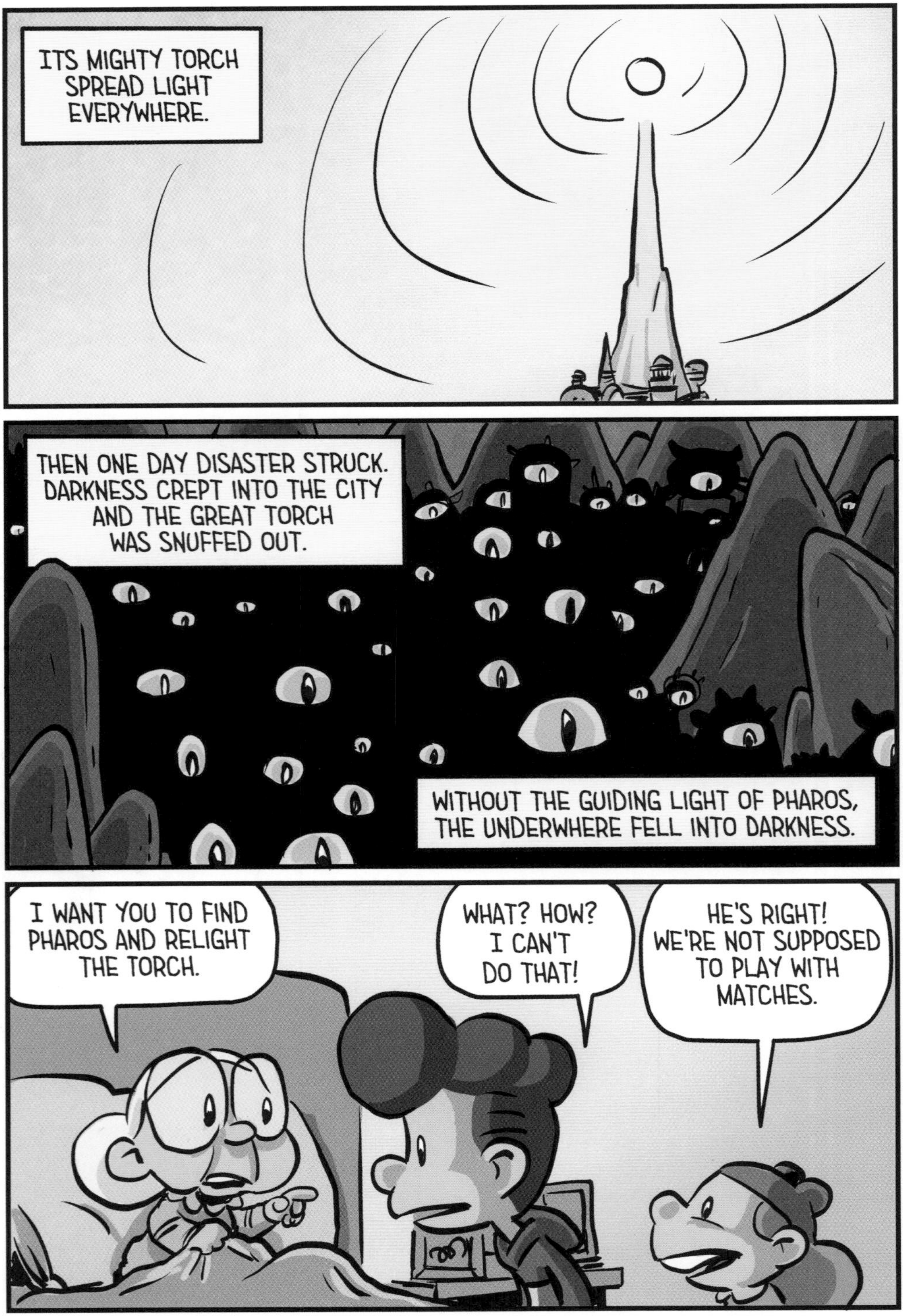
ITS MIGHTY TORCH SPREAD LIGHT EVERYWHERE.
THEN ONE DAY DISASTER STRUCK. DARKNESS CREPT INTO THE CITY AND THE GREAT TORCH WAS SNUFFED OUT.
WITHOUT THE GUIDING LIGHT OF PHAROS, THE UNDERWHERE FELL INTO DARKNESS.
I WANT YOU TO FIND PHAROS AND RELIGHT THE TORCH.
WHAT? HOW? I CAN'T DO THAT!
HE'S RIGHT! WE'RE NOT SUPPOSED TO PLAY WITH MATCHES.

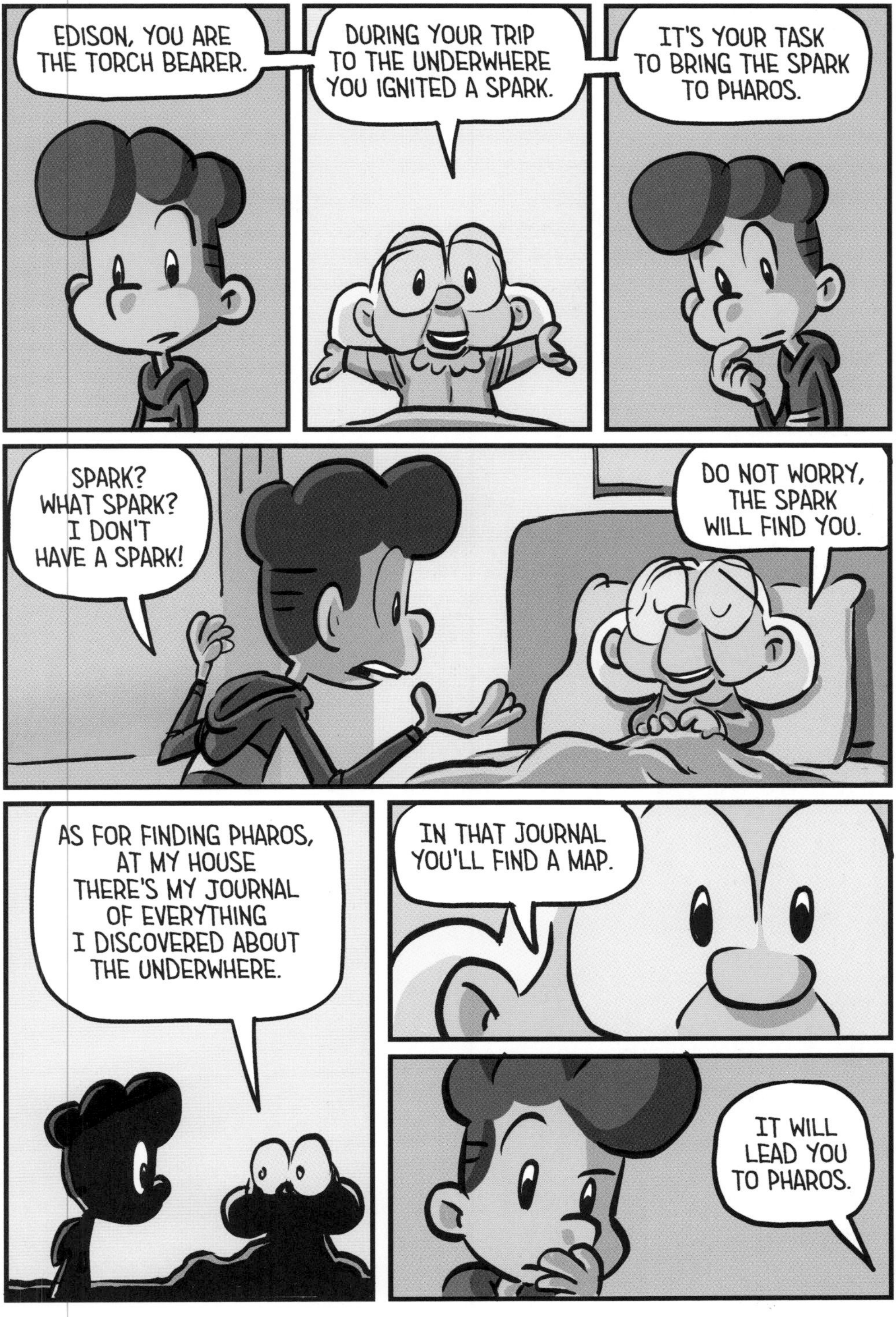
EDISON, YOU ARE THE TORCH BEARER.
DURING YOUR TRIP TO THE UNDERWHERE YOU IGNITED A SPARK.
IT'S YOUR TASK TO BRING THE SPARK TO PHAROS.
SPARK? WHAT SPARK? I DON'T HAVE A SPARK!
DO NOT WORRY, THE SPARK WILL FIND YOU.
AS FOR FINDING PHAROS, AT MY HOUSE THERE'S MY JOURNAL OF EVERYTHING I DISCOVERED ABOUT THE UNDERWHERE.
IN THAT JOURNAL YOU'LL FIND A MAP.
IT WILL LEAD YOU TO PHAROS.

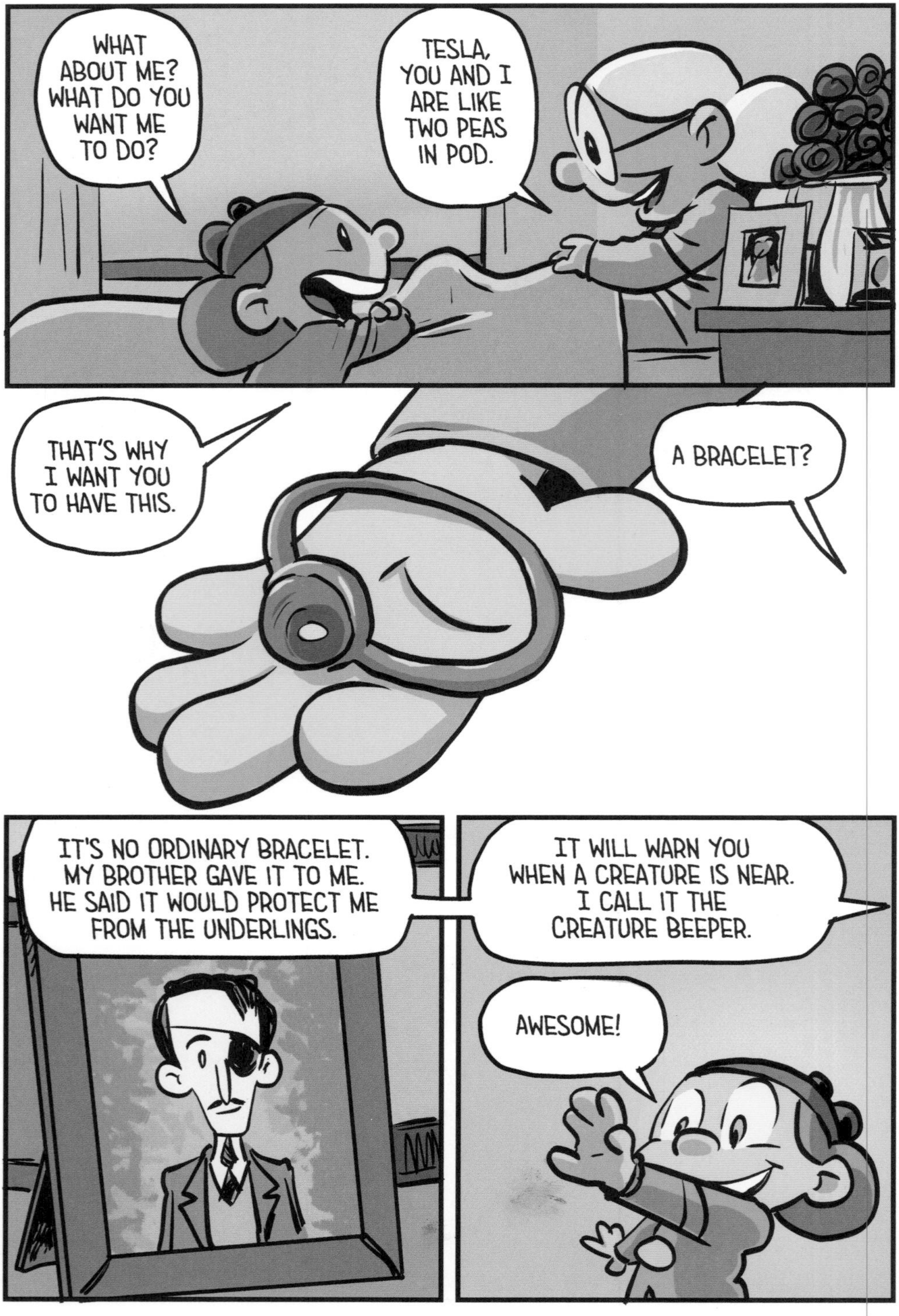
WHAT ABOUT ME? WHAT DO YOU WANT ME TO DO?
TESLA, YOU AND I ARE LIKE TWO PEAS IN POD.
THAT'S WHY I WANT YOU TO HAVE THIS.
A BRACELET?
IT'S NO ORDINARY BRACELET. MY BROTHER GAVE IT TO ME. HE SAID IT WOULD PROTECT ME FROM THE UNDERLINGS.
IT WILL WARN YOU WHEN A CREATURE IS NEAR. I CALL IT THE CREATURE BEEPER.
AWESOME!

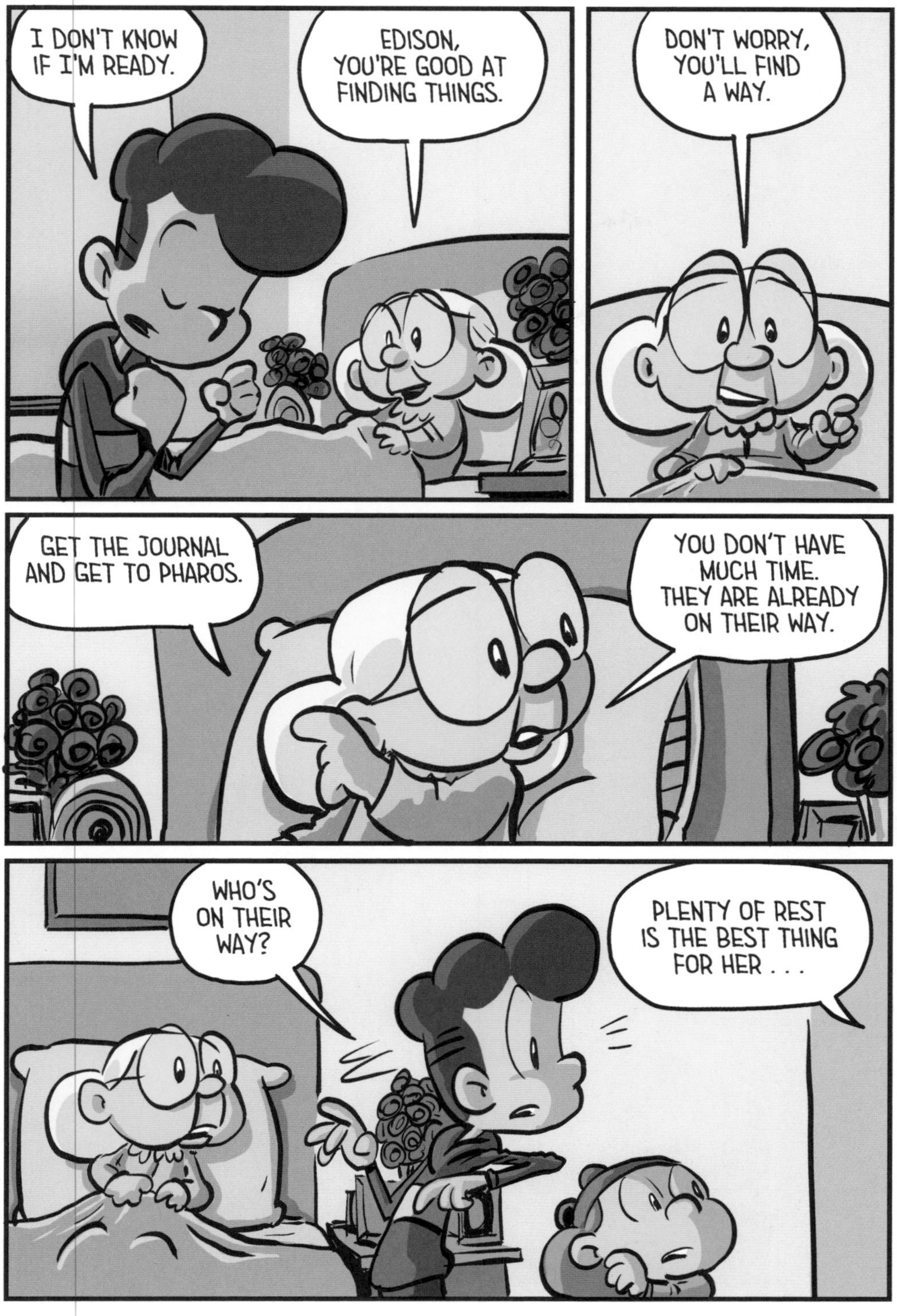
I DON'T KNOW IF I'M READY.
EDISON, YOU'RE GOOD AT FINDING THINGS.
DON'T WORRY, YOU'LL FIND A WAY.
GET THE JOURNAL AND GET TO PHAROS.
YOU DON'T HAVE MUCH TIME. THEY ARE ALREADY ON THEIR WAY.
WHO'S ON THEIR WAY?
PLENTY OF REST IS THE BEST THING FOR HER . . .

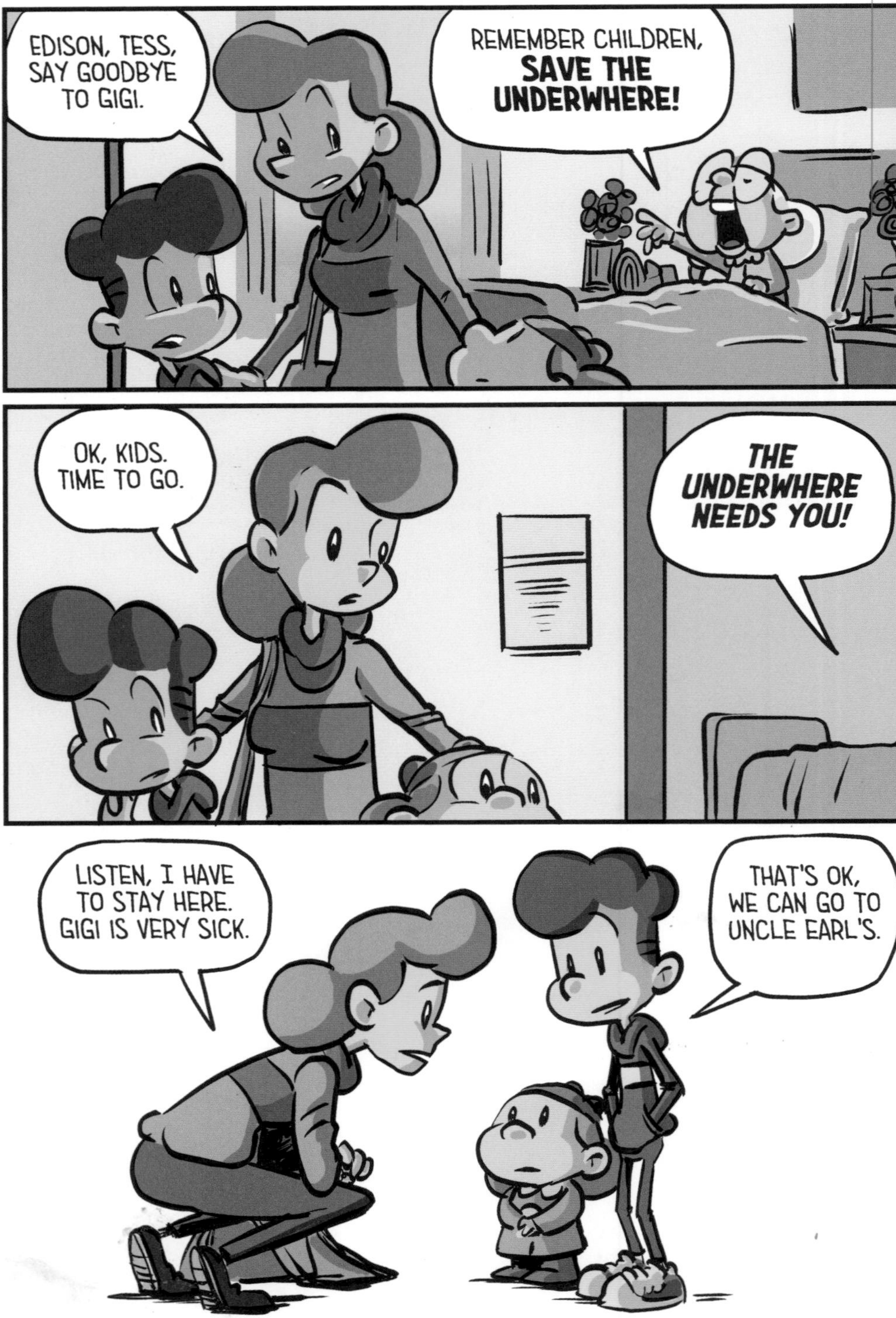
EDISON, TESS, SAY GOODBYE TO GIGI.
REMEMBER CHILDREN, **SAVE THE UNDERWHERE!**
OK, KIDS. TIME TO GO.
THE UNDERWHERE NEEDS YOU!
LISTEN, I HAVE TO STAY HERE. GIGI IS VERY SICK.
THAT'S OK, WE CAN GO TO UNCLE EARL'S.

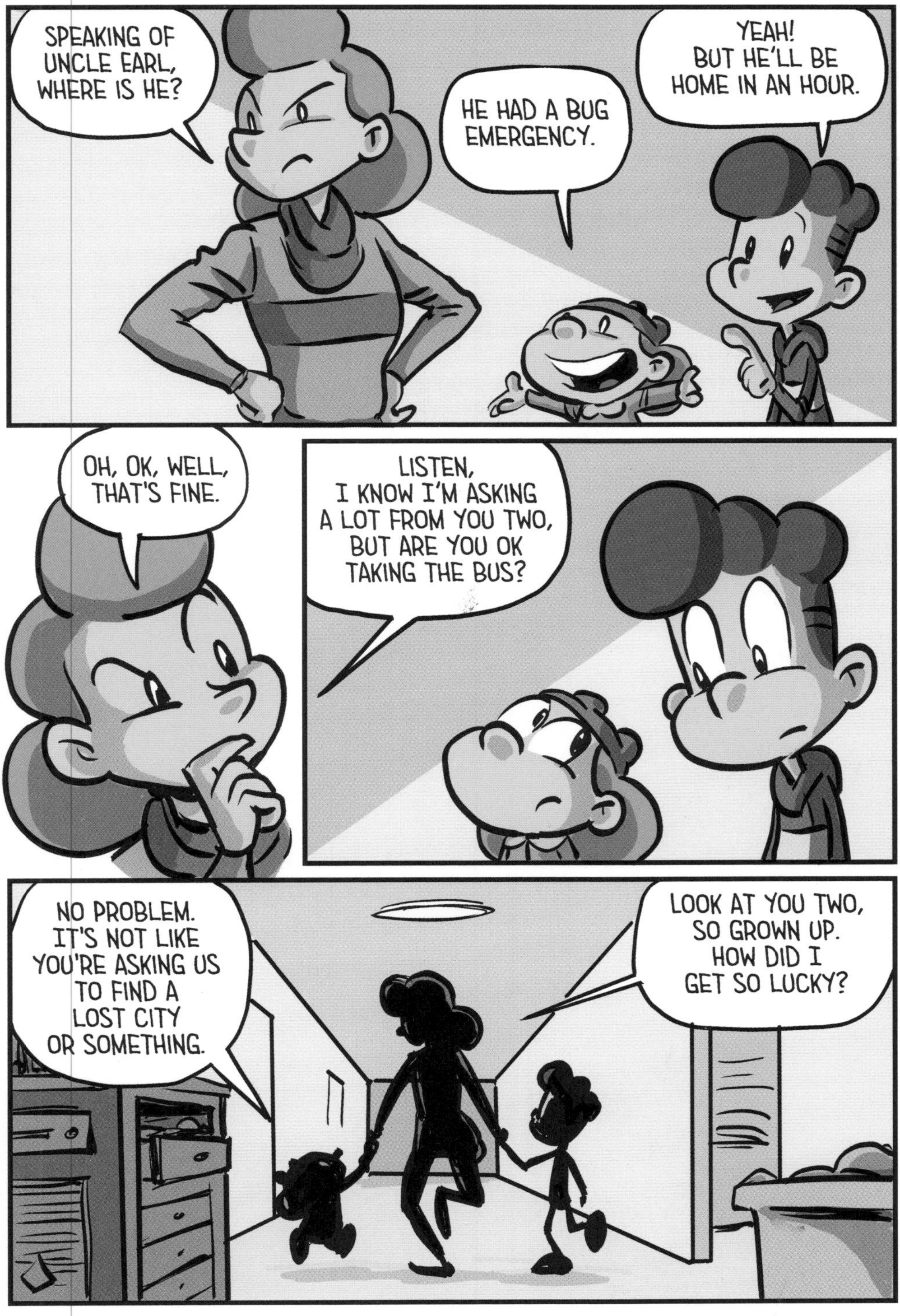
SPEAKING OF UNCLE EARL, WHERE IS HE?
HE HAD A BUG EMERGENCY.
YEAH! BUT HE'LL BE HOME IN AN HOUR.
OH, OK, WELL, THAT'S FINE.
LISTEN, I KNOW I'M ASKING A LOT FROM YOU TWO, BUT ARE YOU OK TAKING THE BUS?
NO PROBLEM. IT'S NOT LIKE YOU'RE ASKING US TO FIND A LOST CITY OR SOMETHING.
LOOK AT YOU TWO, SO GROWN UP. HOW DID I GET SO LUCKY?

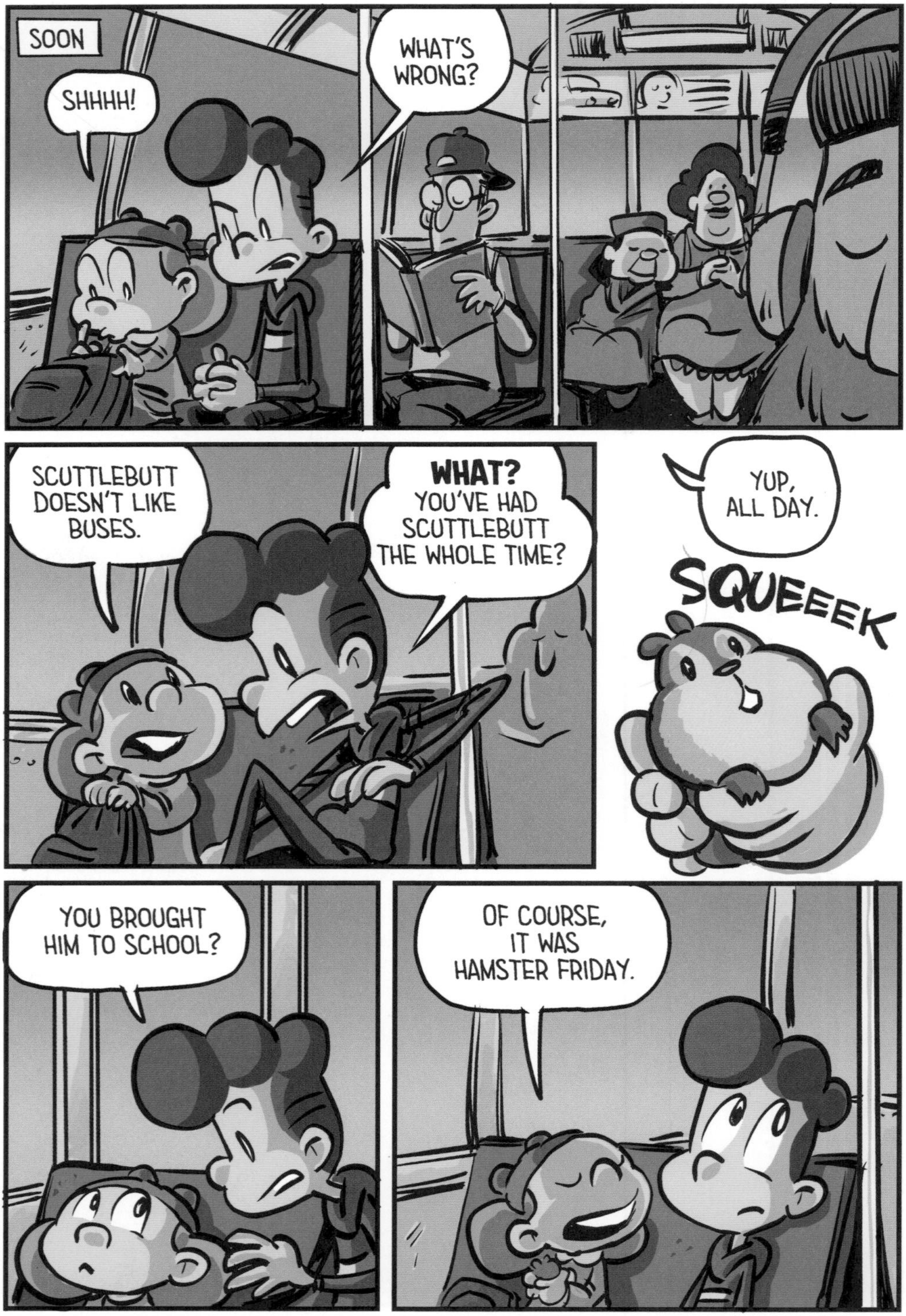
SOON
SHHHH!
WHAT'S WRONG?
SCUTTLEBUTT DOESN'T LIKE BUSES.
WHAT? YOU'VE HAD SCUTTLEBUTT THE WHOLE TIME?
YUP, ALL DAY.
SQUEEEK
YOU BROUGHT HIM TO SCHOOL?
OF COURSE, IT WAS HAMSTER FRIDAY.

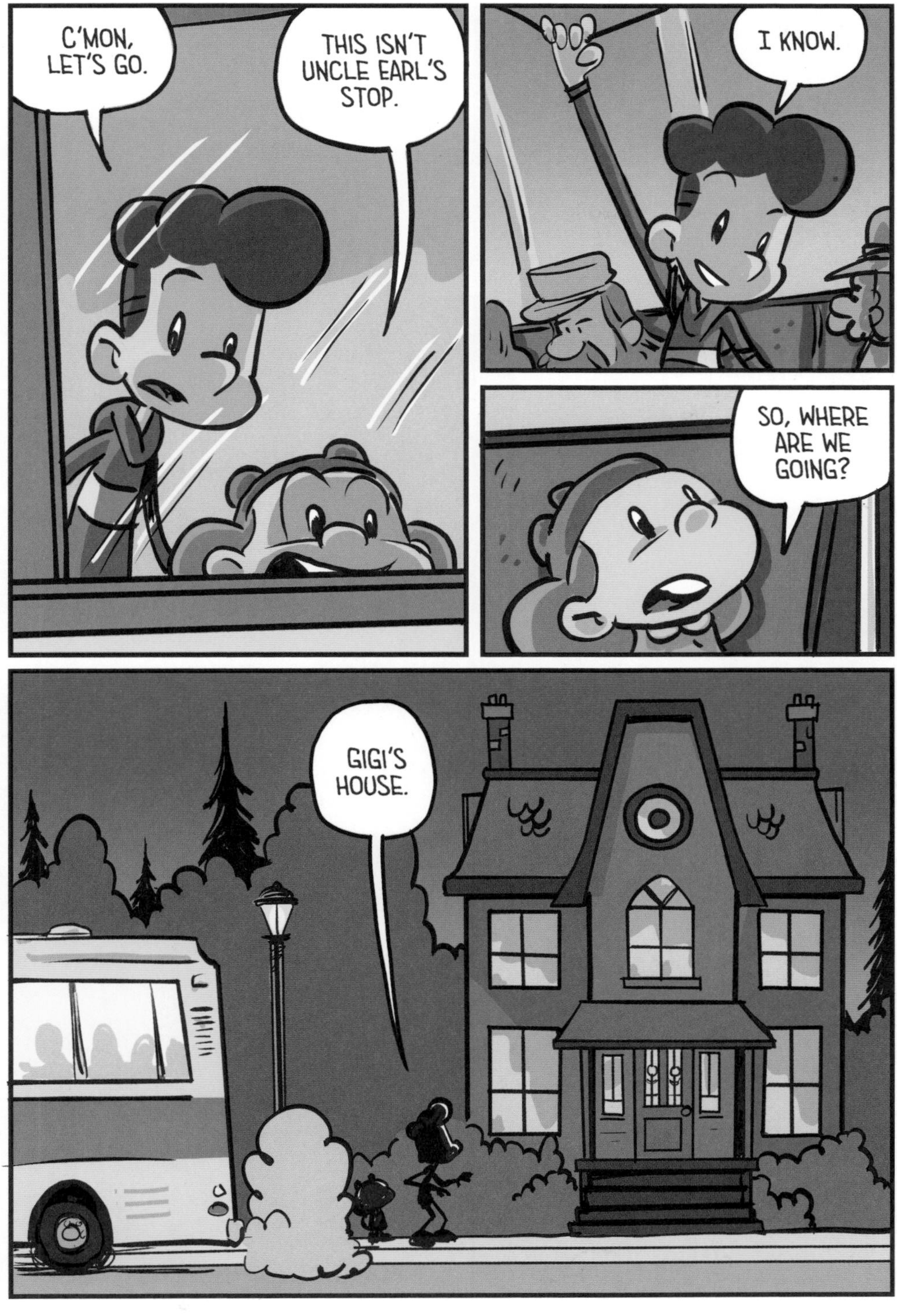
C'MON, LET'S GO.
THIS ISN'T UNCLE EARL'S STOP.
I KNOW.
SO, WHERE ARE WE GOING?
GIGI'S HOUSE.

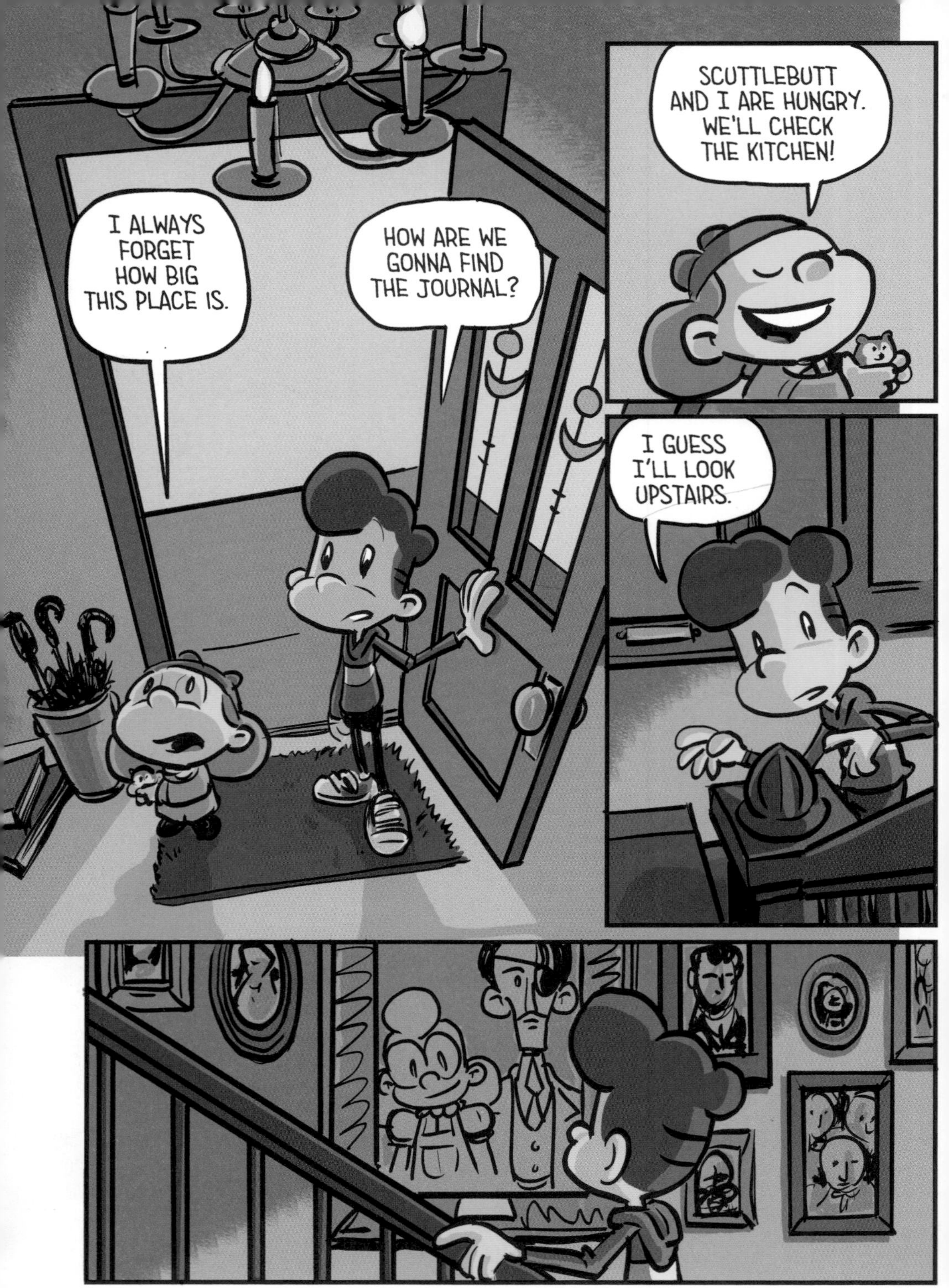
I ALWAYS FORGET HOW BIG THIS PLACE IS.
HOW ARE WE GONNA FIND THE JOURNAL?
SCUTTLEBUTT AND I ARE HUNGRY. WE'LL CHECK THE KITCHEN!
I GUESS I'LL LOOK UPSTAIRS.

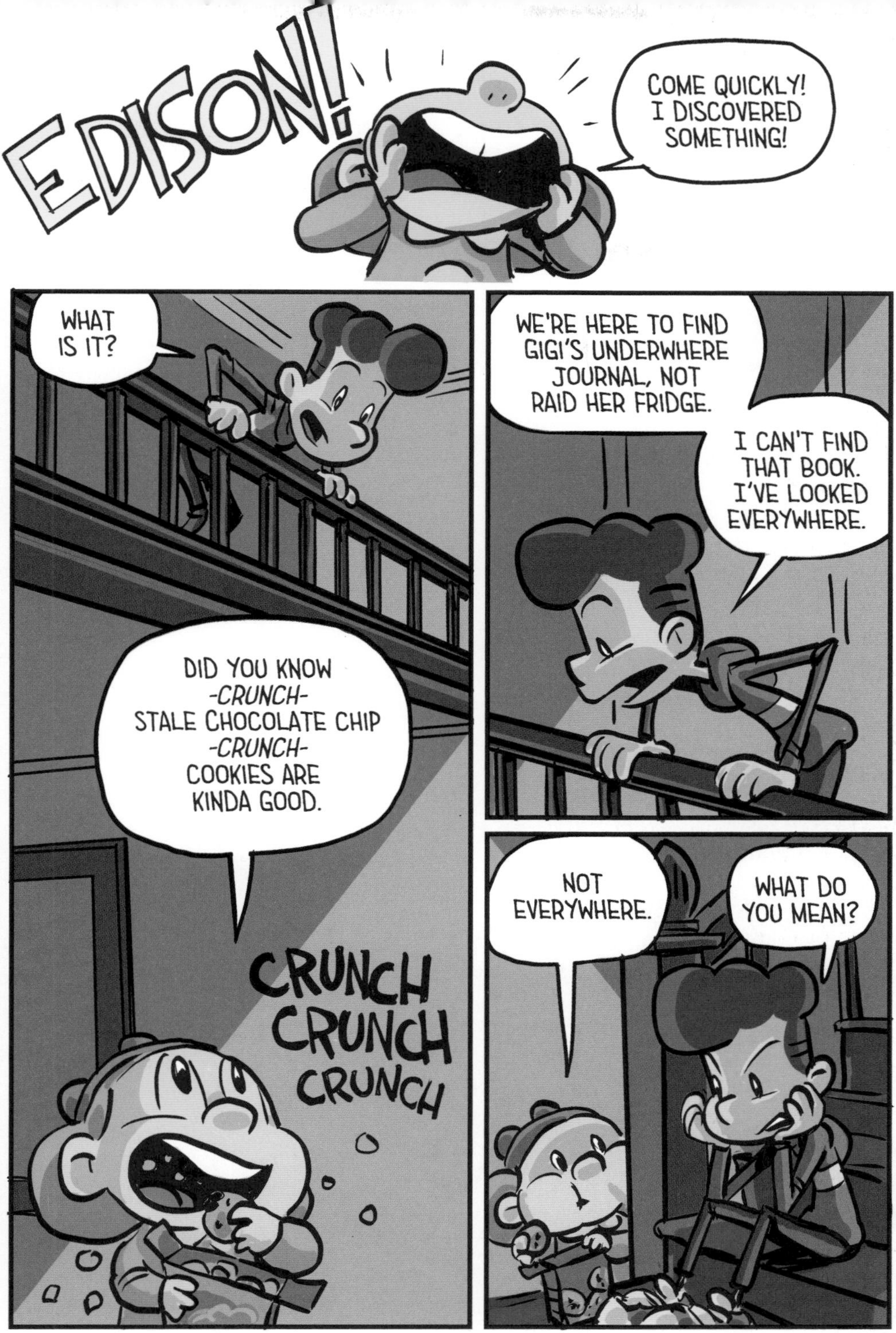
EDISON!
COME QUICKLY! I DISCOVERED SOMETHING!
WHAT IS IT?
DID YOU KNOW -CRUNCH- STALE CHOCOLATE CHIP -CRUNCH- COOKIES ARE KINDA GOOD.
CRUNCH CRUNCH CRUNCH
WE'RE HERE TO FIND GIGI'S UNDERWHERE JOURNAL, NOT RAID HER FRIDGE.
I CAN'T FIND THAT BOOK. I'VE LOOKED EVERYWHERE.
NOT EVERYWHERE.
WHAT DO YOU MEAN?

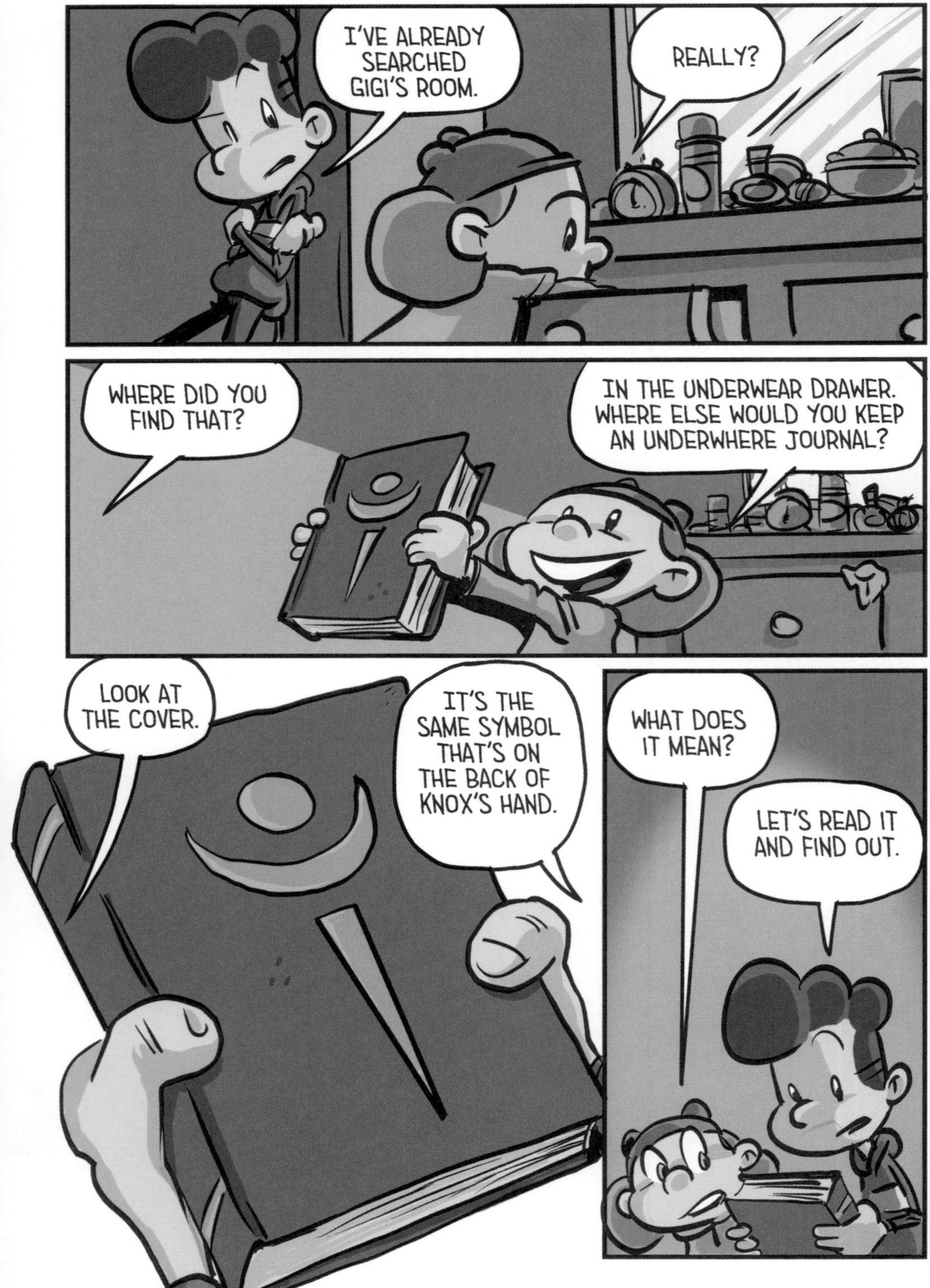
I'VE ALREADY SEARCHED GIGI'S ROOM.
REALLY?
WHERE DID YOU FIND THAT?
IN THE UNDERWEAR DRAWER. WHERE ELSE WOULD YOU KEEP AN UNDERWHERE JOURNAL?
LOOK AT THE COVER.
IT'S THE SAME SYMBOL THAT'S ON THE BACK OF KNOX'S HAND.
WHAT DOES IT MEAN?
LET'S READ IT AND FIND OUT.

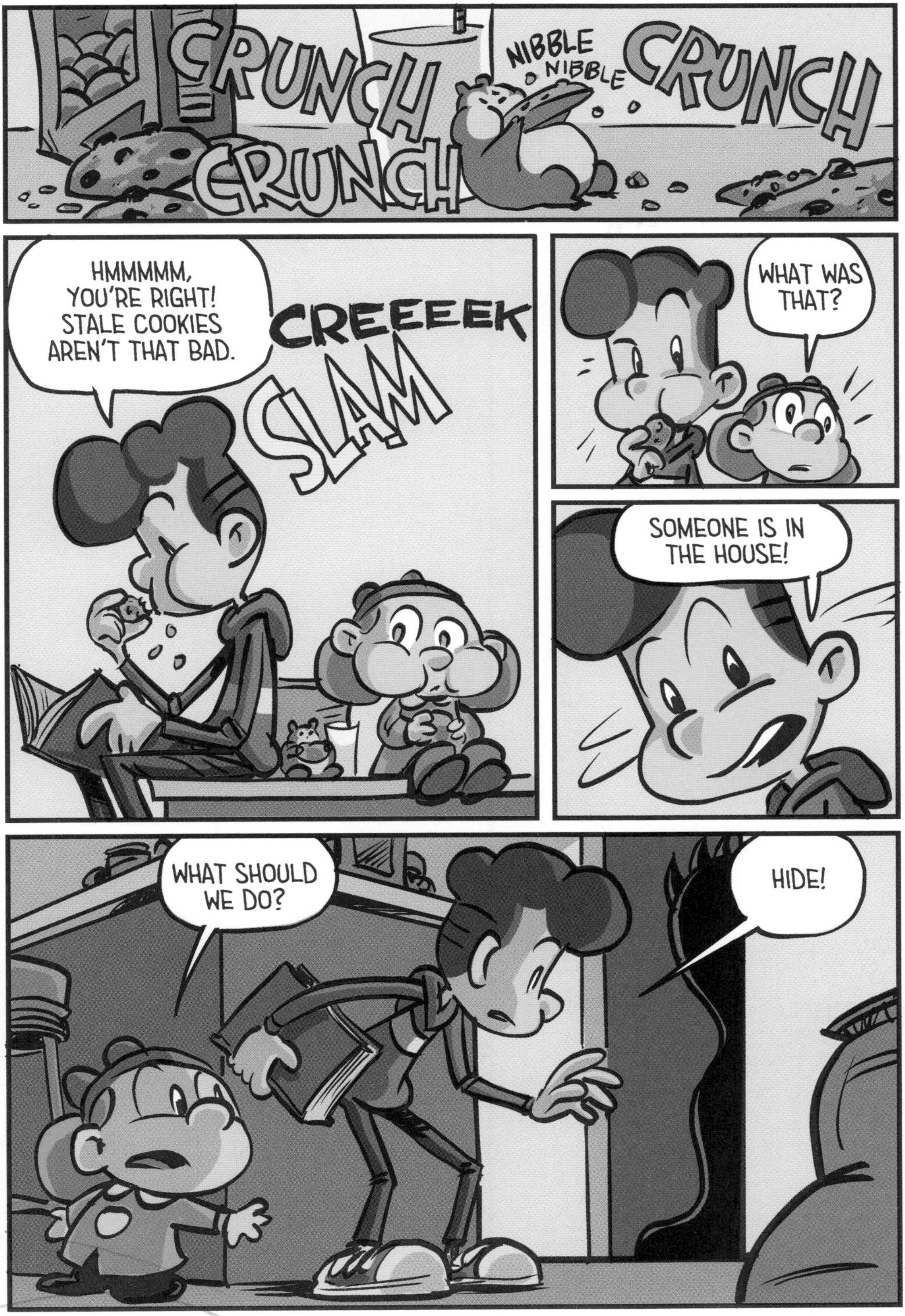
CRUNCH
CRUNCH
NIBBLE NIBBLE
CRUNCH
HMMMMM, YOU'RE RIGHT! STALE COOKIES AREN'T THAT BAD.
CREEEEK
SLAM
WHAT WAS THAT?
SOMEONE IS IN THE HOUSE!
WHAT SHOULD WE DO?
HIDE!

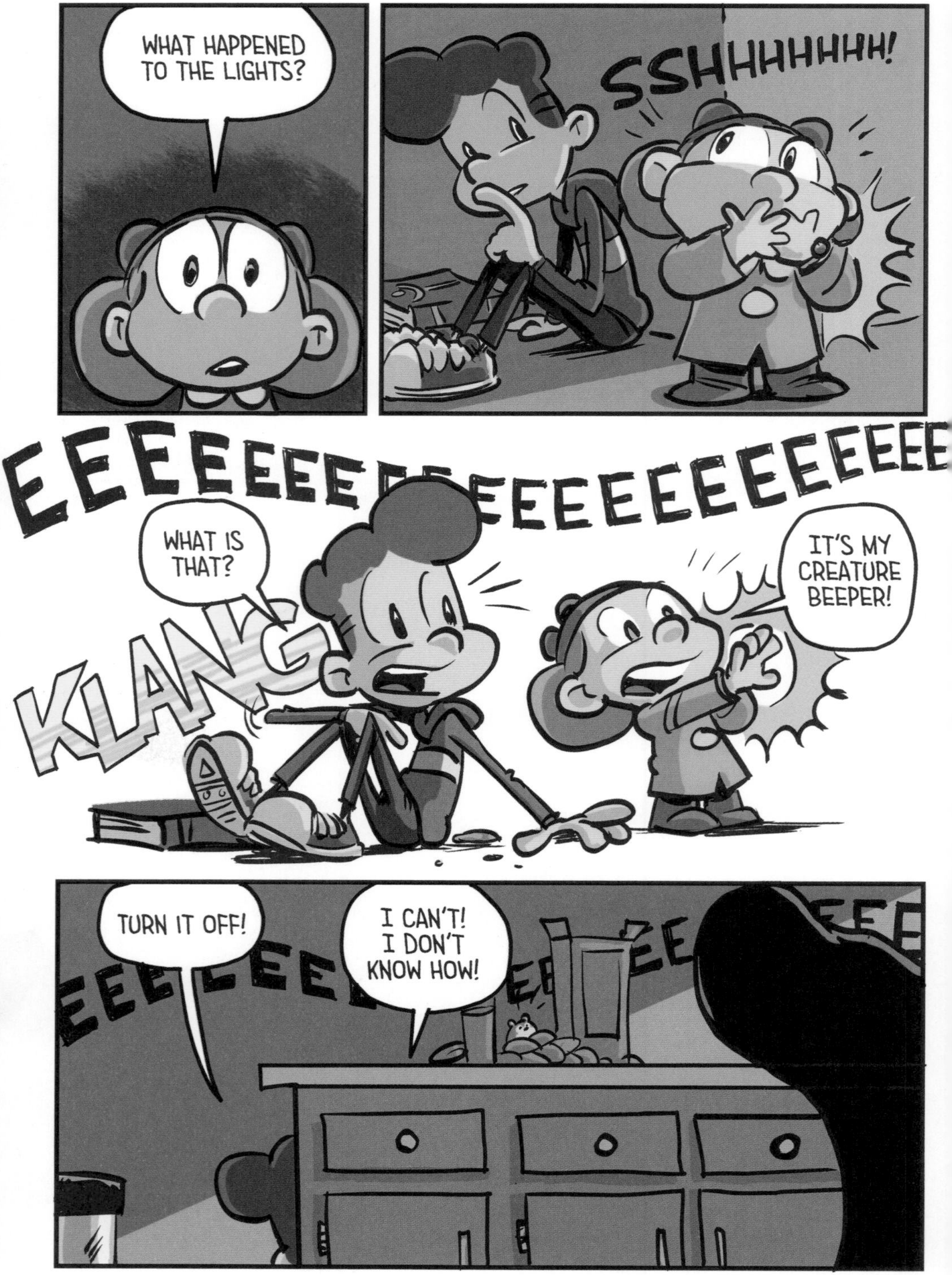
WHAT HAPPENED TO THE LIGHTS?
SSHHHHHHH!
EEEEEEEEEEEEEEEEEEEEE
WHAT IS THAT?
KLANG
IT'S MY CREATURE BEEPER!
TURN IT OFF!
I CAN'T! I DON'T KNOW HOW!

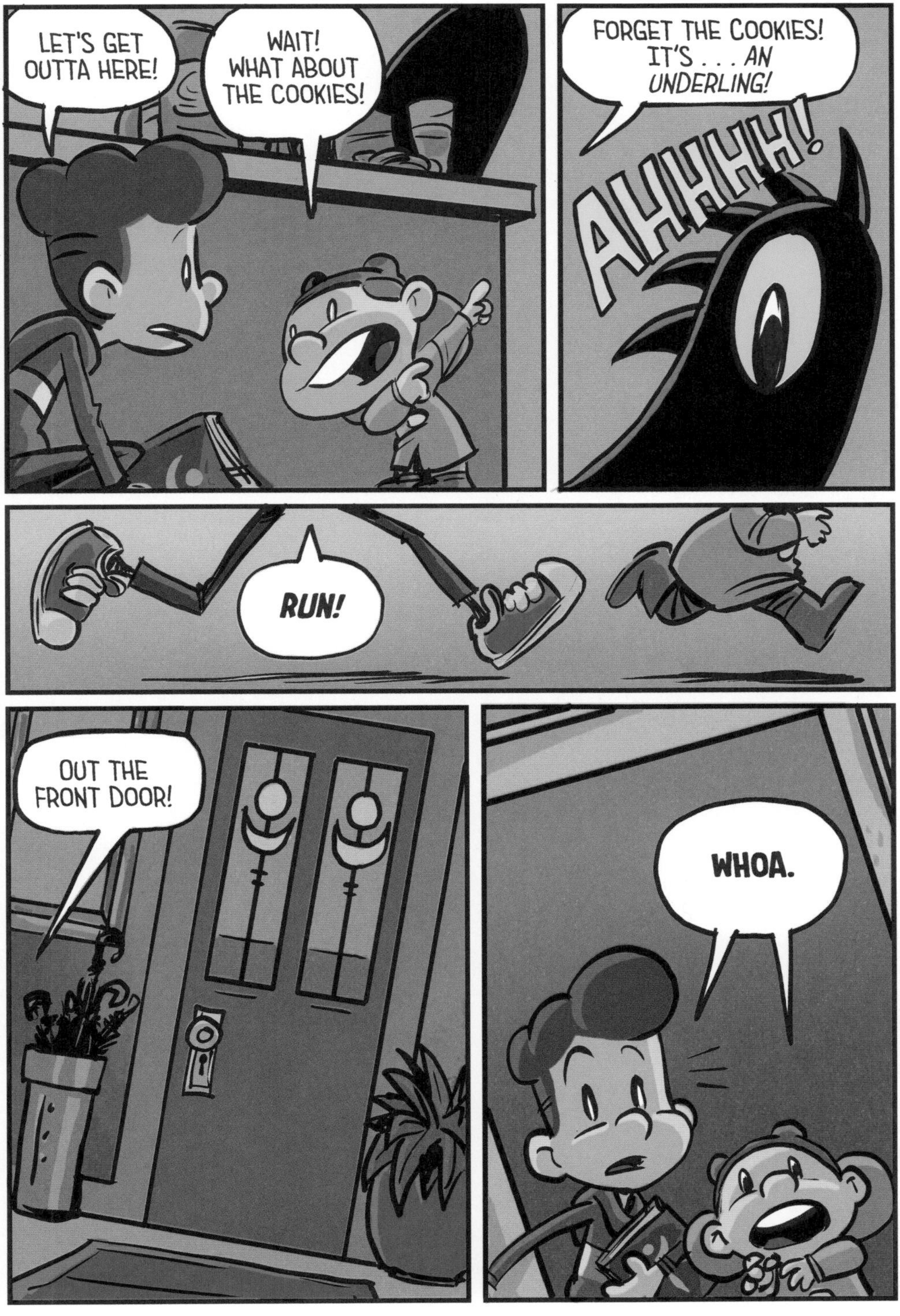
LET'S GET OUTTA HERE!
WAIT! WHAT ABOUT THE COOKIES!
FORGET THE COOKIES! IT'S . . . AN UNDERLING!
AHHHHH!
RUN!
OUT THE FRONT DOOR!
WHOA.

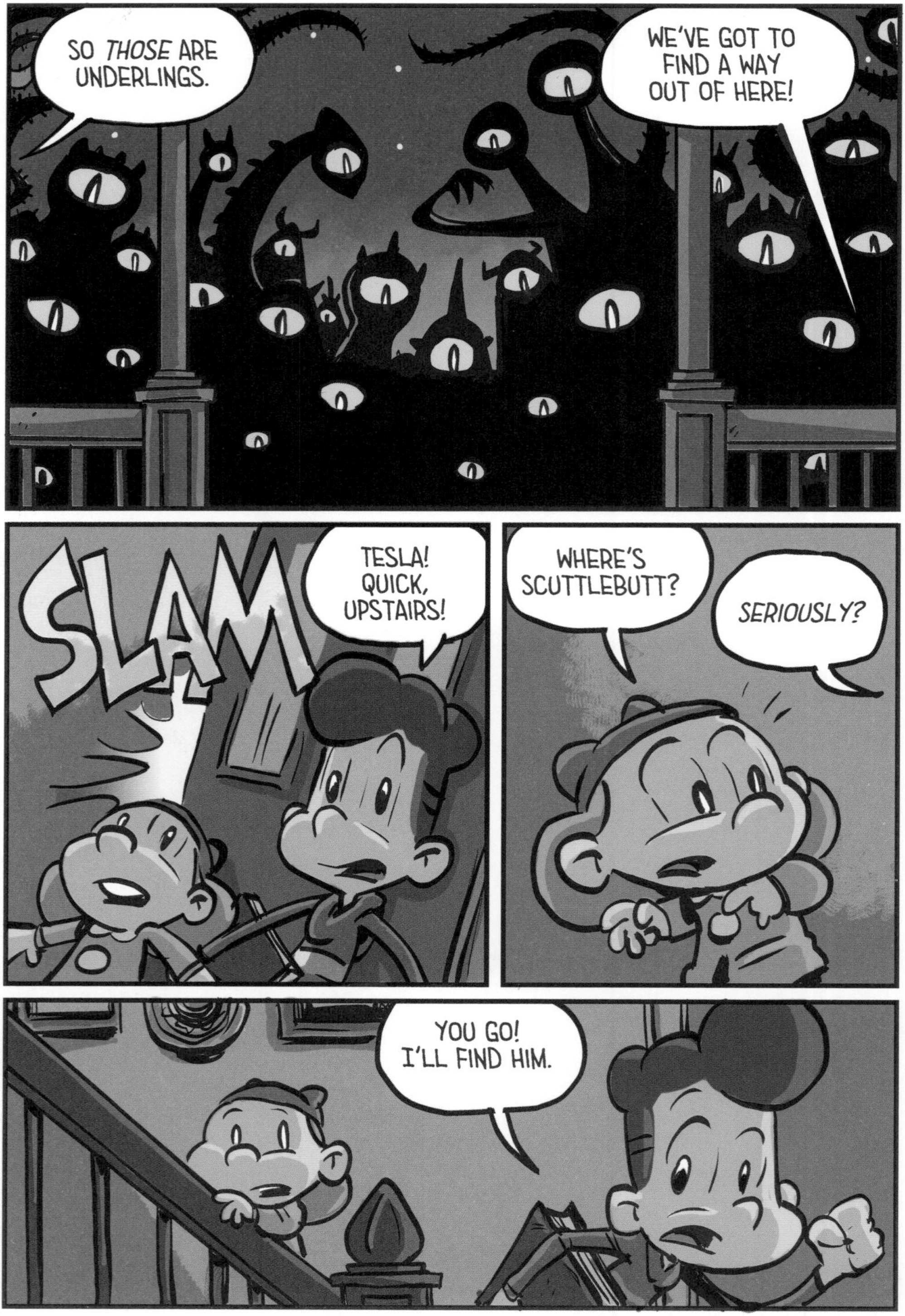
SO *THOSE* ARE UNDERLINGS.
WE'VE GOT TO FIND A WAY OUT OF HERE!
SLAM
TESLA! QUICK, UPSTAIRS!
WHERE'S SCUTTLEBUTT?
SERIOUSLY?
YOU GO! I'LL FIND HIM.

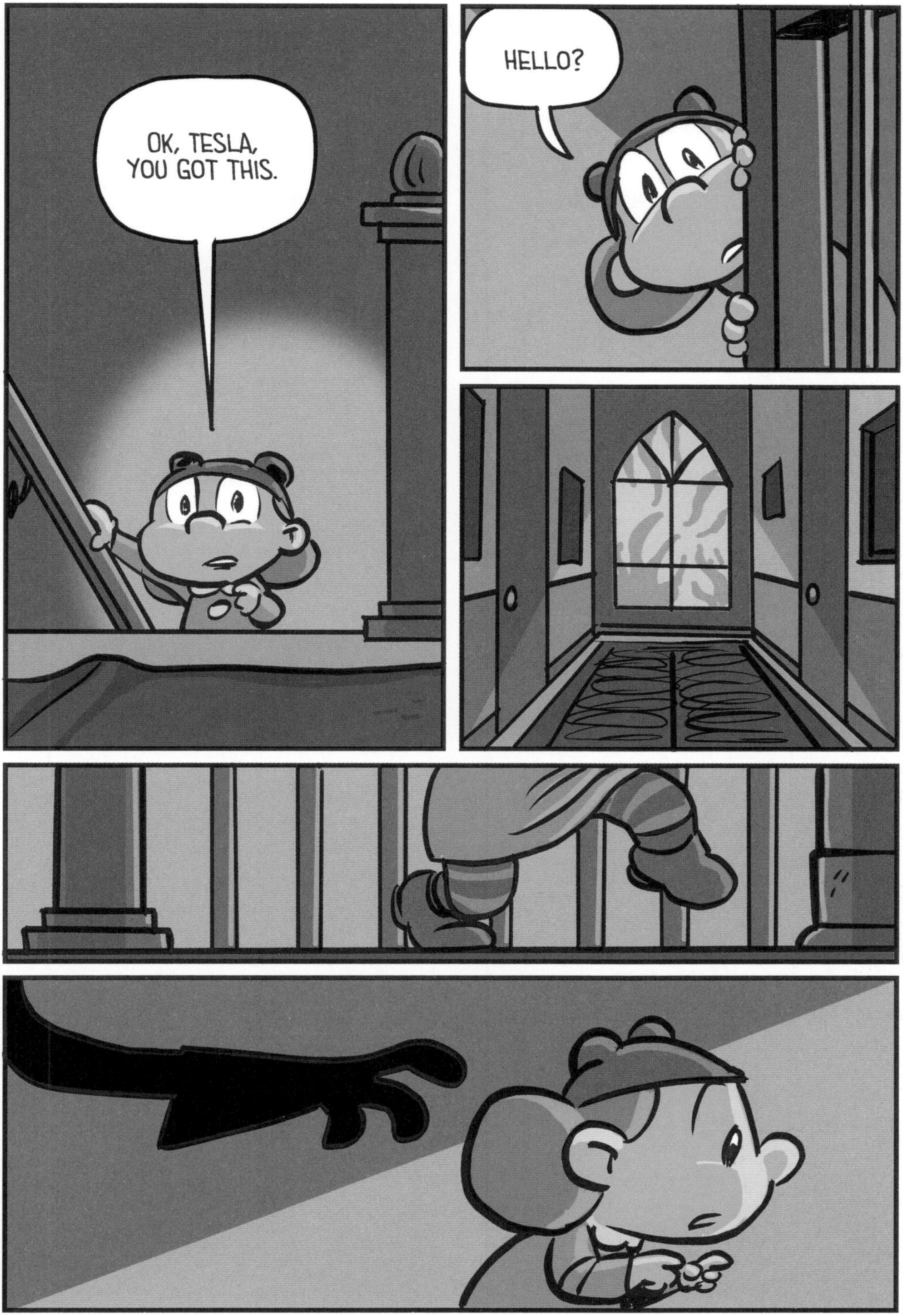
OK, TESLA, YOU GOT THIS.
HELLO?

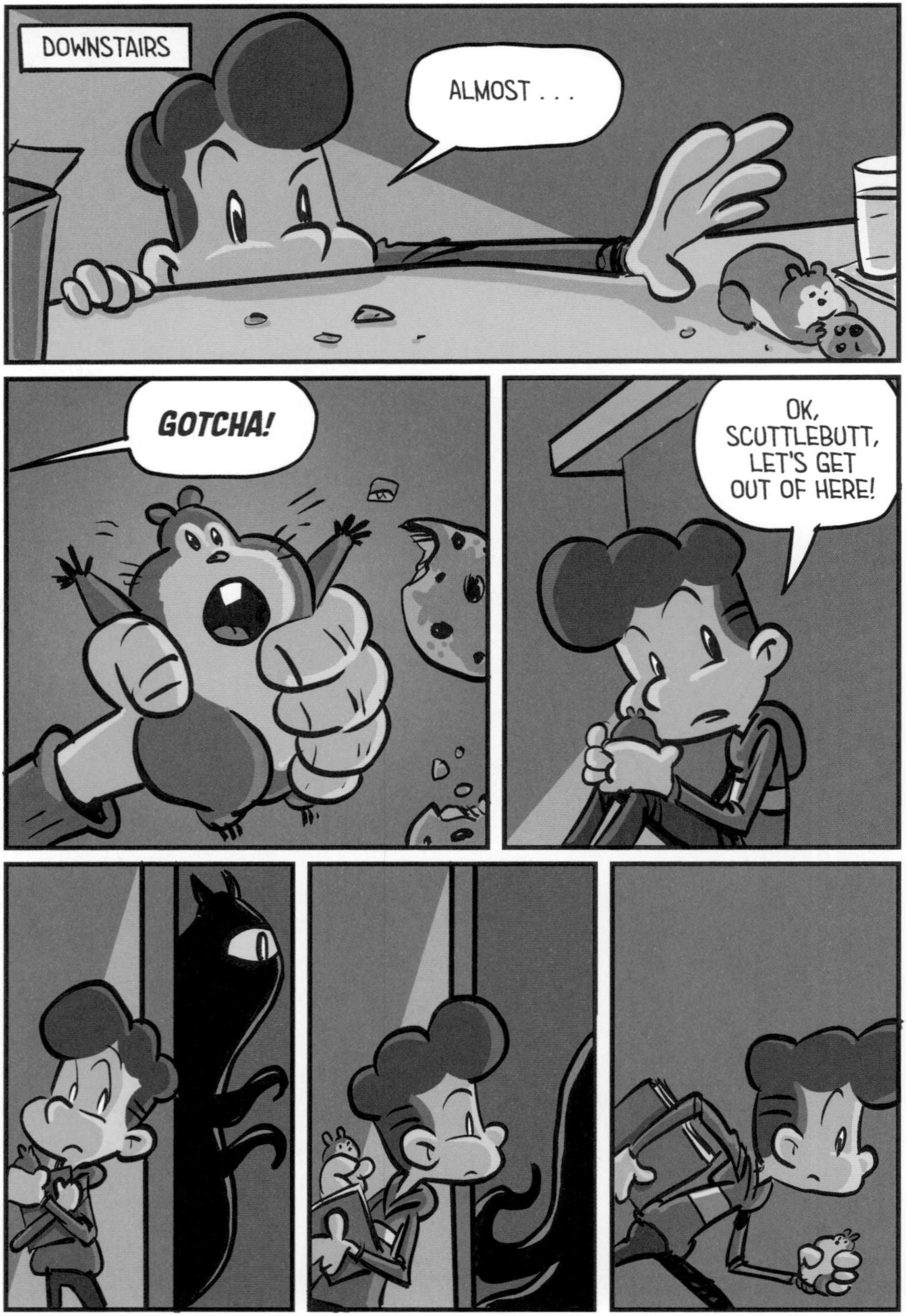
DOWNSTAIRS
ALMOST . . .
GOTCHA!
OK, SCUTTLEBUTT, LET'S GET OUT OF HERE!

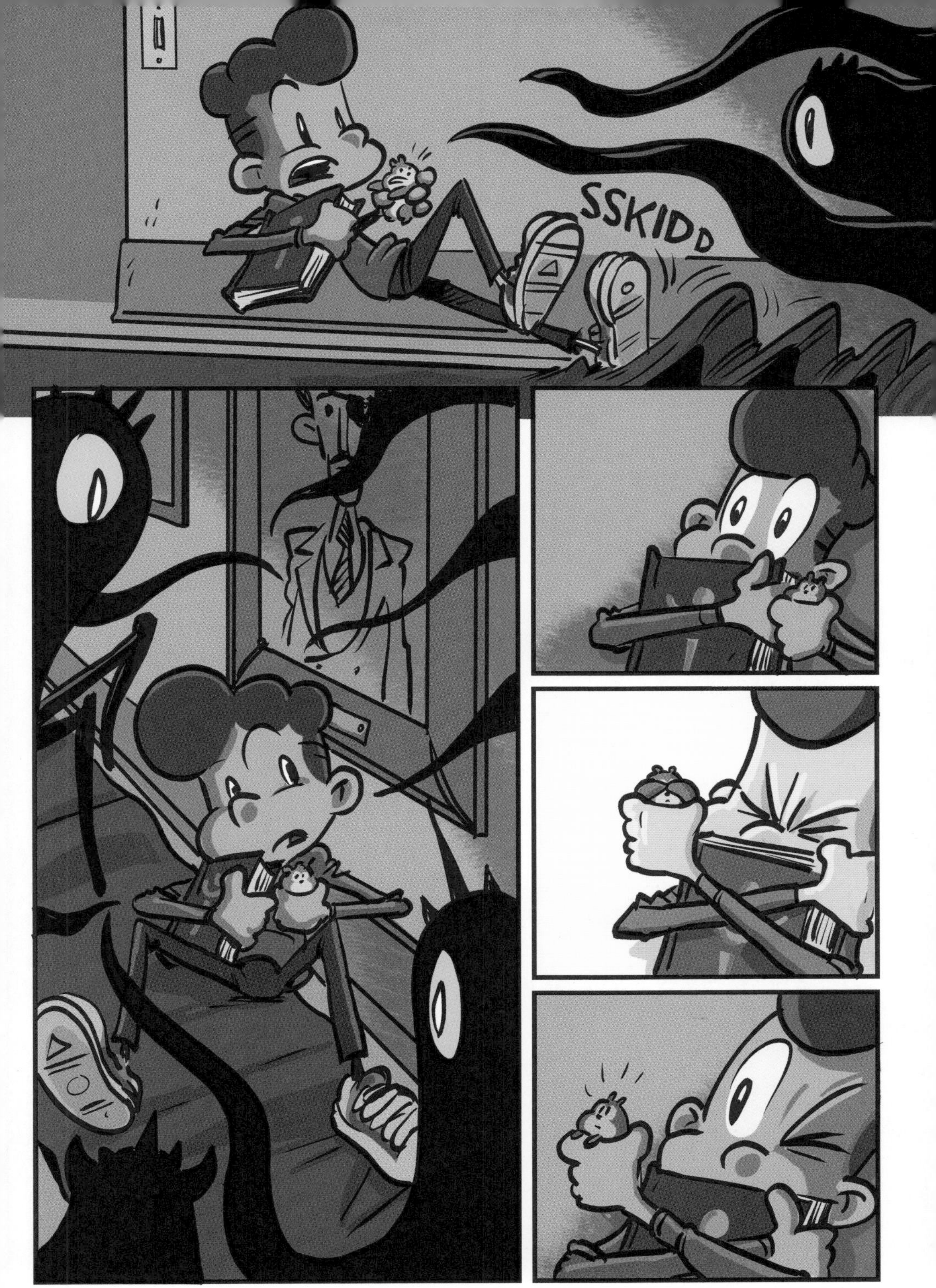
SSKIDD

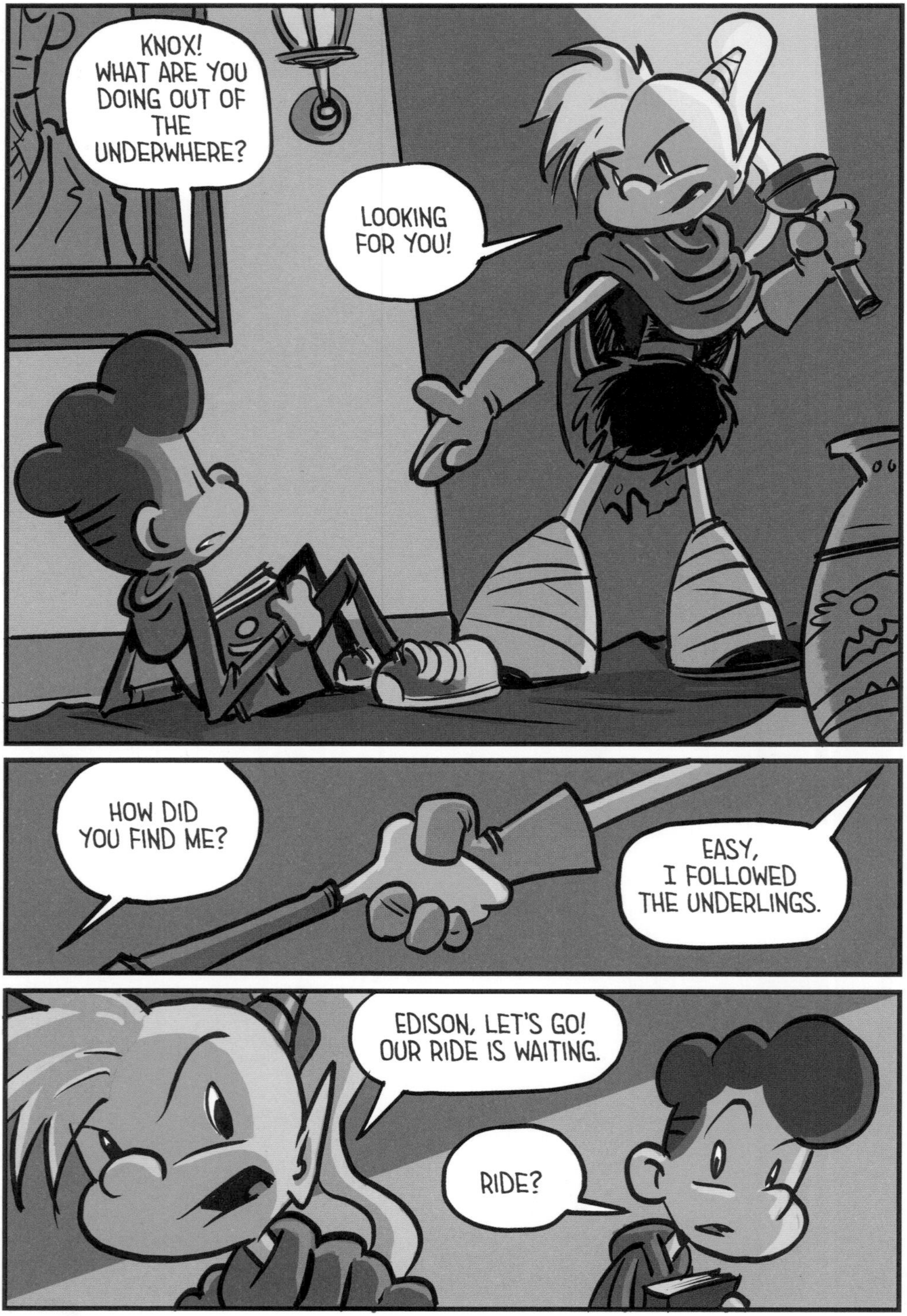
KNOX! WHAT ARE YOU DOING OUT OF THE UNDERWHERE?
LOOKING FOR YOU!
HOW DID YOU FIND ME?
EASY, I FOLLOWED THE UNDERLINGS.
EDISON, LET'S GO! OUR RIDE IS WAITING.
RIDE?

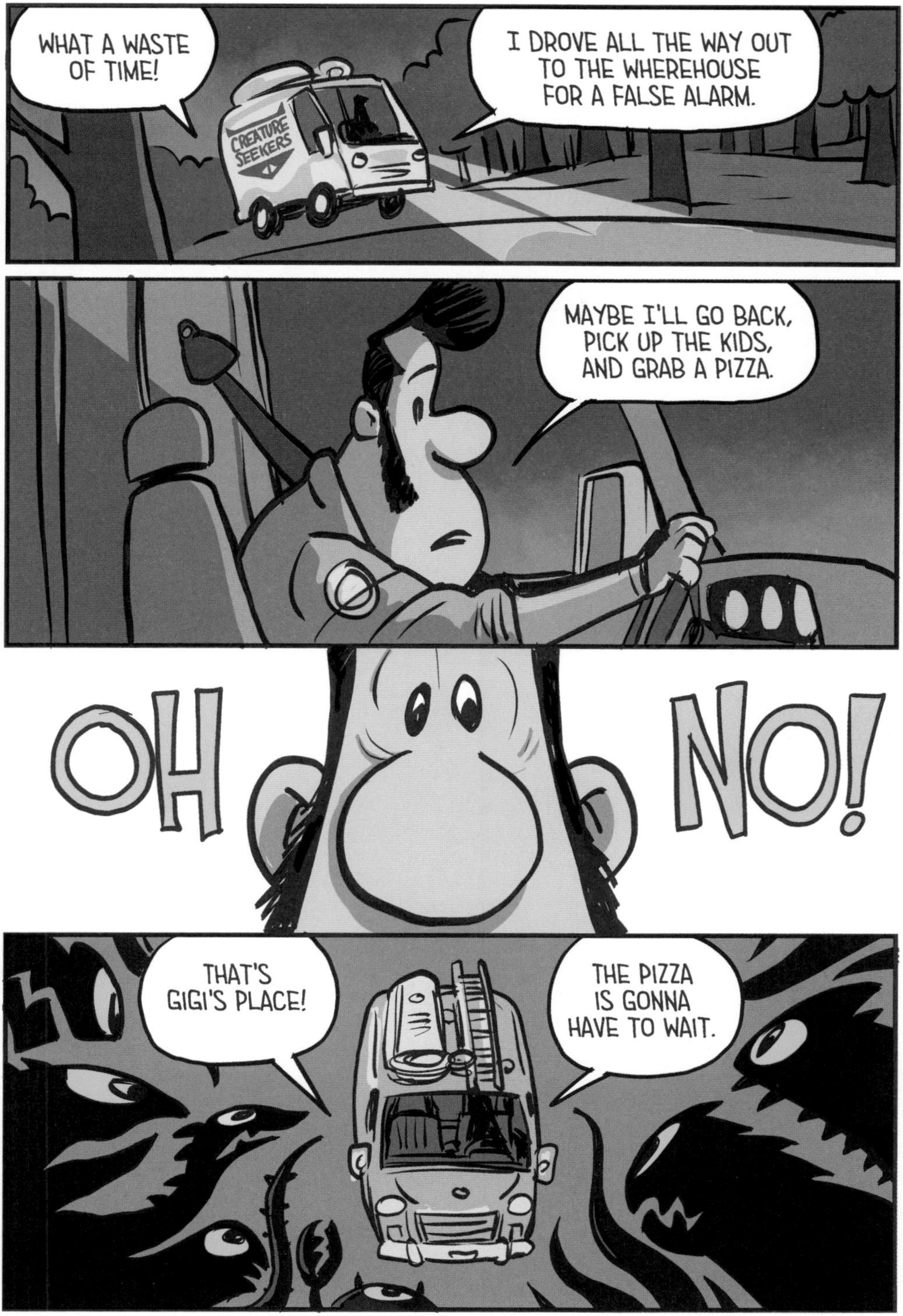
WHAT A WASTE OF TIME!
I DROVE ALL THE WAY OUT TO THE WHEREHOUSE FOR A FALSE ALARM.
CREATURE SEEKERS
MAYBE I'LL GO BACK, PICK UP THE KIDS, AND GRAB A PIZZA.
OH NO!
THAT'S GIGI'S PLACE!
THE PIZZA IS GONNA HAVE TO WAIT.

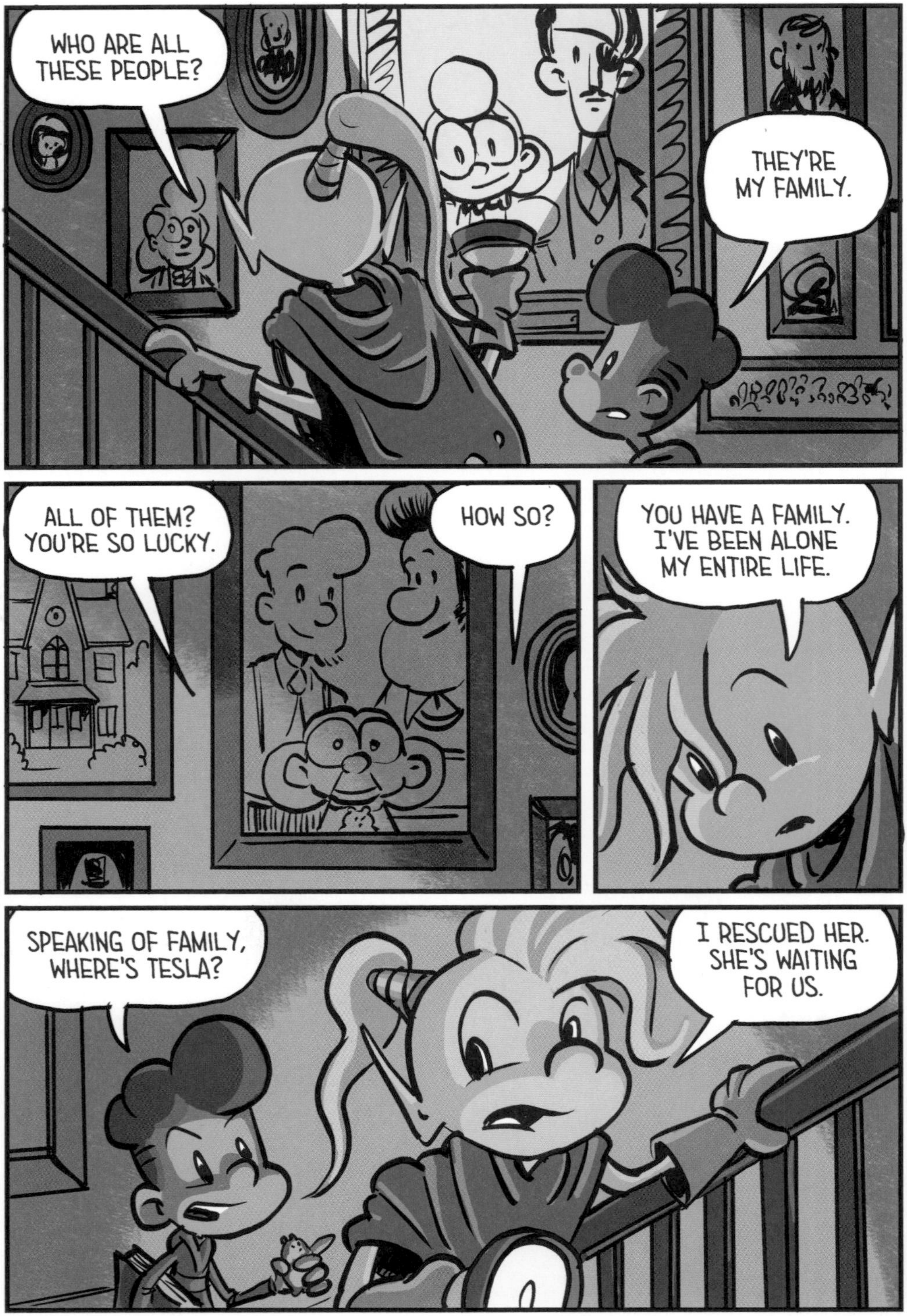
WHO ARE ALL THESE PEOPLE?
THEY'RE MY FAMILY.
ALL OF THEM? YOU'RE SO LUCKY.
HOW SO?
YOU HAVE A FAMILY. I'VE BEEN ALONE MY ENTIRE LIFE.
SPEAKING OF FAMILY, WHERE'S TESLA?
I RESCUED HER. SHE'S WAITING FOR US.

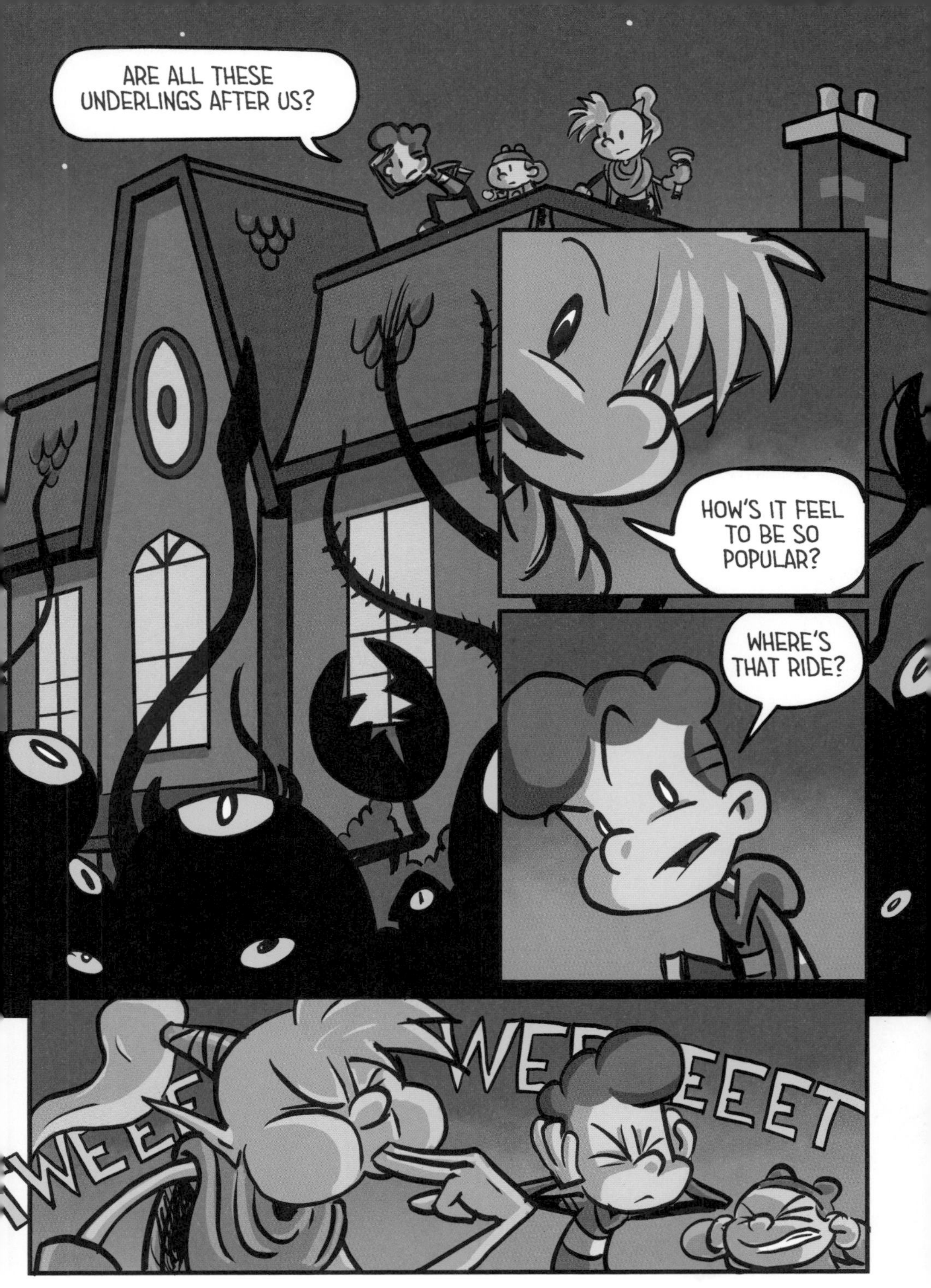
ARE ALL THESE UNDERLINGS AFTER US?
HOW'S IT FEEL TO BE SO POPULAR?
WHERE'S THAT RIDE?
WEEEEEEEEEEEEEET

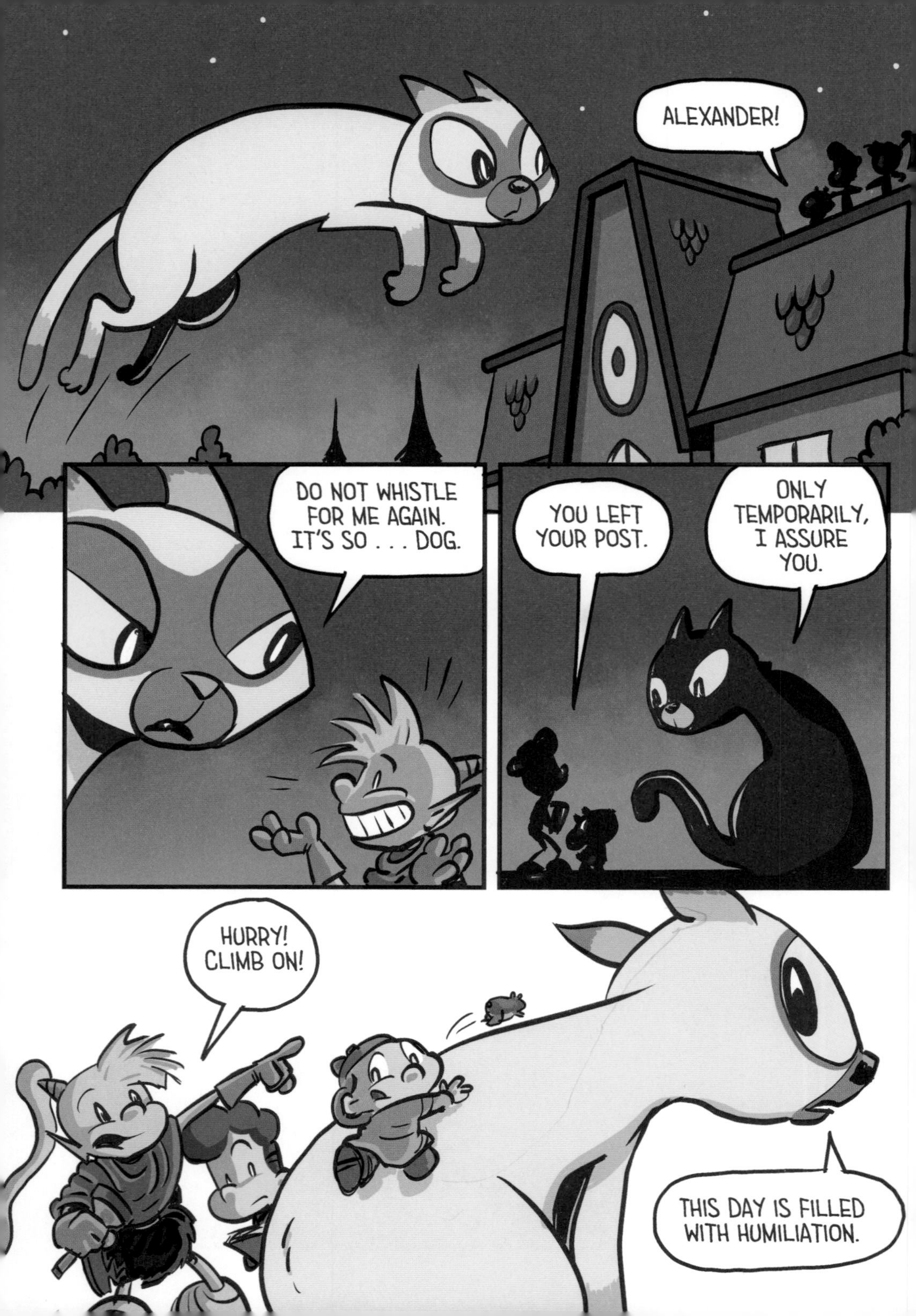
ALEXANDER!
DO NOT WHISTLE FOR ME AGAIN. IT'S SO . . . DOG.
YOU LEFT YOUR POST.
ONLY TEMPORARILY, I ASSURE YOU.
HURRY! CLIMB ON!
THIS DAY IS FILLED WITH HUMILIATION.

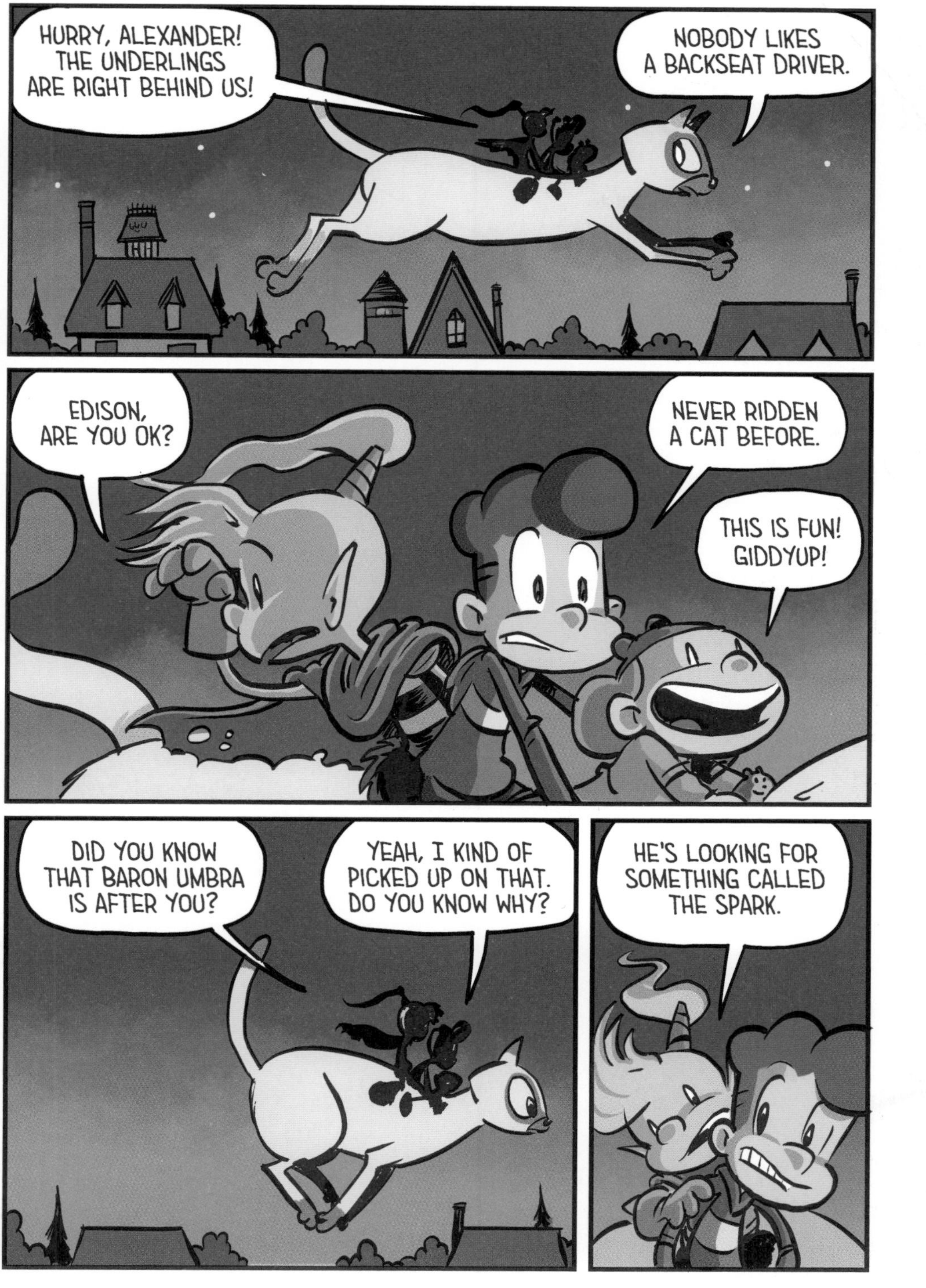
HURRY, ALEXANDER! THE UNDERLINGS ARE RIGHT BEHIND US!
NOBODY LIKES A BACKSEAT DRIVER.
EDISON, ARE YOU OK?
NEVER RIDDEN A CAT BEFORE.
THIS IS FUN! GIDDYUP!
DID YOU KNOW THAT BARON UMBRA IS AFTER YOU?
YEAH, I KIND OF PICKED UP ON THAT. DO YOU KNOW WHY?
HE'S LOOKING FOR SOMETHING CALLED THE SPARK.

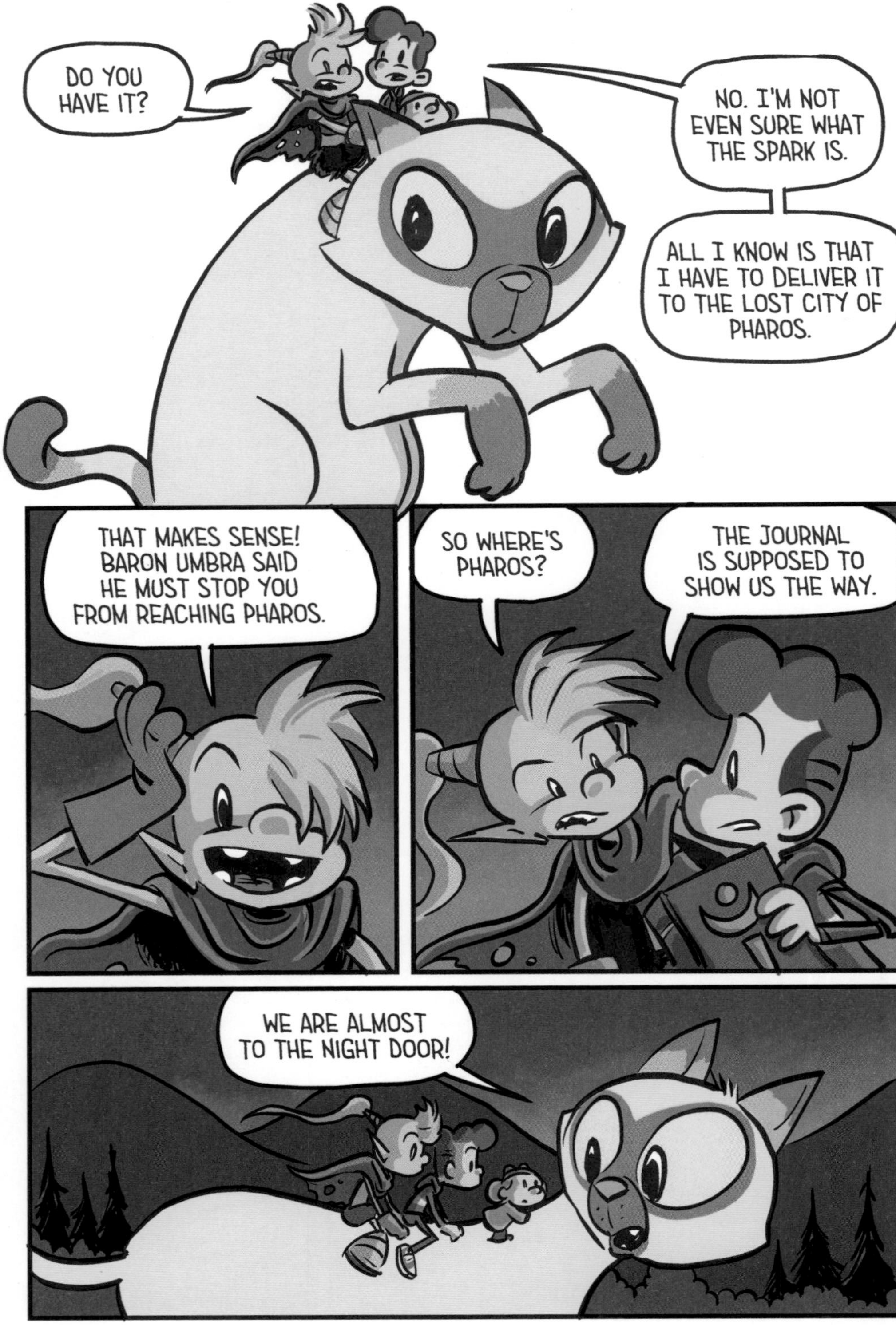
DO YOU HAVE IT?
NO. I'M NOT EVEN SURE WHAT THE SPARK IS.
ALL I KNOW IS THAT I HAVE TO DELIVER IT TO THE LOST CITY OF PHAROS.
THAT MAKES SENSE! BARON UMBRA SAID HE MUST STOP YOU FROM REACHING PHAROS.
SO WHERE'S PHAROS?
THE JOURNAL IS SUPPOSED TO SHOW US THE WAY.
WE ARE ALMOST TO THE NIGHT DOOR!

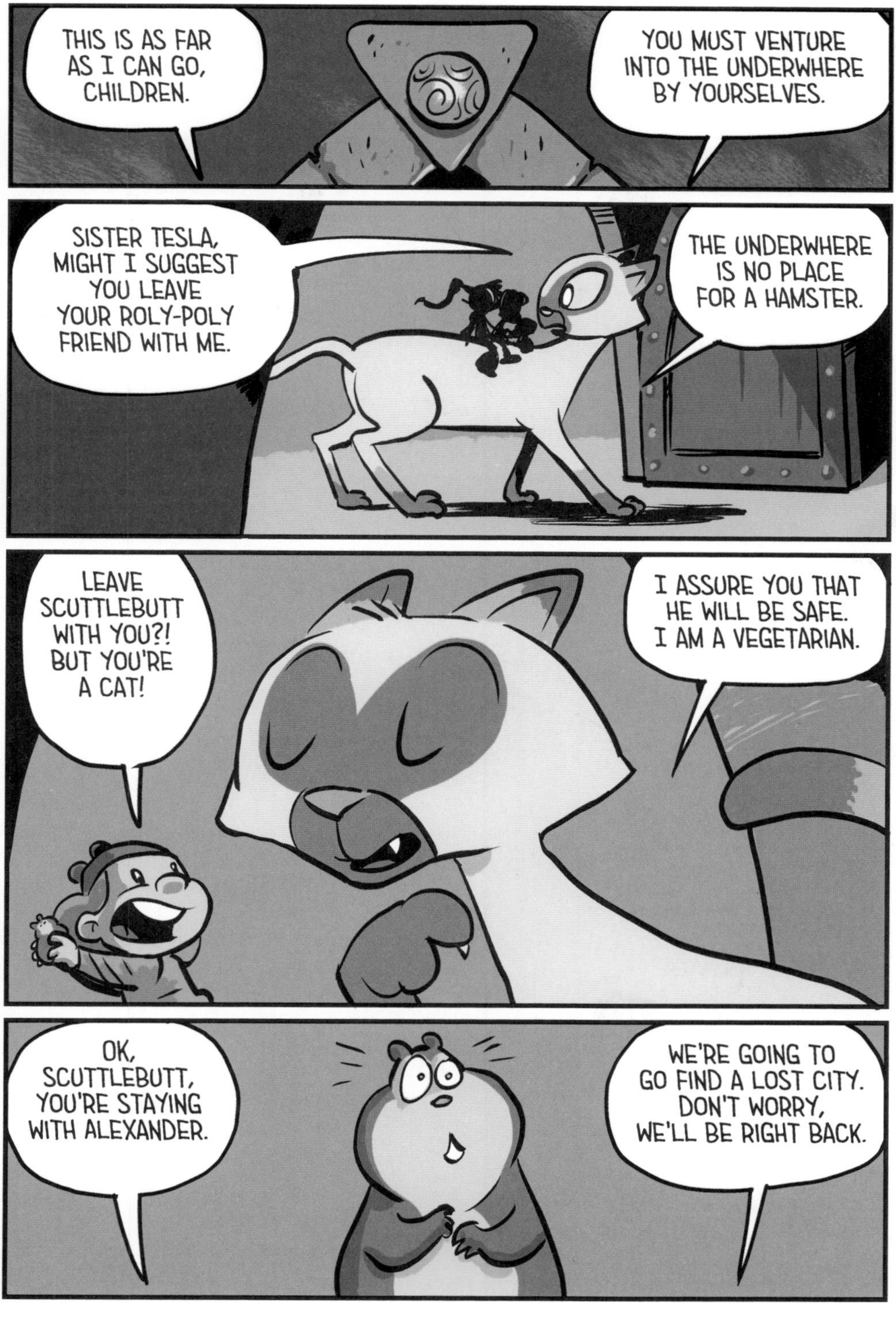
THIS IS AS FAR AS I CAN GO, CHILDREN.
YOU MUST VENTURE INTO THE UNDERWHERE BY YOURSELVES.
SISTER TESLA, MIGHT I SUGGEST YOU LEAVE YOUR ROLY-POLY FRIEND WITH ME.
THE UNDERWHERE IS NO PLACE FOR A HAMSTER.
LEAVE SCUTTLEBUTT WITH YOU?! BUT YOU'RE A CAT!
I ASSURE YOU THAT HE WILL BE SAFE. I AM A VEGETARIAN.
OK, SCUTTLEBUTT, YOU'RE STAYING WITH ALEXANDER.
WE'RE GOING TO GO FIND A LOST CITY. DON'T WORRY, WE'LL BE RIGHT BACK.

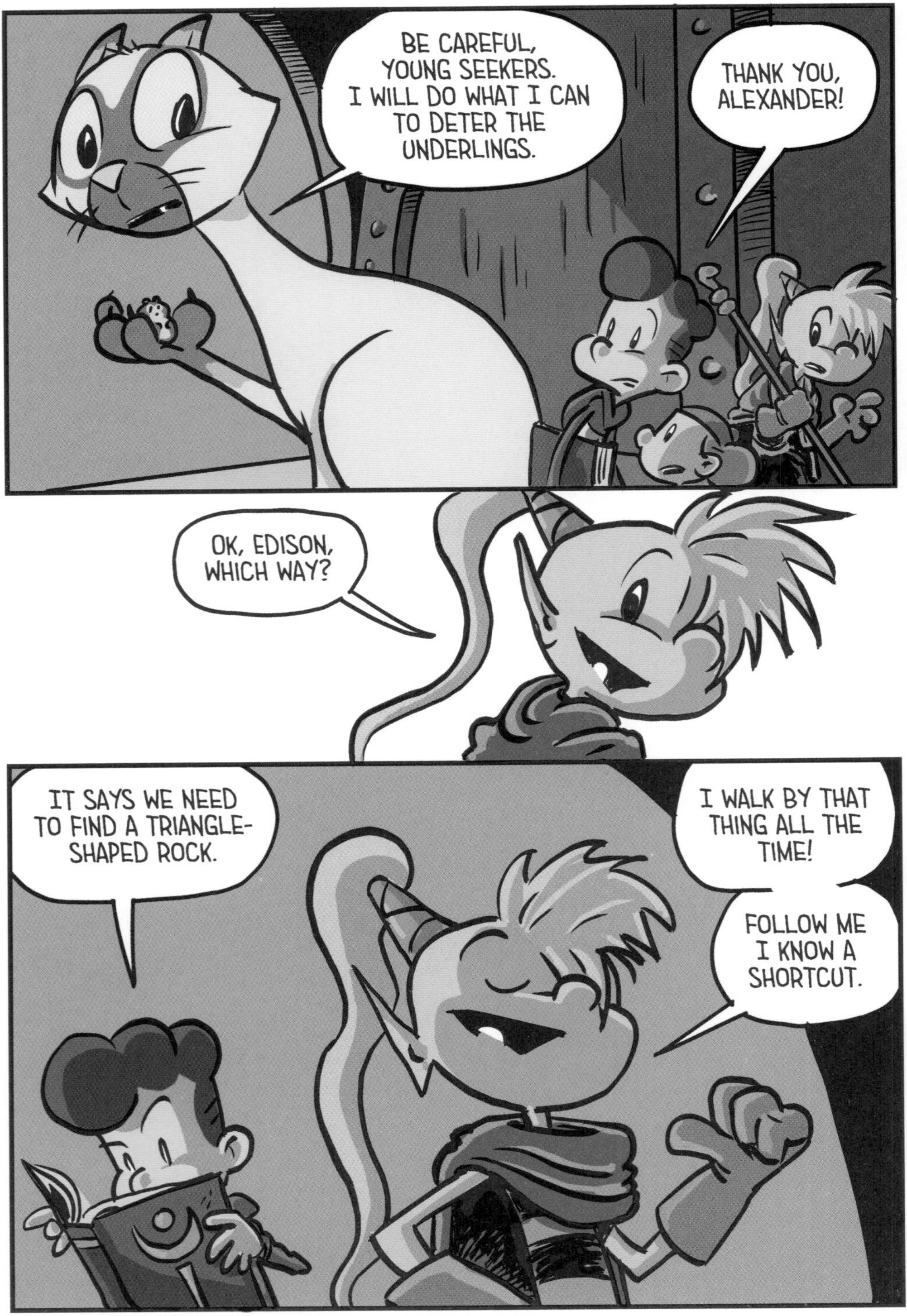
BE CAREFUL, YOUNG SEEKERS. I WILL DO WHAT I CAN TO DETER THE UNDERLINGS.
THANK YOU, ALEXANDER!
OK, EDISON, WHICH WAY?
IT SAYS WE NEED TO FIND A TRIANGLE-SHAPED ROCK.
I WALK BY THAT THING ALL THE TIME!
FOLLOW ME I KNOW A SHORTCUT.

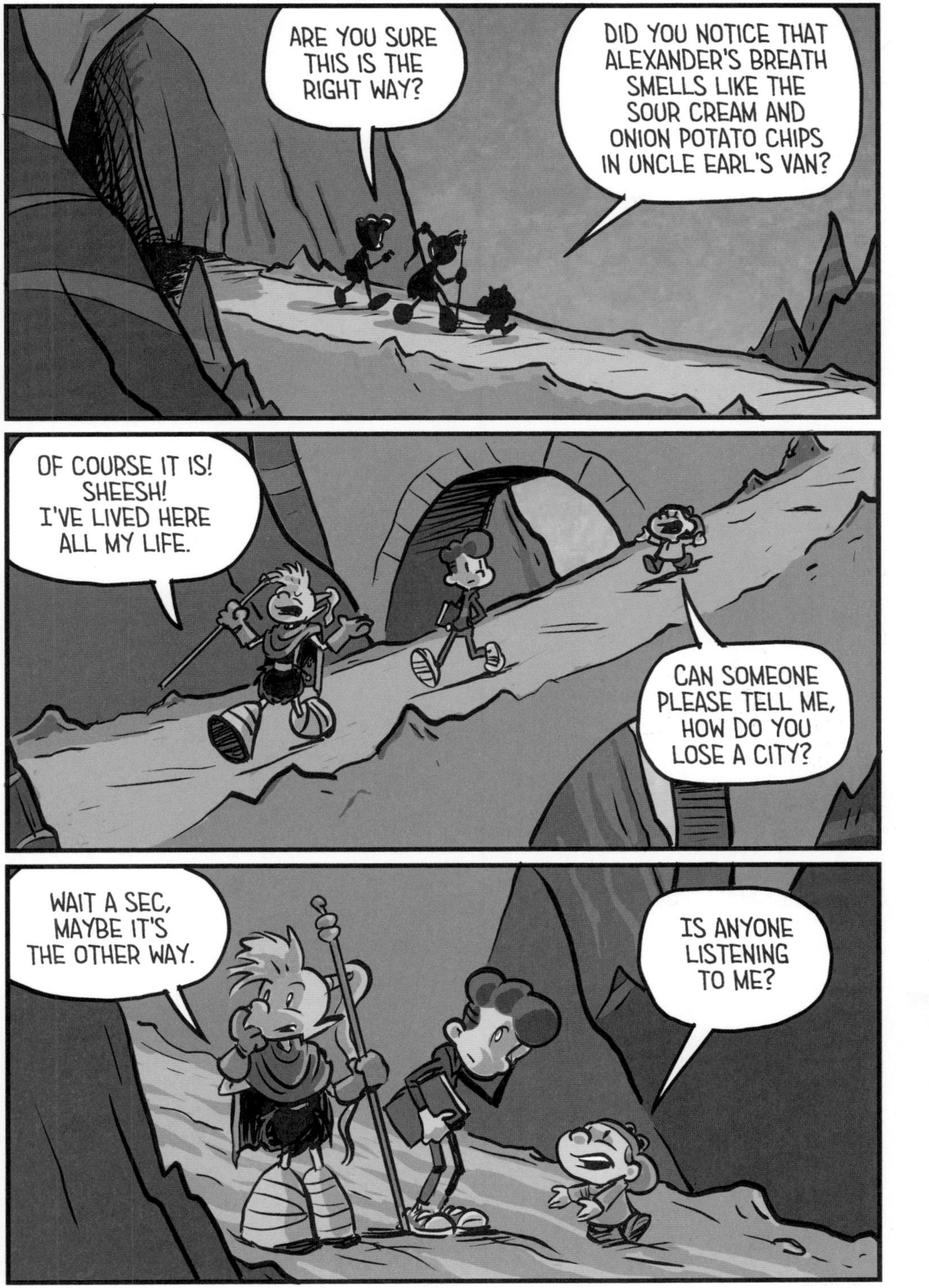
ARE YOU SURE THIS IS THE RIGHT WAY?
DID YOU NOTICE THAT ALEXANDER'S BREATH SMELLS LIKE THE SOUR CREAM AND ONION POTATO CHIPS IN UNCLE EARL'S VAN?
OF COURSE IT IS! SHEESH! I'VE LIVED HERE ALL MY LIFE.
CAN SOMEONE PLEASE TELL ME, HOW DO YOU LOSE A CITY?
WAIT A SEC, MAYBE IT'S THE OTHER WAY.
IS ANYONE LISTENING TO ME?

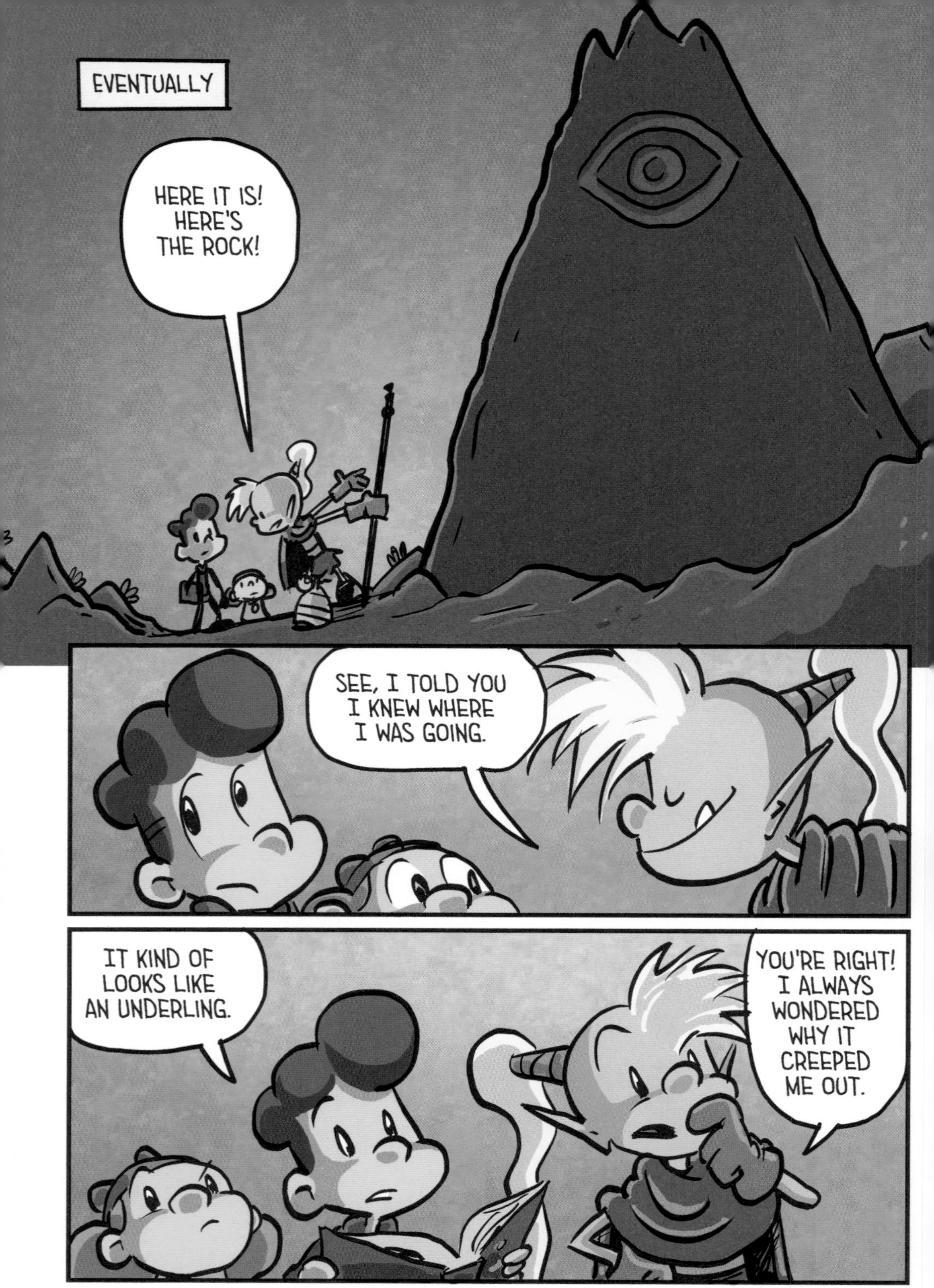
EVENTUALLY
HERE IT IS! HERE'S THE ROCK!
SEE, I TOLD YOU I KNEW WHERE I WAS GOING.
IT KIND OF LOOKS LIKE AN UNDERLING.
YOU'RE RIGHT! I ALWAYS WONDERED WHY IT CREEPED ME OUT.

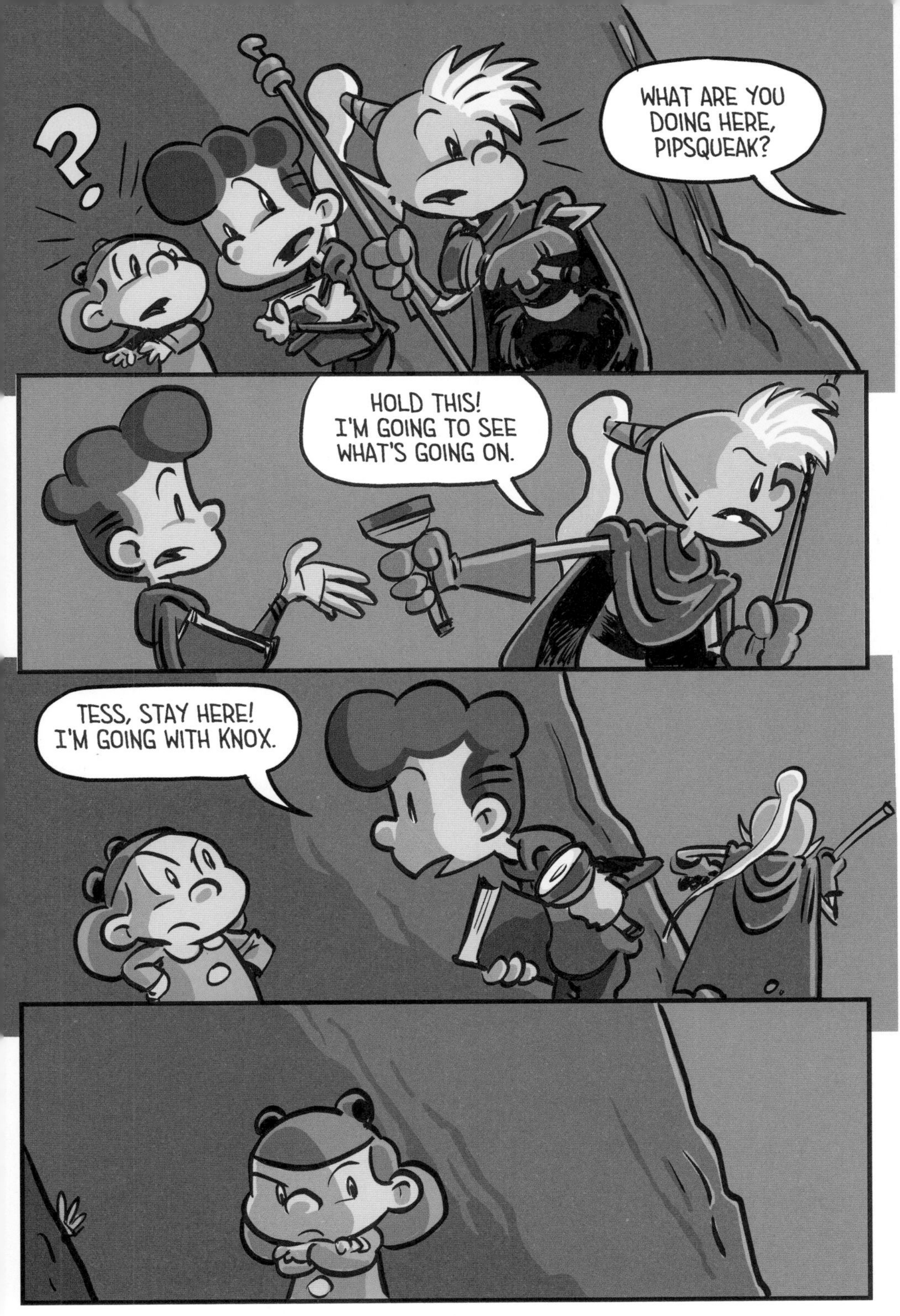
?
WHAT ARE YOU DOING HERE, PIPSQUEAK?
HOLD THIS! I'M GOING TO SEE WHAT'S GOING ON.
TESS, STAY HERE! I'M GOING WITH KNOX.

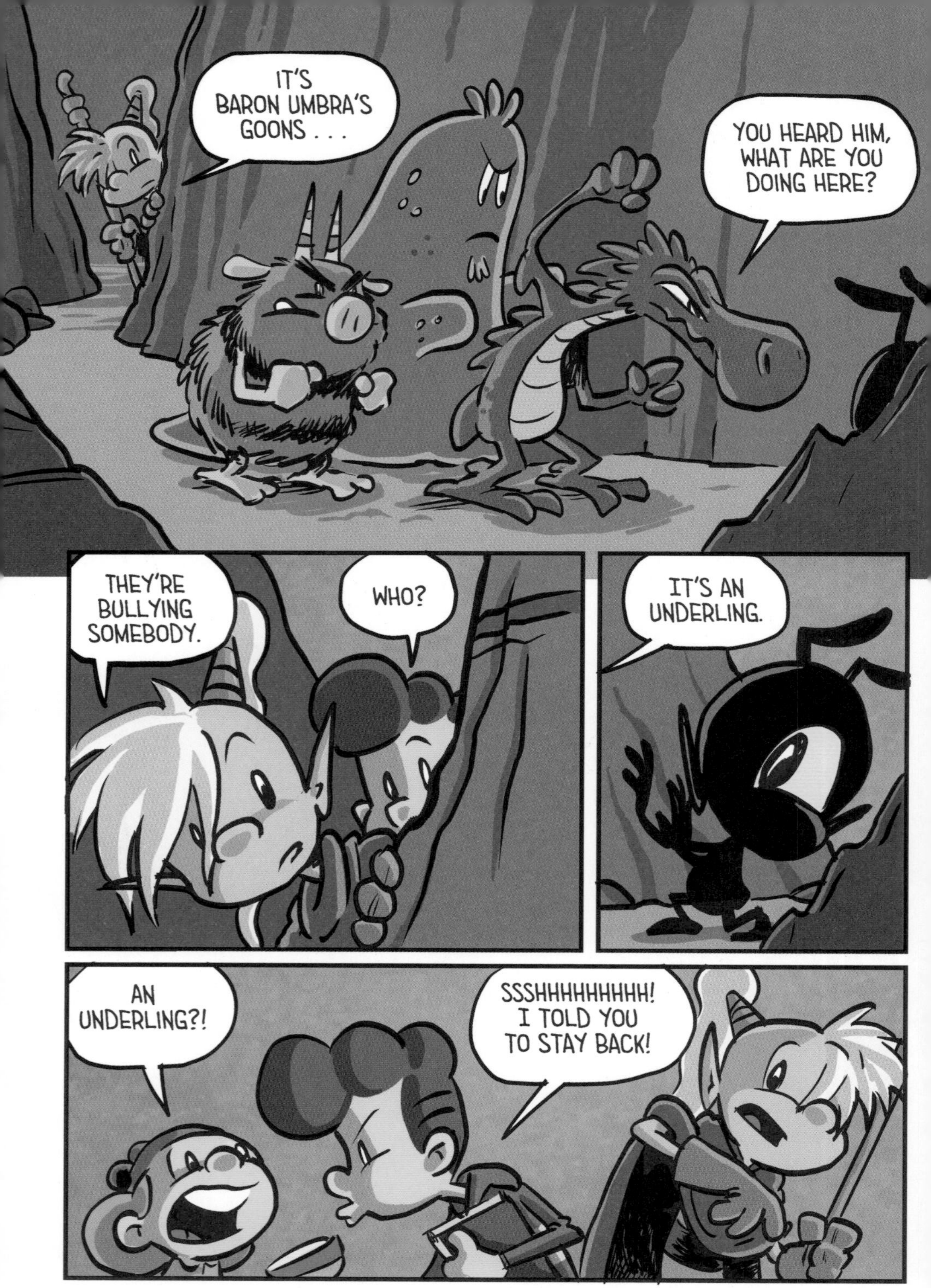
IT'S BARON UMBRA'S GOONS . . .
YOU HEARD HIM, WHAT ARE YOU DOING HERE?
THEY'RE BULLYING SOMEBODY.
WHO?
IT'S AN UNDERLING.
AN UNDERLING?!
SSSHHHHHHHHH! I TOLD YOU TO STAY BACK!

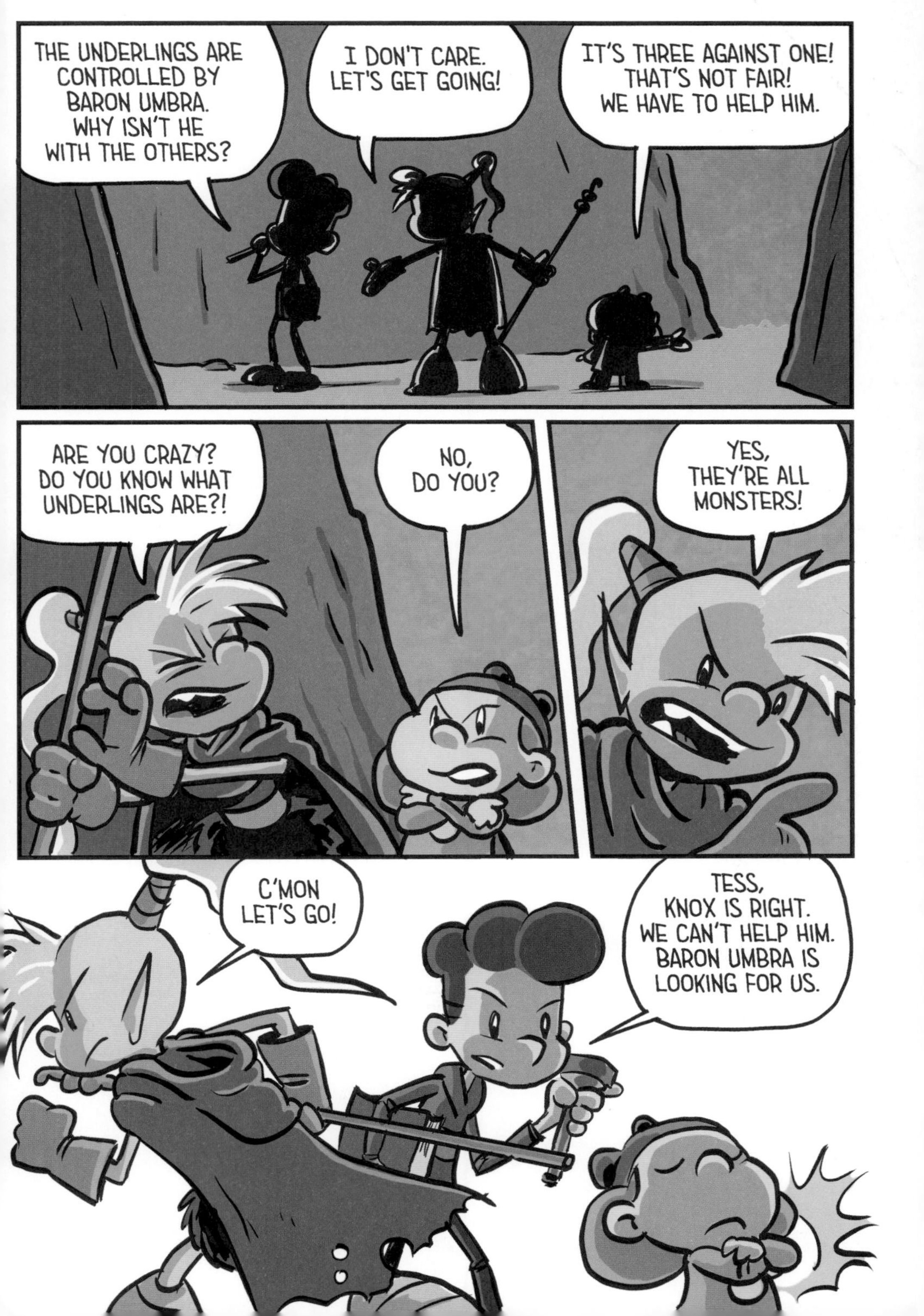
THE UNDERLINGS ARE CONTROLLED BY BARON UMBRA. WHY ISN'T HE WITH THE OTHERS?
I DON'T CARE. LET'S GET GOING!
IT'S THREE AGAINST ONE! THAT'S NOT FAIR! WE HAVE TO HELP HIM.
ARE YOU CRAZY? DO YOU KNOW WHAT UNDERLINGS ARE?!
NO, DO YOU?
YES, THEY'RE ALL MONSTERS!
C'MON LET'S GO!
TESS, KNOX IS RIGHT. WE CAN'T HELP HIM. BARON UMBRA IS LOOKING FOR US.

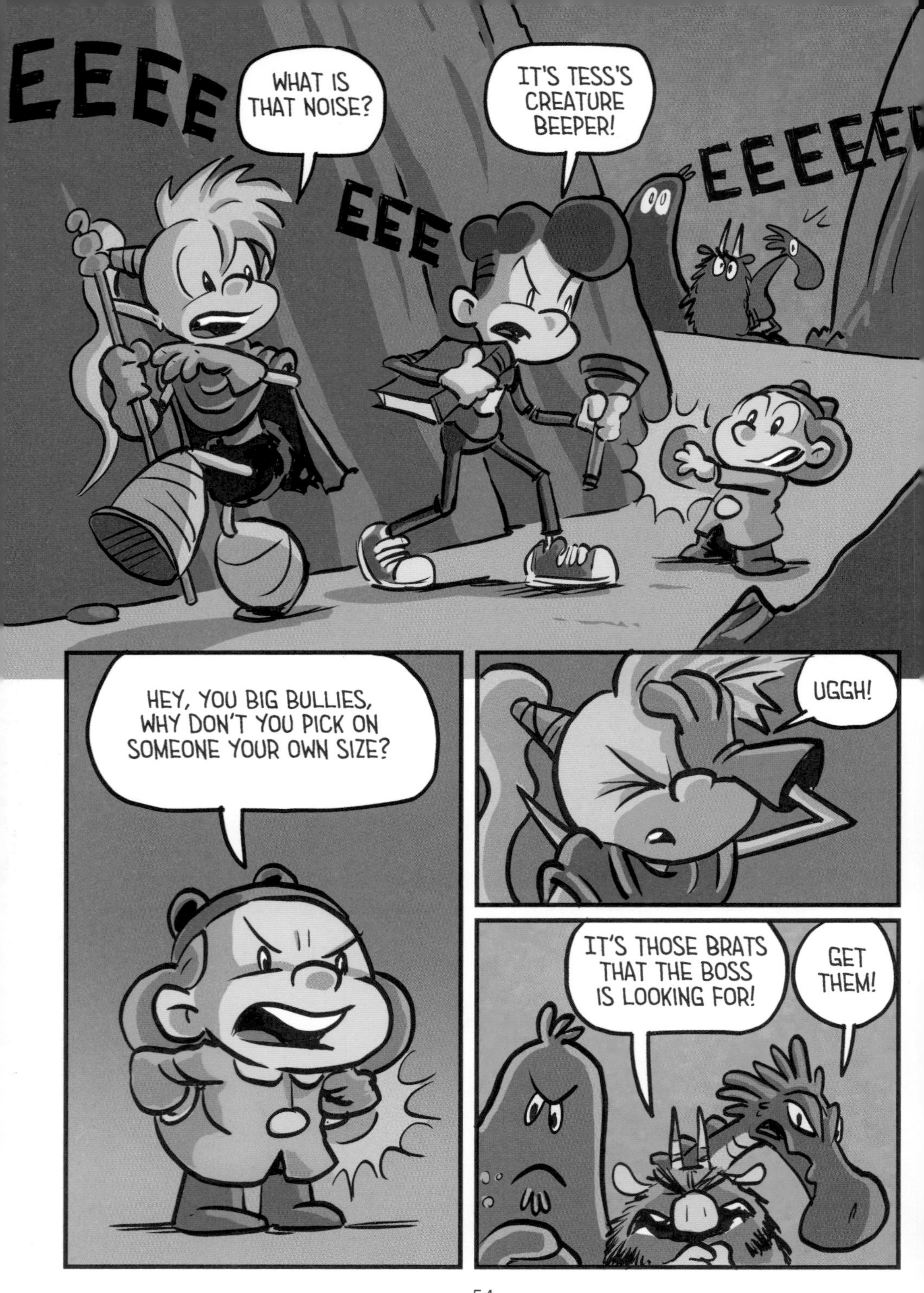
EEEE
WHAT IS THAT NOISE?
EEE
IT'S TESS'S CREATURE BEEPER!
EEEEEE
HEY, YOU BIG BULLIES, WHY DON'T YOU PICK ON SOMEONE YOUR OWN SIZE?
UGGH!
IT'S THOSE BRATS THAT THE BOSS IS LOOKING FOR!
GET THEM!

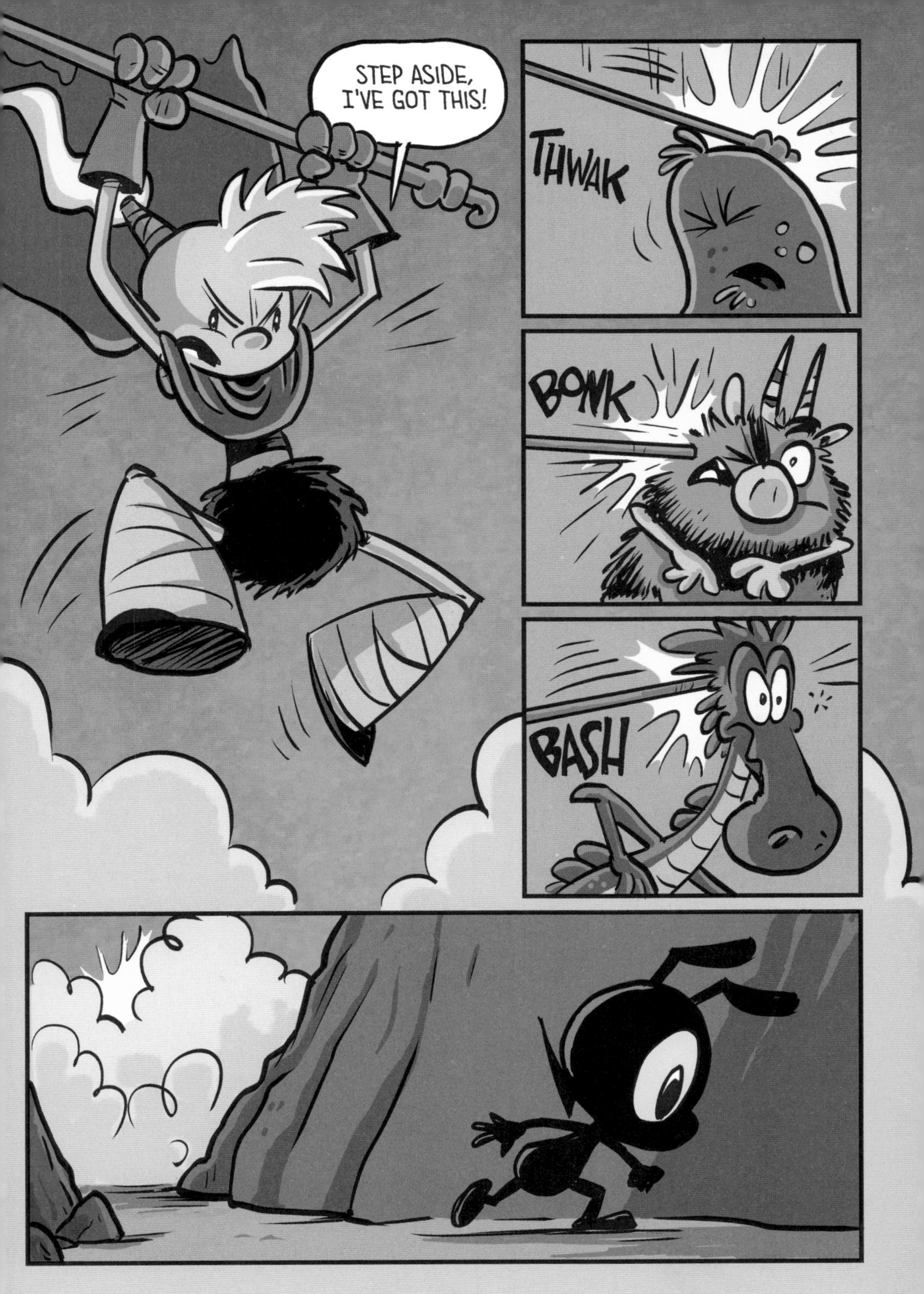
STEP ASIDE, I'VE GOT THIS!
THWAK
BONK
BASH

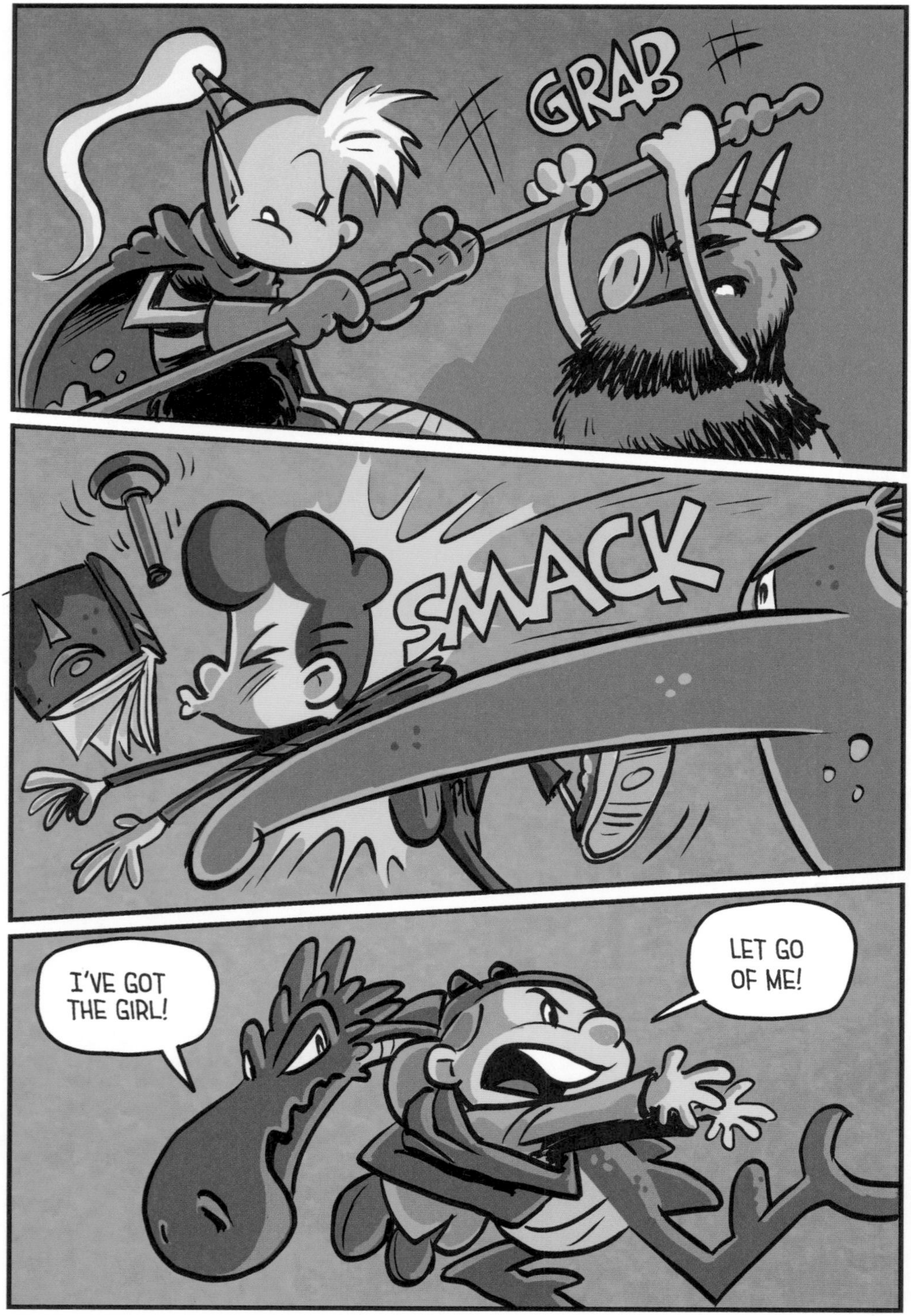
GRAB
SMACK
I'VE GOT THE GIRL!
LET GO OF ME!

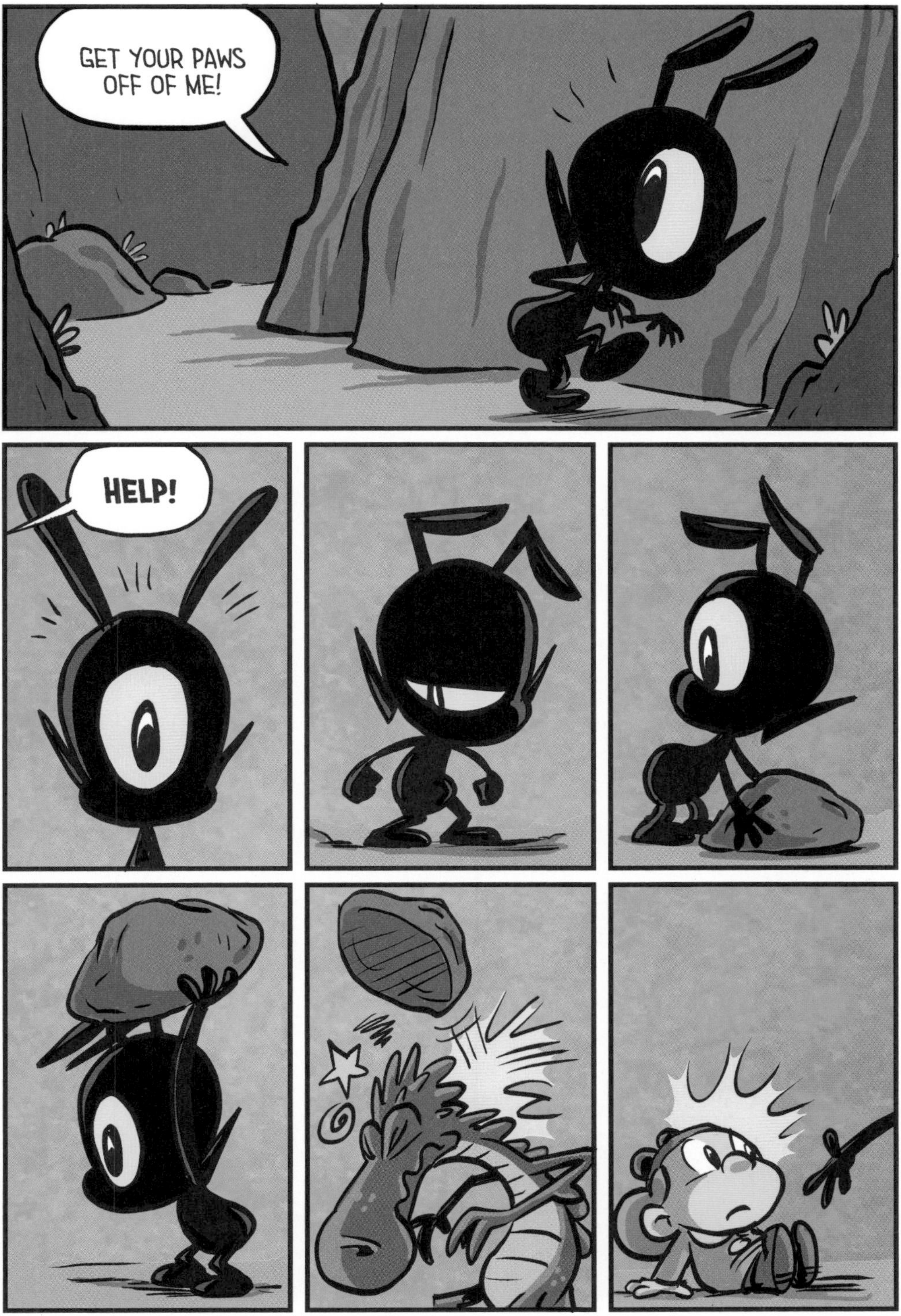
GET YOUR PAWS OFF OF ME!
HELP!

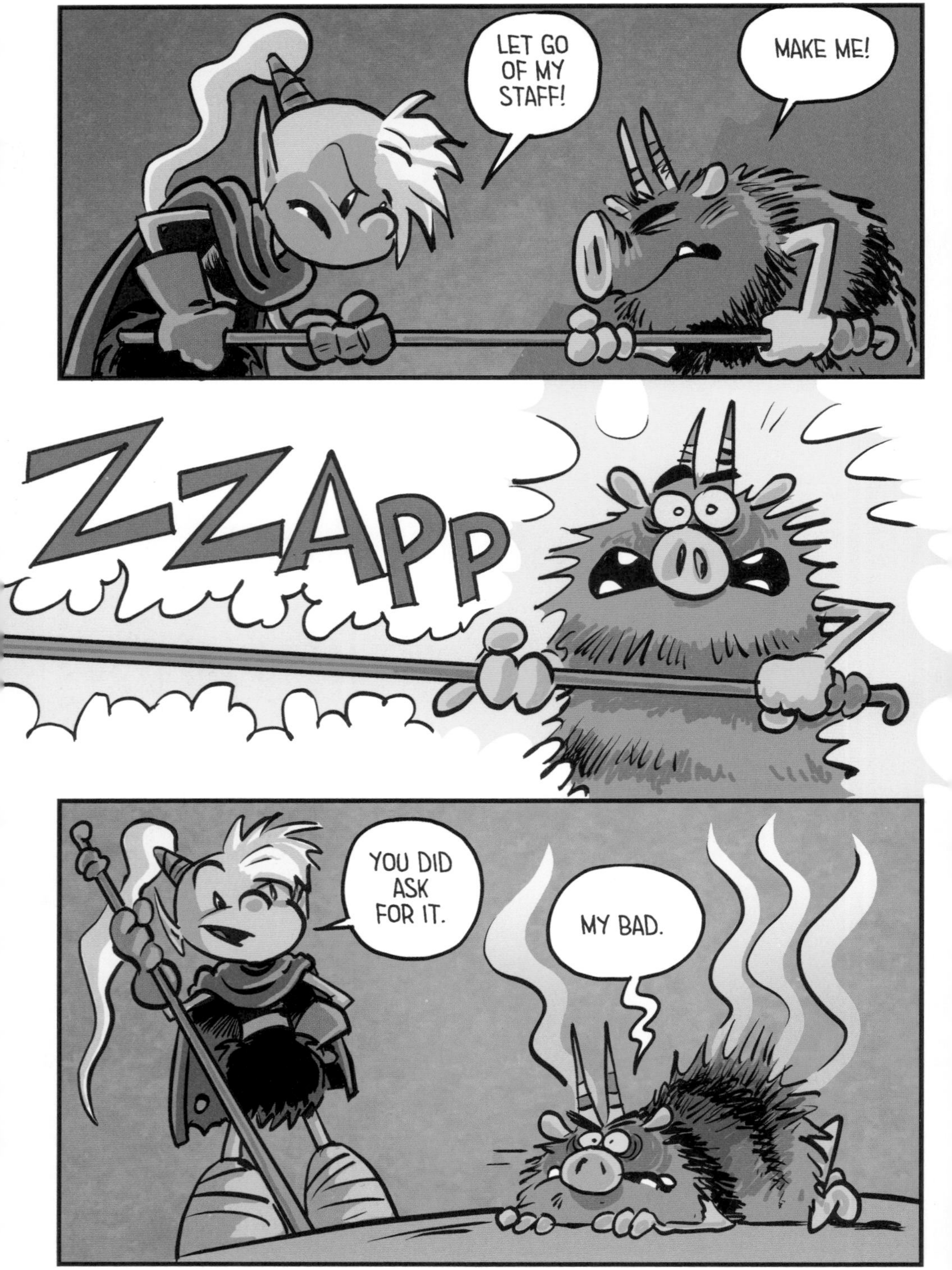
LET GO OF MY STAFF!
MAKE ME!
ZZAPP
YOU DID ASK FOR IT.
MY BAD.

CRUNCH

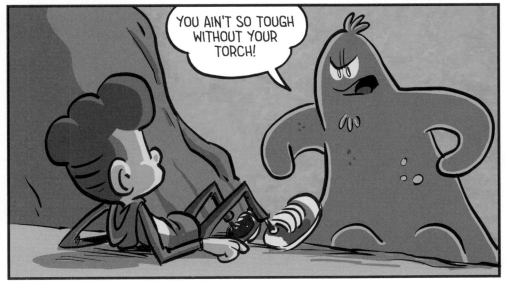

YOU AIN'T SO TOUGH WITHOUT YOUR TORCH!

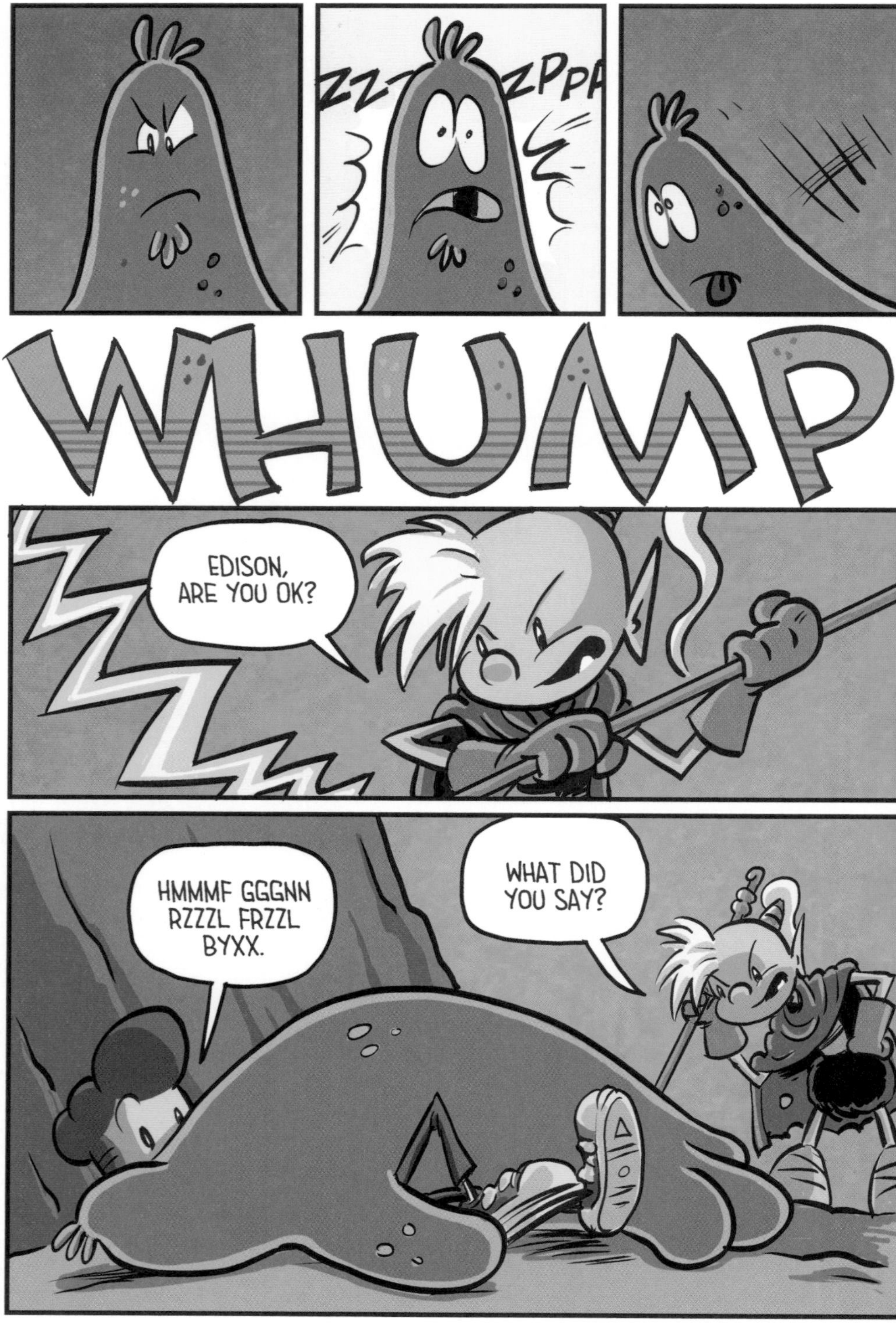
ZZZ
ZPPA
WHUMP
EDISON, ARE YOU OK?
HMMMF GGGNN RZZZL FRZZL BYXX.
WHAT DID YOU SAY?

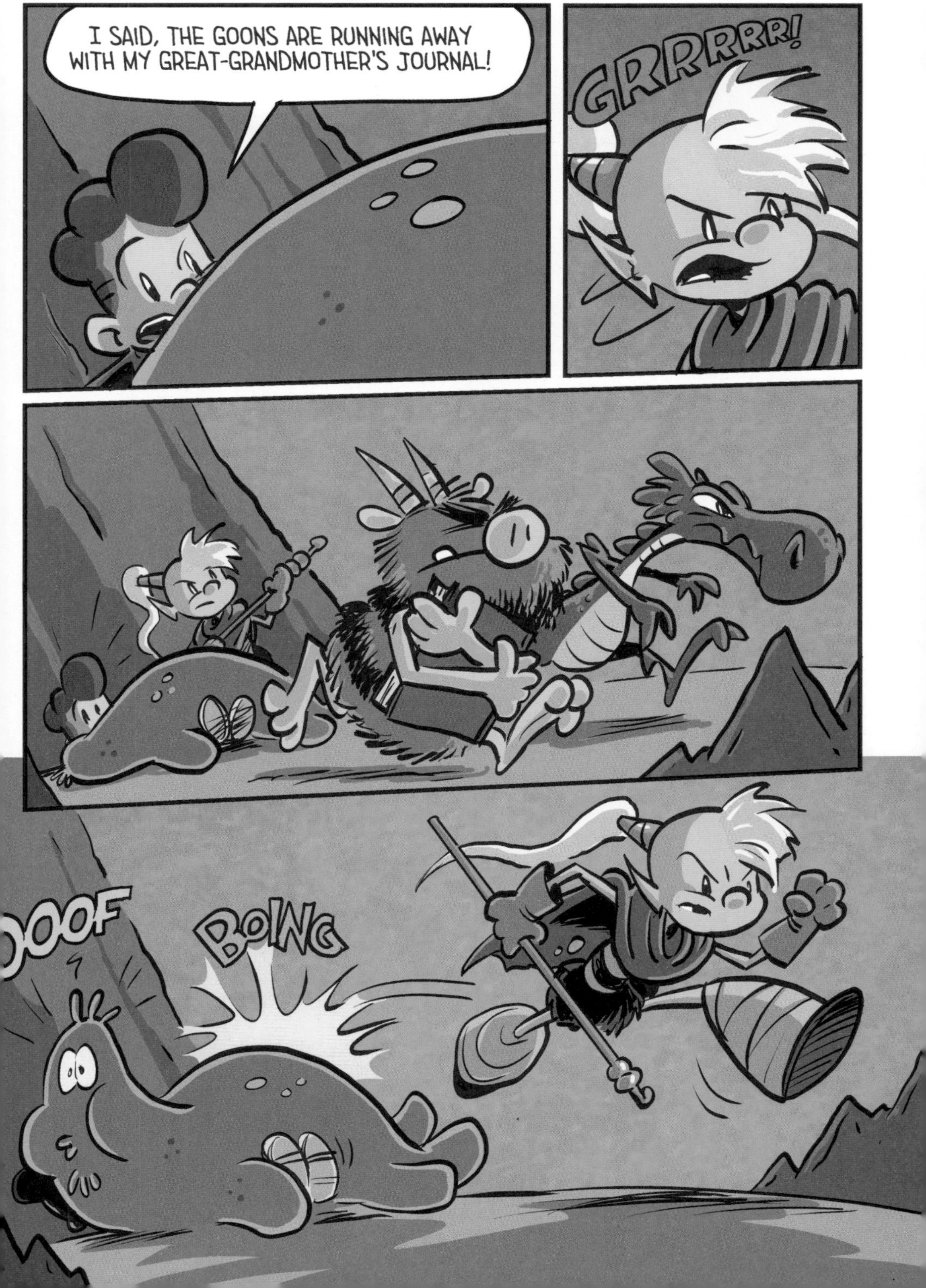
I SAID, THE GOONS ARE RUNNING AWAY WITH MY GREAT-GRANDMOTHER'S JOURNAL!
GRRRRRR!
OOOF
BOING

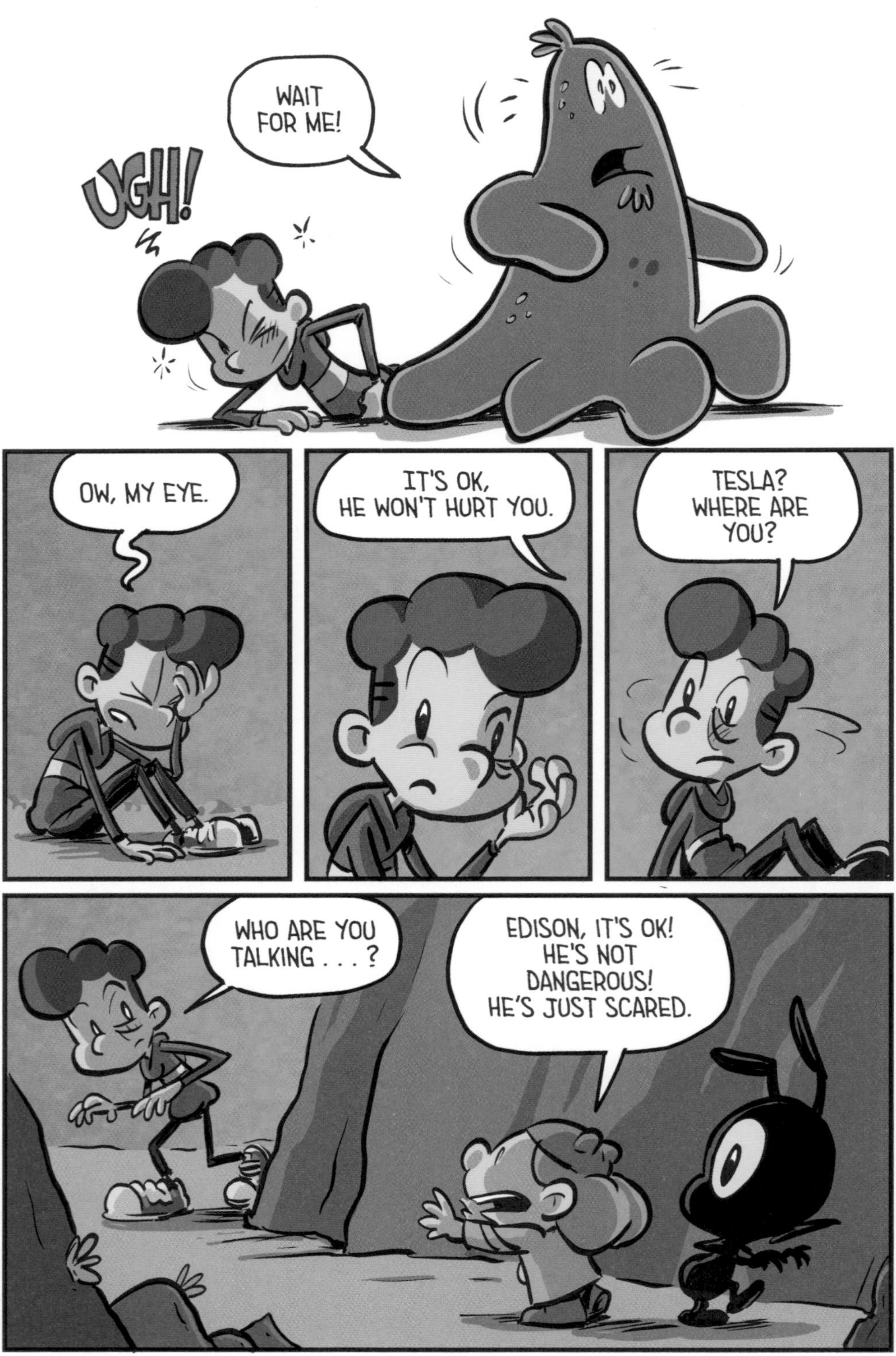
WAIT FOR ME!
UGH!
OW, MY EYE.
IT'S OK, HE WON'T HURT YOU.
TESLA? WHERE ARE YOU?
WHO ARE YOU TALKING . . . ?
EDISON, IT'S OK! HE'S NOT DANGEROUS! HE'S JUST SCARED.

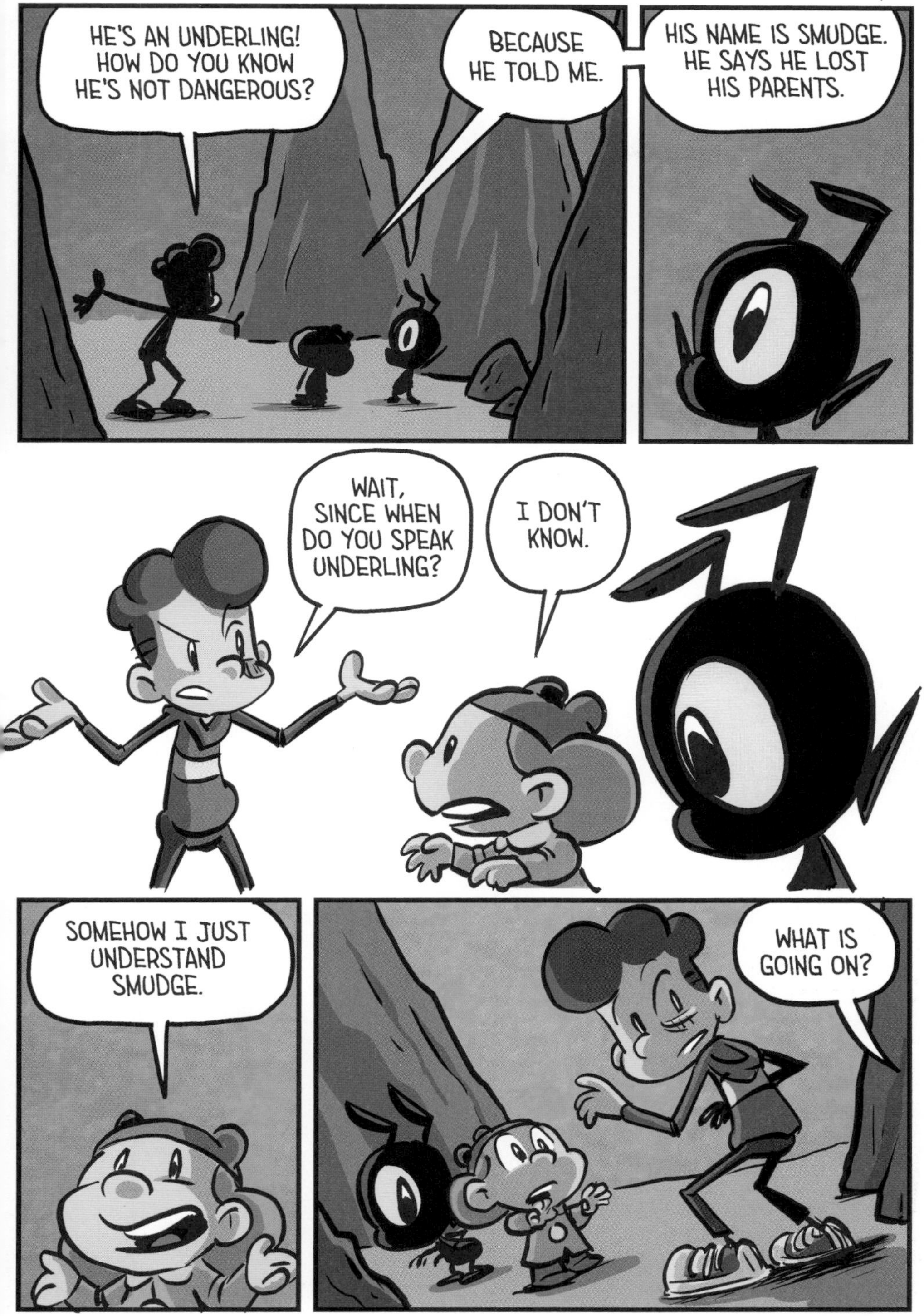
HE'S AN UNDERLING! HOW DO YOU KNOW HE'S NOT DANGEROUS?
BECAUSE HE TOLD ME.
HIS NAME IS SMUDGE. HE SAYS HE LOST HIS PARENTS.
WAIT, SINCE WHEN DO YOU SPEAK UNDERLING?
I DON'T KNOW.
SOMEHOW I JUST UNDERSTAND SMUDGE.
WHAT IS GOING ON?

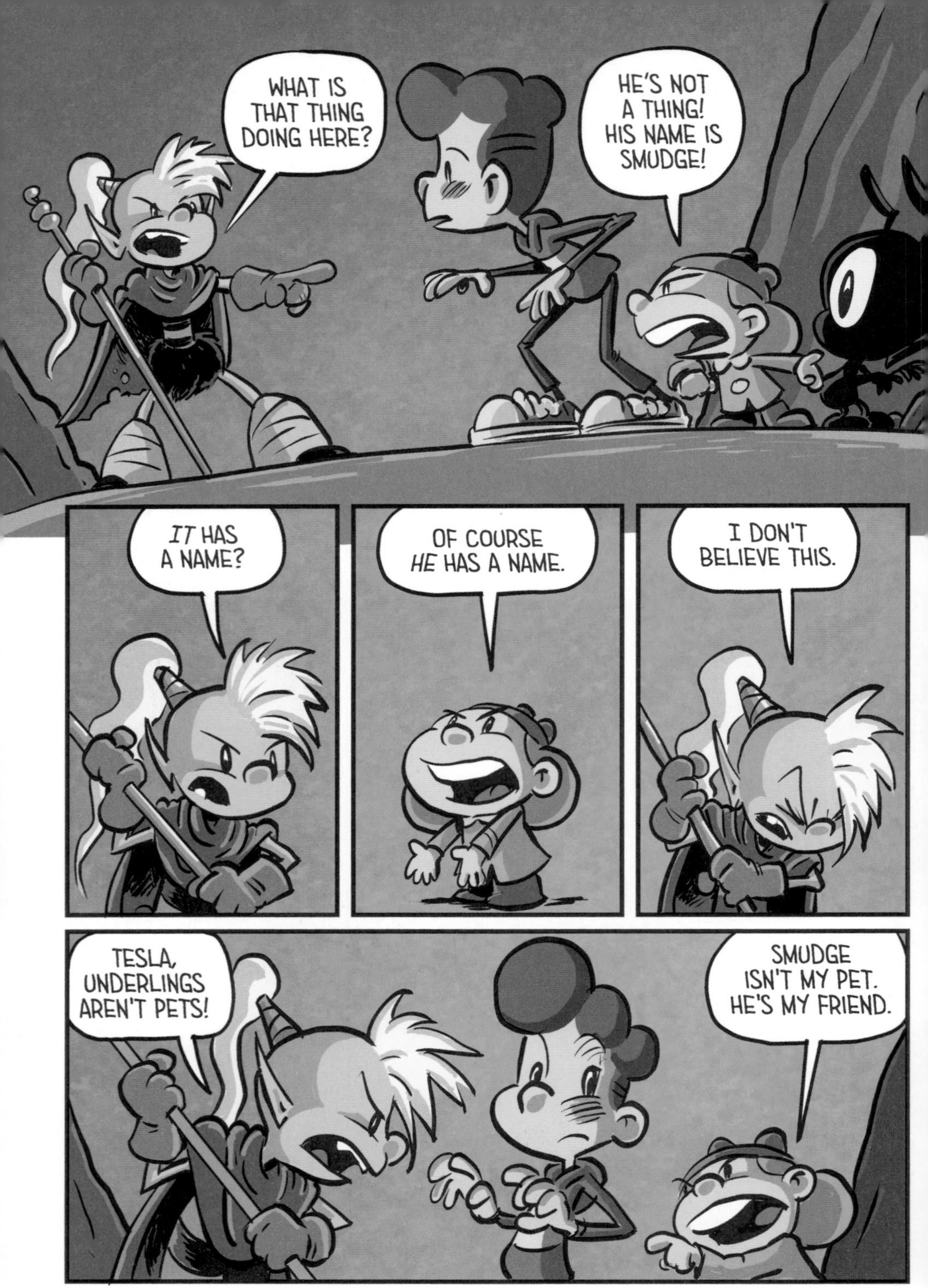
WHAT IS THAT THING DOING HERE?
HE'S NOT A THING! HIS NAME IS SMUDGE!
IT HAS A NAME?
OF COURSE *HE* HAS A NAME.
I DON'T BELIEVE THIS.
TESLA, UNDERLINGS AREN'T PETS!
SMUDGE ISN'T MY PET. HE'S MY FRIEND.

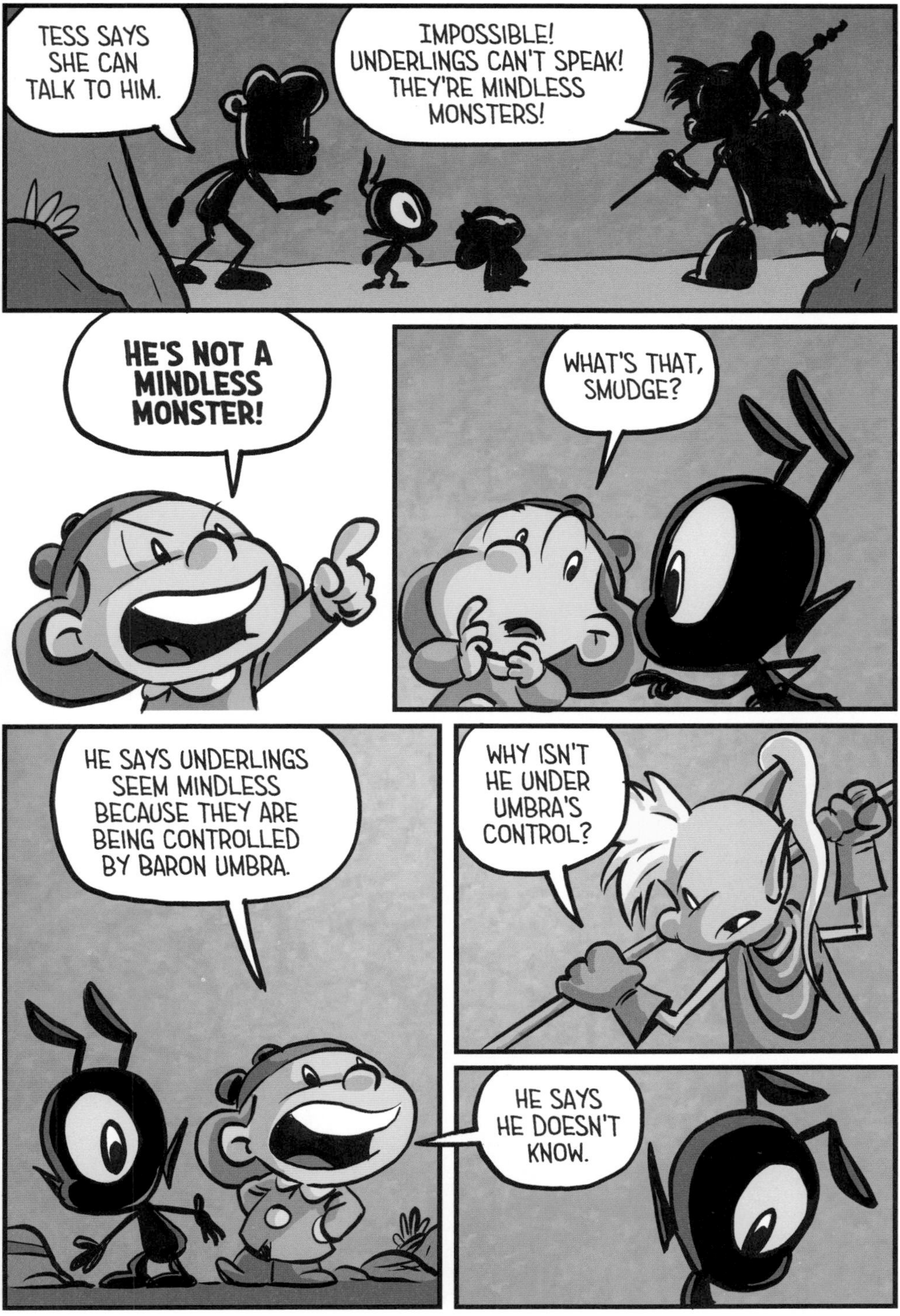
TESS SAYS SHE CAN TALK TO HIM.
IMPOSSIBLE! UNDERLINGS CAN'T SPEAK! THEY'RE MINDLESS MONSTERS!
HE'S NOT A MINDLESS MONSTER!
WHAT'S THAT, SMUDGE?
HE SAYS UNDERLINGS SEEM MINDLESS BECAUSE THEY ARE BEING CONTROLLED BY BARON UMBRA.
WHY ISN'T HE UNDER UMBRA'S CONTROL?
HE SAYS HE DOESN'T KNOW.

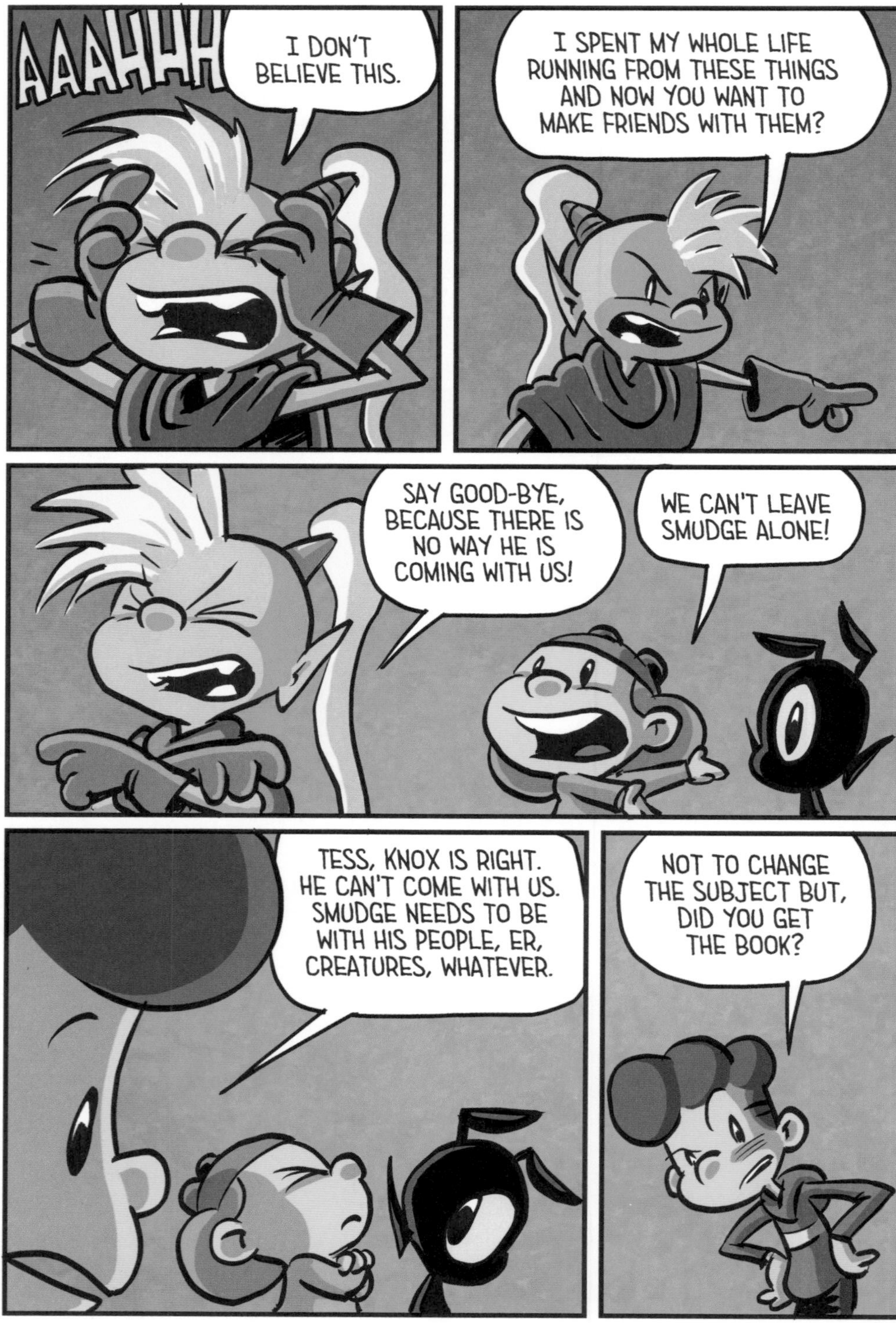
AAAHHH
I DON'T BELIEVE THIS.
I SPENT MY WHOLE LIFE RUNNING FROM THESE THINGS AND NOW YOU WANT TO MAKE FRIENDS WITH THEM?
SAY GOOD-BYE, BECAUSE THERE IS NO WAY HE IS COMING WITH US!
WE CAN'T LEAVE SMUDGE ALONE!
TESS, KNOX IS RIGHT. HE CAN'T COME WITH US. SMUDGE NEEDS TO BE WITH HIS PEOPLE, ER, CREATURES, WHATEVER.
NOT TO CHANGE THE SUBJECT BUT, DID YOU GET THE BOOK?

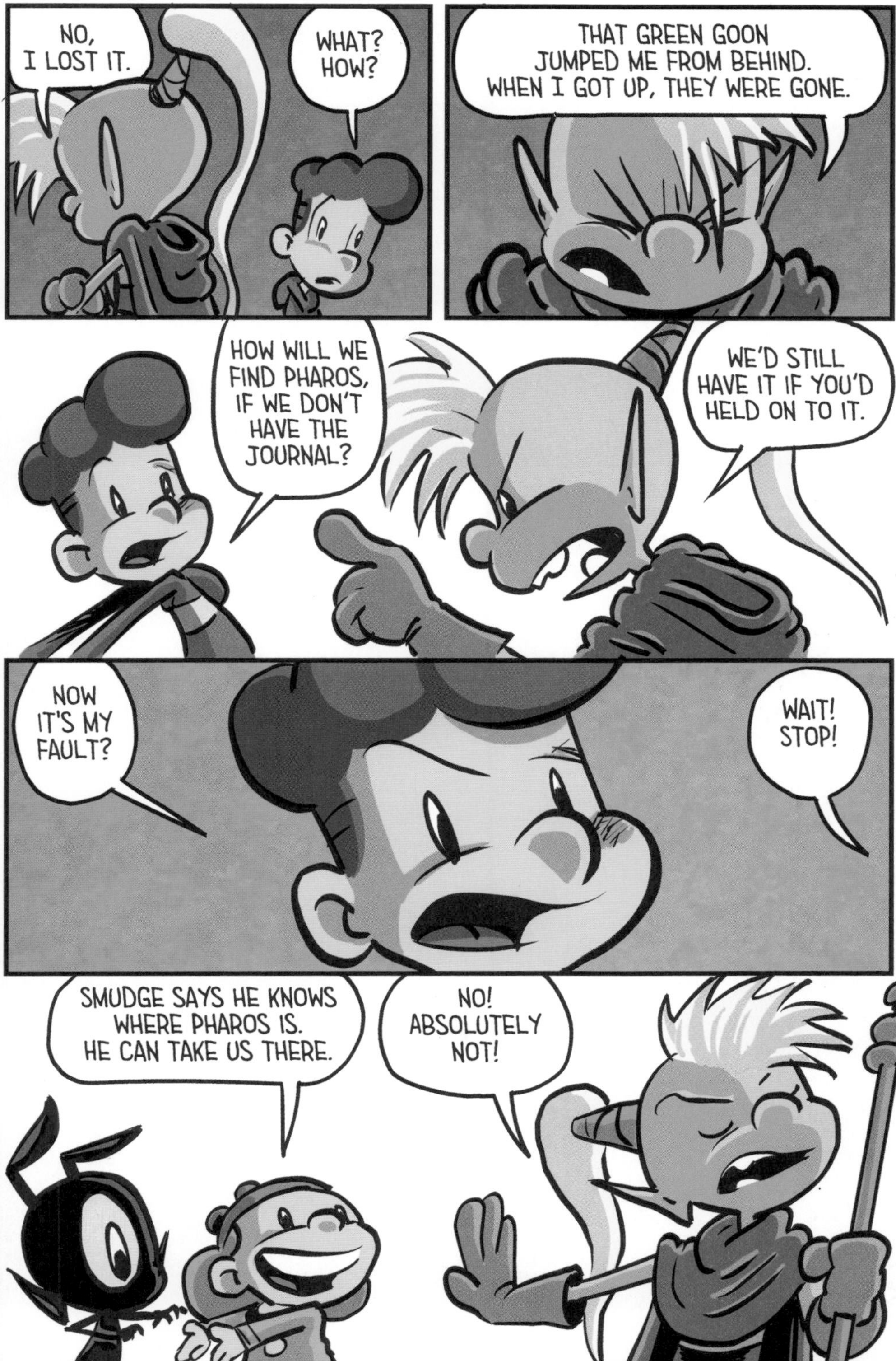
NO, I LOST IT.
WHAT? HOW?
THAT GREEN GOON JUMPED ME FROM BEHIND. WHEN I GOT UP, THEY WERE GONE.
HOW WILL WE FIND PHAROS, IF WE DON'T HAVE THE JOURNAL?
WE'D STILL HAVE IT IF YOU'D HELD ON TO IT.
NOW IT'S MY FAULT?
WAIT! STOP!
SMUDGE SAYS HE KNOWS WHERE PHAROS IS. HE CAN TAKE US THERE.
NO! ABSOLUTELY NOT!

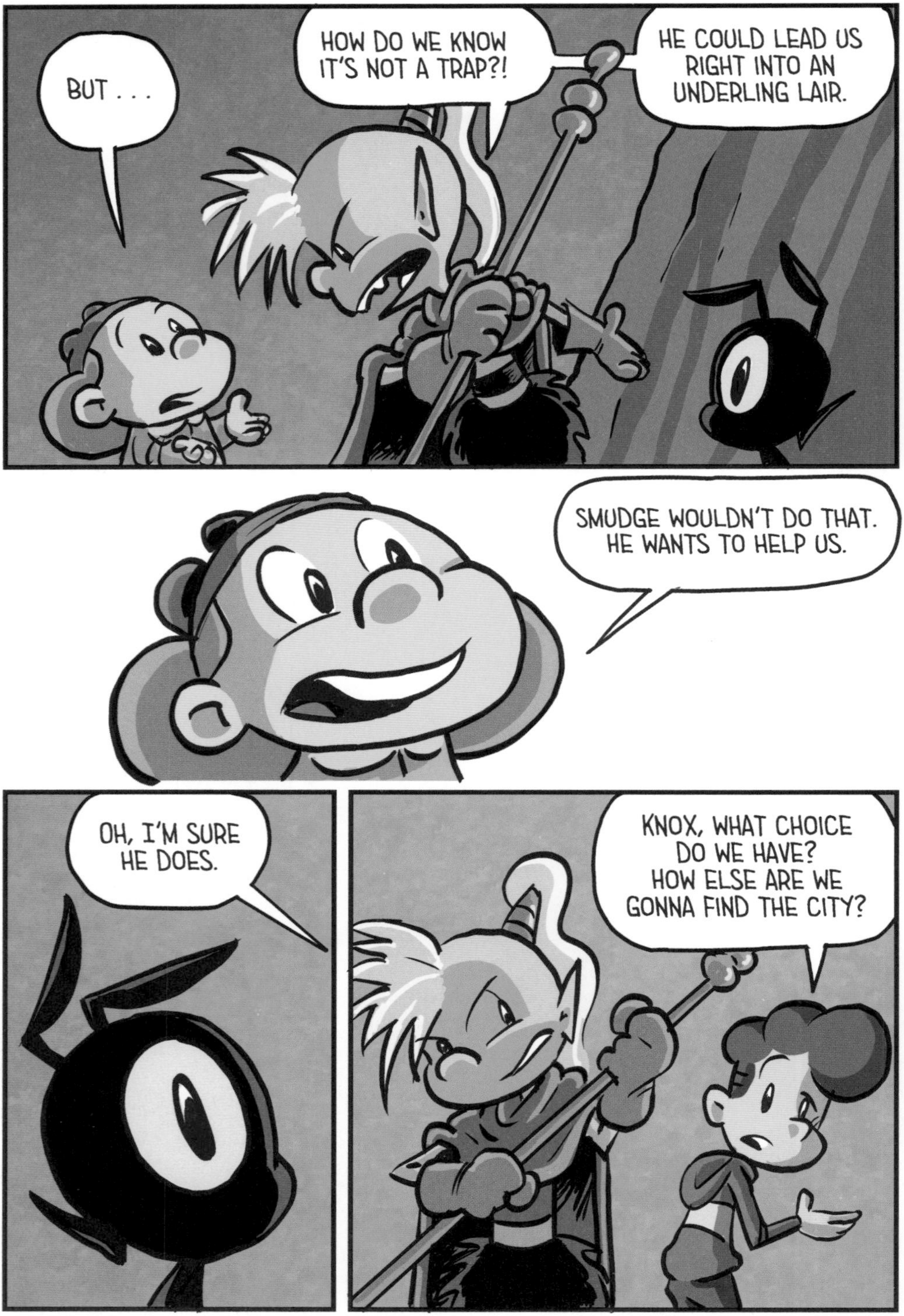
BUT . . .
HOW DO WE KNOW IT'S NOT A TRAP?!
HE COULD LEAD US RIGHT INTO AN UNDERLING LAIR.
SMUDGE WOULDN'T DO THAT. HE WANTS TO HELP US.
OH, I'M SURE HE DOES.
KNOX, WHAT CHOICE DO WE HAVE? HOW ELSE ARE WE GONNA FIND THE CITY?

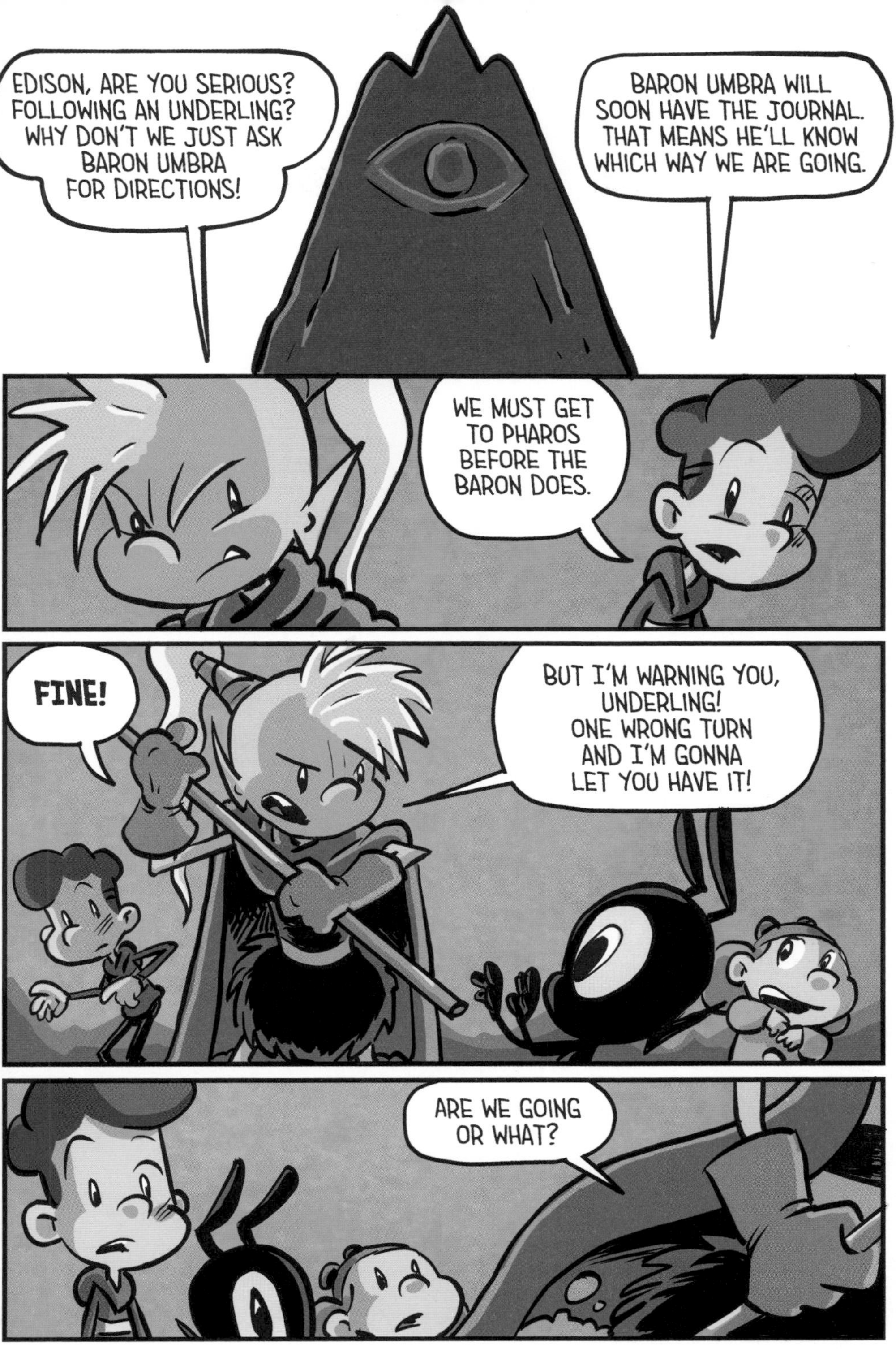

EDISON, ARE YOU SERIOUS? FOLLOWING AN UNDERLING? WHY DON'T WE JUST ASK BARON UMBRA FOR DIRECTIONS!
BARON UMBRA WILL SOON HAVE THE JOURNAL. THAT MEANS HE'LL KNOW WHICH WAY WE ARE GOING.
WE MUST GET TO PHAROS BEFORE THE BARON DOES.
FINE!
BUT I'M WARNING YOU, UNDERLING! ONE WRONG TURN AND I'M GONNA LET YOU HAVE IT!
ARE WE GOING OR WHAT?

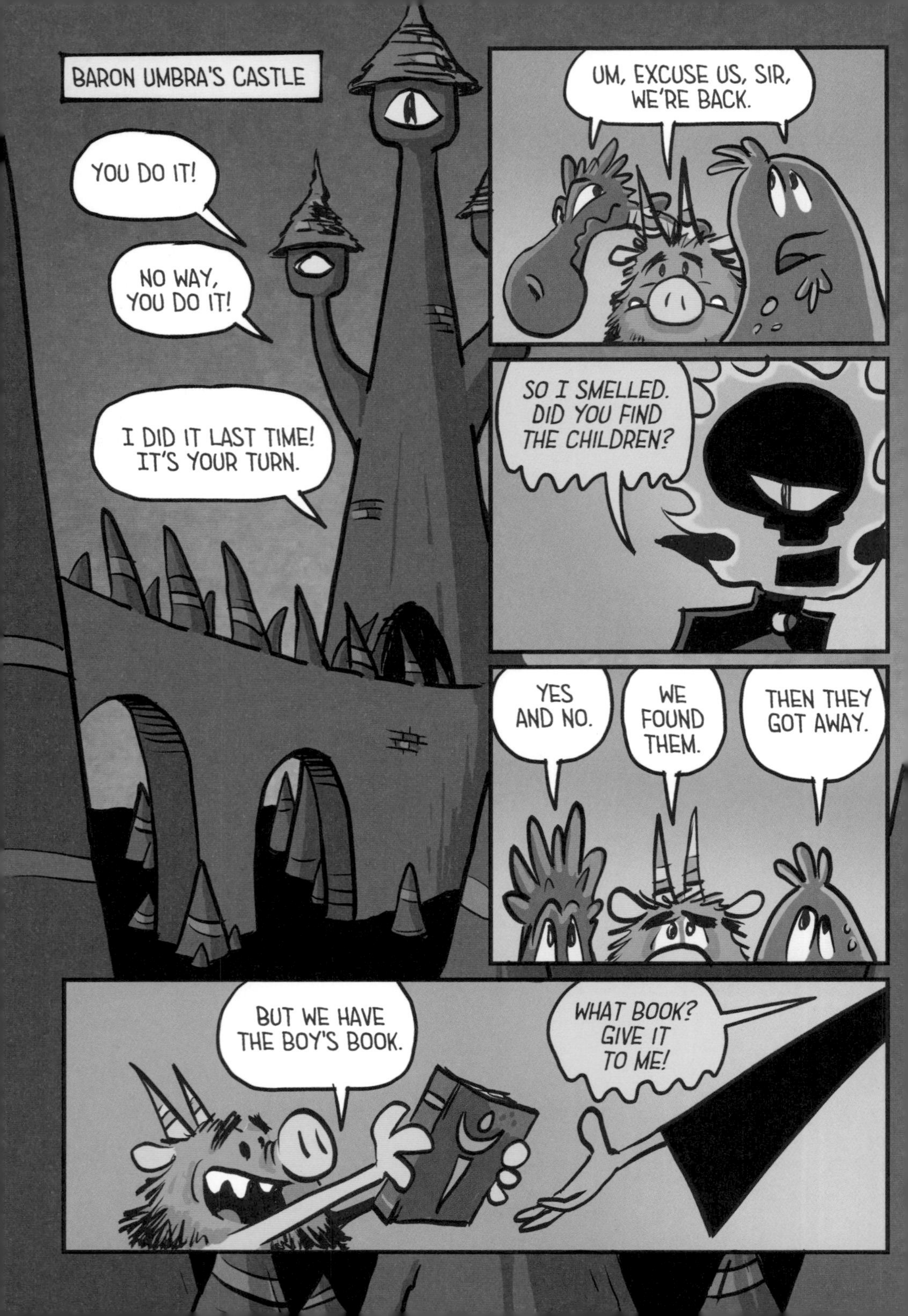
BARON UMBRA'S CASTLE
YOU DO IT!
NO WAY, YOU DO IT!
I DID IT LAST TIME! IT'S YOUR TURN.
UM, EXCUSE US, SIR, WE'RE BACK.
SO I SMELLED. DID YOU FIND THE CHILDREN?
YES AND NO.
WE FOUND THEM.
THEN THEY GOT AWAY.
BUT WE HAVE THE BOY'S BOOK.
WHAT BOOK? GIVE IT TO ME!

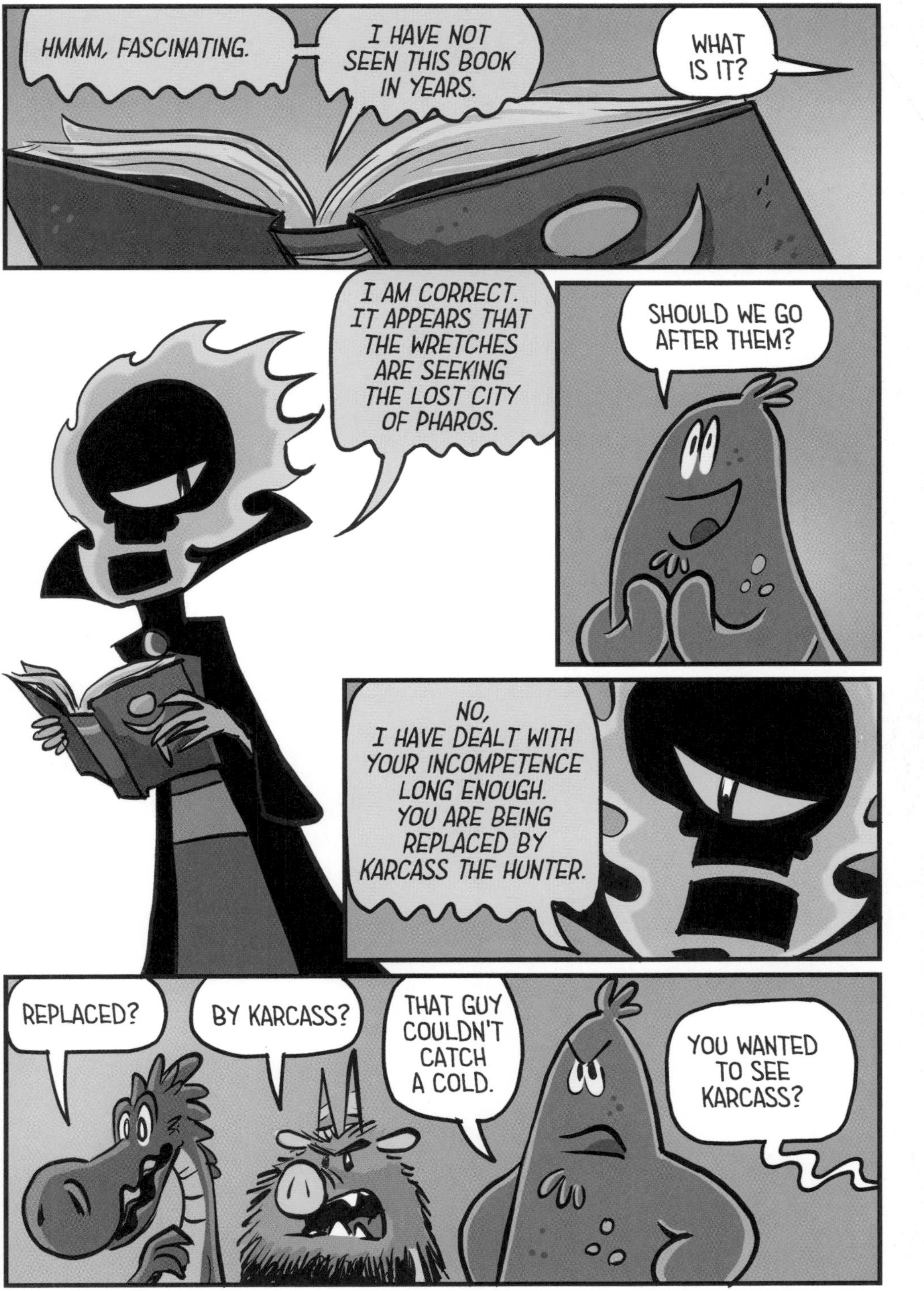
HMMM, FASCINATING.
I HAVE NOT SEEN THIS BOOK IN YEARS.
WHAT IS IT?
I AM CORRECT. IT APPEARS THAT THE WRETCHES ARE SEEKING THE LOST CITY OF PHAROS.
SHOULD WE GO AFTER THEM?
NO, I HAVE DEALT WITH YOUR INCOMPETENCE LONG ENOUGH. YOU ARE BEING REPLACED BY KARCASS THE HUNTER.
REPLACED?
BY KARCASS?
THAT GUY COULDN'T CATCH A COLD.
YOU WANTED TO SEE KARCASS?

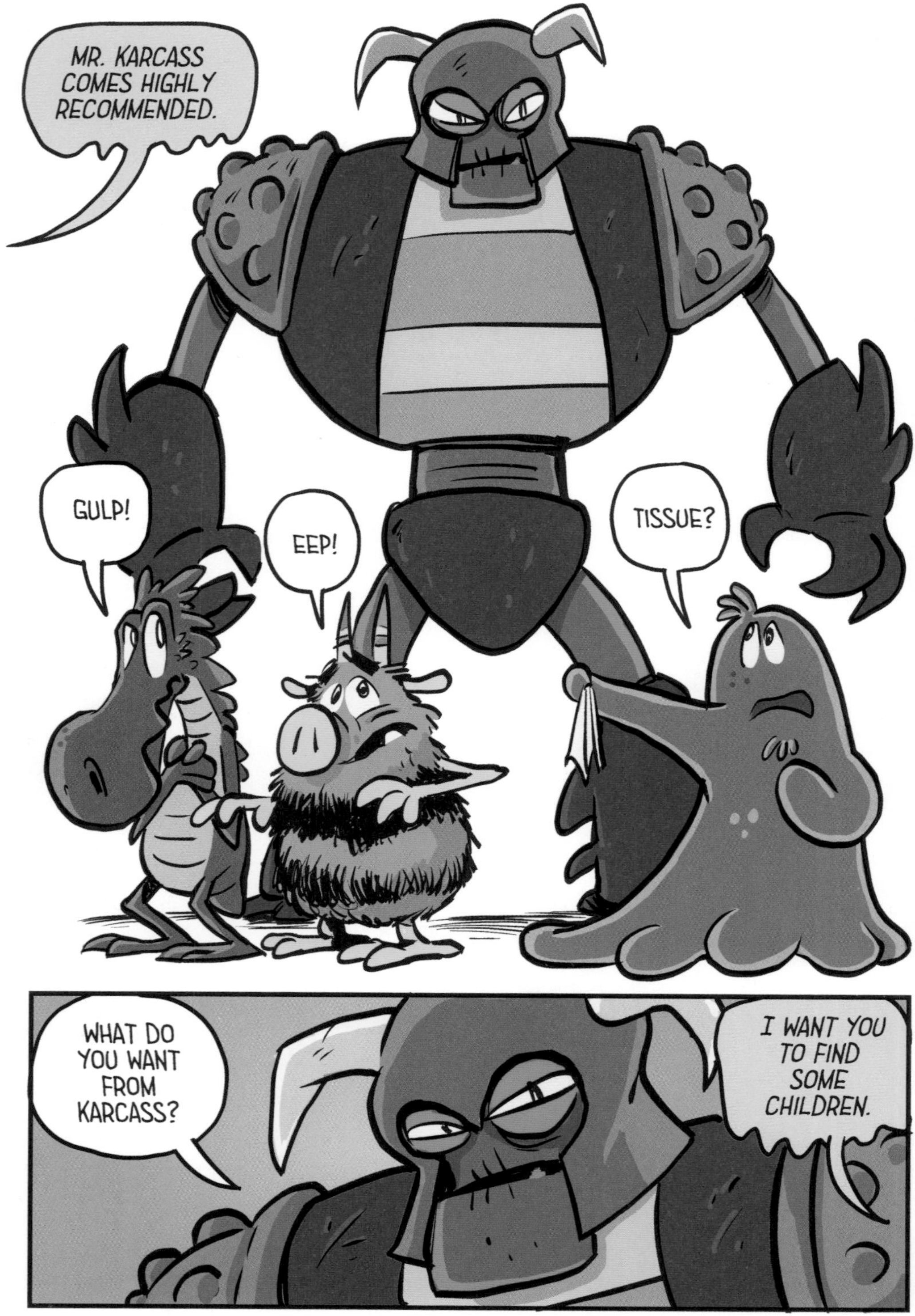
MR. KARCASS COMES HIGHLY RECOMMENDED.
GULP!
EEP!
TISSUE?
WHAT DO YOU WANT FROM KARCASS?
I WANT YOU TO FIND SOME CHILDREN.

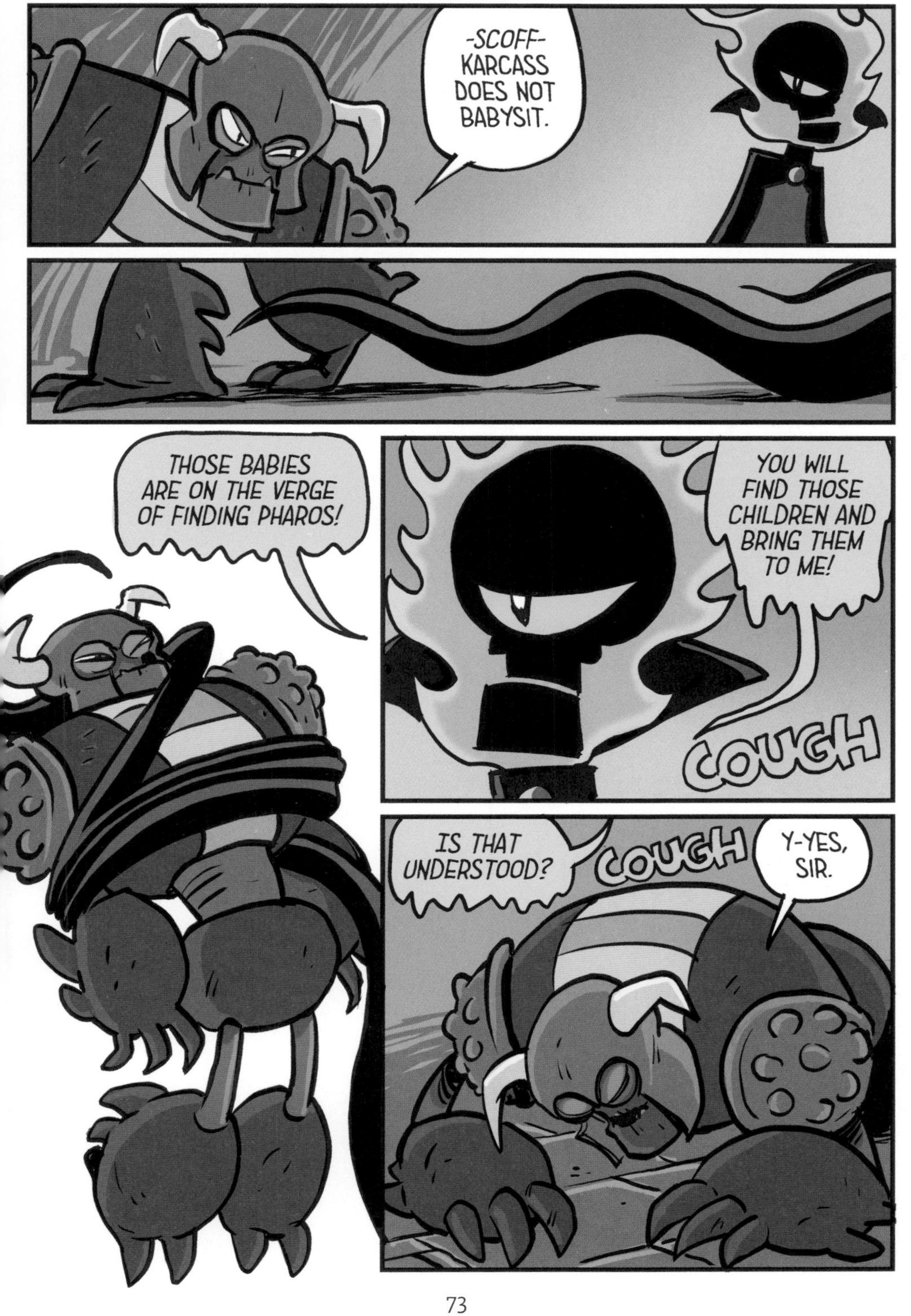
-SCOFF- KARCASS DOES NOT BABYSIT.
THOSE BABIES ARE ON THE VERGE OF FINDING PHAROS!
YOU WILL FIND THOSE CHILDREN AND BRING THEM TO ME!
COUGH
IS THAT UNDERSTOOD?
COUGH
Y-YES, SIR.

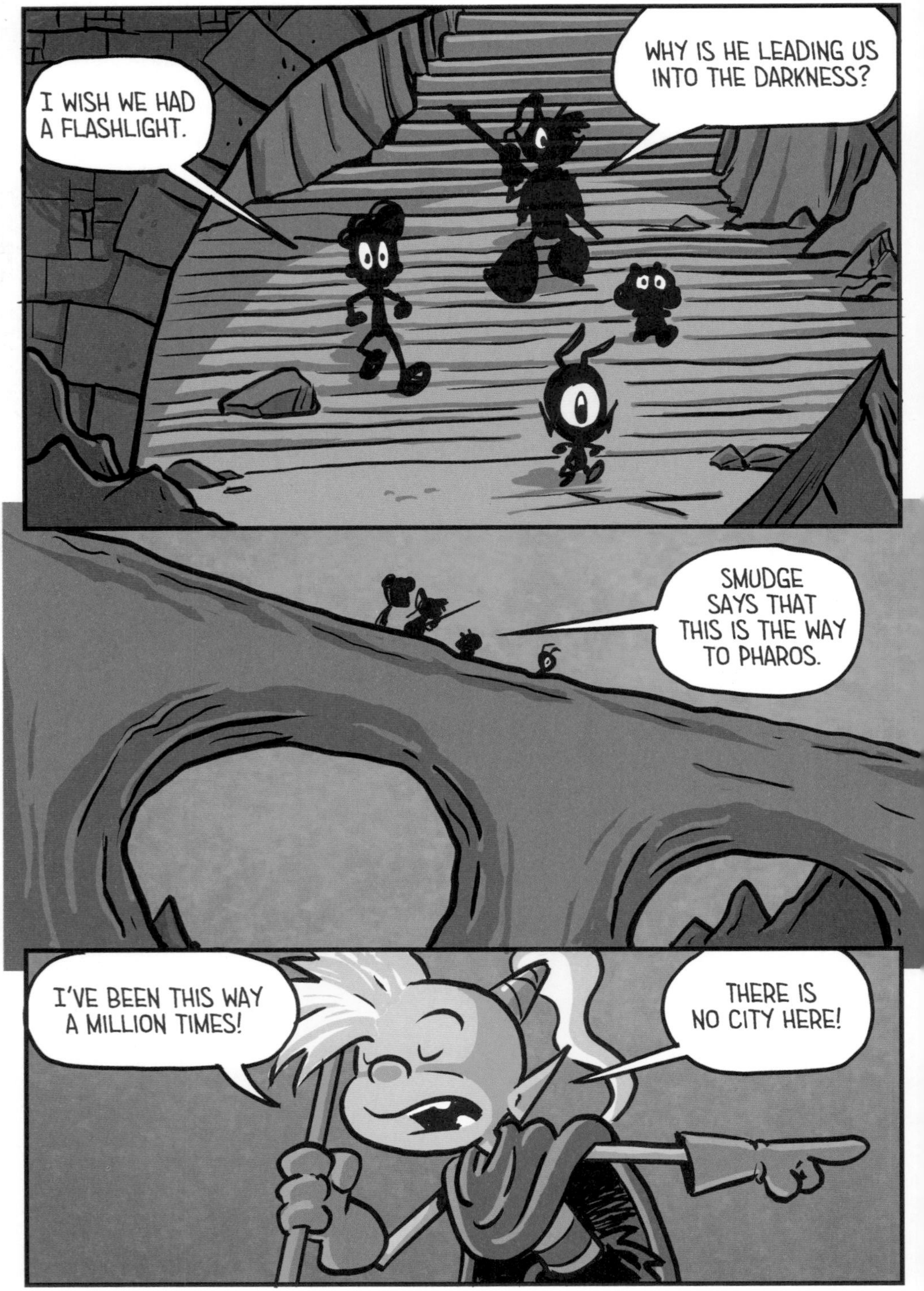

I WISH WE HAD A FLASHLIGHT.
WHY IS HE LEADING US INTO THE DARKNESS?
SMUDGE SAYS THAT THIS IS THE WAY TO PHAROS.
I'VE BEEN THIS WAY A MILLION TIMES!
THERE IS NO CITY HERE!

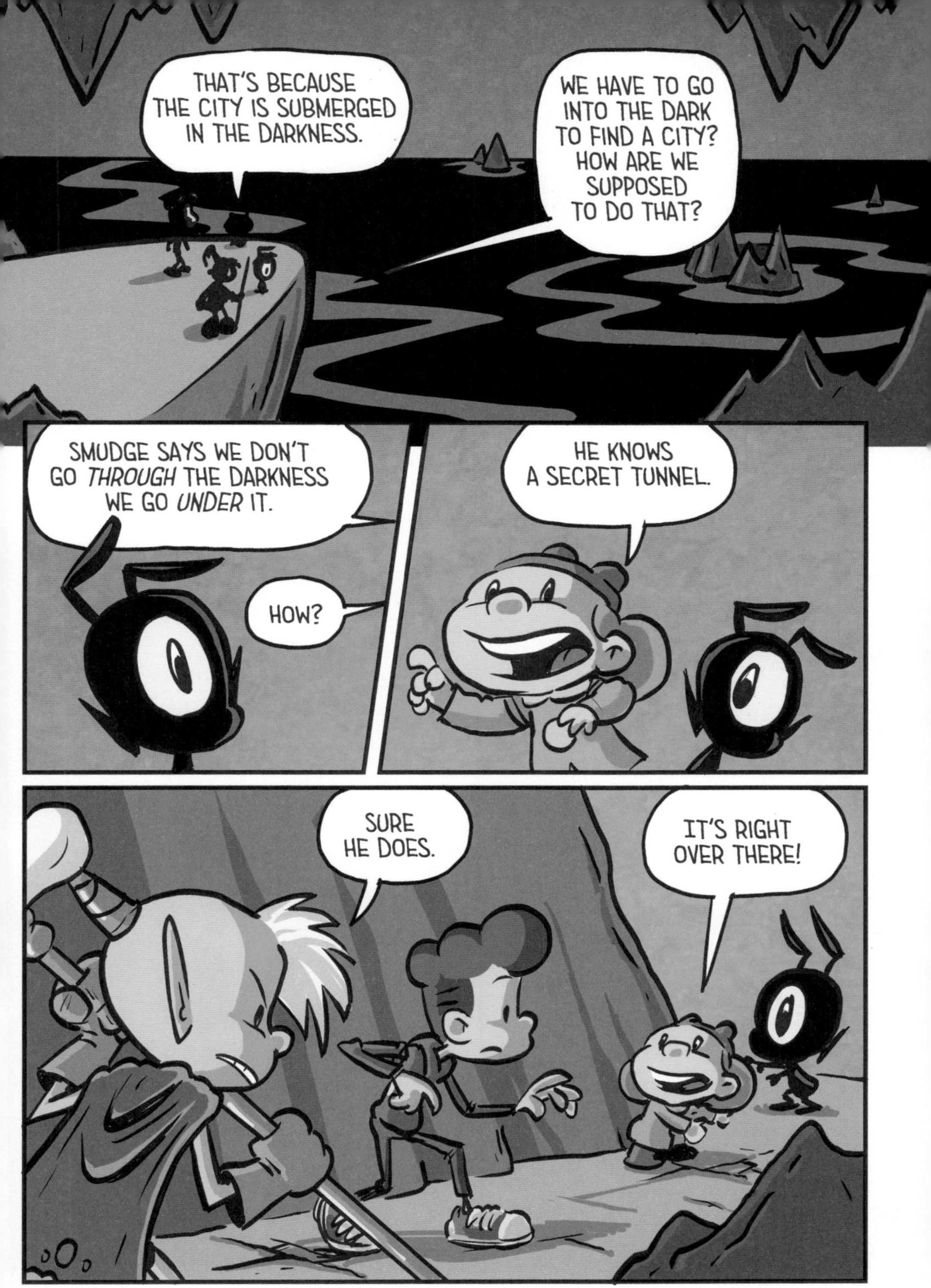
THAT'S BECAUSE THE CITY IS SUBMERGED IN THE DARKNESS.
WE HAVE TO GO INTO THE DARK TO FIND A CITY? HOW ARE WE SUPPOSED TO DO THAT?
SMUDGE SAYS WE DON'T GO *THROUGH* THE DARKNESS WE GO *UNDER* IT.
HOW?
HE KNOWS A SECRET TUNNEL.
SURE HE DOES.
IT'S RIGHT OVER THERE!

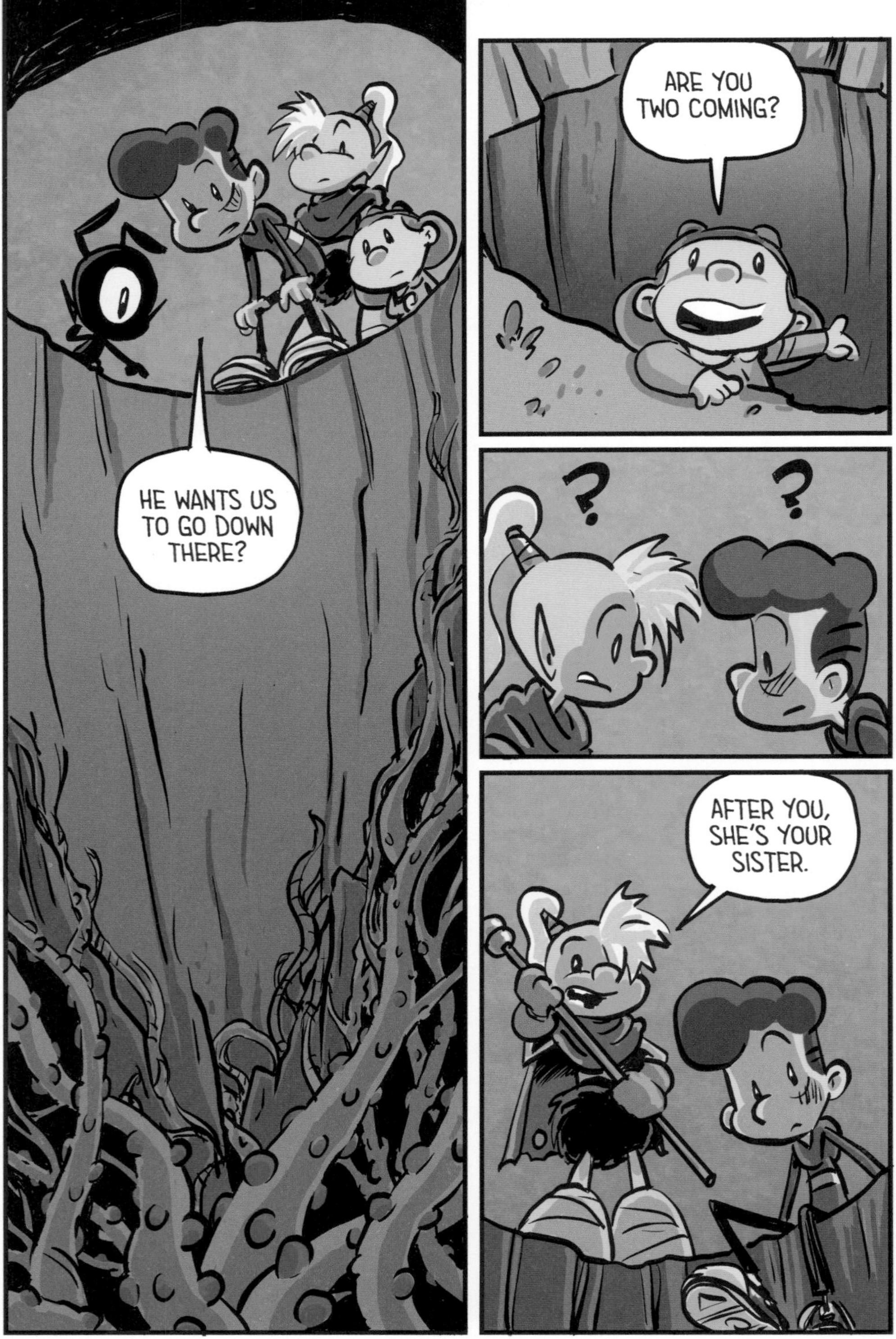
HE WANTS US TO GO DOWN THERE?
ARE YOU TWO COMING?
?
?
AFTER YOU, SHE'S YOUR SISTER.

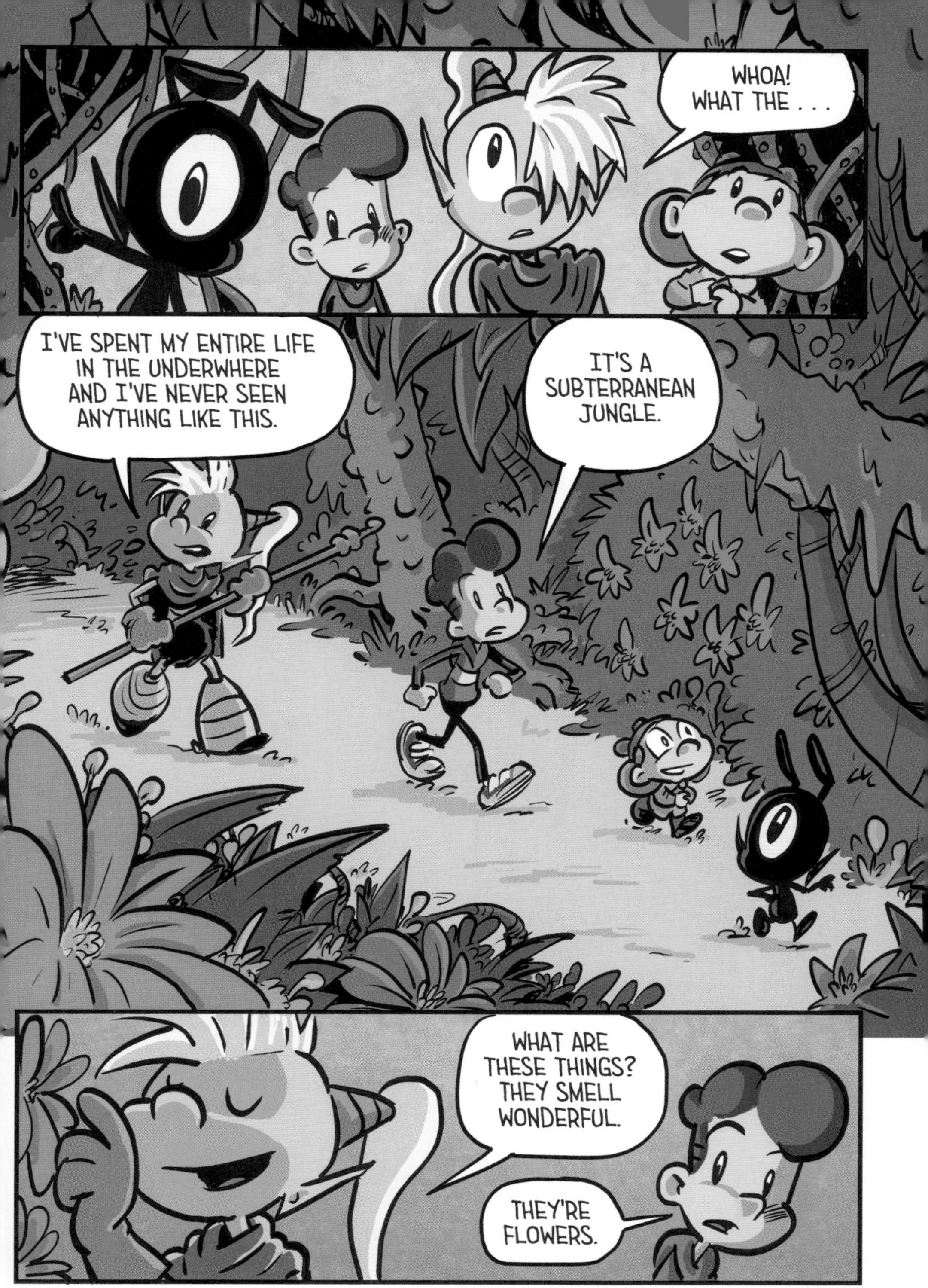
WHOA! WHAT THE . . .
I'VE SPENT MY ENTIRE LIFE IN THE UNDERWHERE AND I'VE NEVER SEEN ANYTHING LIKE THIS.
IT'S A SUBTERRANEAN JUNGLE.
WHAT ARE THESE THINGS? THEY SMELL WONDERFUL.
THEY'RE FLOWERS.

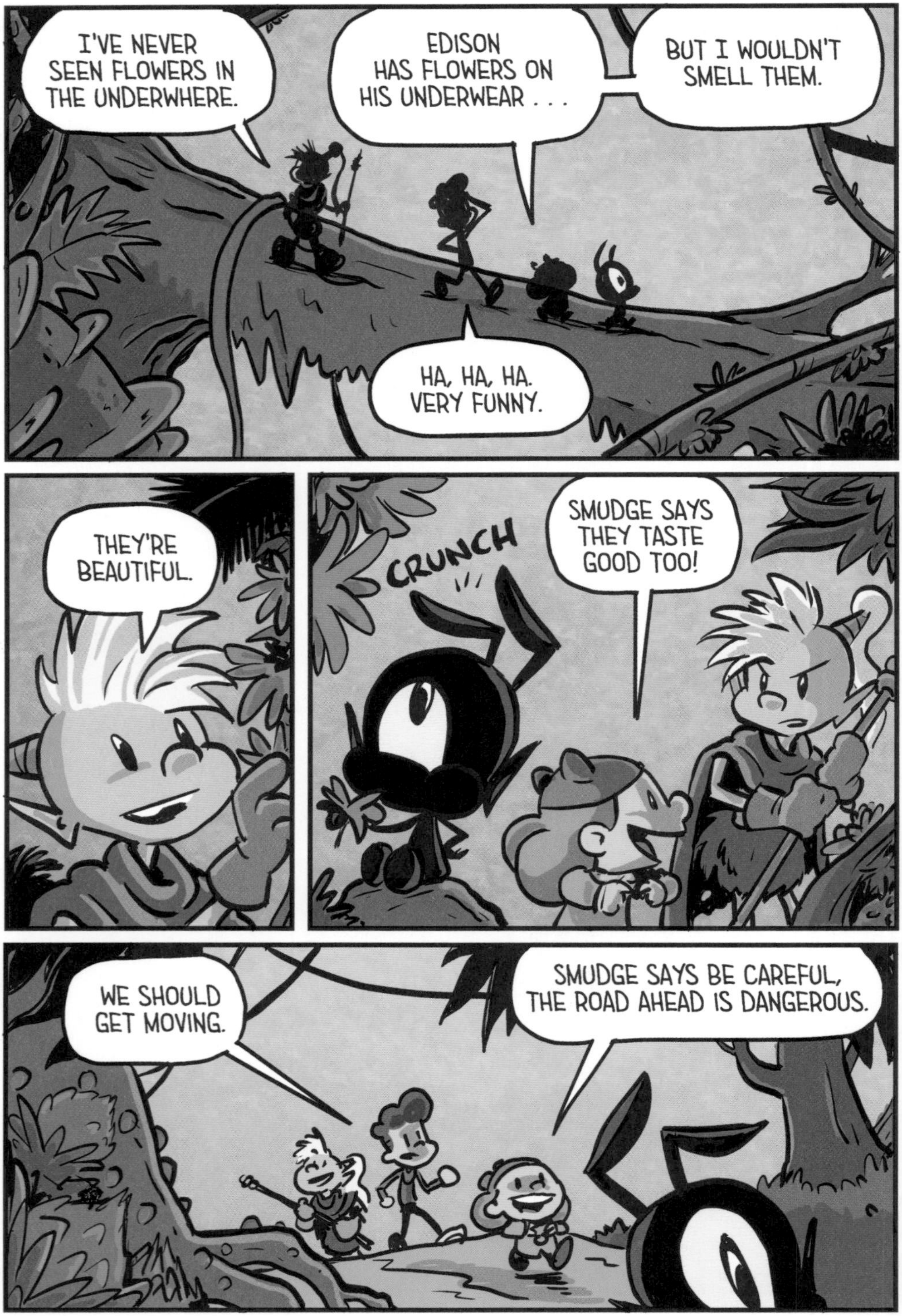
I'VE NEVER SEEN FLOWERS IN THE UNDERWHERE.
EDISON HAS FLOWERS ON HIS UNDERWEAR . . .
BUT I WOULDN'T SMELL THEM.
HA, HA, HA. VERY FUNNY.
THEY'RE BEAUTIFUL.
CRUNCH
SMUDGE SAYS THEY TASTE GOOD TOO!
WE SHOULD GET MOVING.
SMUDGE SAYS BE CAREFUL, THE ROAD AHEAD IS DANGEROUS.

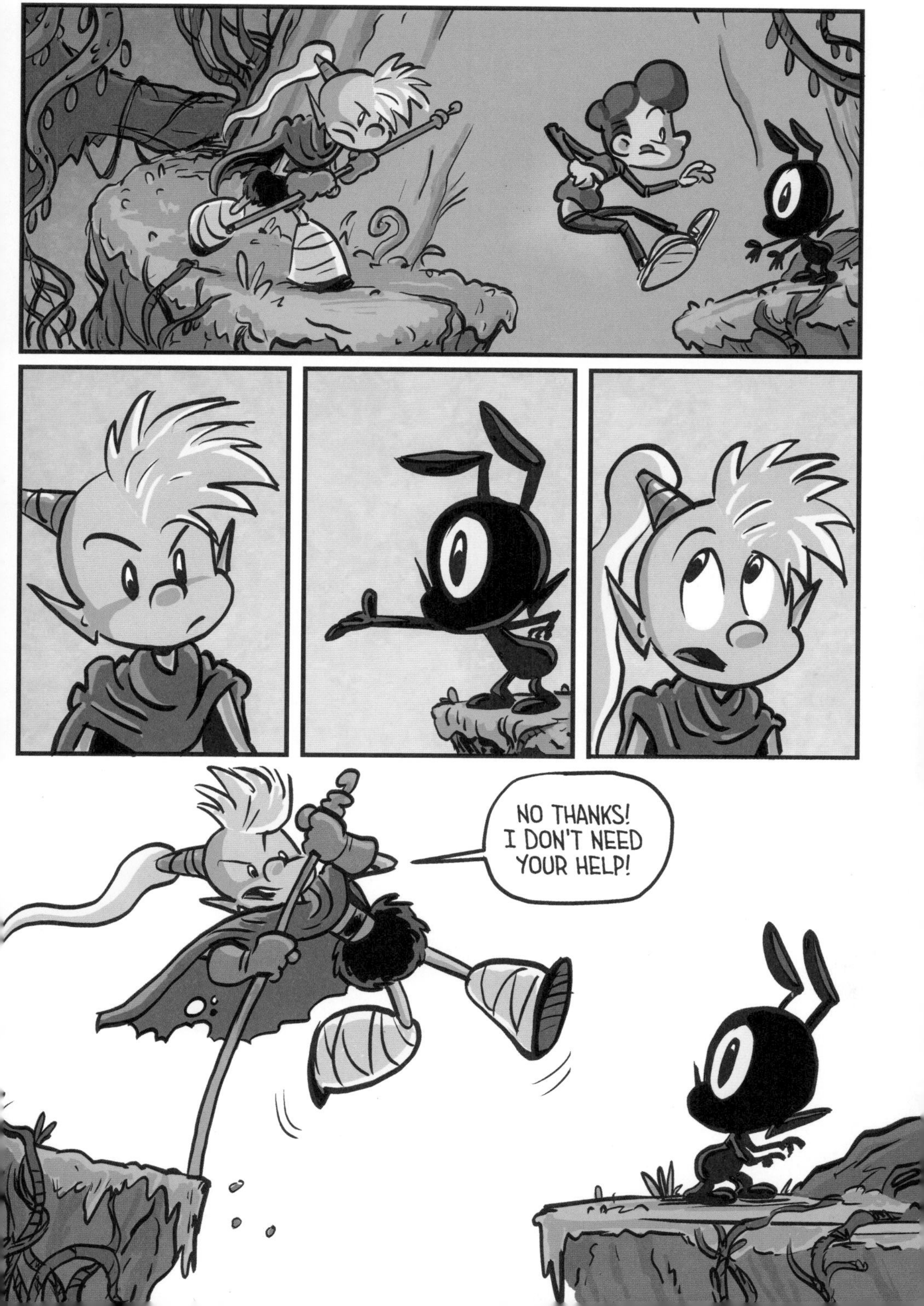
NO THANKS! I DON'T NEED YOUR HELP!

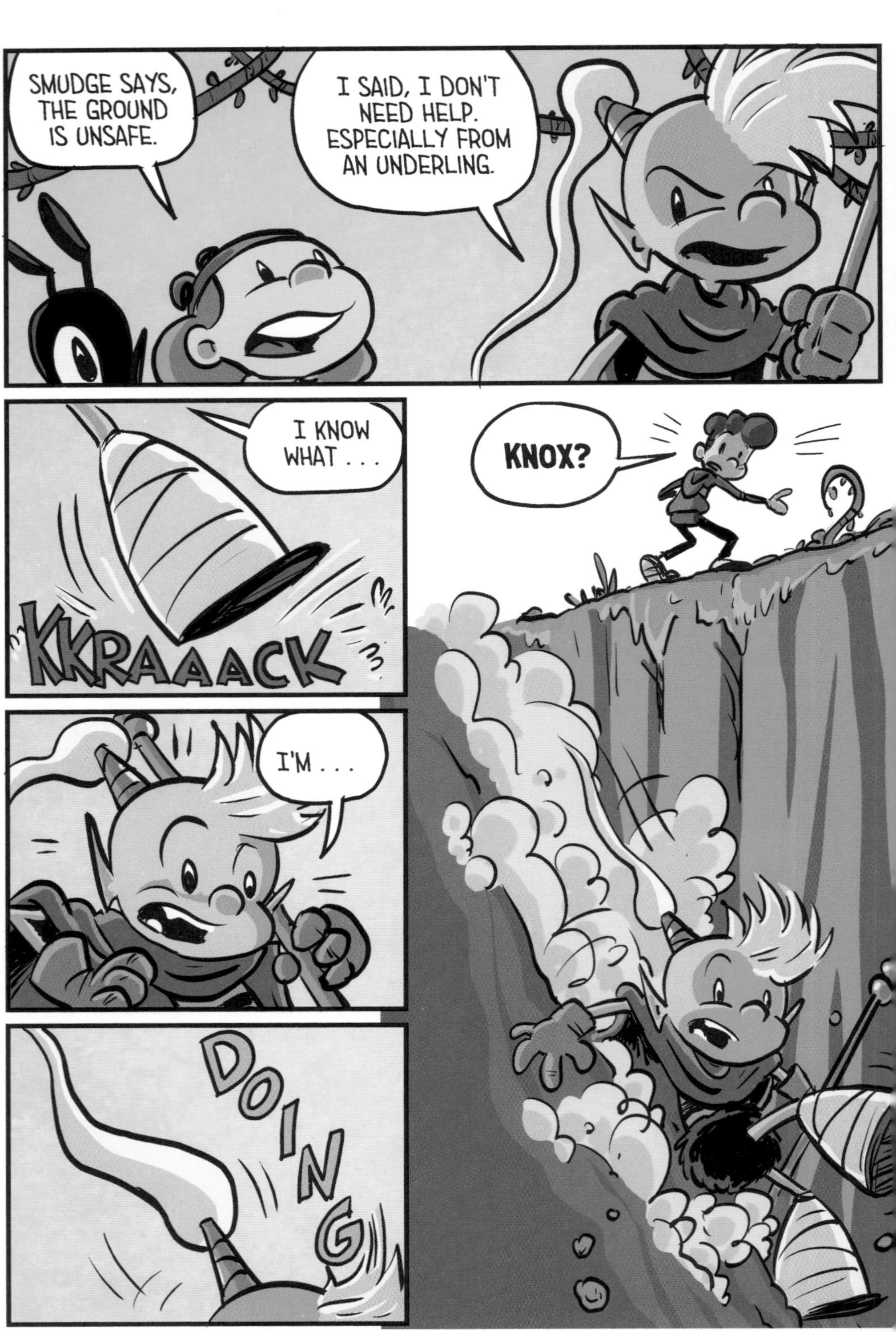
SMUDGE SAYS, THE GROUND IS UNSAFE.
I SAID, I DON'T NEED HELP. ESPECIALLY FROM AN UNDERLING.
I KNOW WHAT . . .
KKRAAACK
KNOX?
I'M . . .
DOING

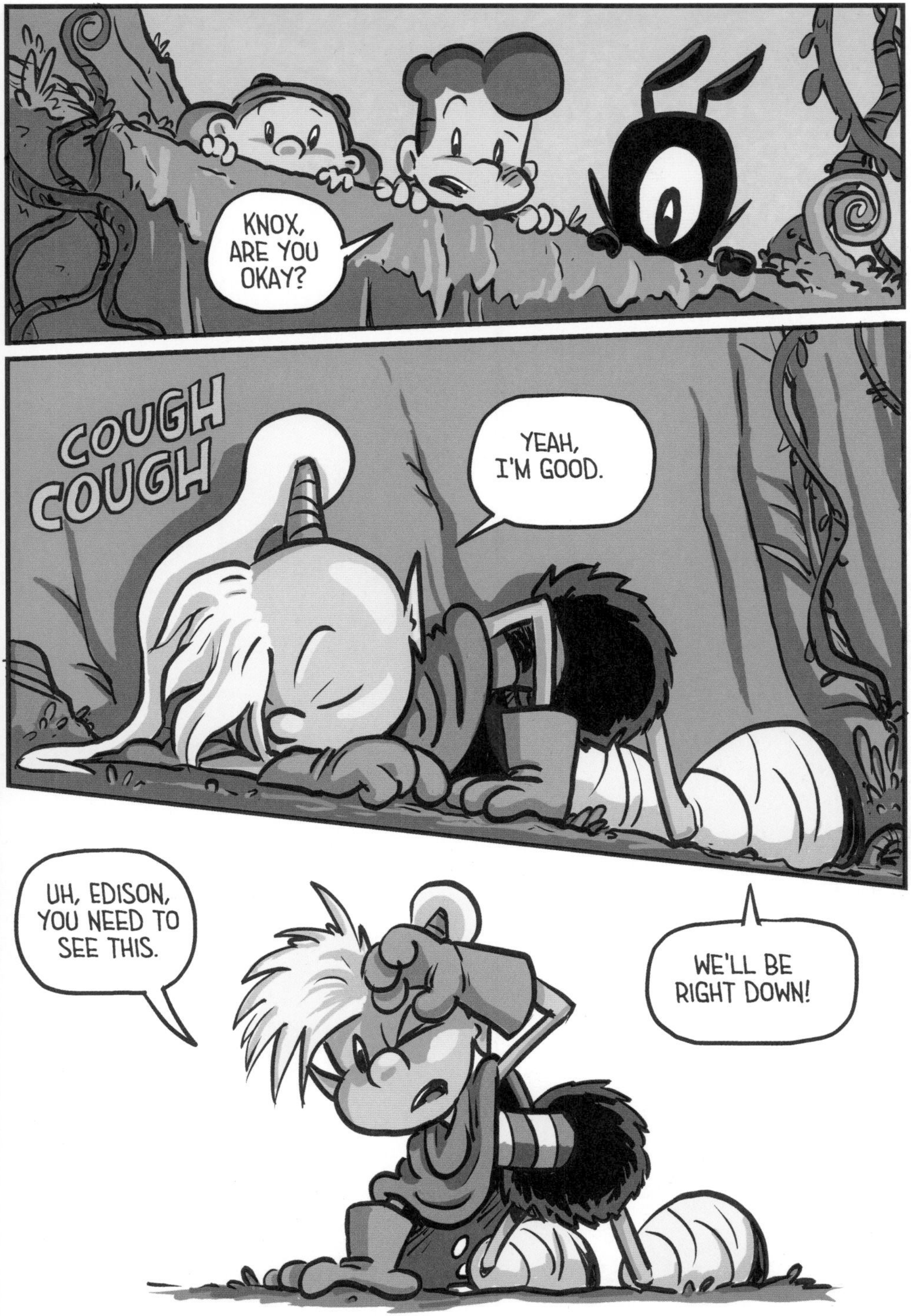
KNOX, ARE YOU OKAY?
COUGH COUGH
YEAH, I'M GOOD.
UH, EDISON, YOU NEED TO SEE THIS.
WE'LL BE RIGHT DOWN!

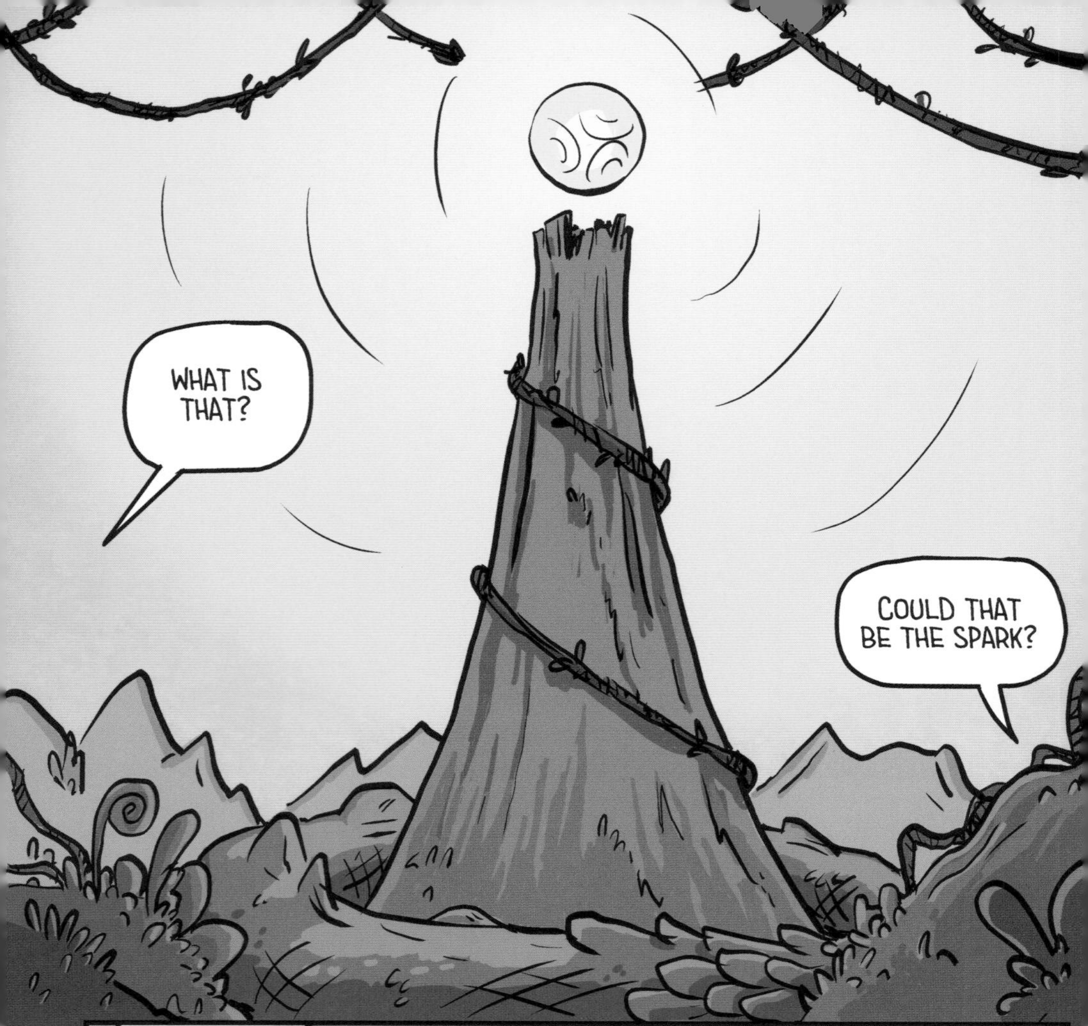
WHAT IS THAT?
COULD THAT BE THE SPARK?

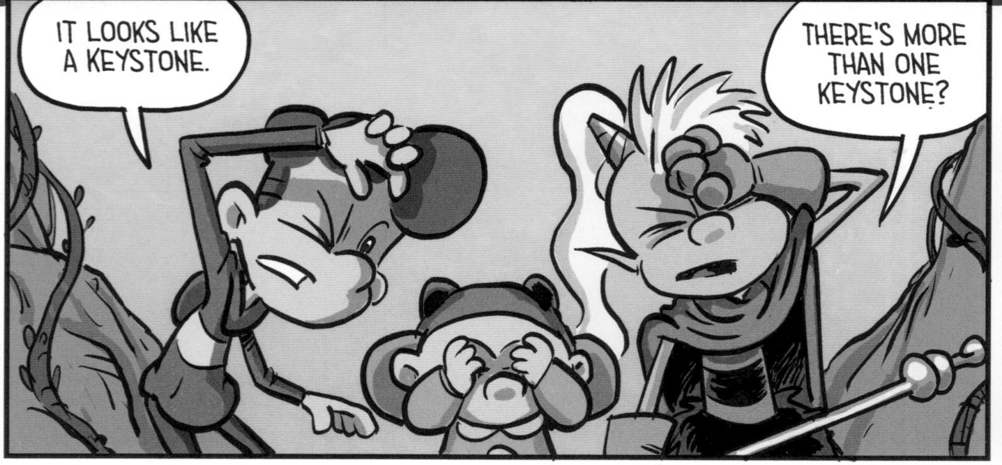
IT LOOKS LIKE A KEYSTONE.
THERE'S MORE THAN ONE KEYSTONE?

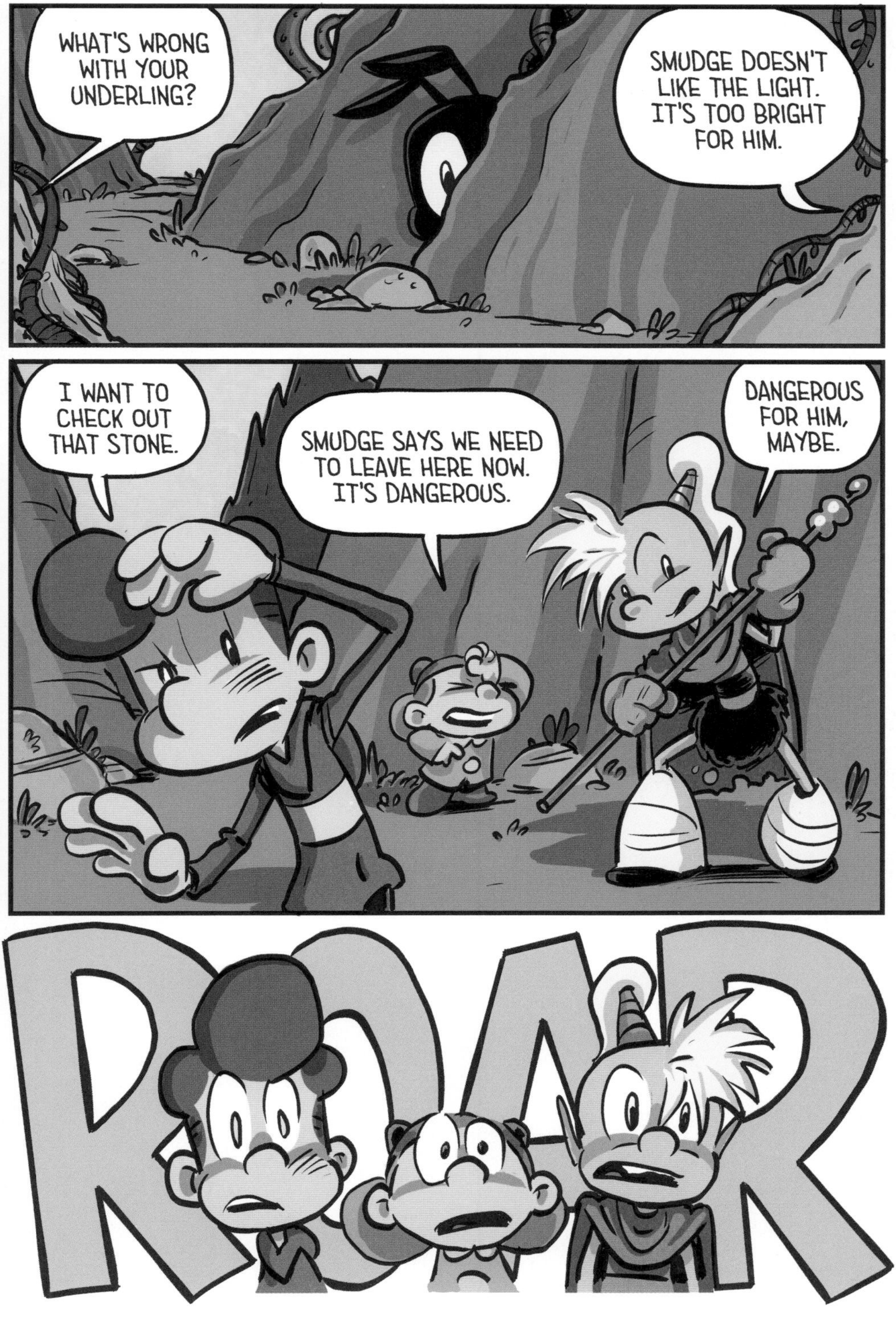
WHAT'S WRONG WITH YOUR UNDERLING?
SMUDGE DOESN'T LIKE THE LIGHT. IT'S TOO BRIGHT FOR HIM.
I WANT TO CHECK OUT THAT STONE.
SMUDGE SAYS WE NEED TO LEAVE HERE NOW. IT'S DANGEROUS.
DANGEROUS FOR HIM, MAYBE.
ROAR

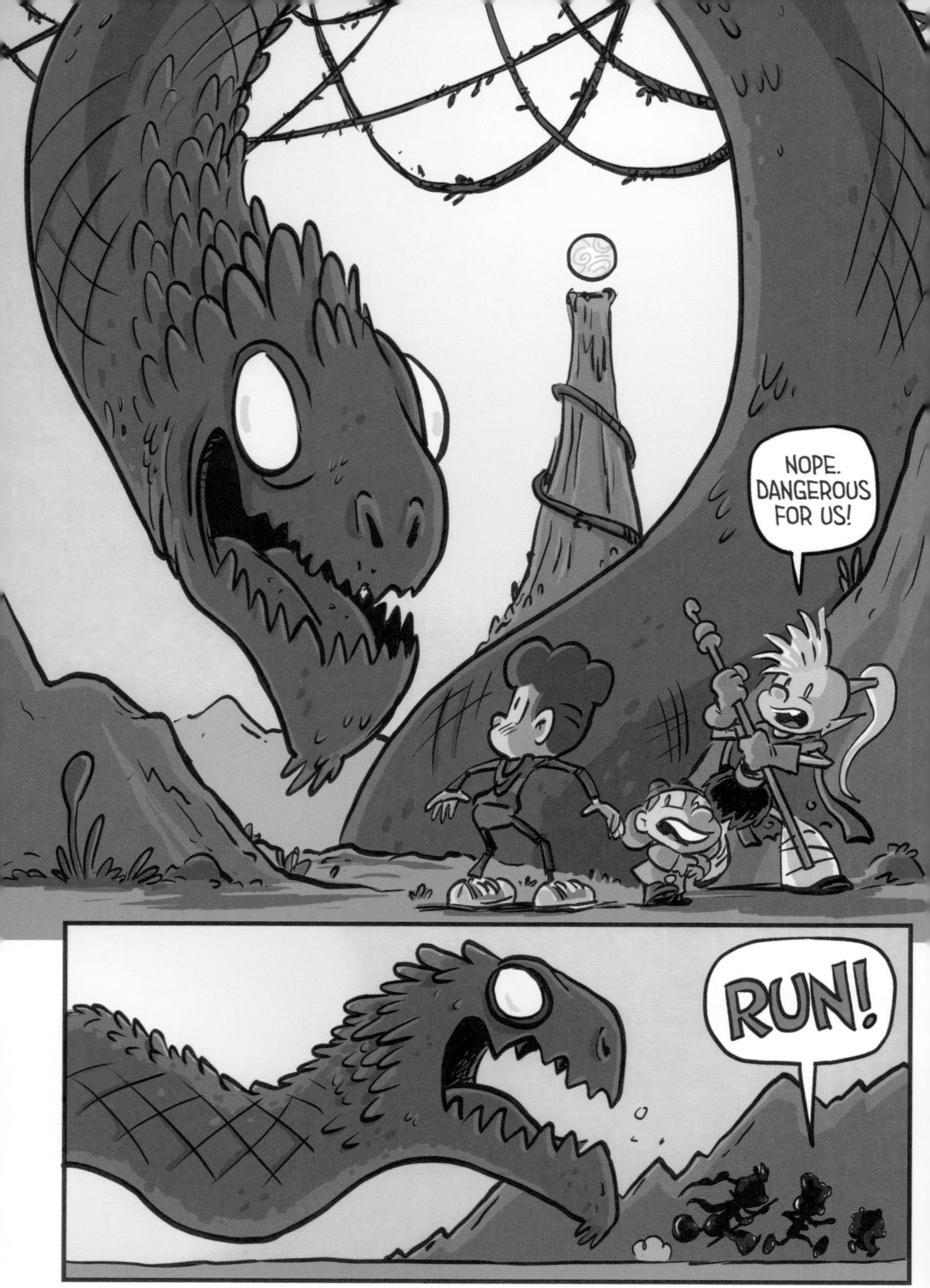
NOPE. DANGEROUS FOR US!
RUN!

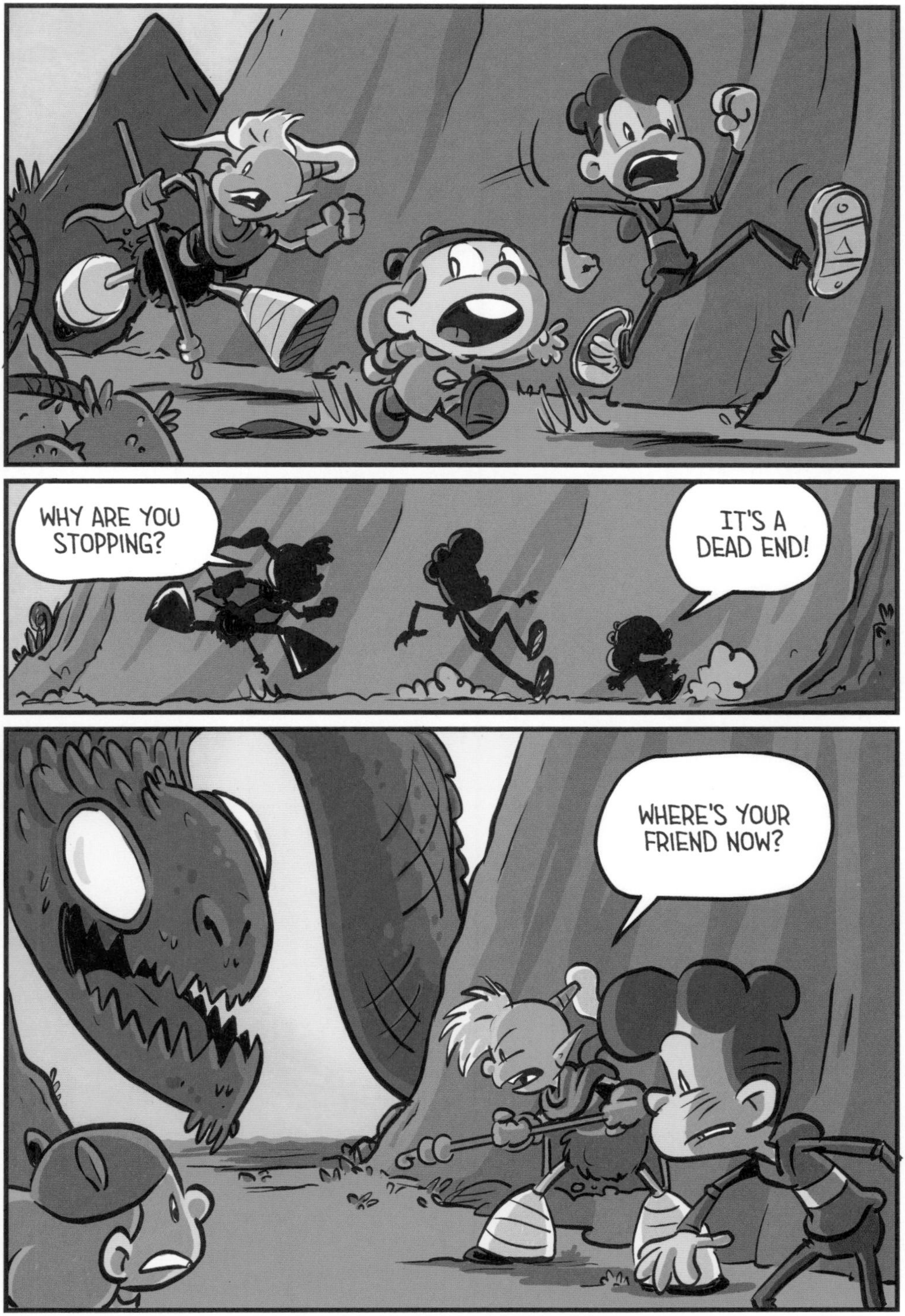

WHY ARE YOU STOPPING?
IT'S A DEAD END!
WHERE'S YOUR FRIEND NOW?

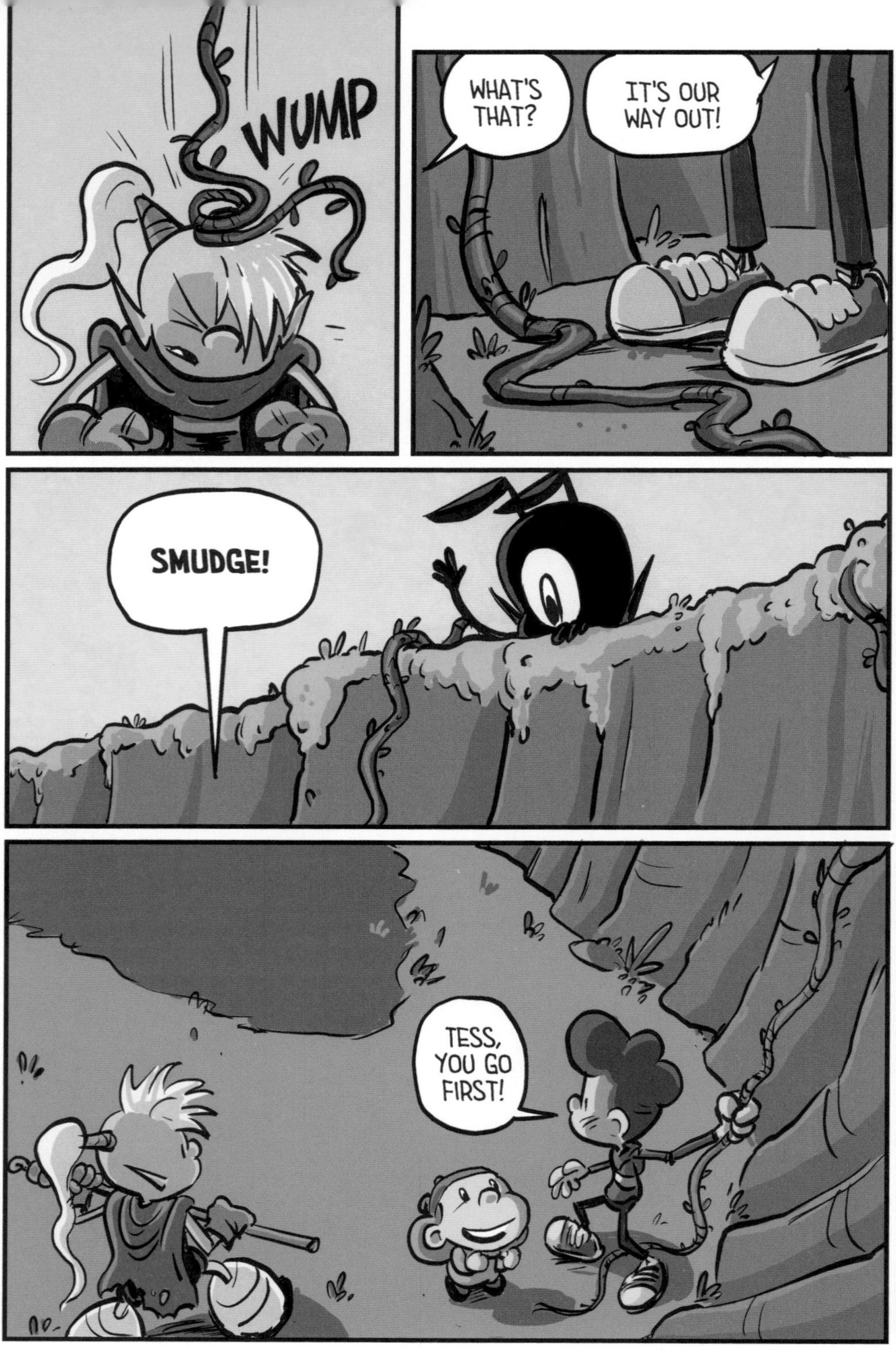
WUMP
WHAT'S THAT?
IT'S OUR WAY OUT!
SMUDGE!
TESS, YOU GO FIRST!

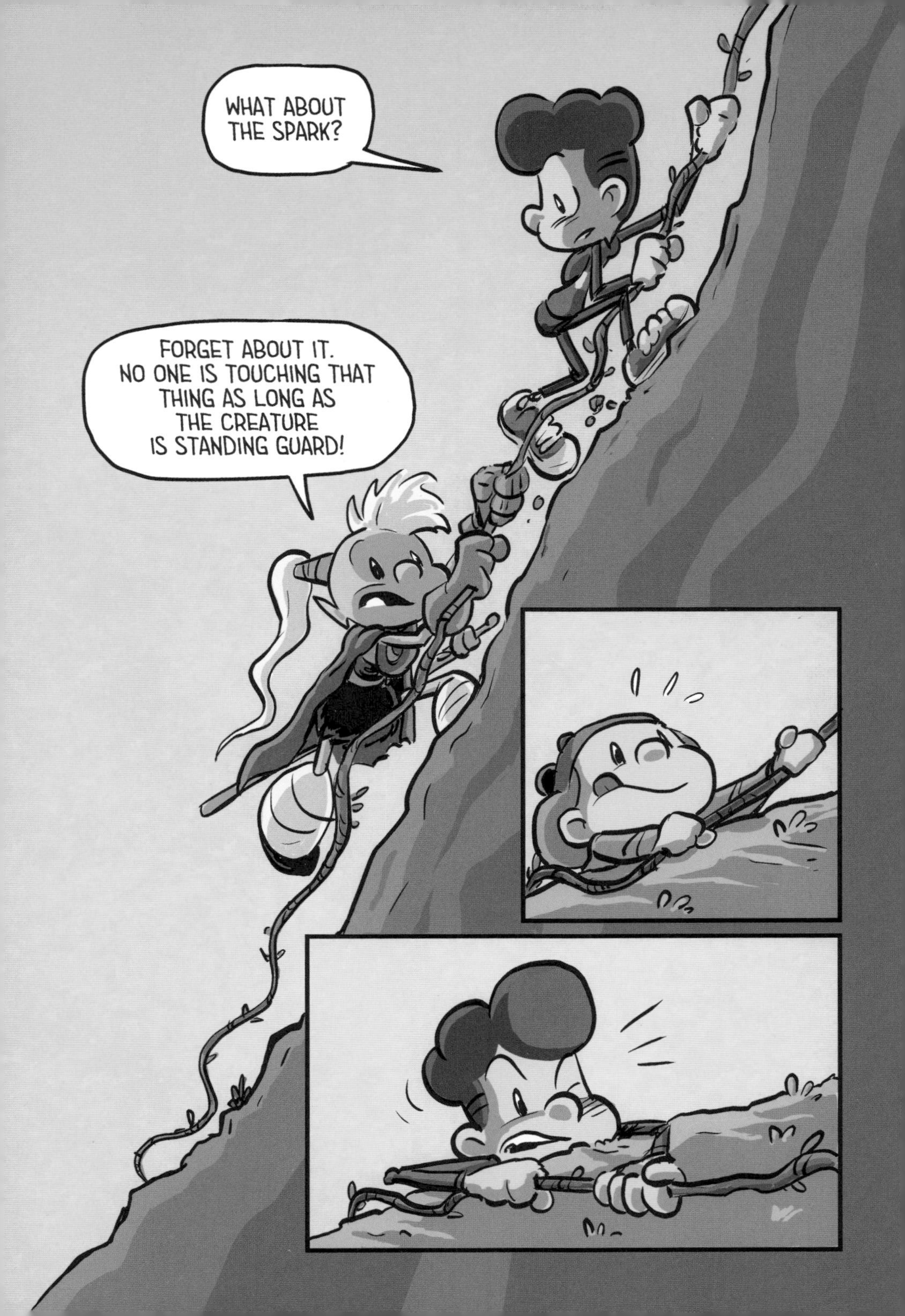
WHAT ABOUT THE SPARK?
FORGET ABOUT IT. NO ONE IS TOUCHING THAT THING AS LONG AS THE CREATURE IS STANDING GUARD!

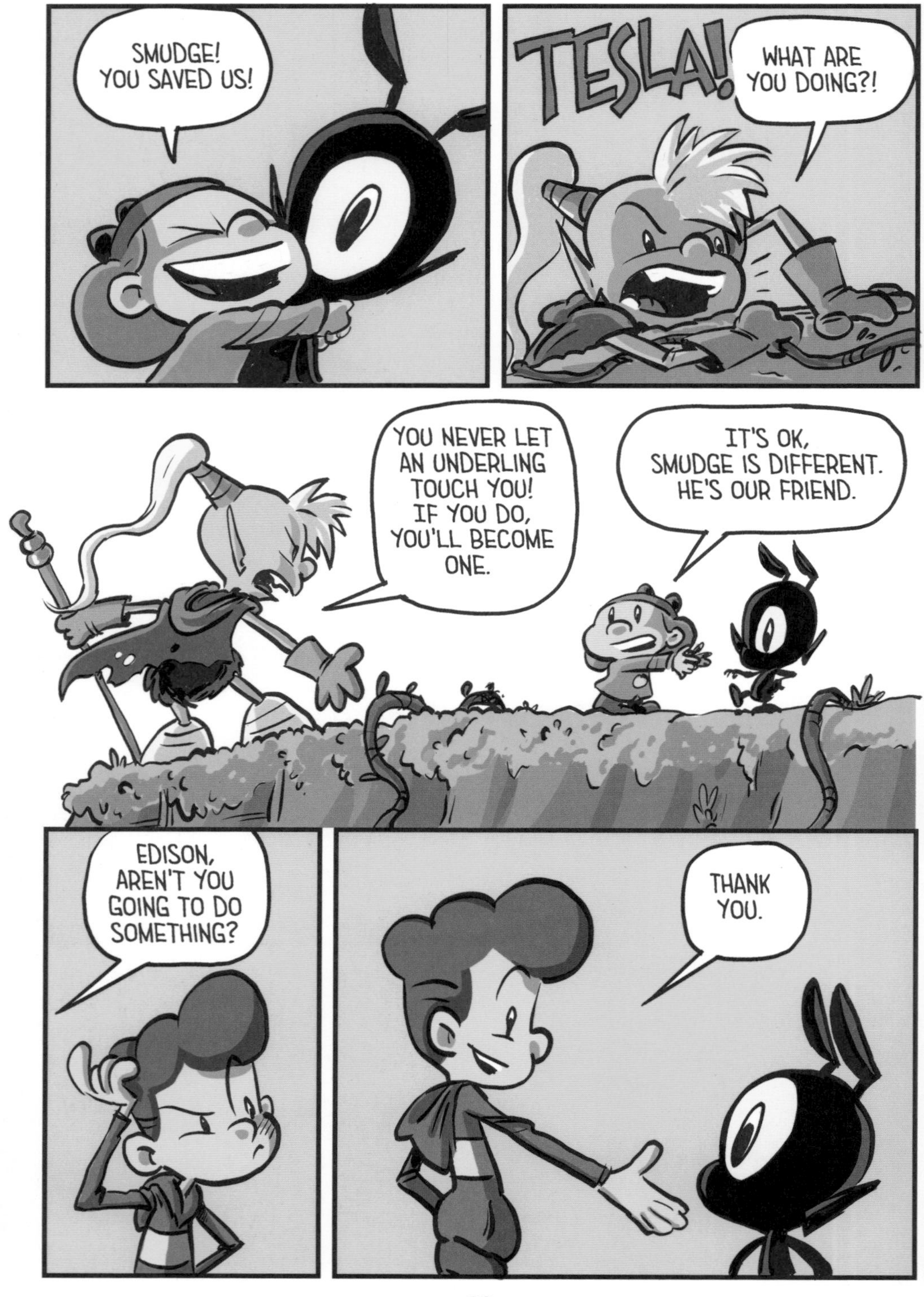
SMUDGE! YOU SAVED US!
TESLA!
WHAT ARE YOU DOING?!
YOU NEVER LET AN UNDERLING TOUCH YOU! IF YOU DO, YOU'LL BECOME ONE.
IT'S OK, SMUDGE IS DIFFERENT. HE'S OUR FRIEND.
EDISON, AREN'T YOU GOING TO DO SOMETHING?
THANK YOU.

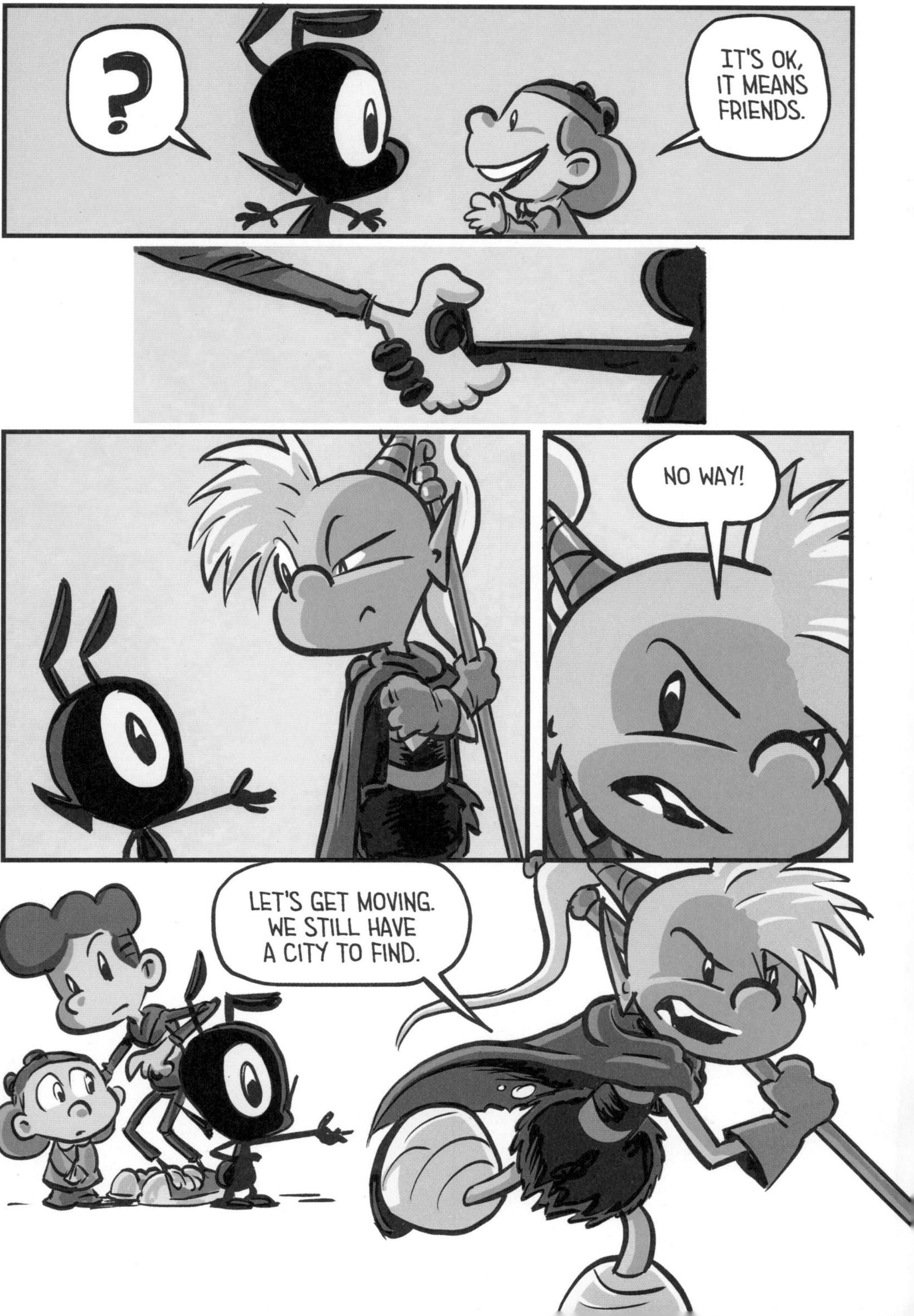
?
IT'S OK, IT MEANS FRIENDS.
NO WAY!
LET'S GET MOVING. WE STILL HAVE A CITY TO FIND.

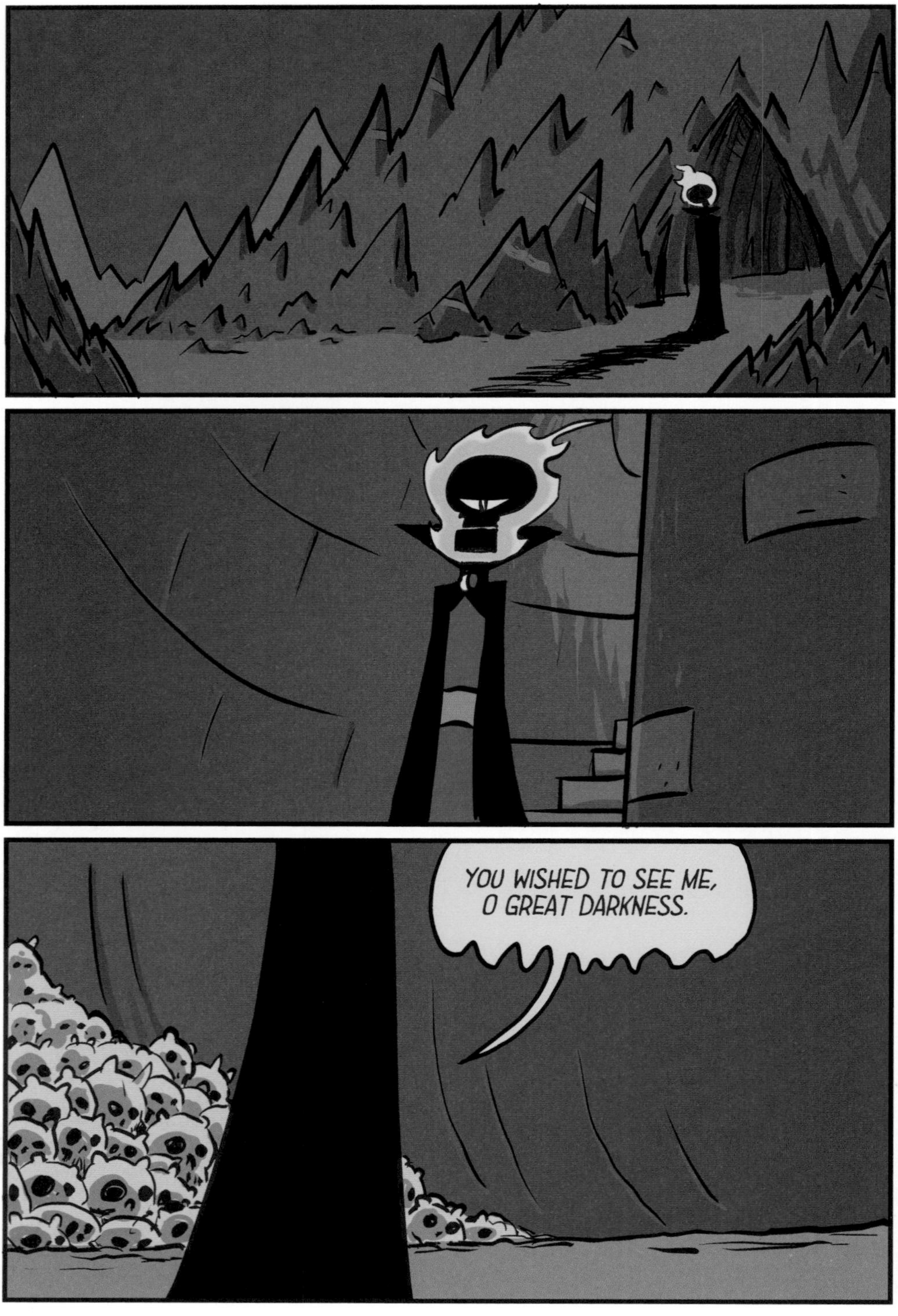
YOU WISHED TO SEE ME, O GREAT DARKNESS.

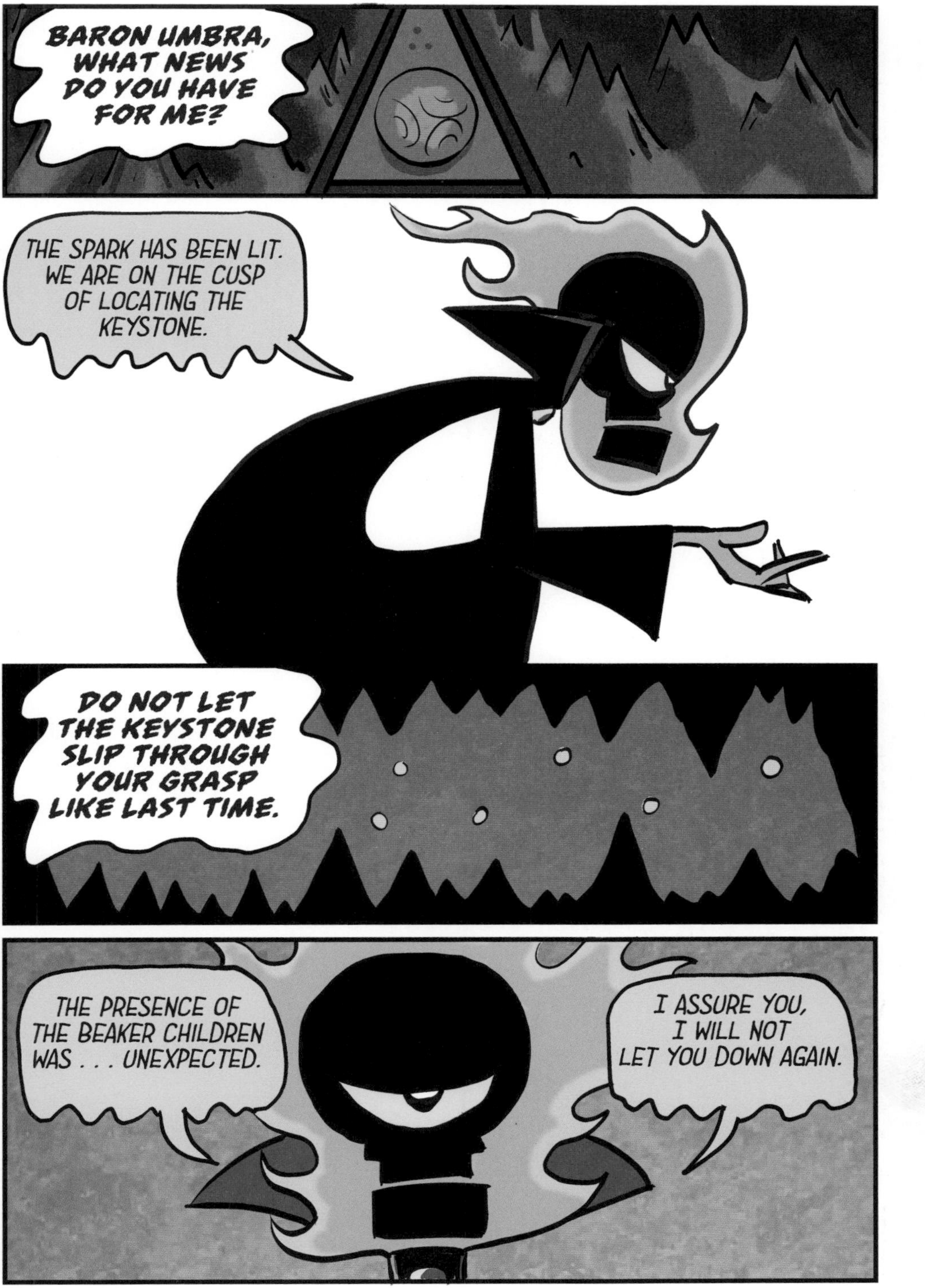
BARON UMBRA, WHAT NEWS DO YOU HAVE FOR ME?
THE SPARK HAS BEEN LIT. WE ARE ON THE CUSP OF LOCATING THE KEYSTONE.
DO NOT LET THE KEYSTONE SLIP THROUGH YOUR GRASP LIKE LAST TIME.
THE PRESENCE OF THE BEAKER CHILDREN WAS . . . UNEXPECTED.
I ASSURE YOU, I WILL NOT LET YOU DOWN AGAIN.

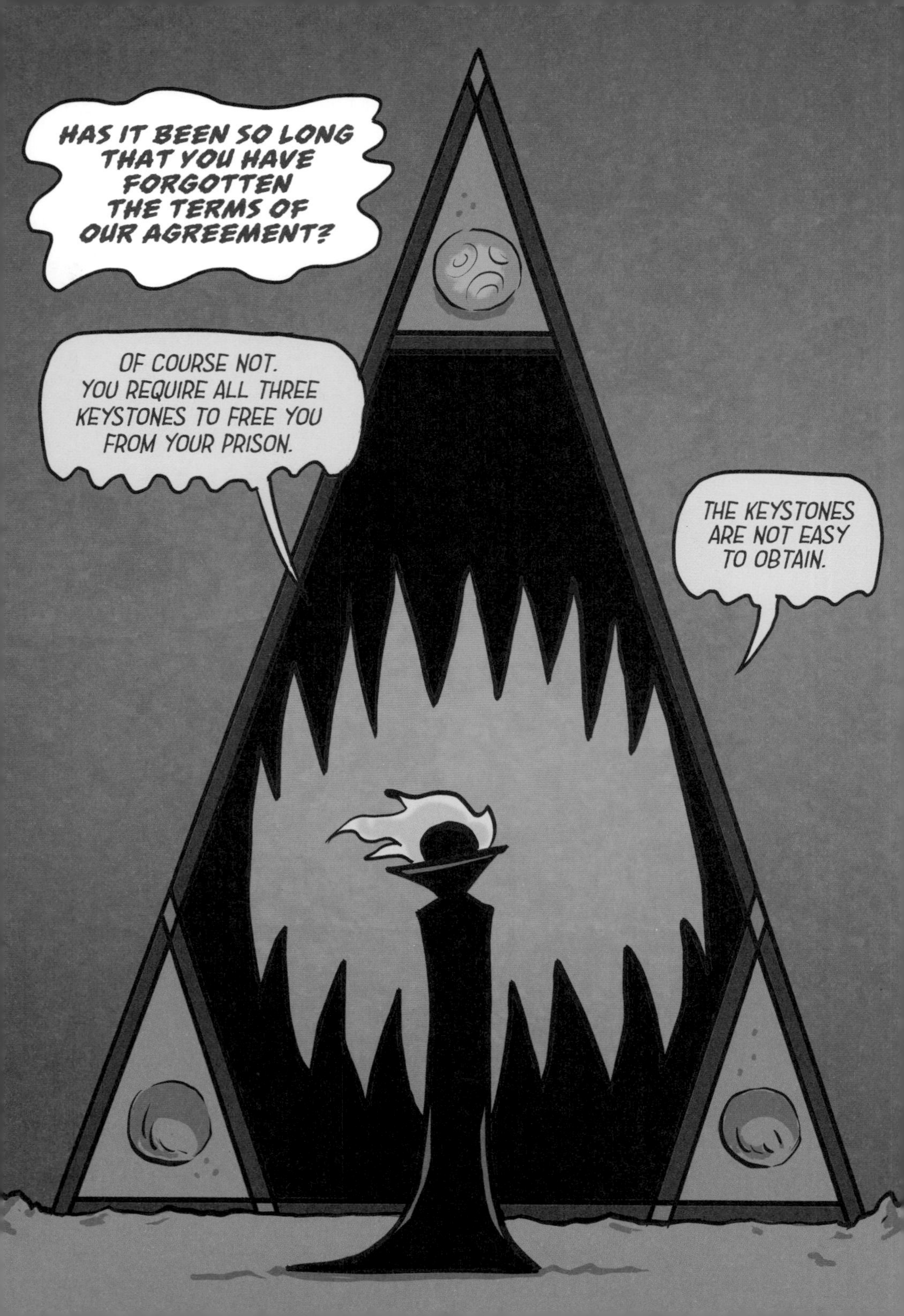
HAS IT BEEN SO LONG THAT YOU HAVE FORGOTTEN THE TERMS OF OUR AGREEMENT?
OF COURSE NOT. YOU REQUIRE ALL THREE KEYSTONES TO FREE YOU FROM YOUR PRISON.
THE KEYSTONES ARE NOT EASY TO OBTAIN.

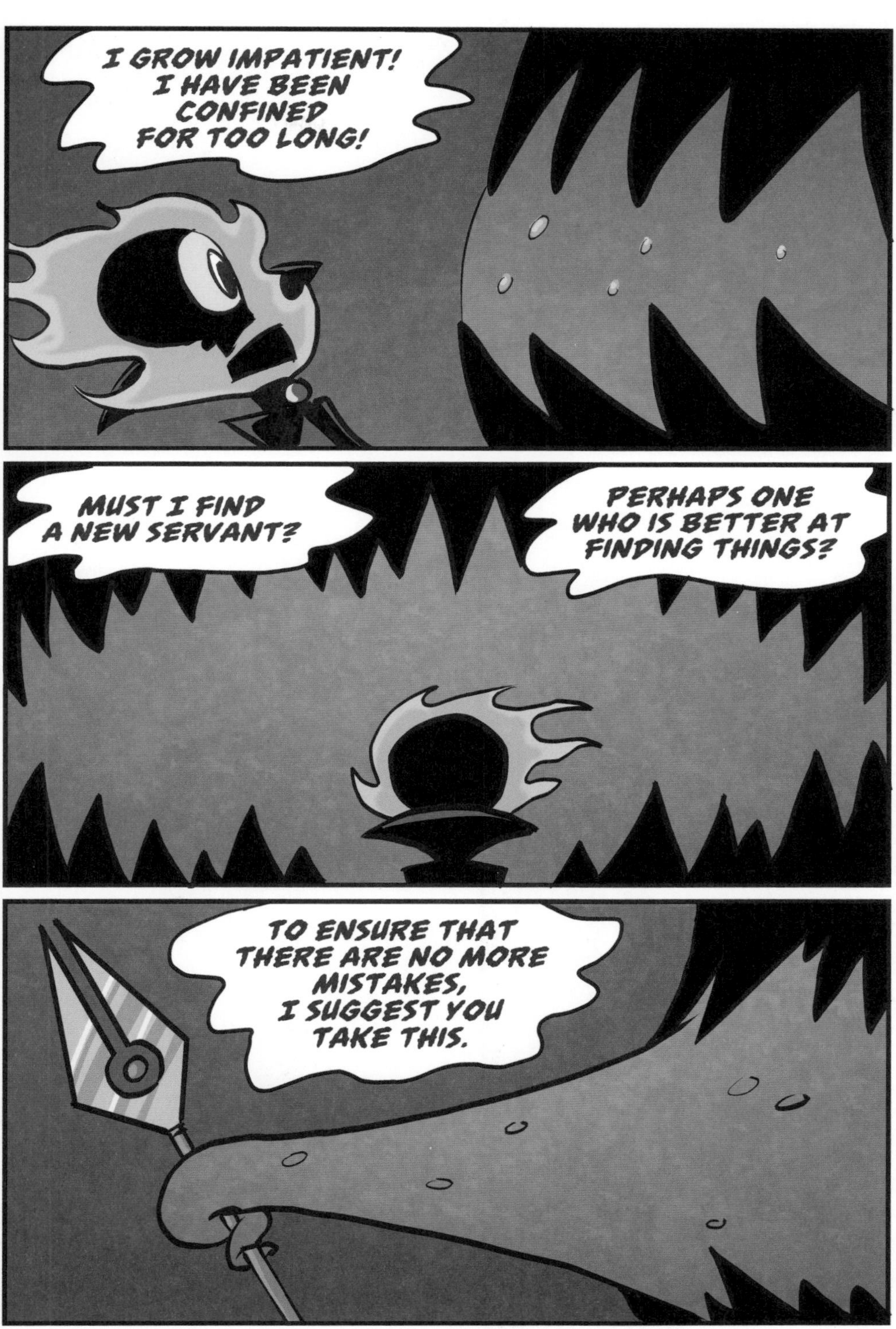
I GROW IMPATIENT! I HAVE BEEN CONFINED FOR TOO LONG!
MUST I FIND A NEW SERVANT?
PERHAPS ONE WHO IS BETTER AT FINDING THINGS?
TO ENSURE THAT THERE ARE NO MORE MISTAKES, I SUGGEST YOU TAKE THIS.

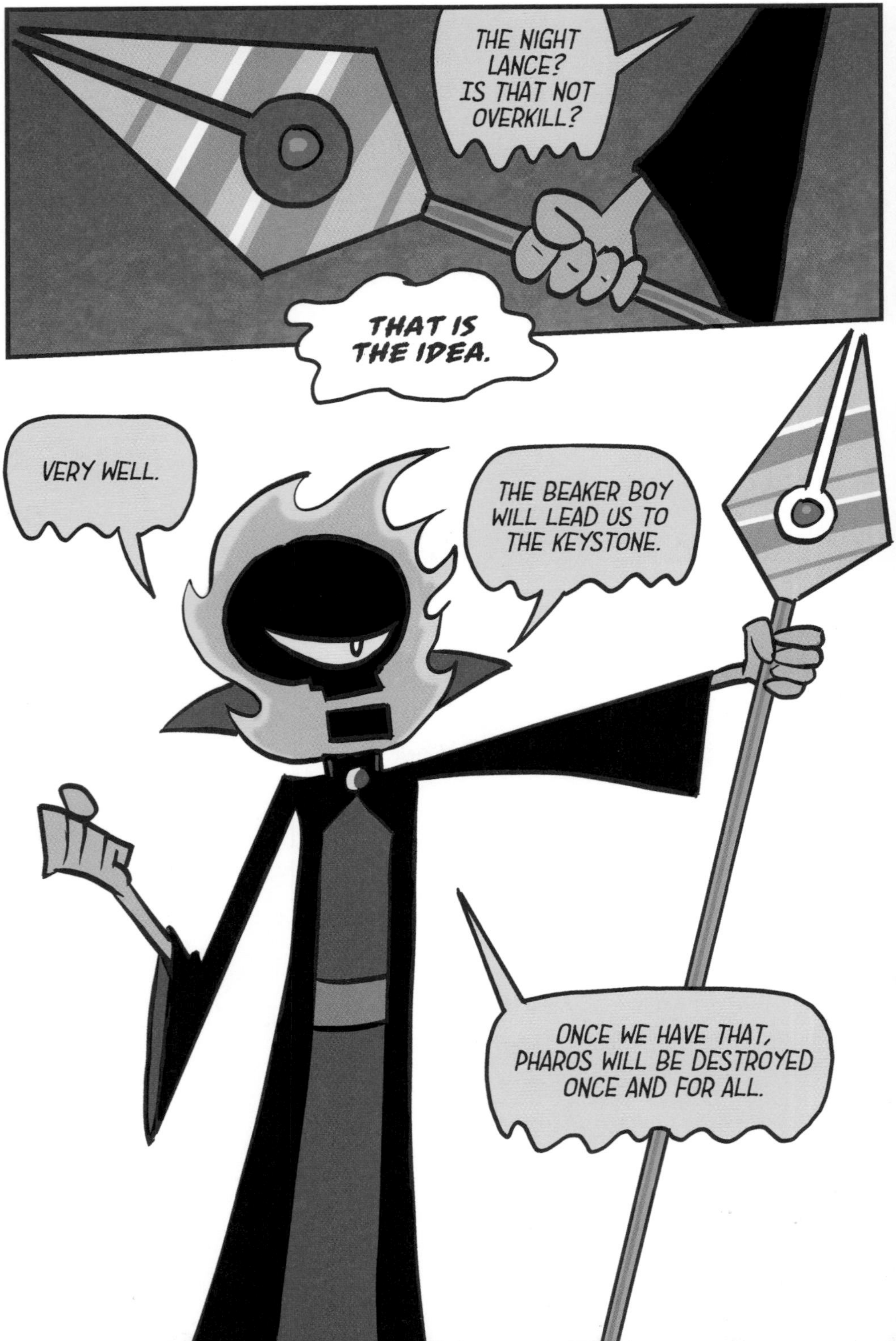
THE NIGHT LANCE? IS THAT NOT OVERKILL?
THAT IS THE IDEA.
VERY WELL.
THE BEAKER BOY WILL LEAD US TO THE KEYSTONE.
ONCE WE HAVE THAT, PHAROS WILL BE DESTROYED ONCE AND FOR ALL.

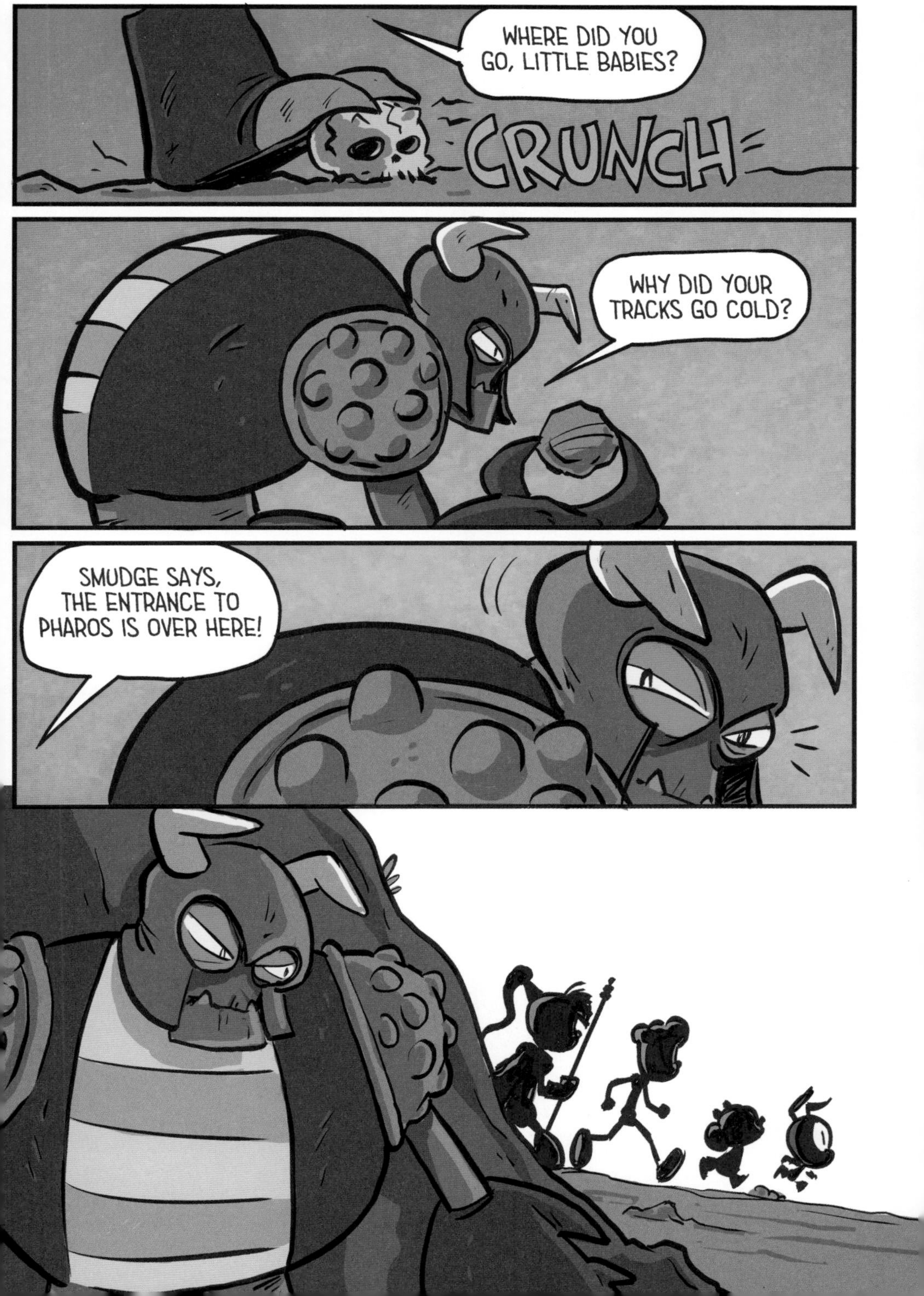
WHERE DID YOU GO, LITTLE BABIES?
CRUNCH
WHY DID YOUR TRACKS GO COLD?
SMUDGE SAYS, THE ENTRANCE TO PHAROS IS OVER HERE!

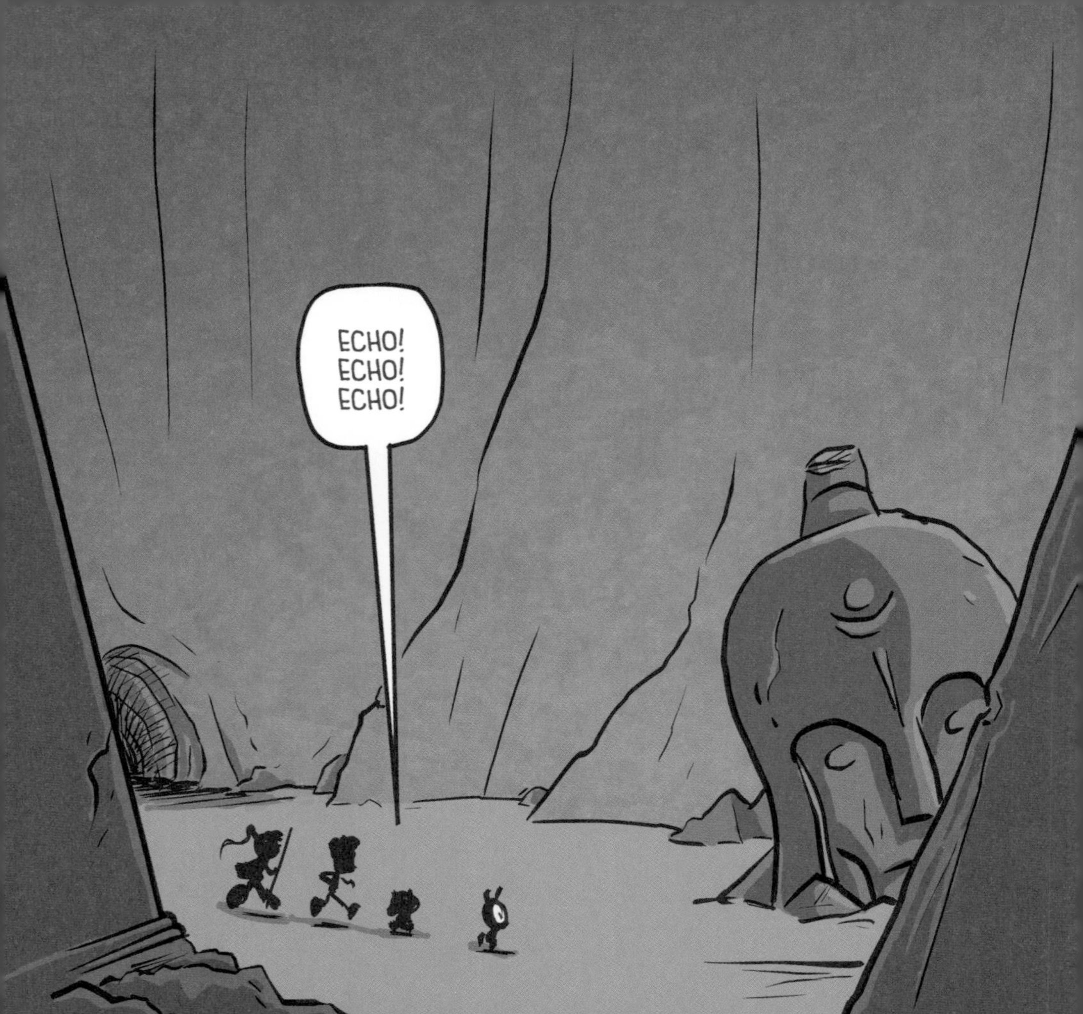
ECHO!
ECHO!
ECHO!

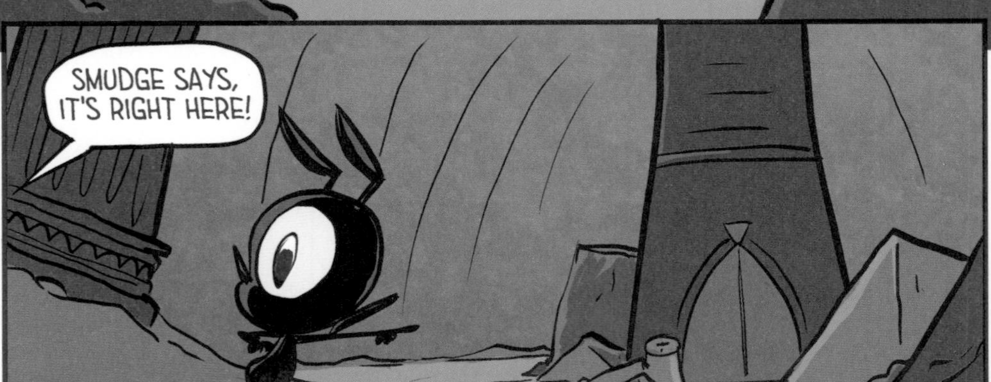
SMUDGE SAYS, IT'S RIGHT HERE!

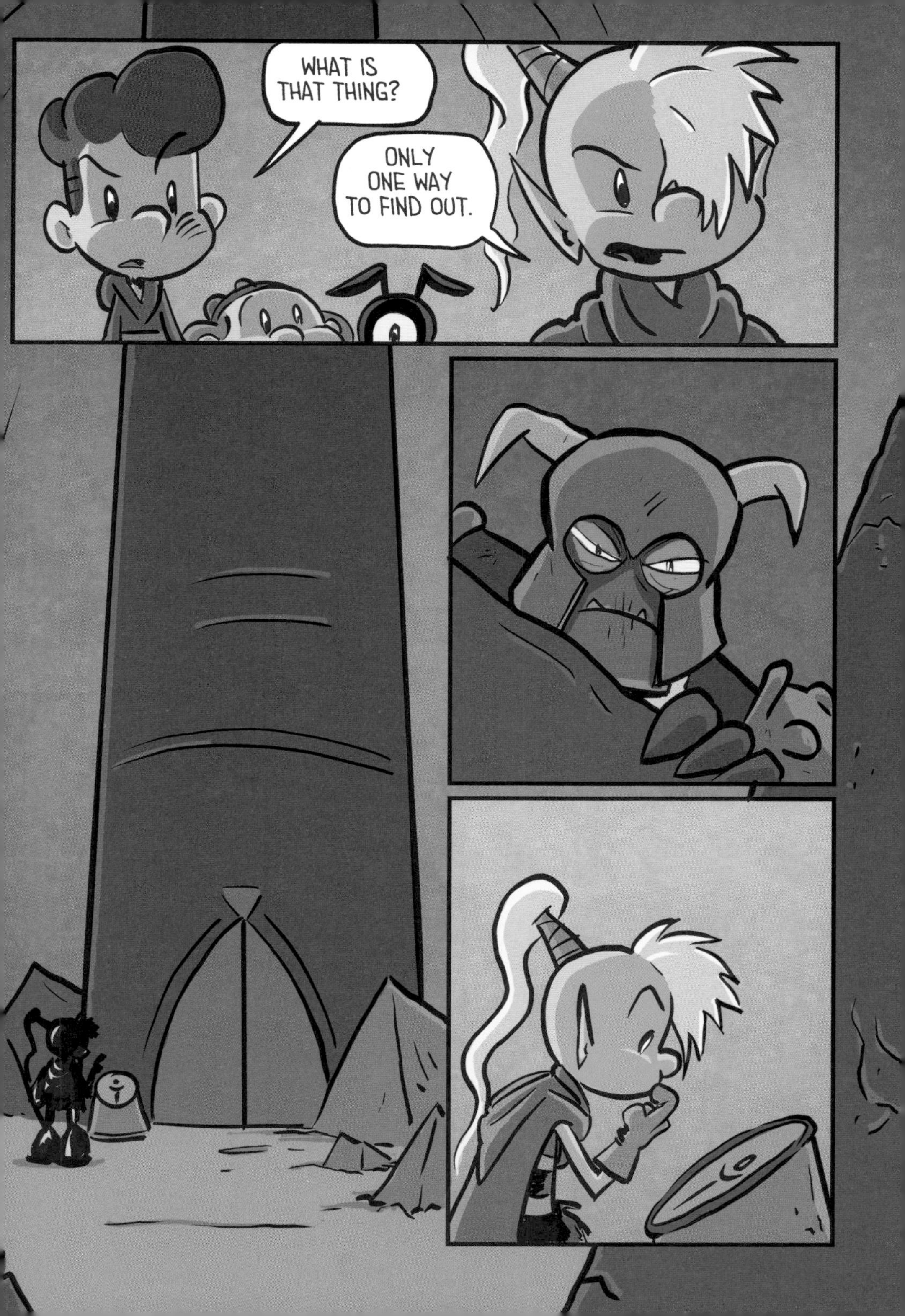
WHAT IS THAT THING?
ONLY ONE WAY TO FIND OUT.

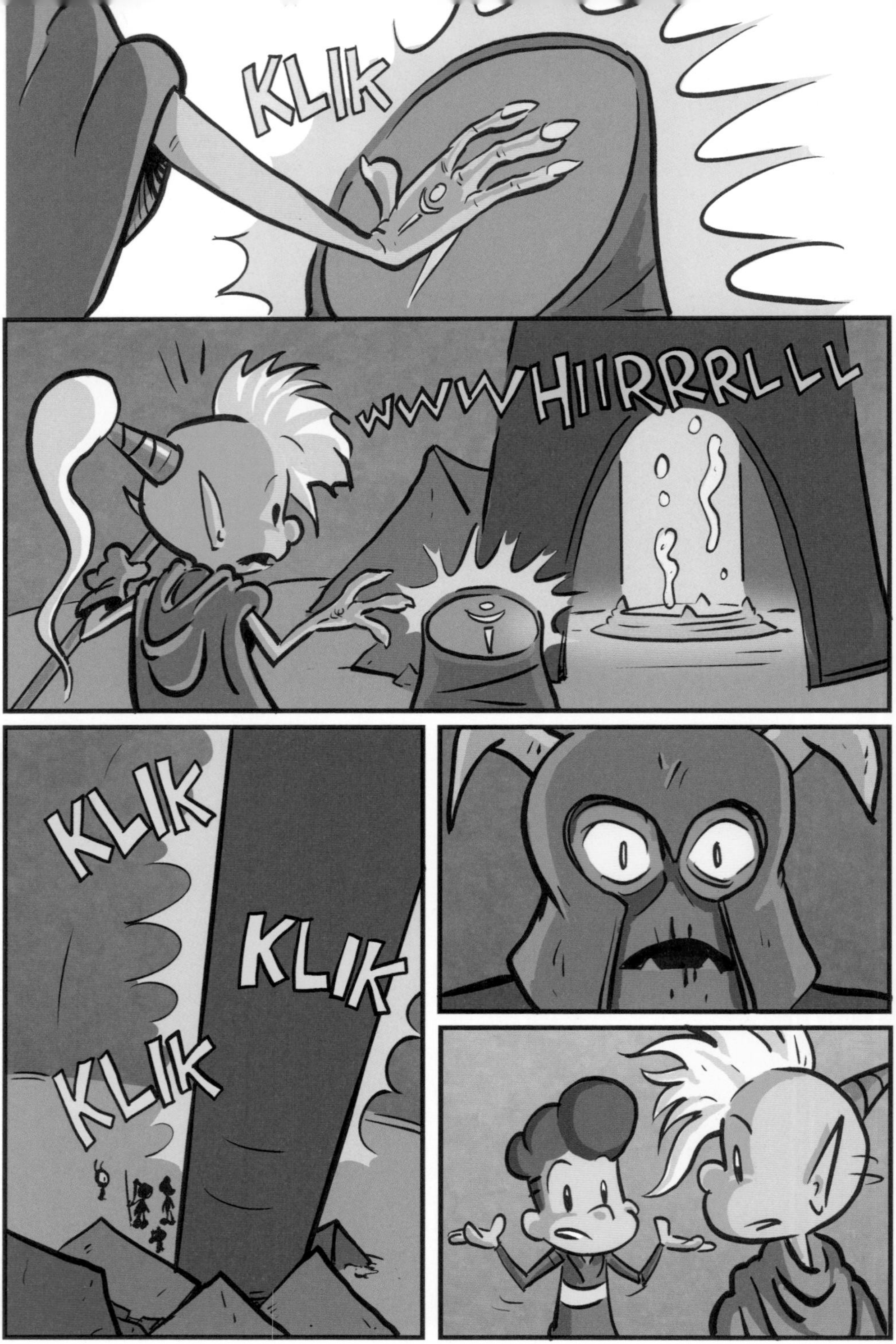
KLIK
WWWHIIRRRLLL
KLIK
KLIK
KLIK

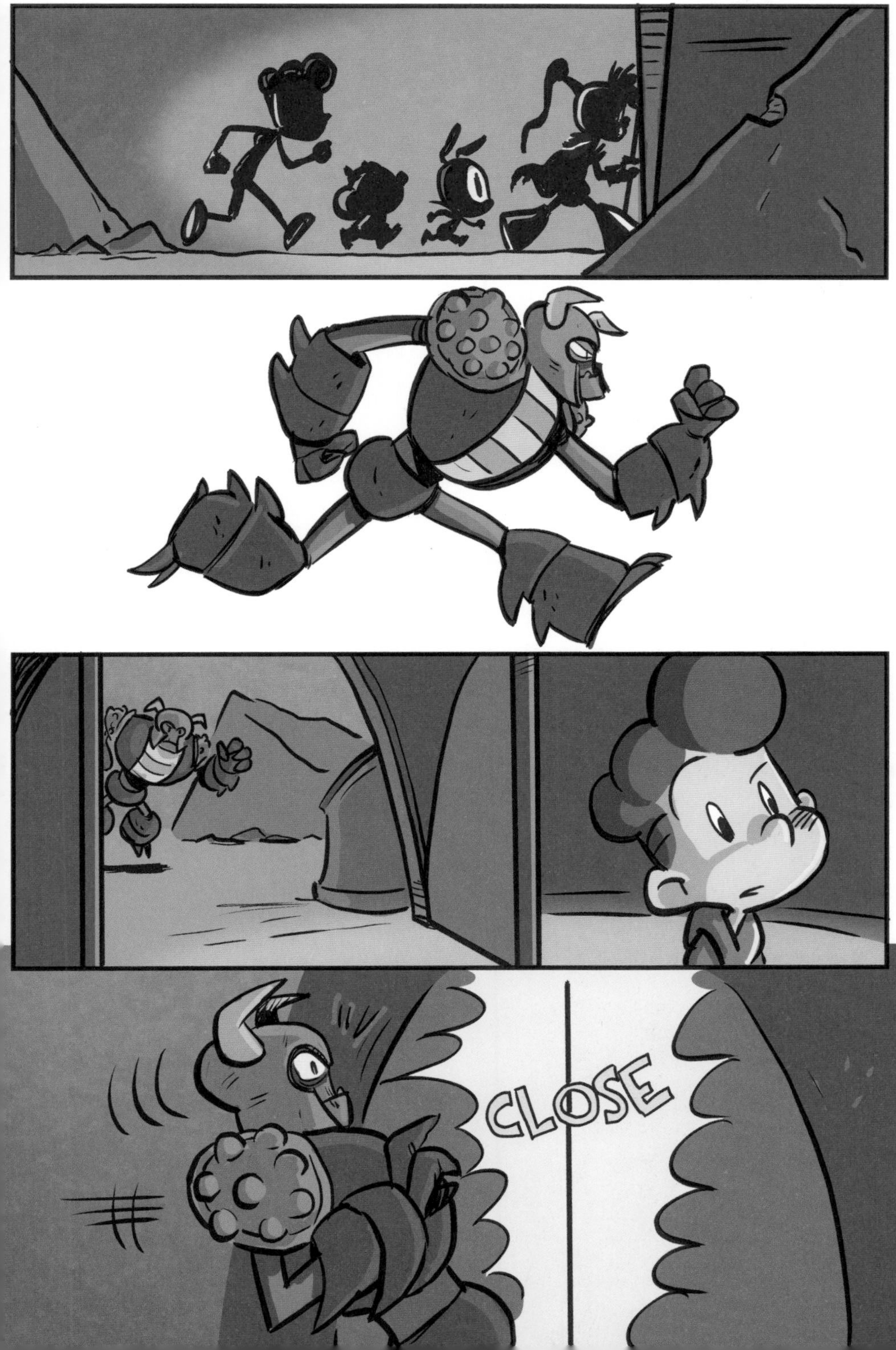
CLOSE

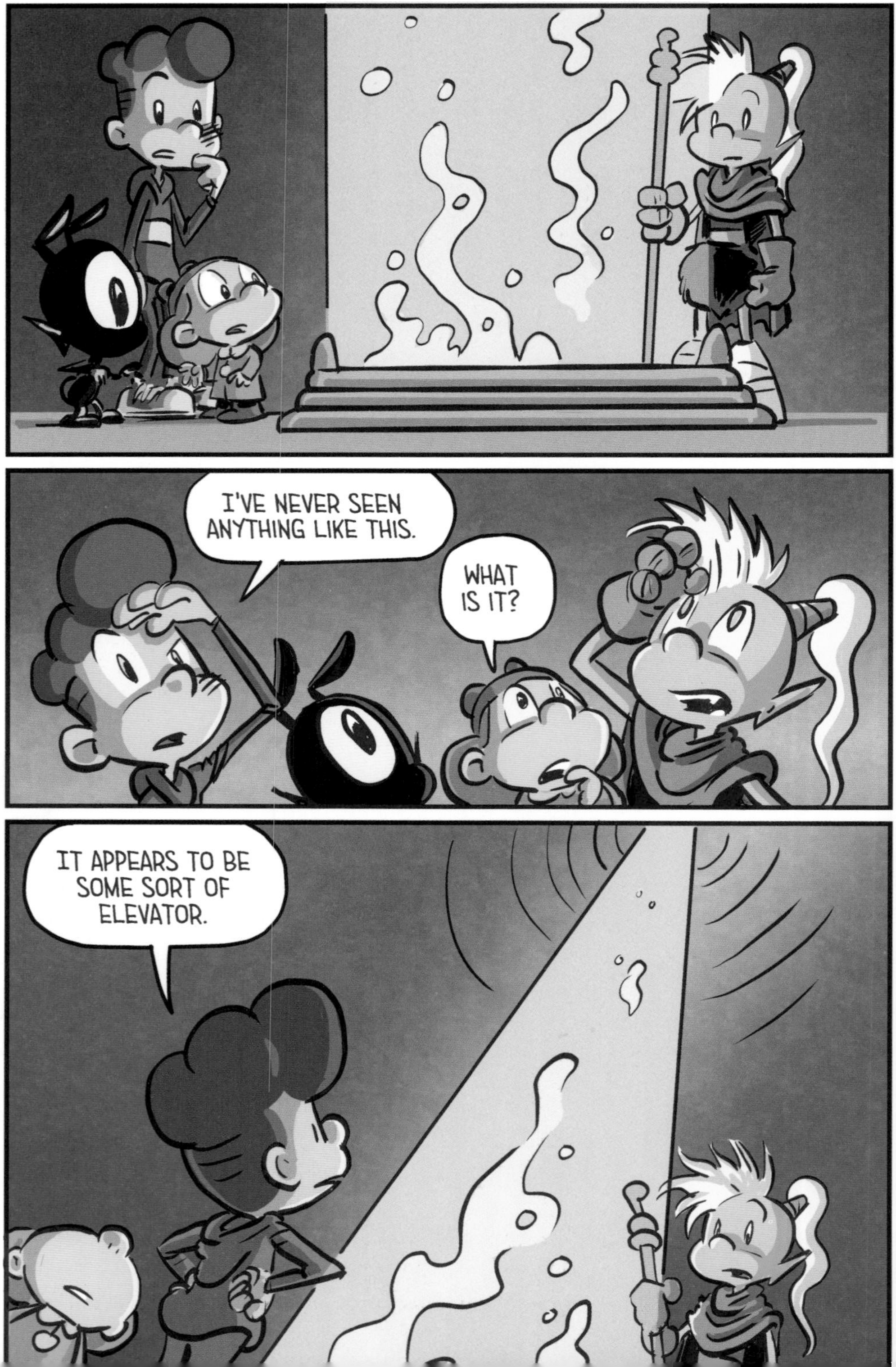
I'VE NEVER SEEN ANYTHING LIKE THIS.
WHAT IS IT?
IT APPEARS TO BE SOME SORT OF ELEVATOR.

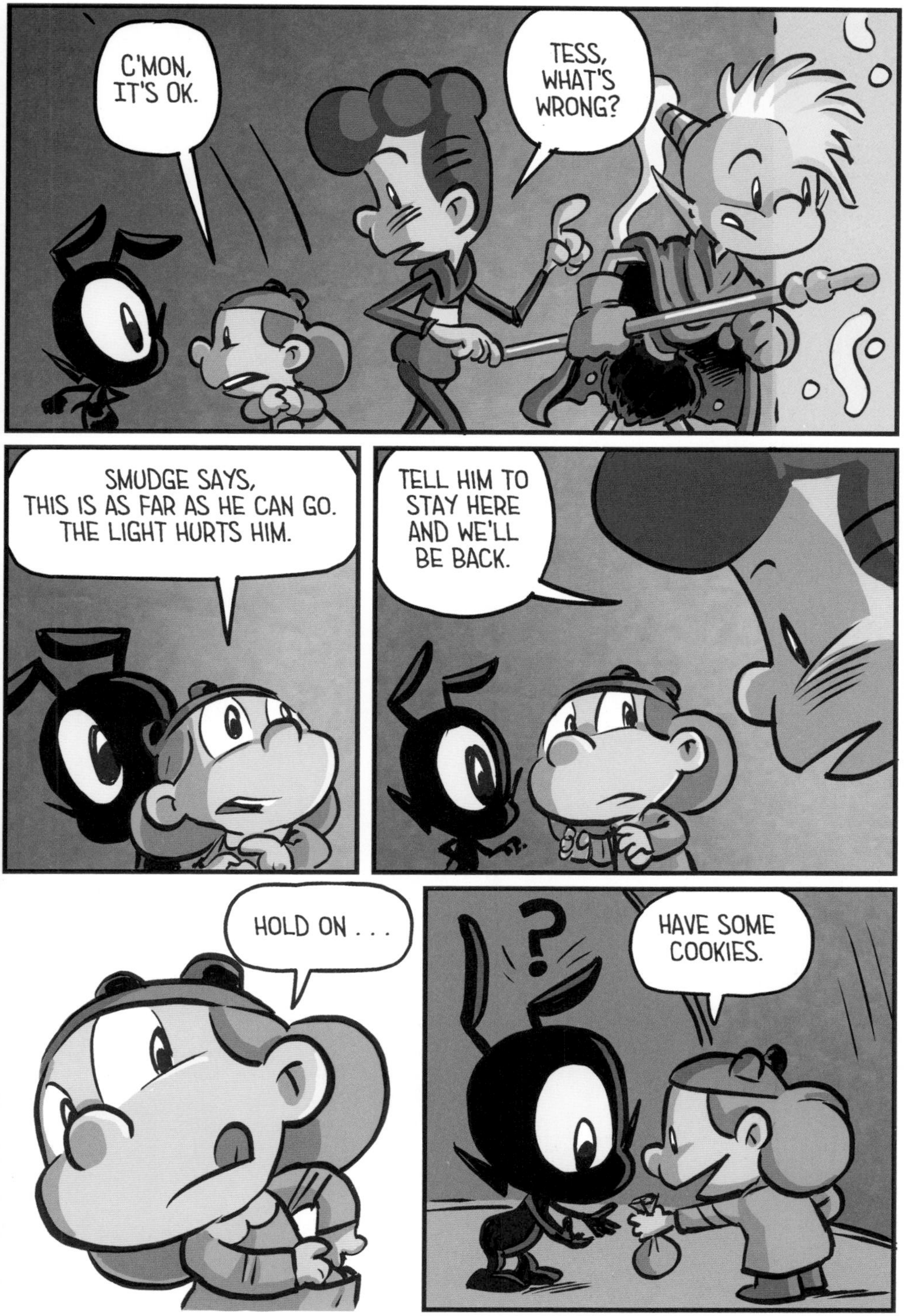
C'MON, IT'S OK.
TESS, WHAT'S WRONG?
SMUDGE SAYS, THIS IS AS FAR AS HE CAN GO. THE LIGHT HURTS HIM.
TELL HIM TO STAY HERE AND WE'LL BE BACK.
HOLD ON . . .
?
HAVE SOME COOKIES.

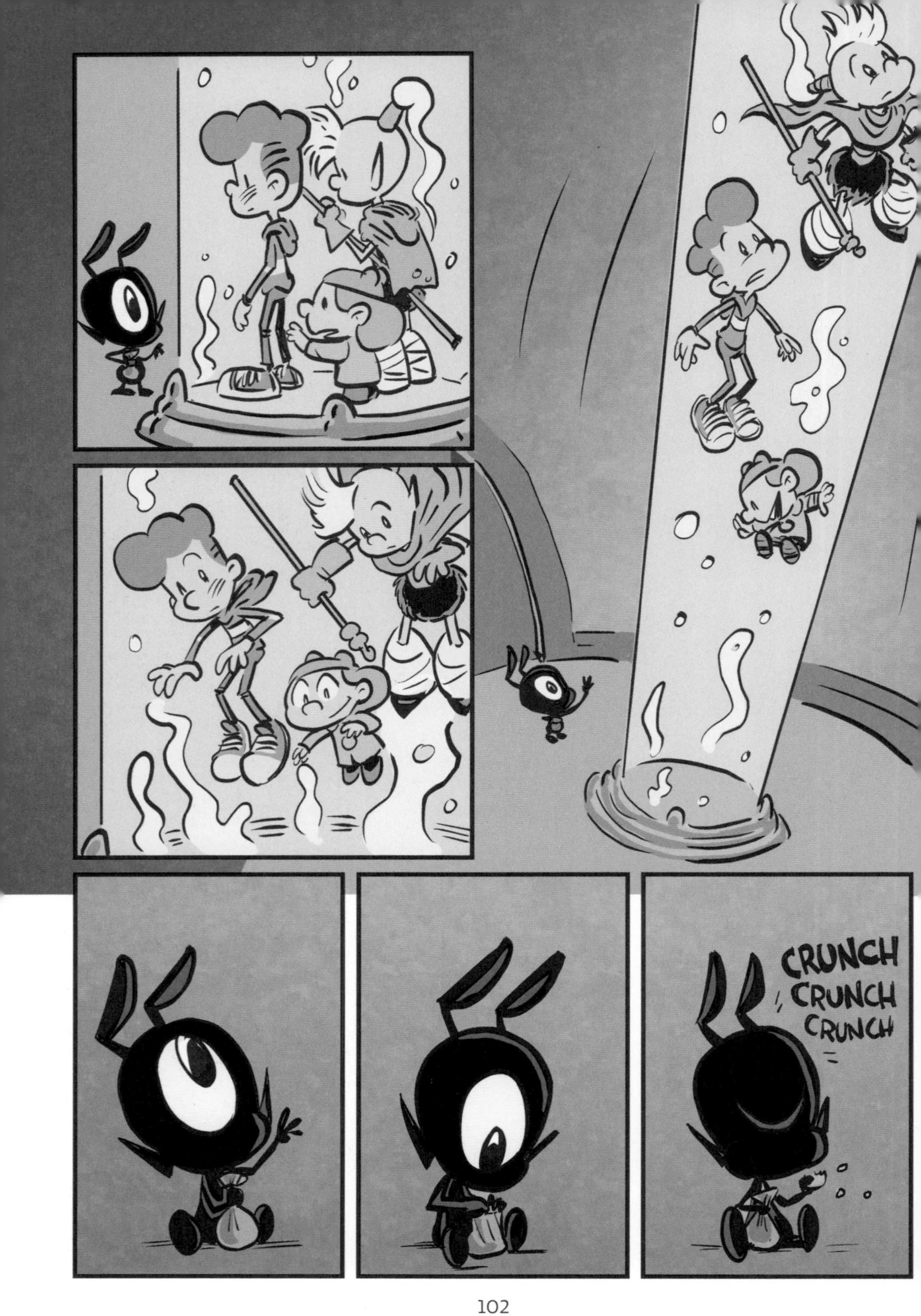
CRUNCH
CRUNCH
CRUNCH

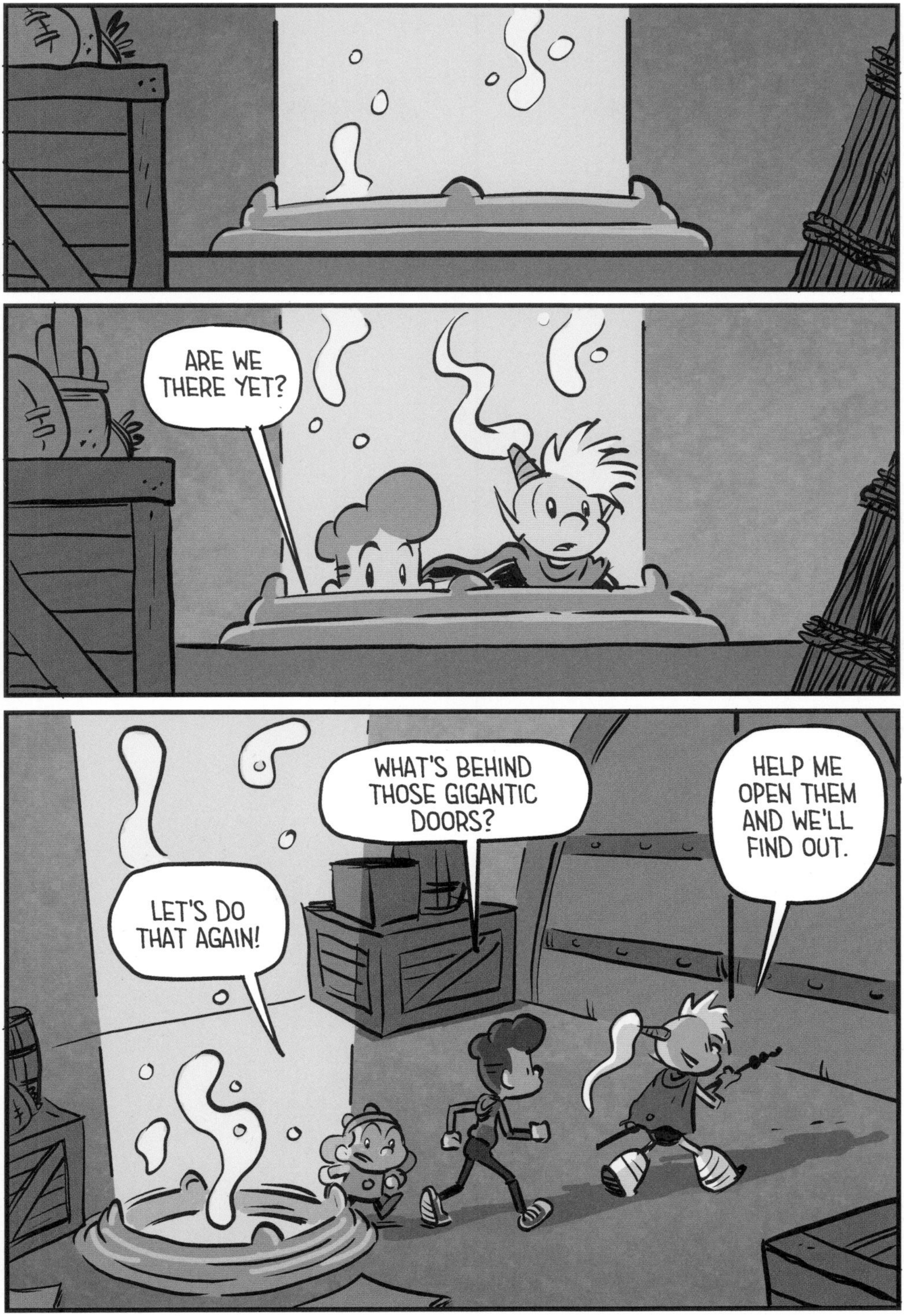
ARE WE THERE YET?
WHAT'S BEHIND THOSE GIGANTIC DOORS?
HELP ME OPEN THEM AND WE'LL FIND OUT.
LET'S DO THAT AGAIN!

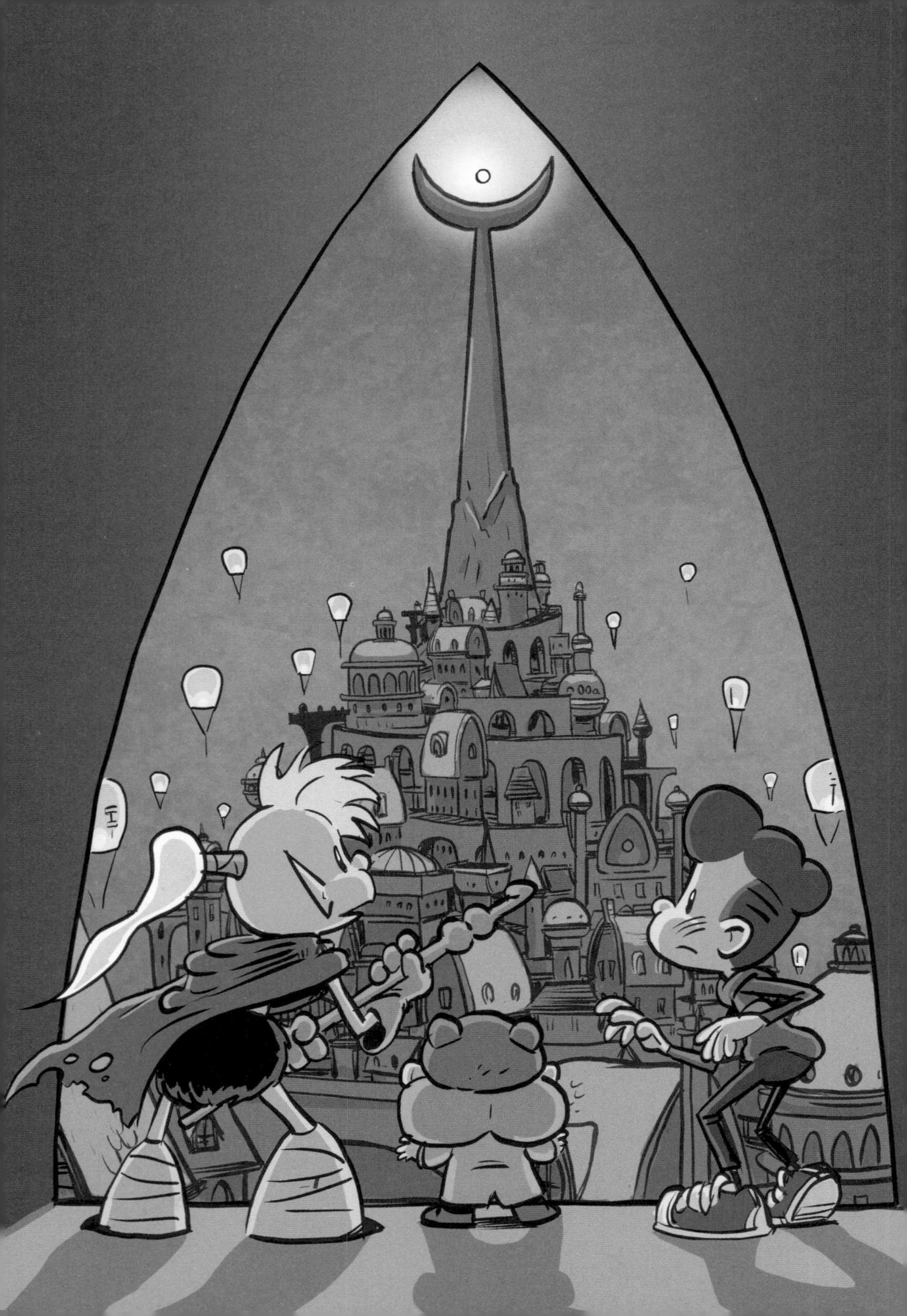

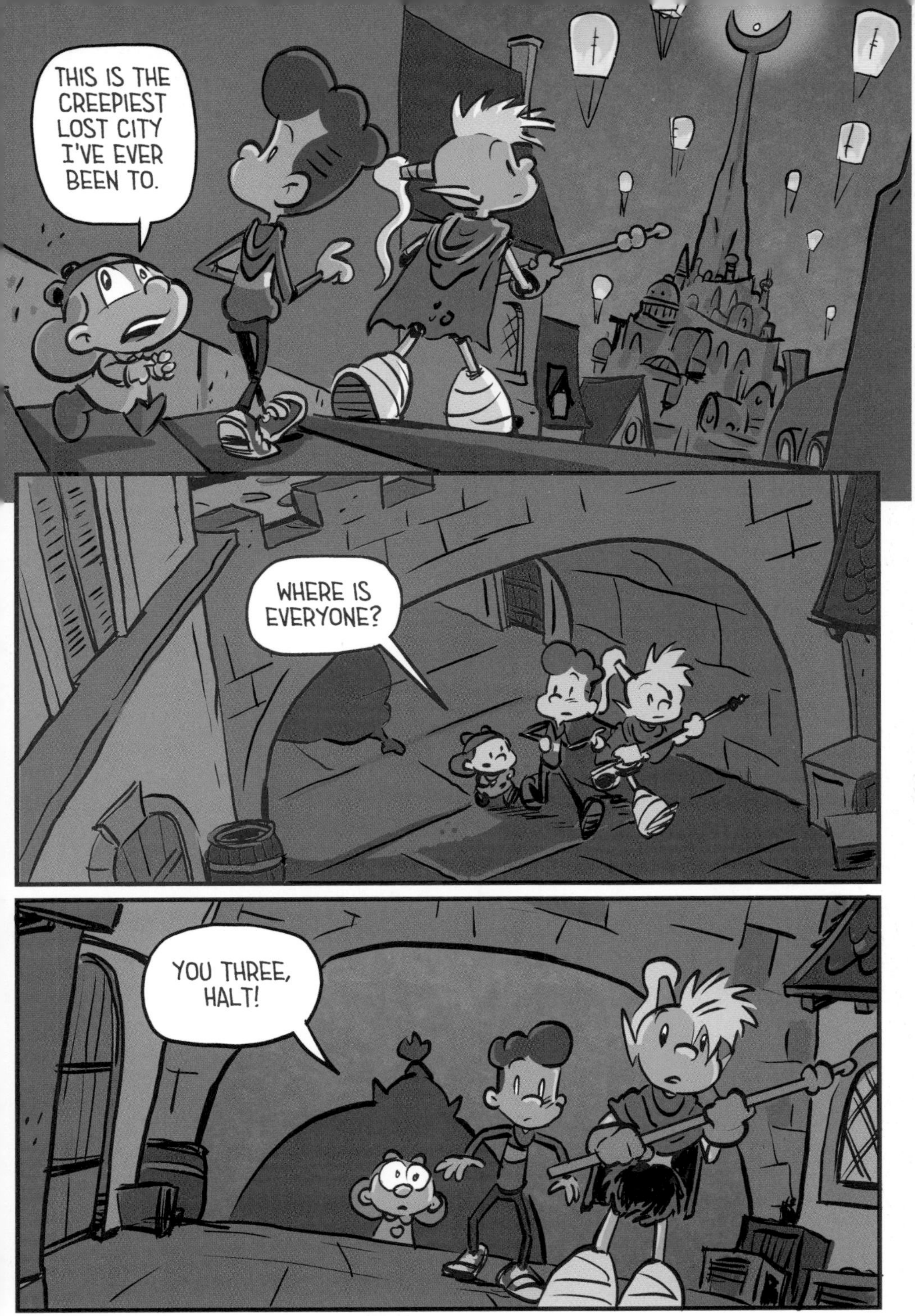
THIS IS THE CREEPIEST LOST CITY I'VE EVER BEEN TO.
WHERE IS EVERYONE?
YOU THREE, HALT!

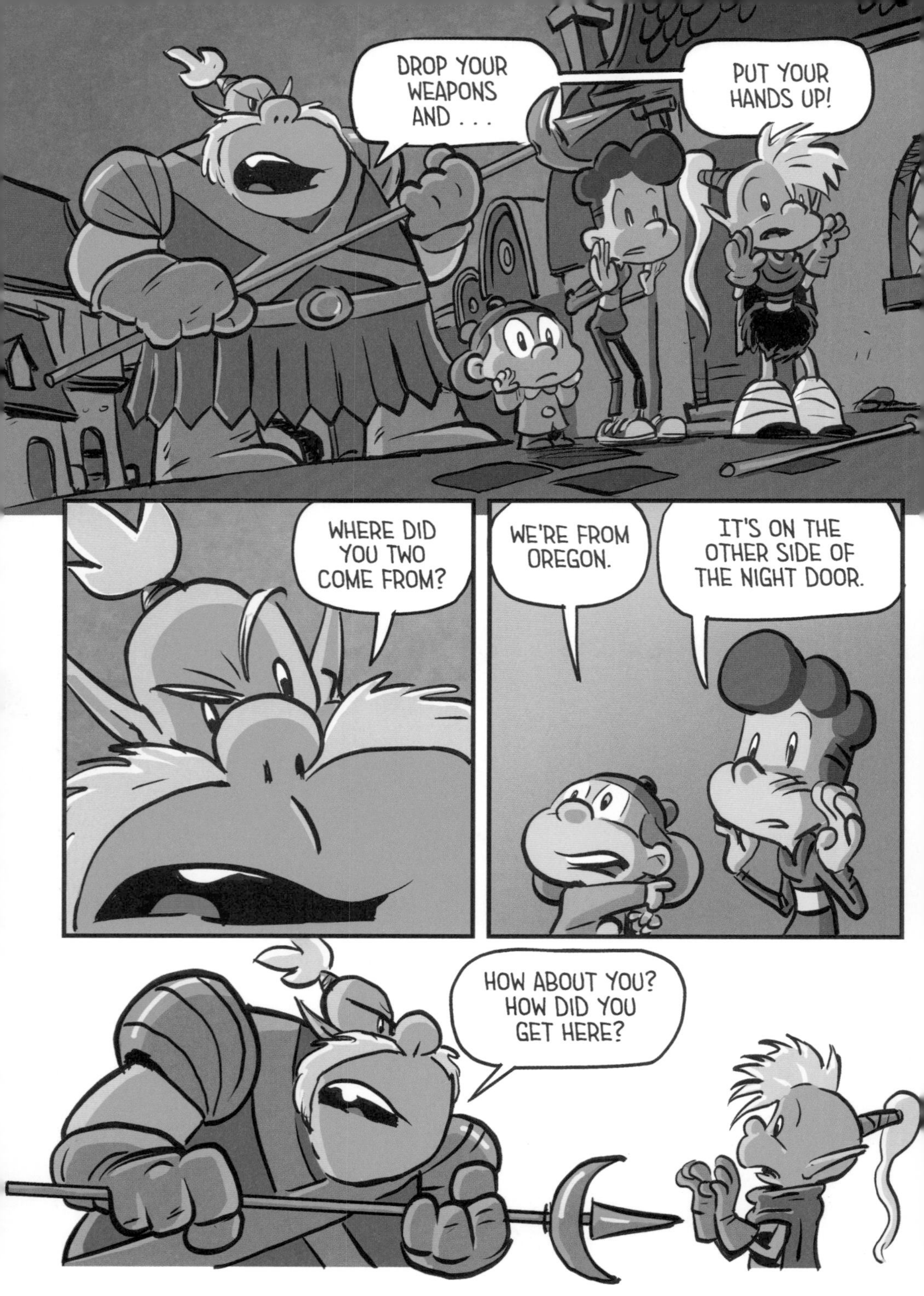
DROP YOUR WEAPONS AND . . .
PUT YOUR HANDS UP!
WHERE DID YOU TWO COME FROM?
WE'RE FROM OREGON.
IT'S ON THE OTHER SIDE OF THE NIGHT DOOR.
HOW ABOUT YOU? HOW DID YOU GET HERE?

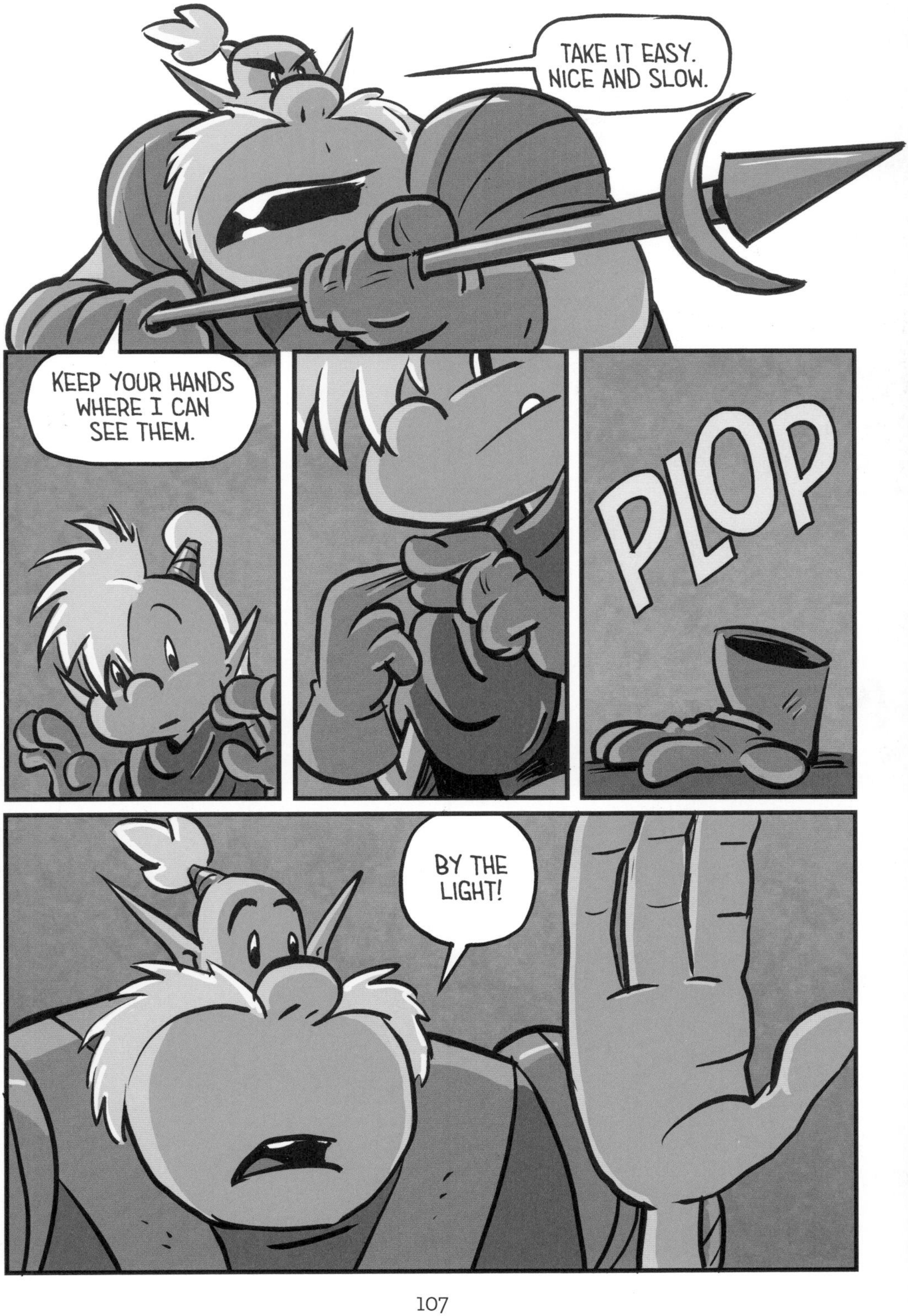
TAKE IT EASY. NICE AND SLOW.
KEEP YOUR HANDS WHERE I CAN SEE THEM.
PLOP
BY THE LIGHT!

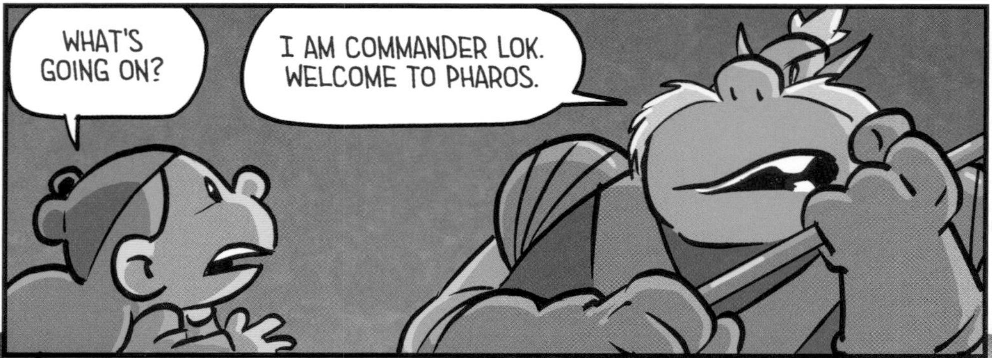
WHAT'S GOING ON?
I AM COMMANDER LOK. WELCOME TO PHAROS.

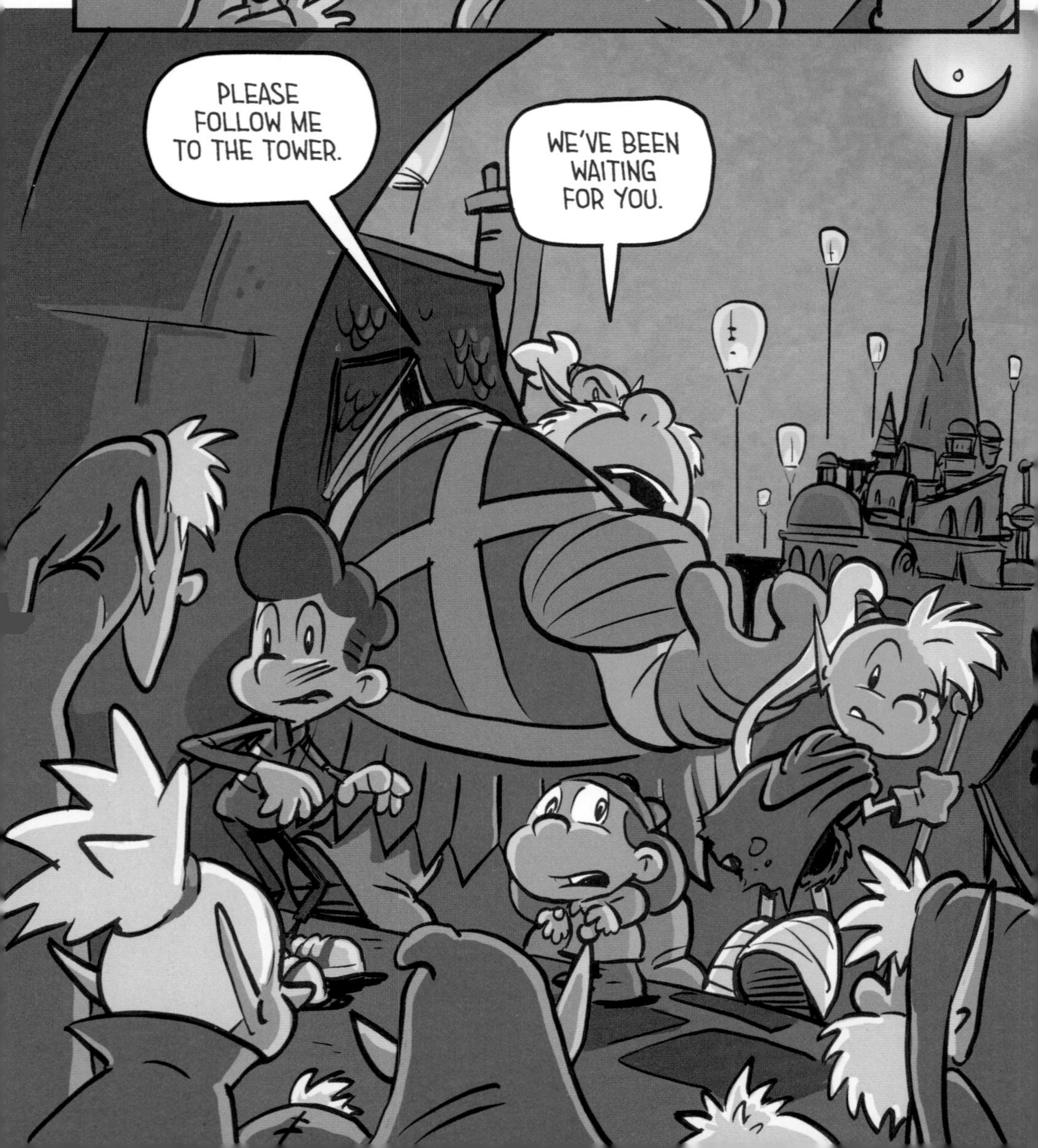
PLEASE FOLLOW ME TO THE TOWER.
WE'VE BEEN WAITING FOR YOU.

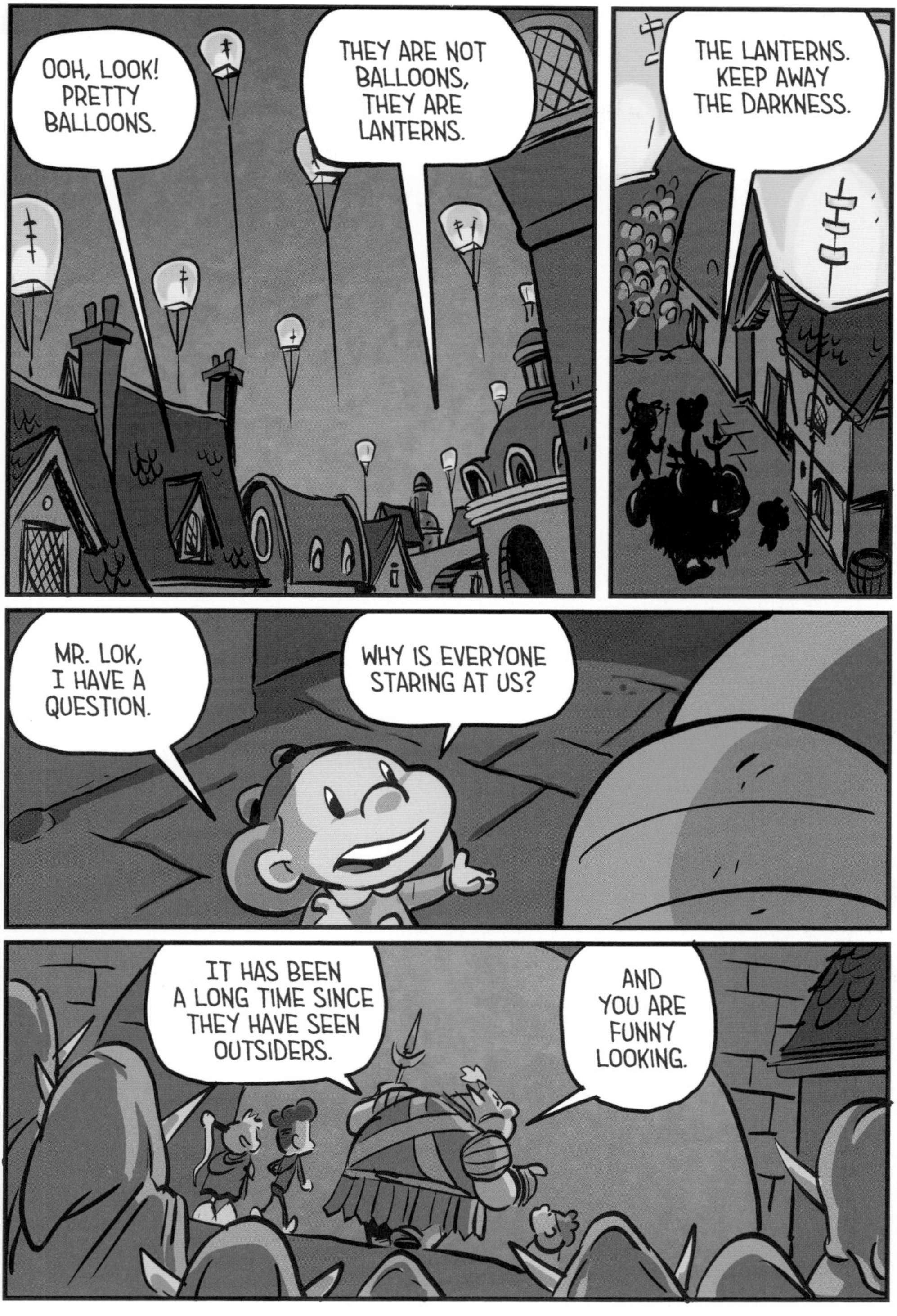
OOH, LOOK! PRETTY BALLOONS.
THEY ARE NOT BALLOONS, THEY ARE LANTERNS.
THE LANTERNS. KEEP AWAY THE DARKNESS.
MR. LOK, I HAVE A QUESTION.
WHY IS EVERYONE STARING AT US?
IT HAS BEEN A LONG TIME SINCE THEY HAVE SEEN OUTSIDERS.
AND YOU ARE FUNNY LOOKING.

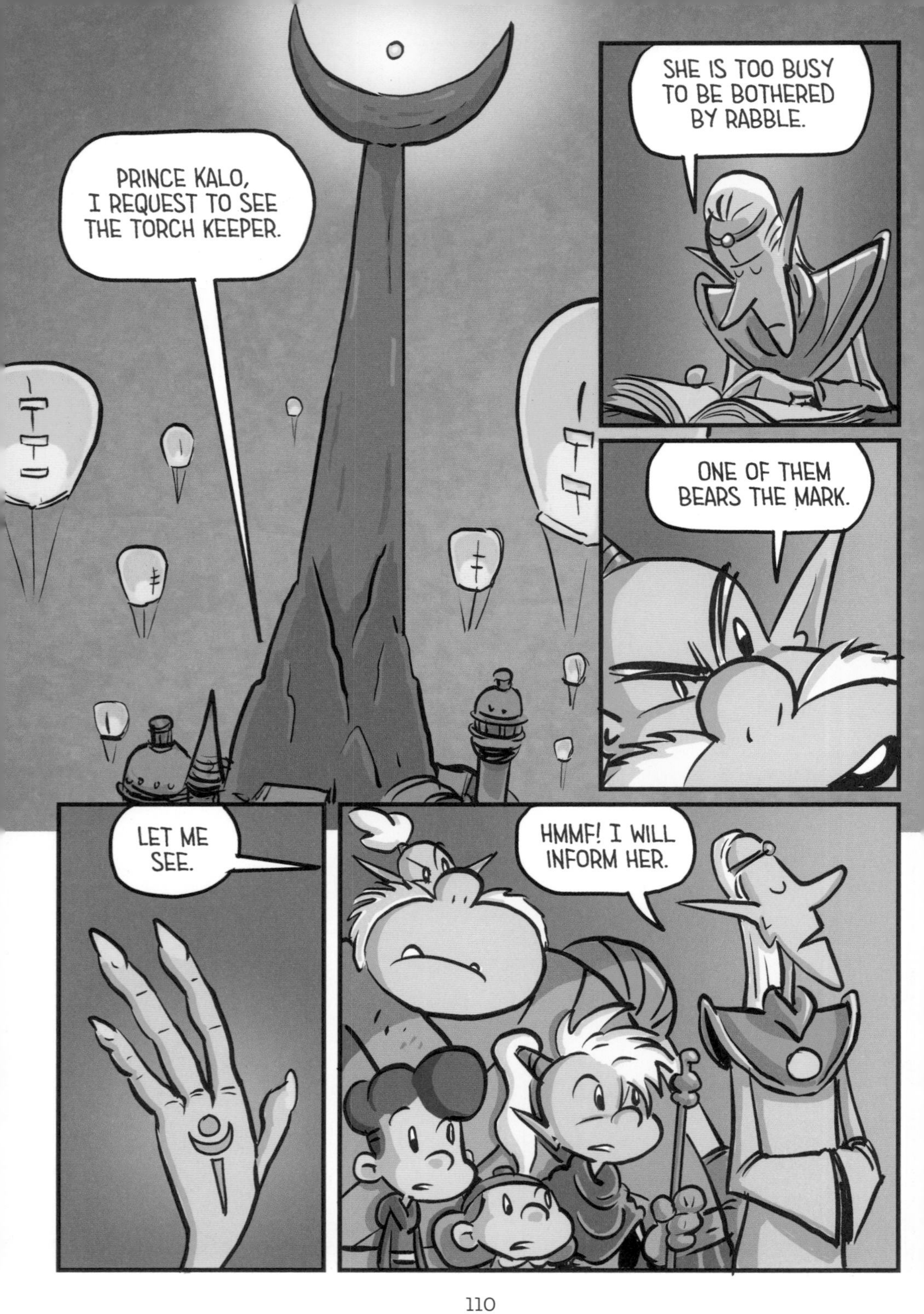
PRINCE KALO, I REQUEST TO SEE THE TORCH KEEPER.
SHE IS TOO BUSY TO BE BOTHERED BY RABBLE.
ONE OF THEM BEARS THE MARK.
LET ME SEE.
HMMF! I WILL INFORM HER.

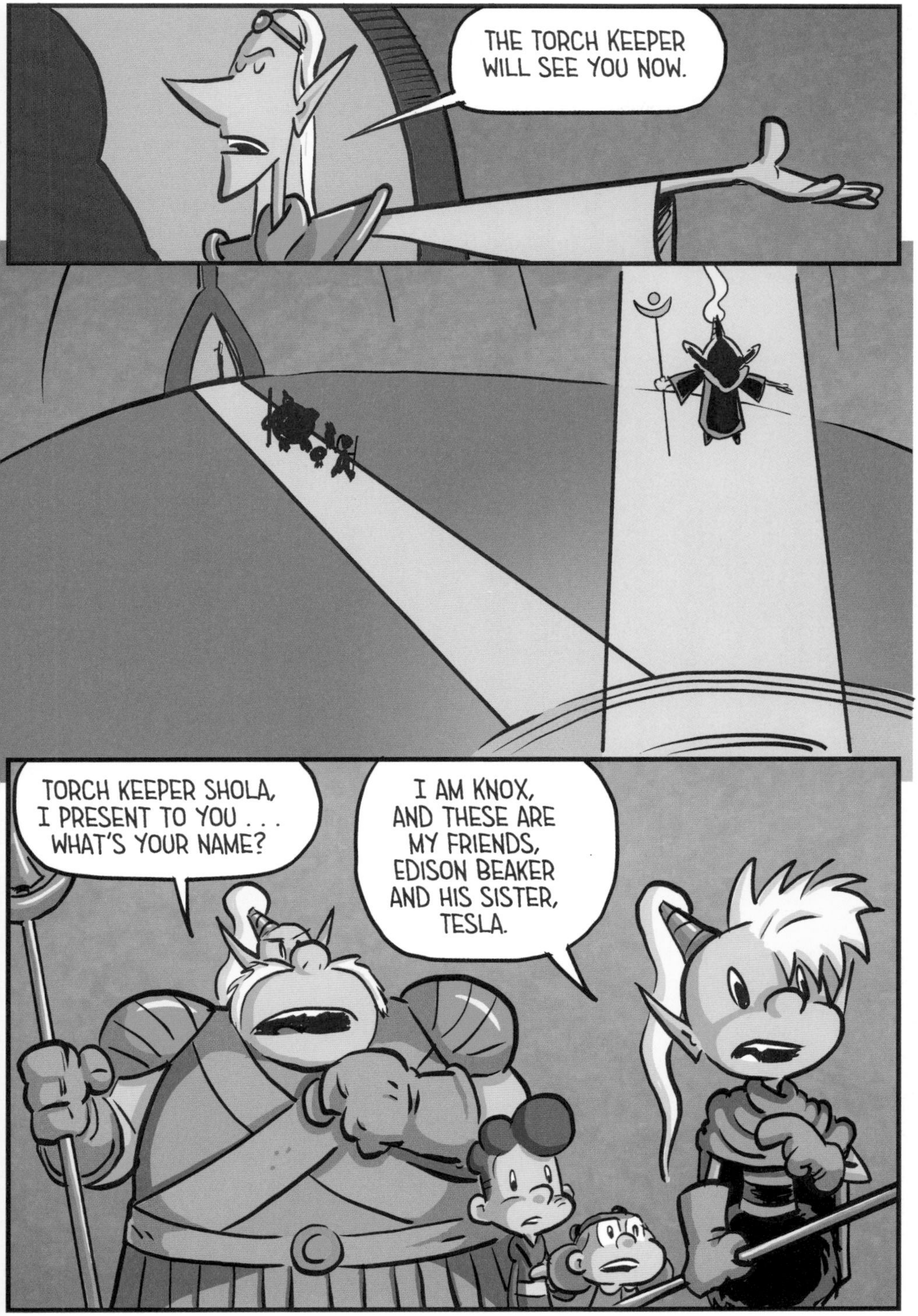
THE TORCH KEEPER WILL SEE YOU NOW.
TORCH KEEPER SHOLA, I PRESENT TO YOU . . . WHAT'S YOUR NAME?
I AM KNOX, AND THESE ARE MY FRIENDS, EDISON BEAKER AND HIS SISTER, TESLA.

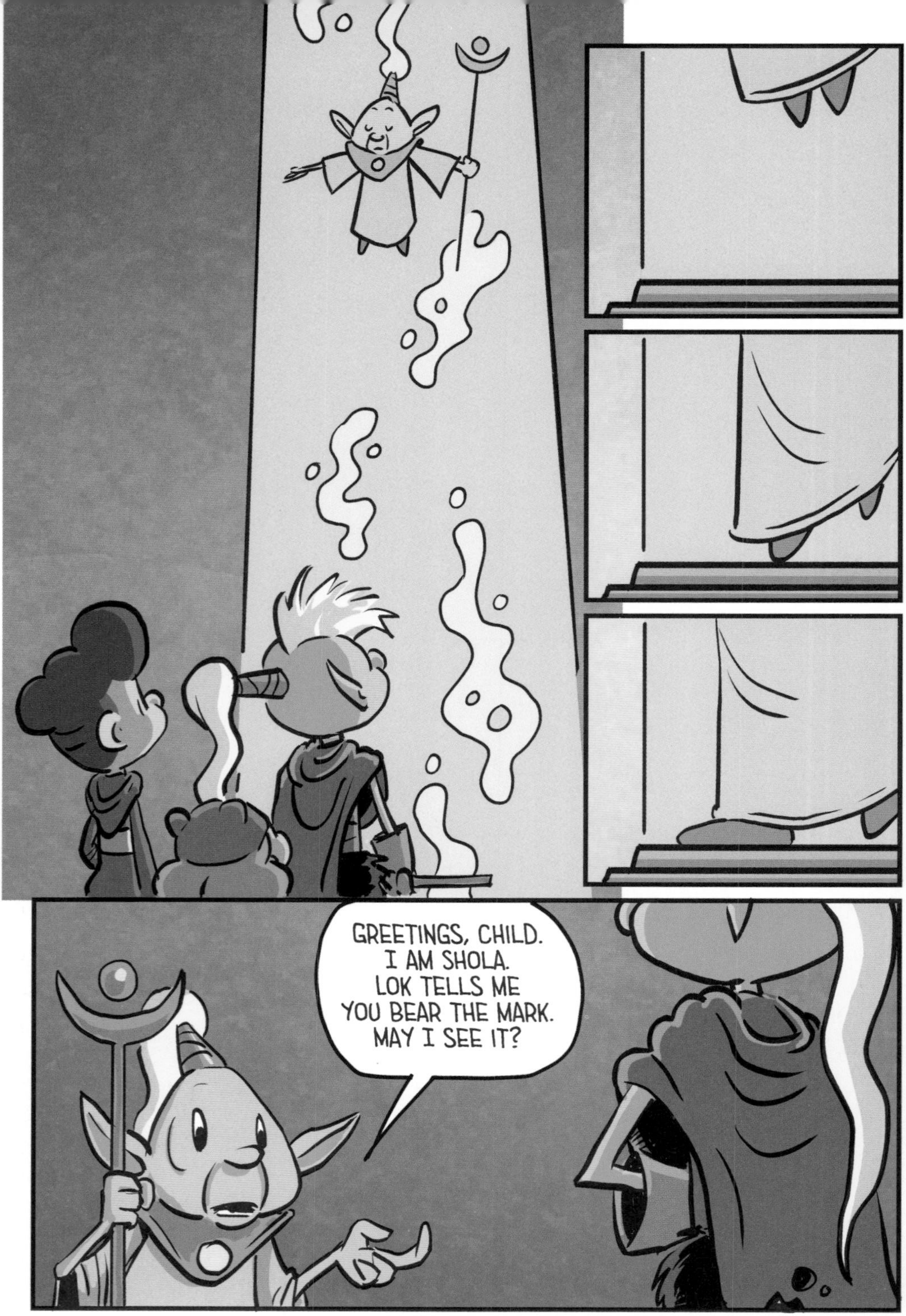
GREETINGS, CHILD. I AM SHOLA. LOK TELLS ME YOU BEAR THE MARK. MAY I SEE IT?

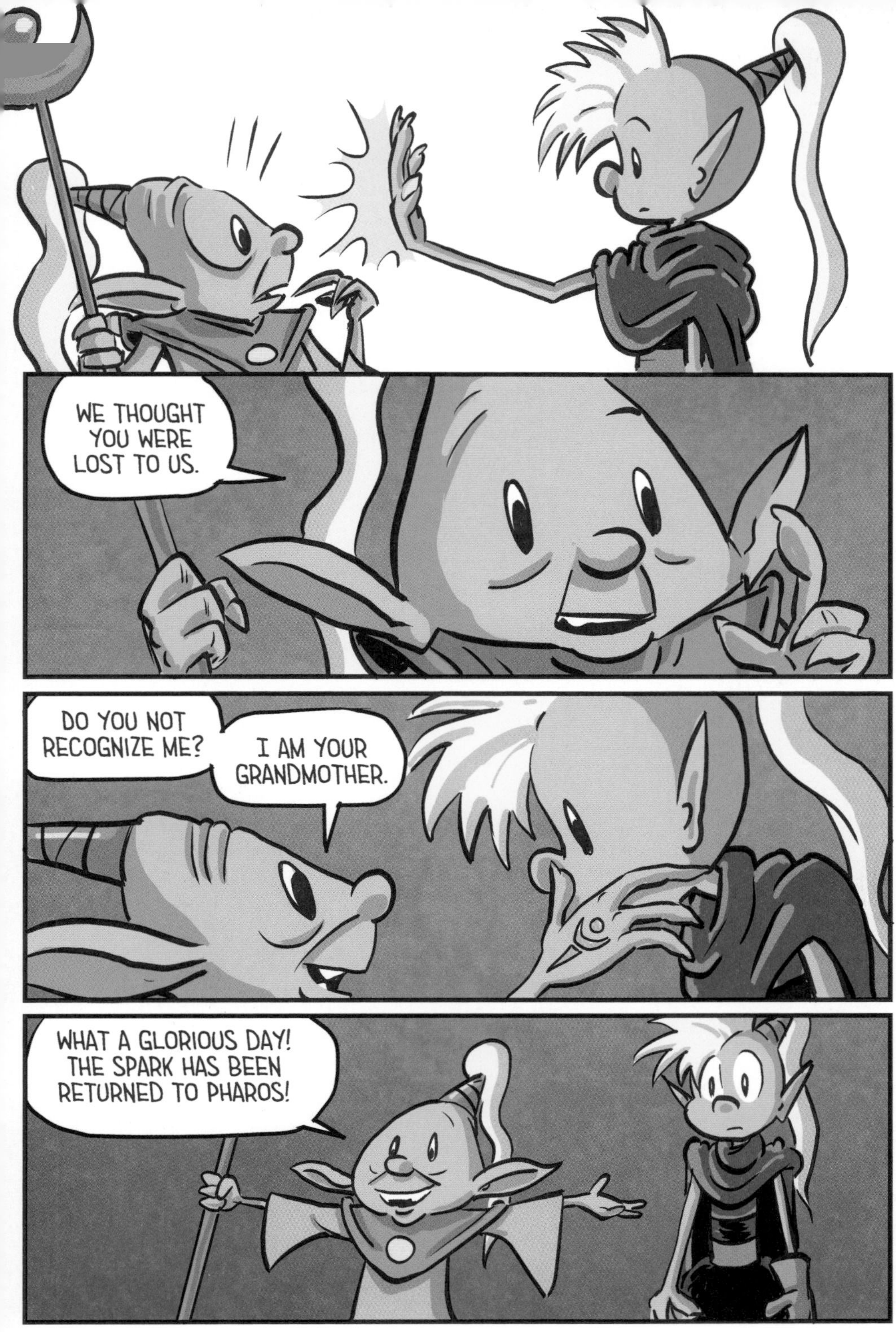
WE THOUGHT YOU WERE LOST TO US.
DO YOU NOT RECOGNIZE ME?
I AM YOUR GRANDMOTHER.
WHAT A GLORIOUS DAY! THE SPARK HAS BEEN RETURNED TO PHAROS!

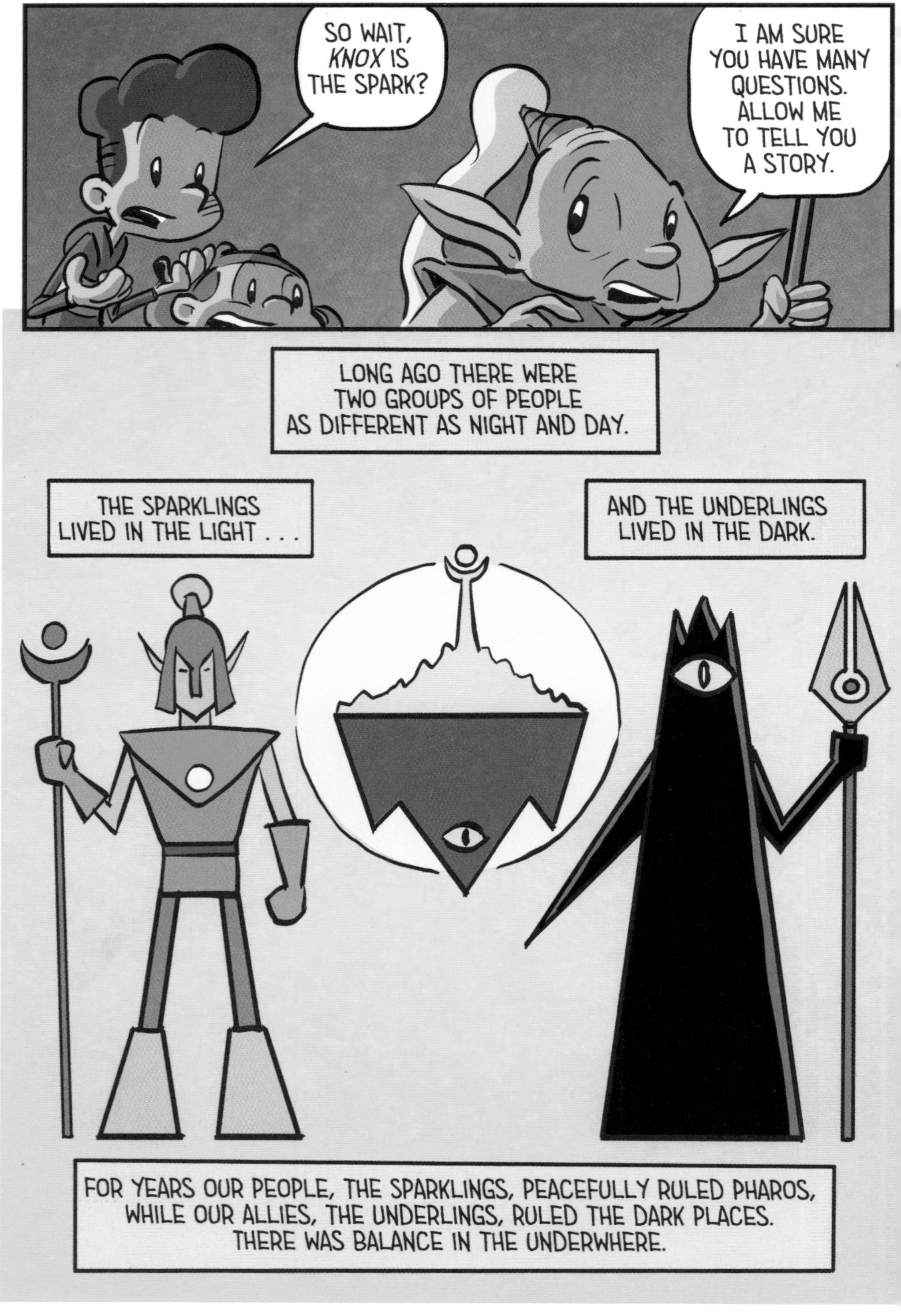
SO WAIT, *KNOX* IS THE SPARK?
I AM SURE YOU HAVE MANY QUESTIONS. ALLOW ME TO TELL YOU A STORY.
LONG AGO THERE WERE TWO GROUPS OF PEOPLE AS DIFFERENT AS NIGHT AND DAY.
THE SPARKLINGS LIVED IN THE LIGHT . . .
AND THE UNDERLINGS LIVED IN THE DARK.
FOR YEARS OUR PEOPLE, THE SPARKLINGS, PEACEFULLY RULED PHAROS, WHILE OUR ALLIES, THE UNDERLINGS, RULED THE DARK PLACES. THERE WAS BALANCE IN THE UNDERWHERE.

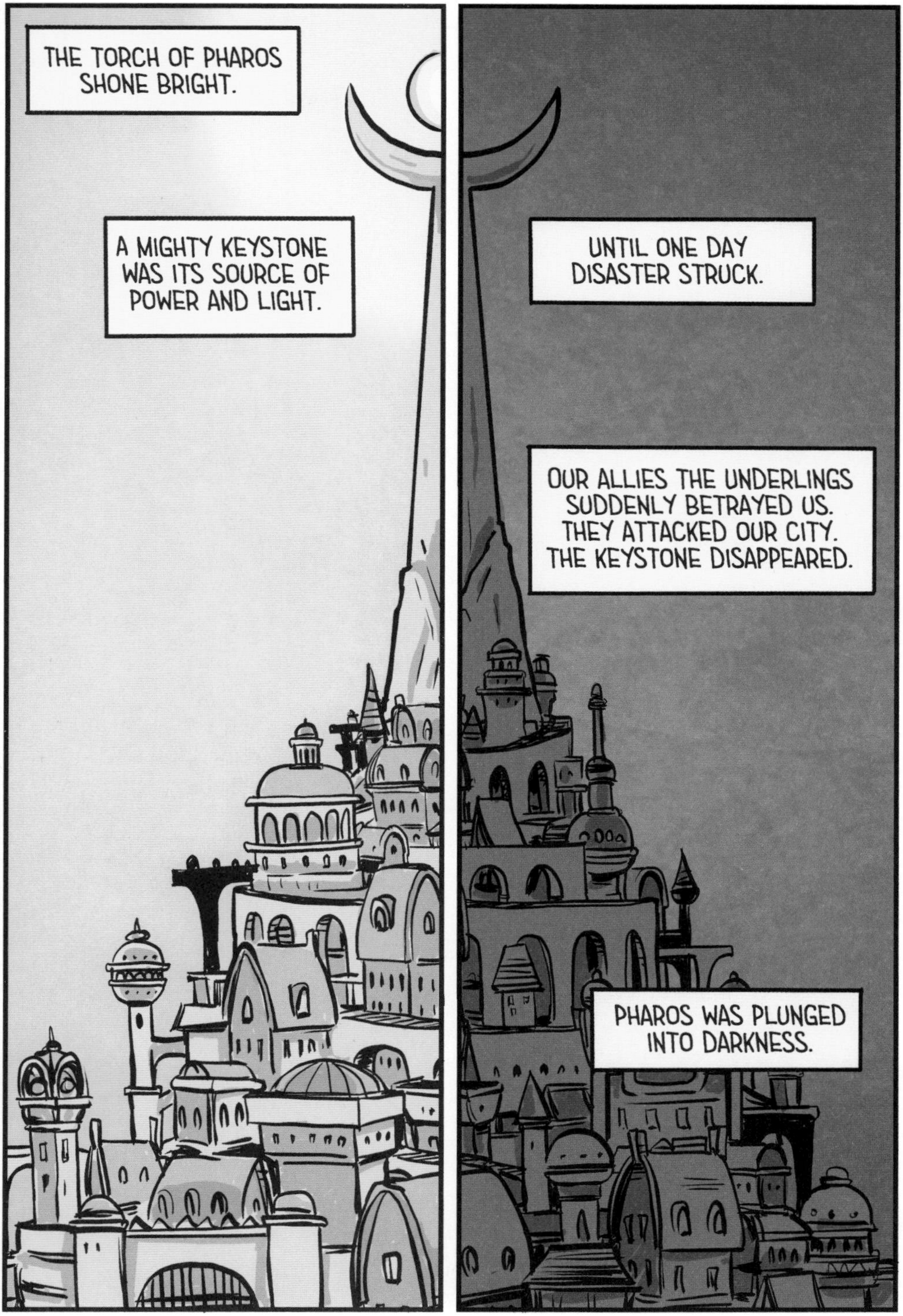
THE TORCH OF PHAROS SHONE BRIGHT.
A MIGHTY KEYSTONE WAS ITS SOURCE OF POWER AND LIGHT.
UNTIL ONE DAY DISASTER STRUCK.
OUR ALLIES THE UNDERLINGS SUDDENLY BETRAYED US. THEY ATTACKED OUR CITY. THE KEYSTONE DISAPPEARED.
PHAROS WAS PLUNGED INTO DARKNESS.

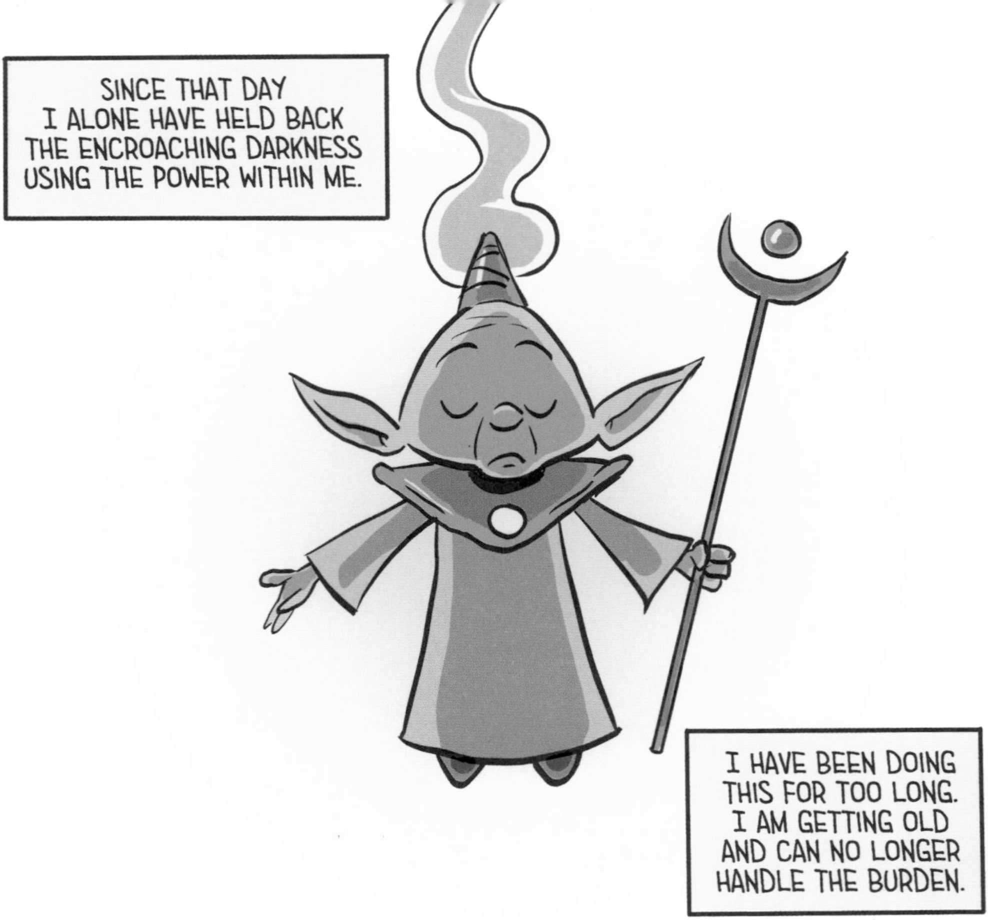
SINCE THAT DAY I ALONE HAVE HELD BACK THE ENCROACHING DARKNESS USING THE POWER WITHIN ME.
I HAVE BEEN DOING THIS FOR TOO LONG. I AM GETTING OLD AND CAN NO LONGER HANDLE THE BURDEN.

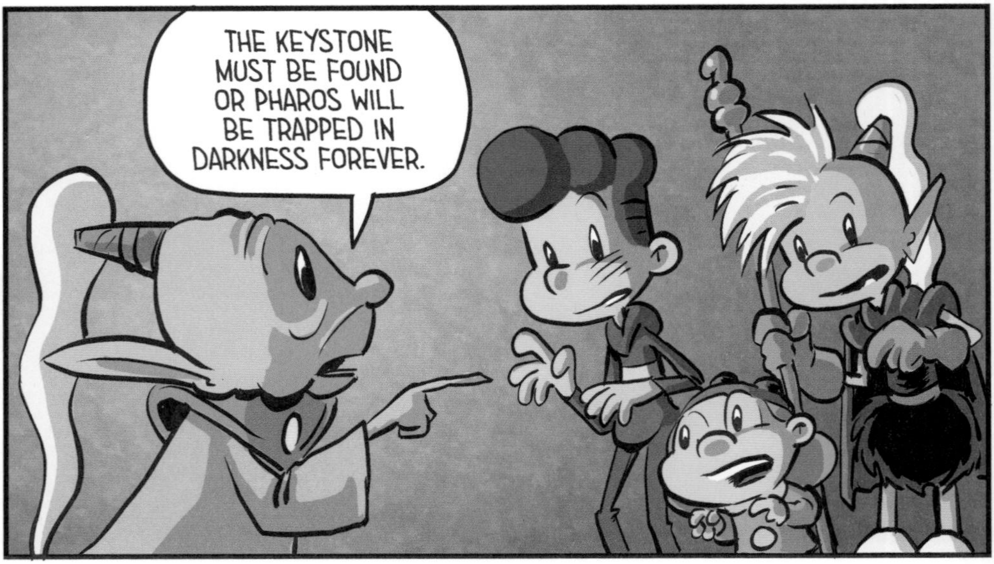
THE KEYSTONE MUST BE FOUND OR PHAROS WILL BE TRAPPED IN DARKNESS FOREVER.

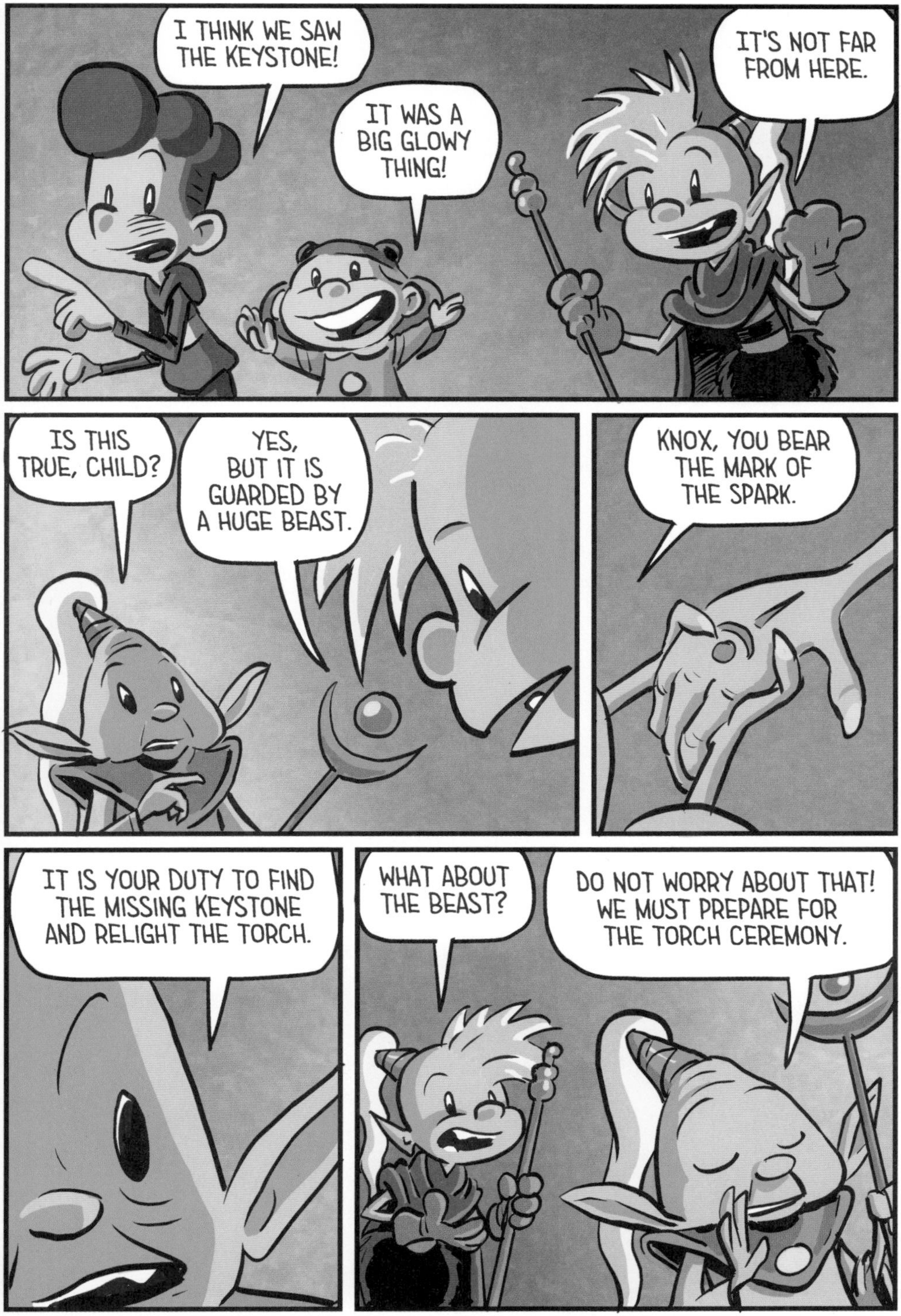
I THINK WE SAW THE KEYSTONE!
IT WAS A BIG GLOWY THING!
IT'S NOT FAR FROM HERE.
IS THIS TRUE, CHILD?
YES, BUT IT IS GUARDED BY A HUGE BEAST.
KNOX, YOU BEAR THE MARK OF THE SPARK.
IT IS YOUR DUTY TO FIND THE MISSING KEYSTONE AND RELIGHT THE TORCH.
WHAT ABOUT THE BEAST?
DO NOT WORRY ABOUT THAT! WE MUST PREPARE FOR THE TORCH CEREMONY.

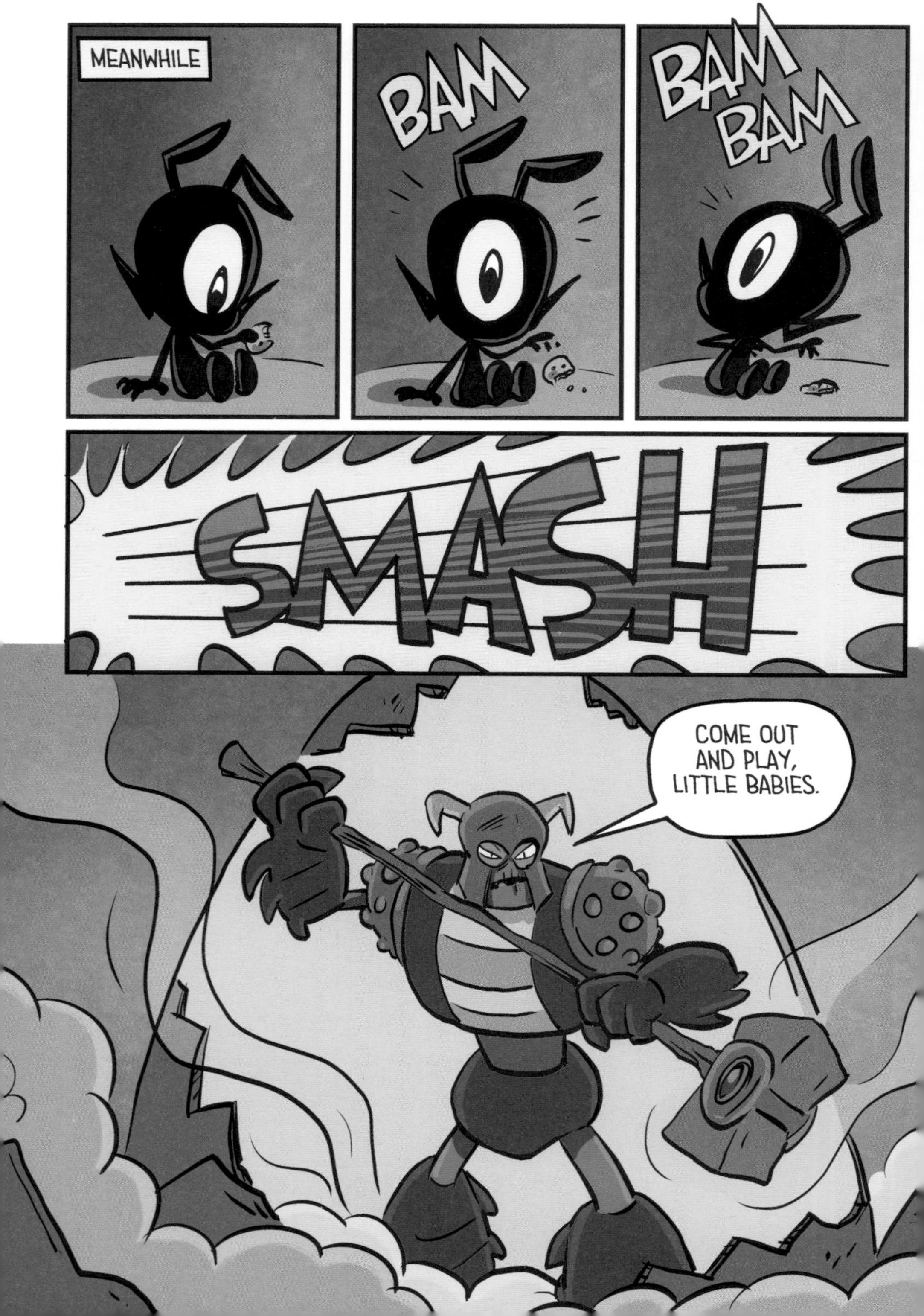

MEANWHILE
BAM
BAM
BAM
SMASH
COME OUT AND PLAY, LITTLE BABIES.

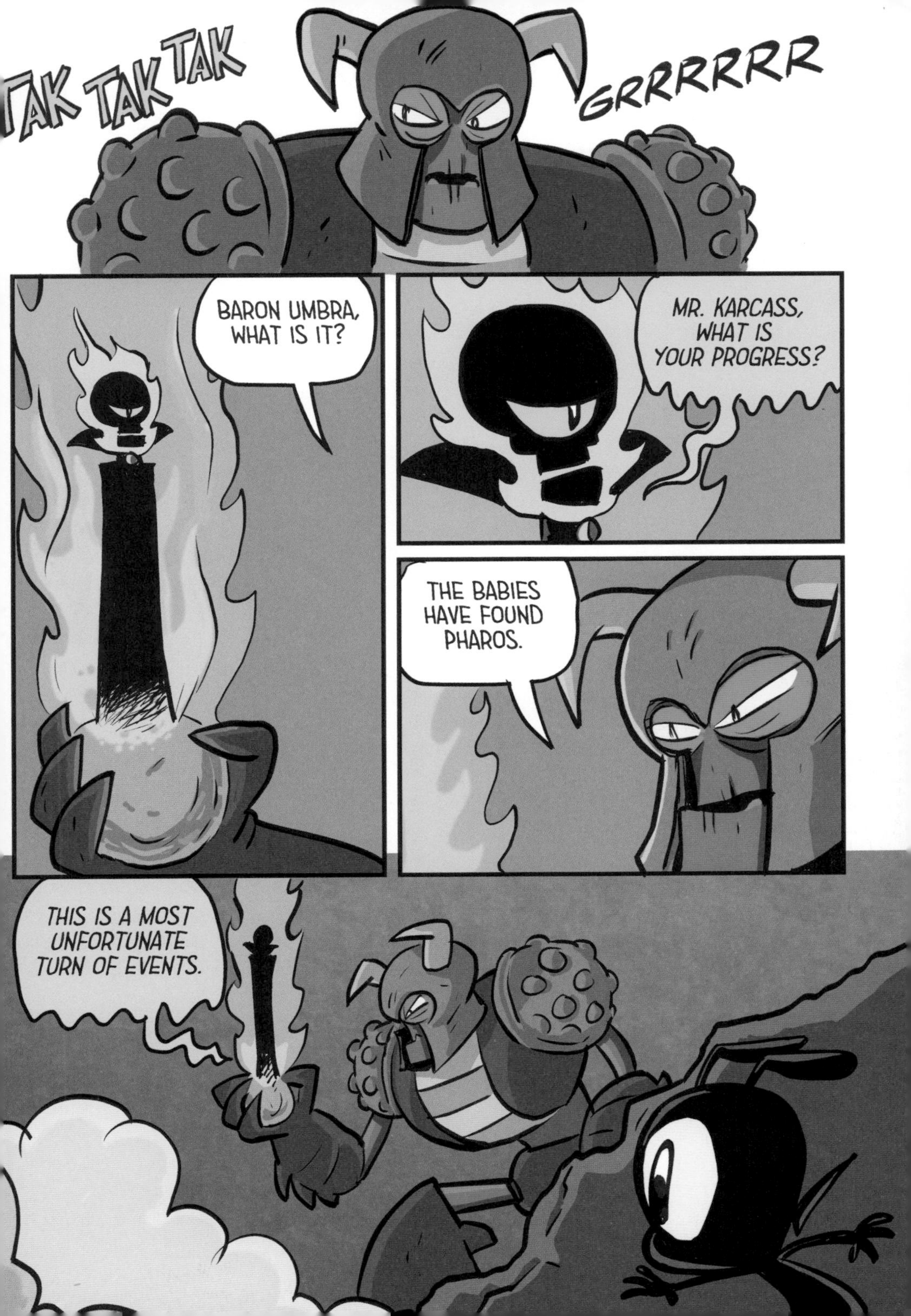
TAK TAK TAK
GRRRRRR
BARON UMBRA, WHAT IS IT?
MR. KARCASS, WHAT IS YOUR PROGRESS?
THE BABIES HAVE FOUND PHAROS.
THIS IS A MOST UNFORTUNATE TURN OF EVENTS.

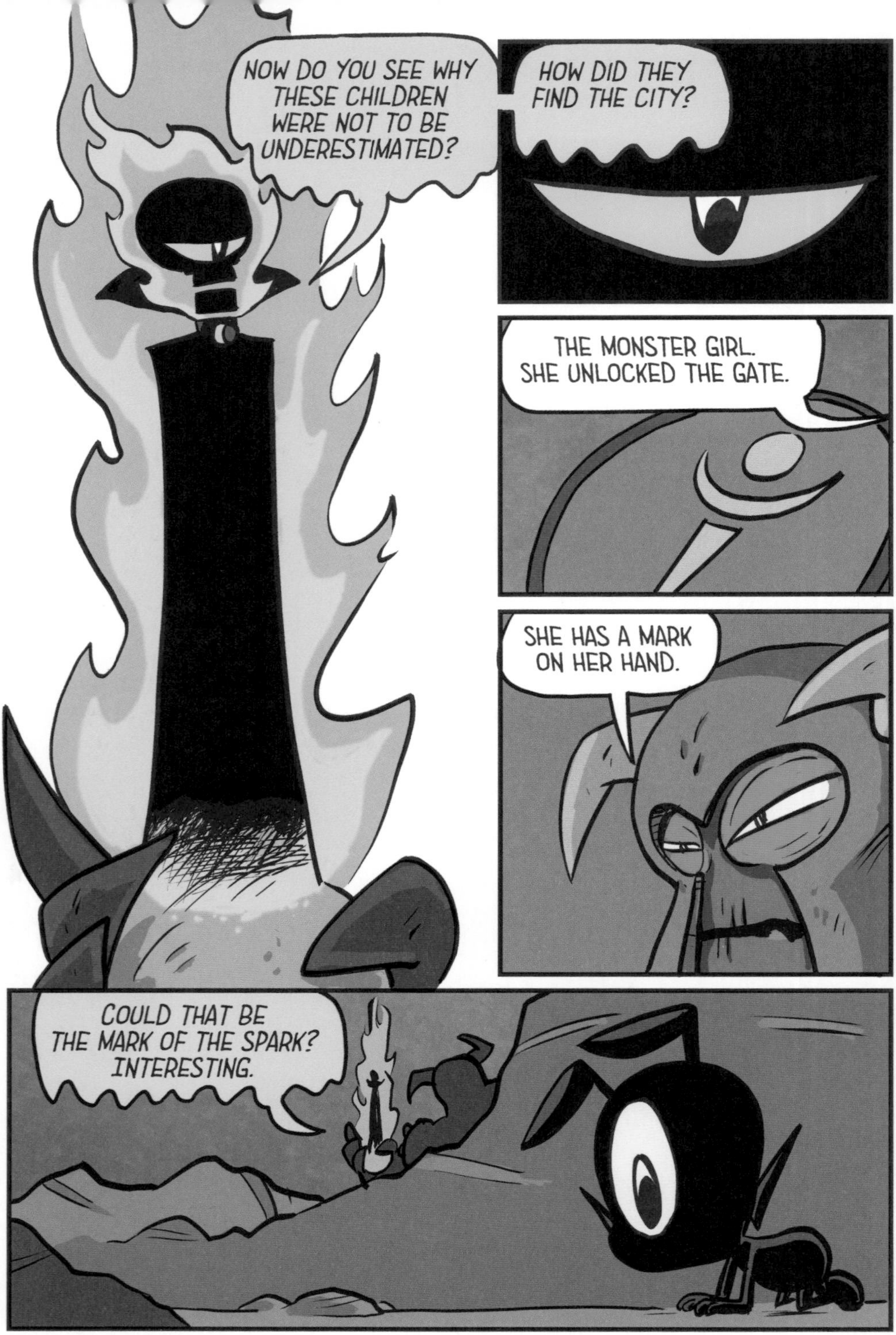
NOW DO YOU SEE WHY THESE CHILDREN WERE NOT TO BE UNDERESTIMATED?
HOW DID THEY FIND THE CITY?
THE MONSTER GIRL. SHE UNLOCKED THE GATE.
SHE HAS A MARK ON HER HAND.
COULD THAT BE THE MARK OF THE SPARK? INTERESTING.

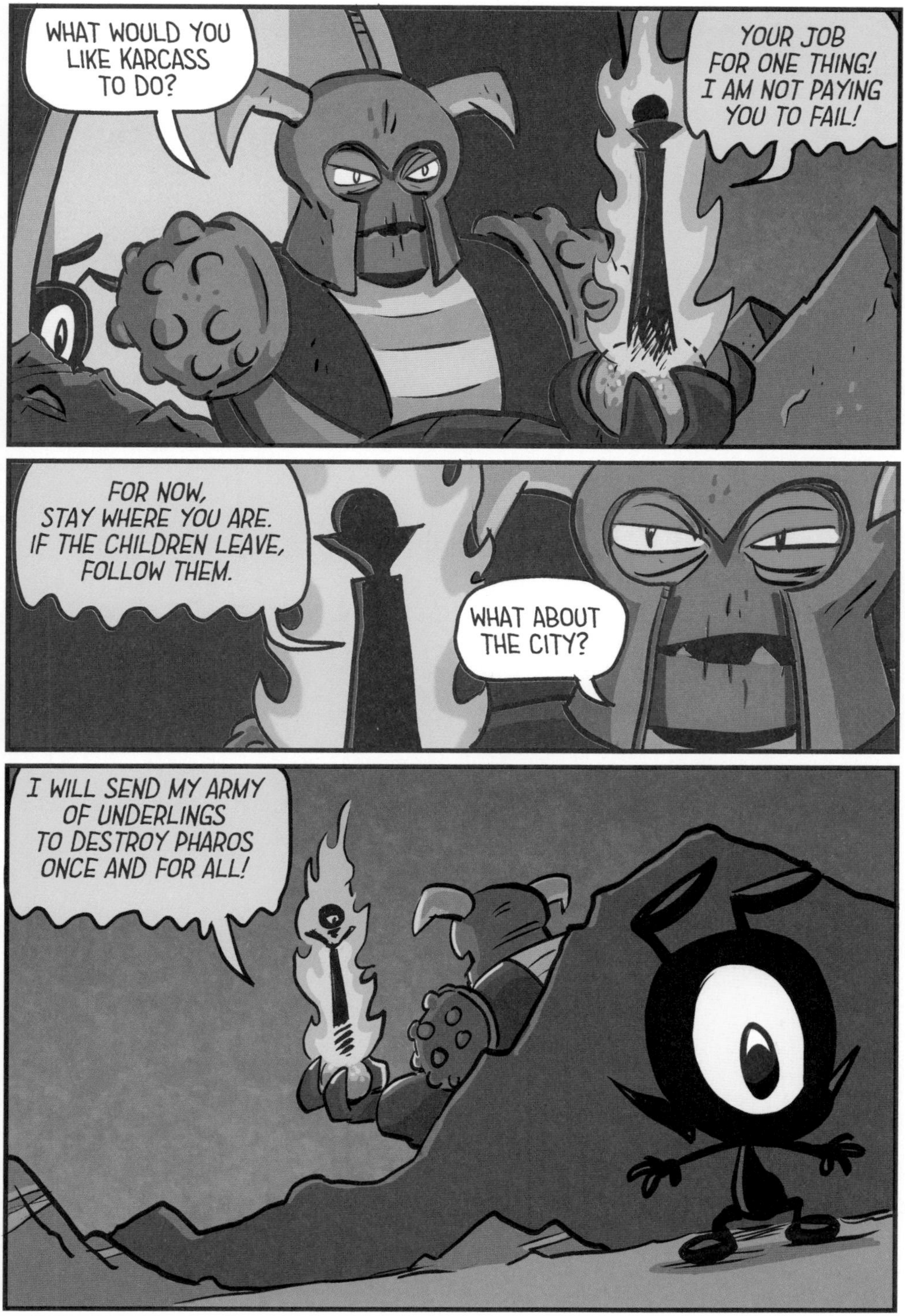
WHAT WOULD YOU LIKE KARCASS TO DO?
YOUR JOB FOR ONE THING! I AM NOT PAYING YOU TO FAIL!
FOR NOW, STAY WHERE YOU ARE. IF THE CHILDREN LEAVE, FOLLOW THEM.
WHAT ABOUT THE CITY?
I WILL SEND MY ARMY OF UNDERLINGS TO DESTROY PHAROS ONCE AND FOR ALL!

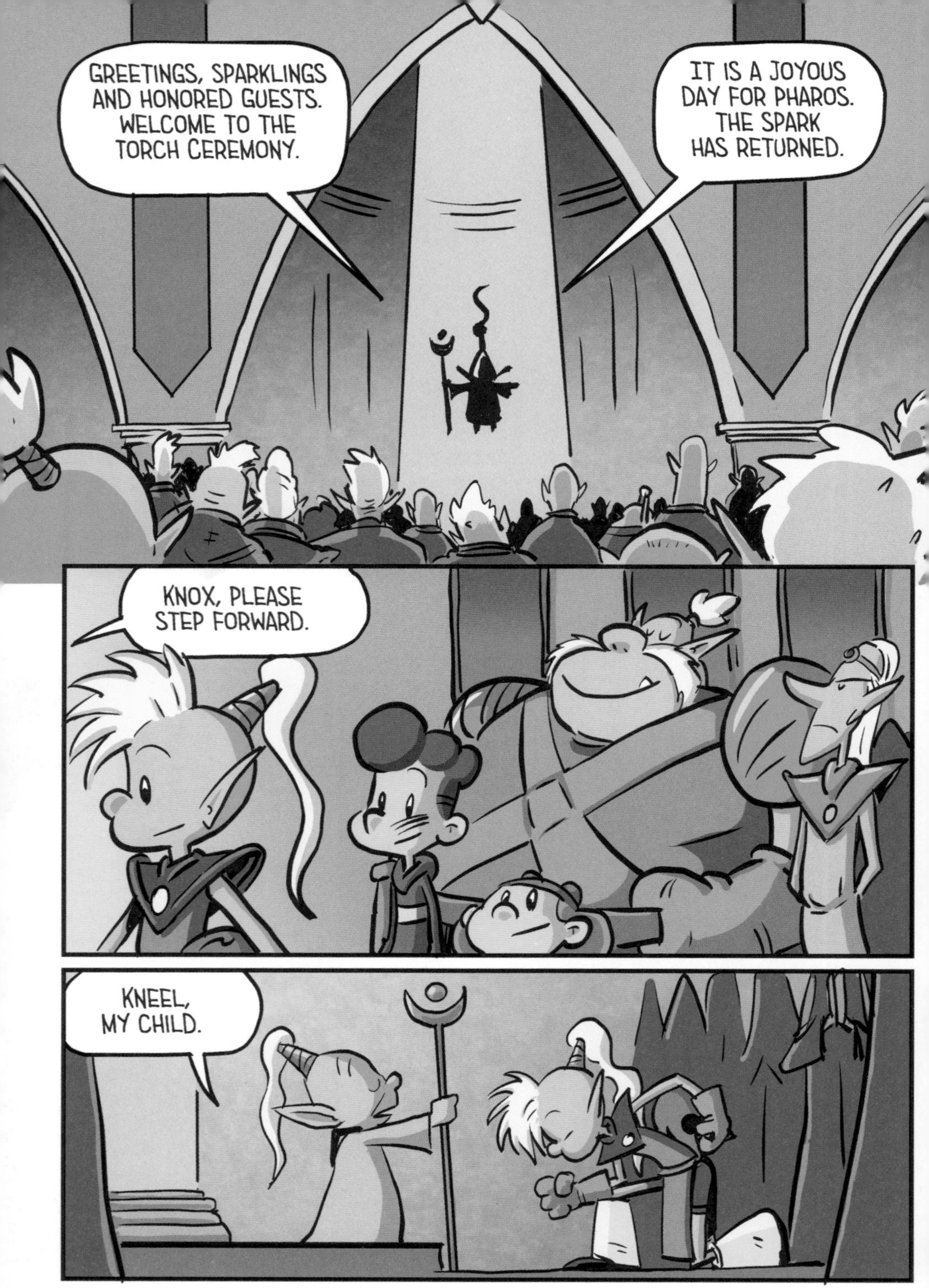
GREETINGS, SPARKLINGS AND HONORED GUESTS. WELCOME TO THE TORCH CEREMONY.
IT IS A JOYOUS DAY FOR PHAROS. THE SPARK HAS RETURNED.
KNOX, PLEASE STEP FORWARD.
KNEEL, MY CHILD.

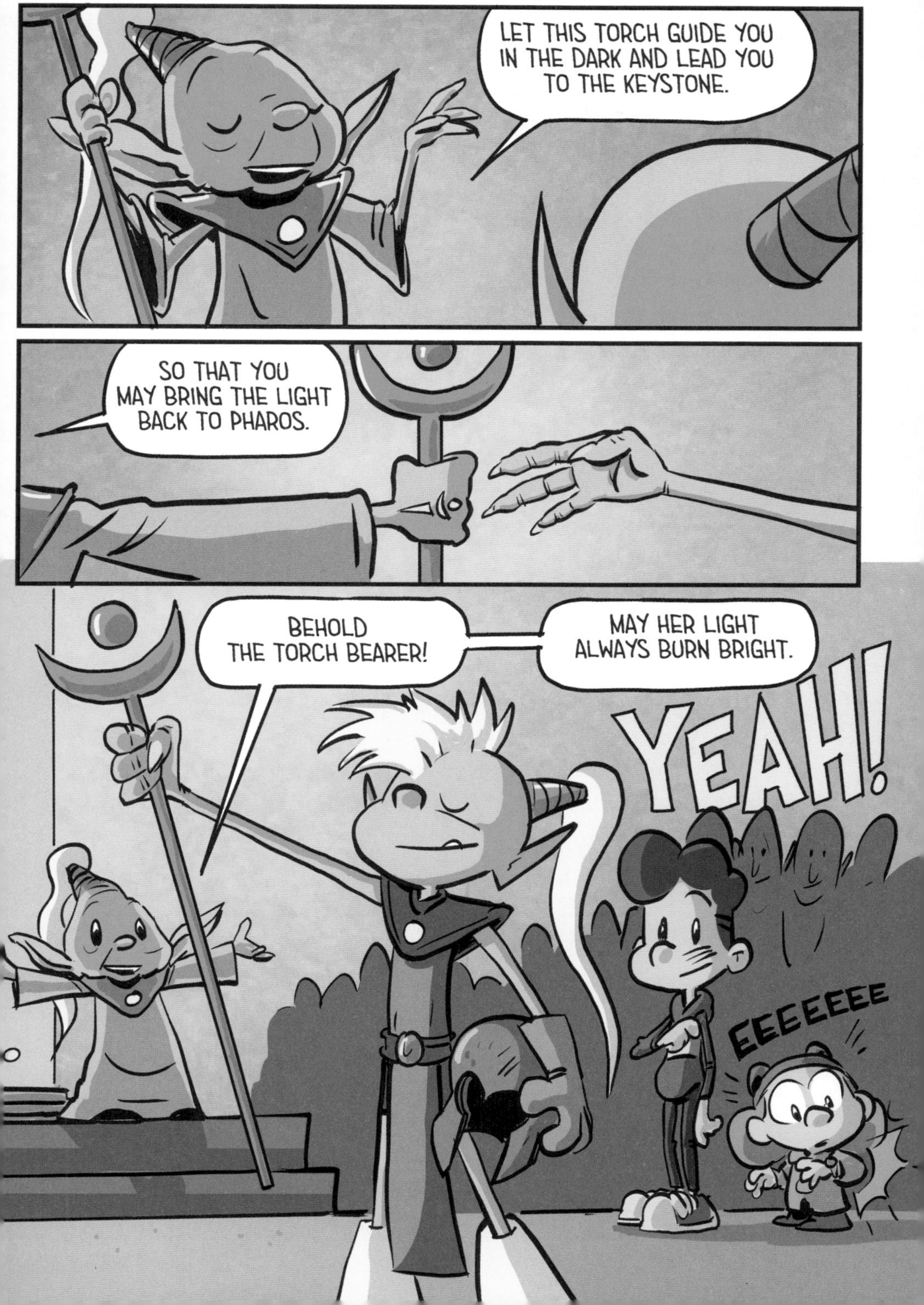
LET THIS TORCH GUIDE YOU IN THE DARK AND LEAD YOU TO THE KEYSTONE.
SO THAT YOU MAY BRING THE LIGHT BACK TO PHAROS.
BEHOLD THE TORCH BEARER!
MAY HER LIGHT ALWAYS BURN BRIGHT.
YEAH!
EEEEEEE

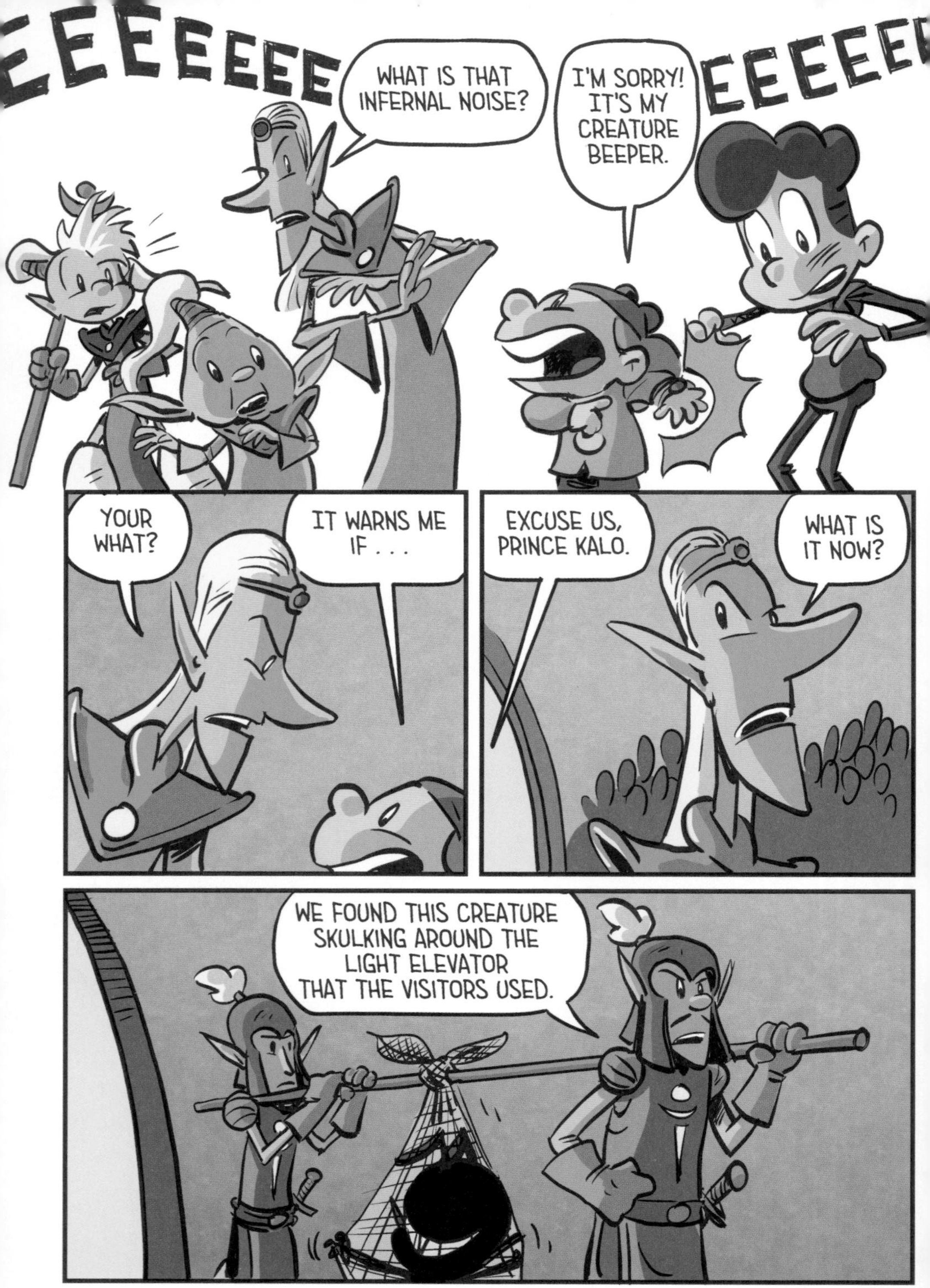
EEEEEEE
WHAT IS THAT INFERNAL NOISE?
I'M SORRY! IT'S MY CREATURE BEEPER.
EEEEEEE
YOUR WHAT?
IT WARNS ME IF . . .
EXCUSE US, PRINCE KALO.
WHAT IS IT NOW?
WE FOUND THIS CREATURE SKULKING AROUND THE LIGHT ELEVATOR THAT THE VISITORS USED.

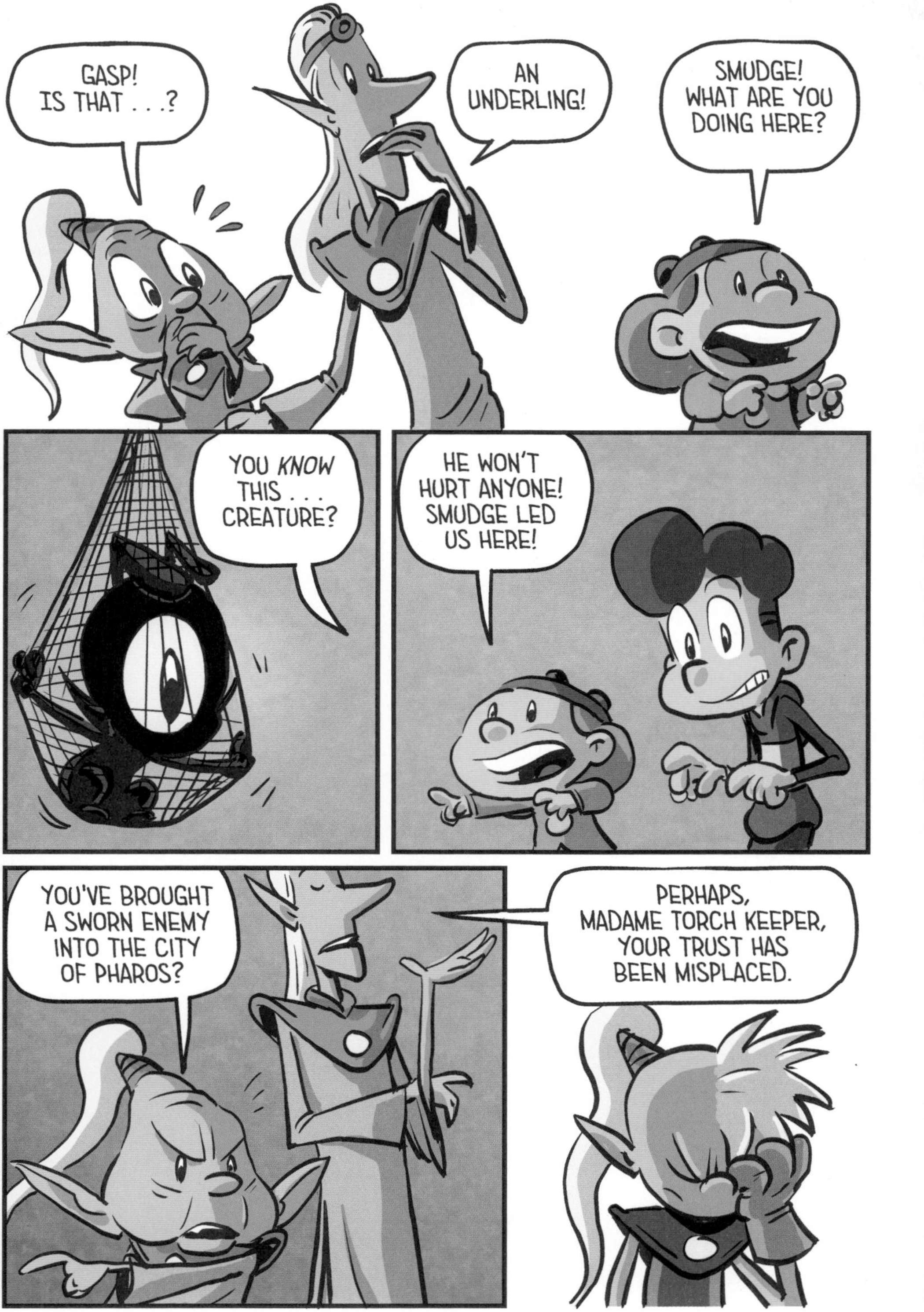
GASP! IS THAT . . .?
AN UNDERLING!
SMUDGE! WHAT ARE YOU DOING HERE?
YOU *KNOW* THIS . . . CREATURE?
HE WON'T HURT ANYONE! SMUDGE LED US HERE!
YOU'VE BROUGHT A SWORN ENEMY INTO THE CITY OF PHAROS?
PERHAPS, MADAME TORCH KEEPER, YOUR TRUST HAS BEEN MISPLACED.

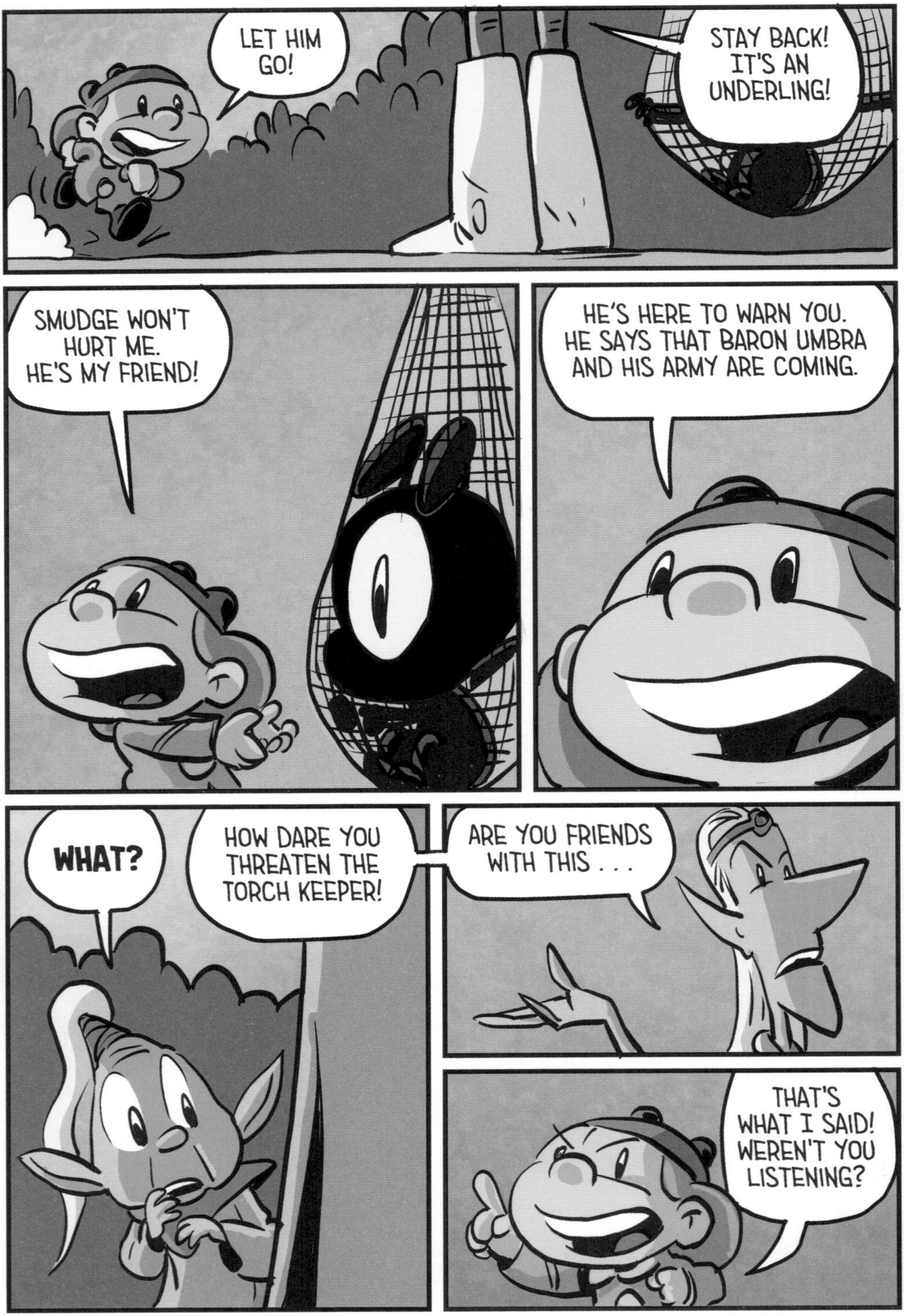
LET HIM GO!
STAY BACK! IT'S AN UNDERLING!
SMUDGE WON'T HURT ME. HE'S MY FRIEND!
HE'S HERE TO WARN YOU. HE SAYS THAT BARON UMBRA AND HIS ARMY ARE COMING.
WHAT?
HOW DARE YOU THREATEN THE TORCH KEEPER!
ARE YOU FRIENDS WITH THIS . . .
THAT'S WHAT I SAID! WEREN'T YOU LISTENING?

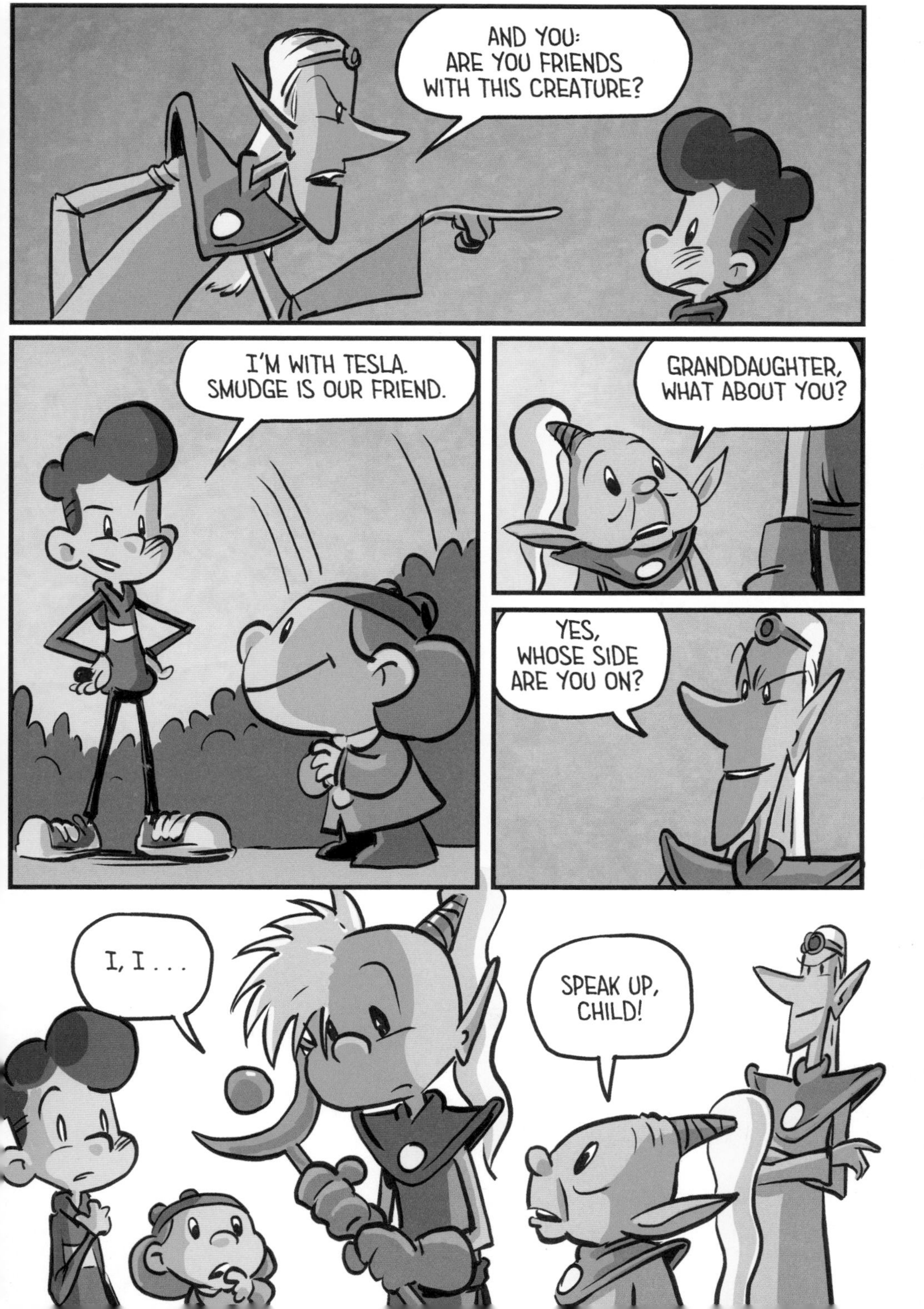
AND YOU: ARE YOU FRIENDS WITH THIS CREATURE?
I'M WITH TESLA. SMUDGE IS OUR FRIEND.
GRANDDAUGHTER, WHAT ABOUT YOU?
YES, WHOSE SIDE ARE YOU ON?
I, I . . .
SPEAK UP, CHILD!

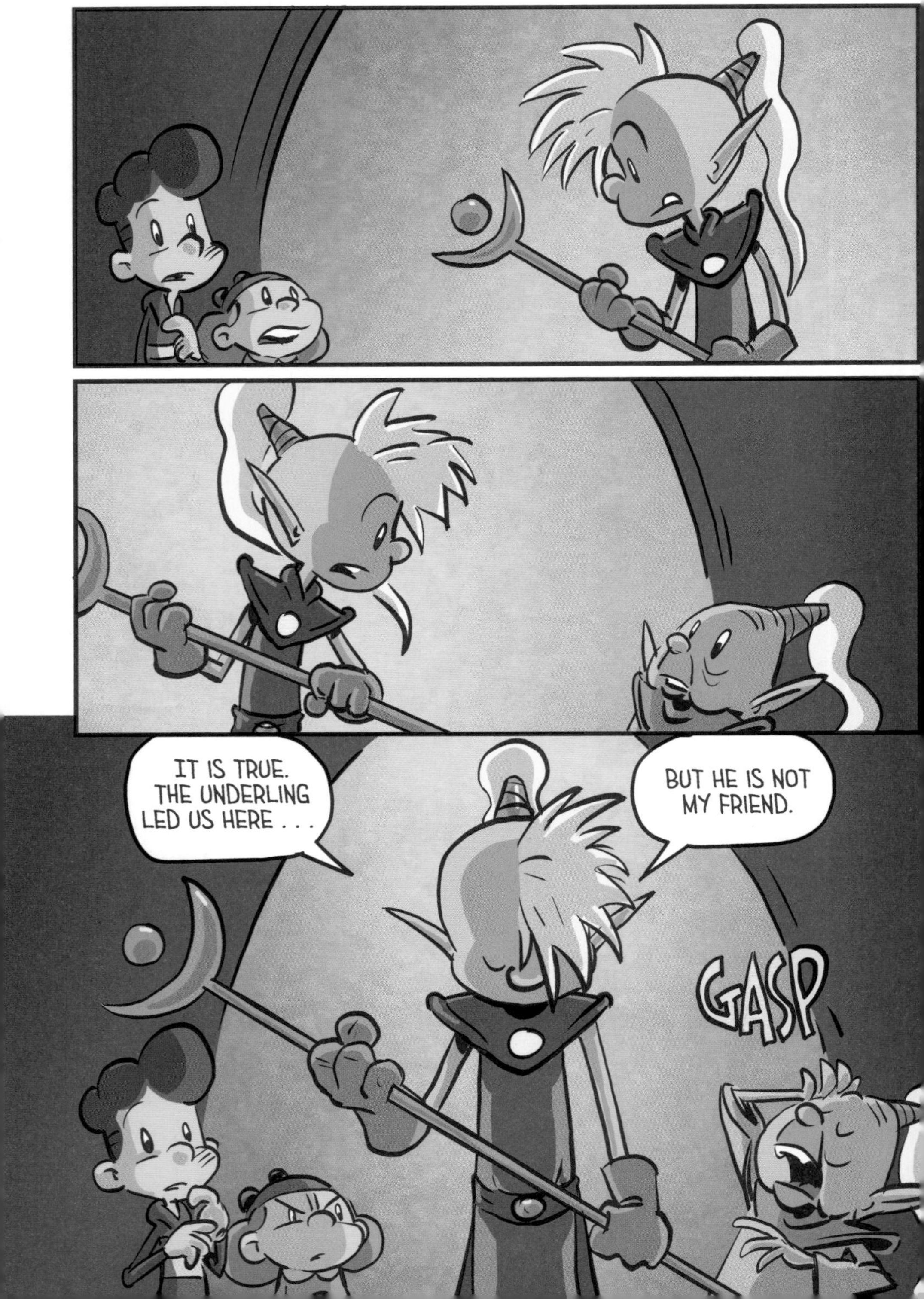
IT IS TRUE. THE UNDERLING LED US HERE . . .
BUT HE IS NOT MY FRIEND.
GASP

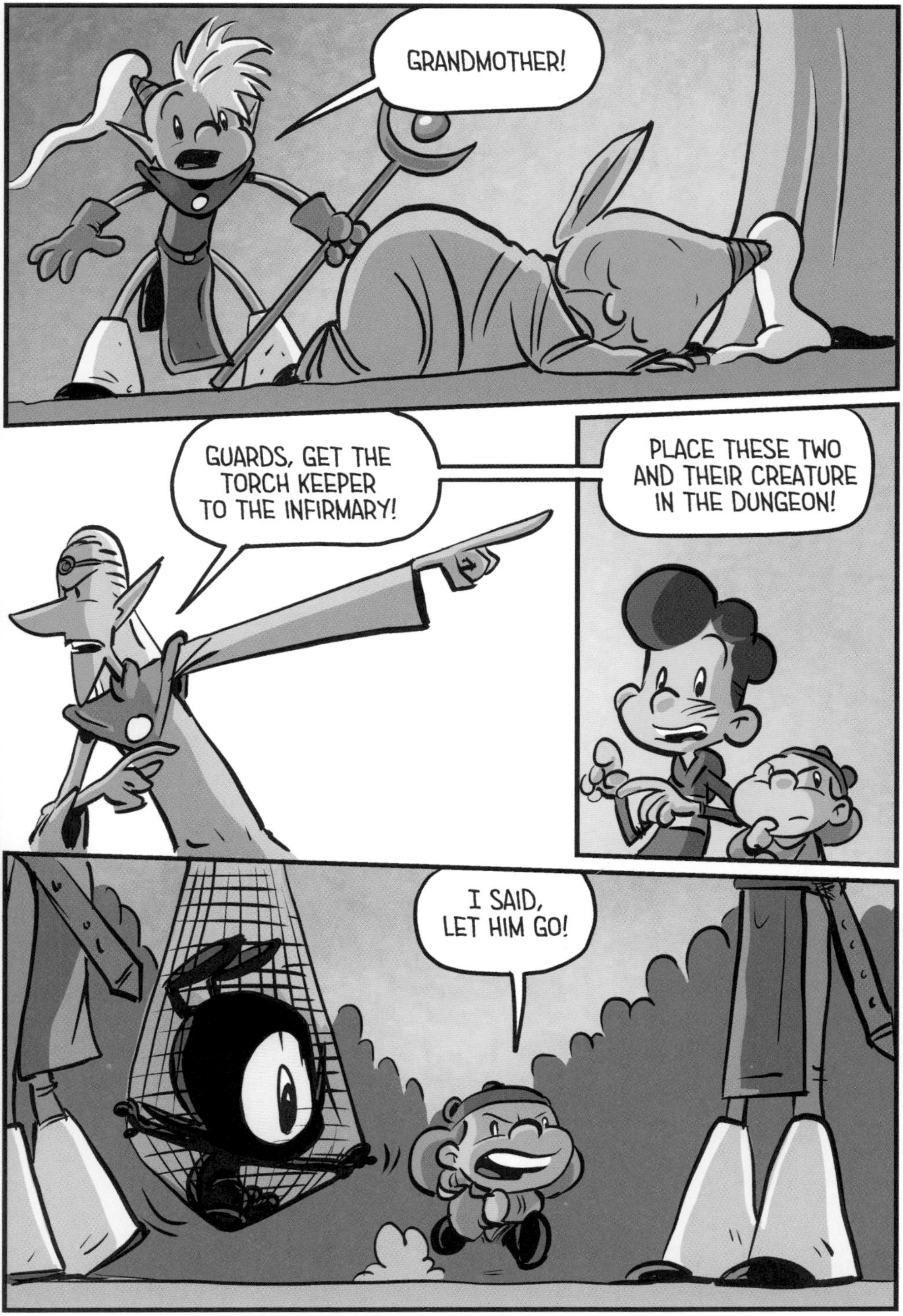
GRANDMOTHER!
GUARDS, GET THE TORCH KEEPER TO THE INFIRMARY!
PLACE THESE TWO AND THEIR CREATURE IN THE DUNGEON!
I SAID, LET HIM GO!

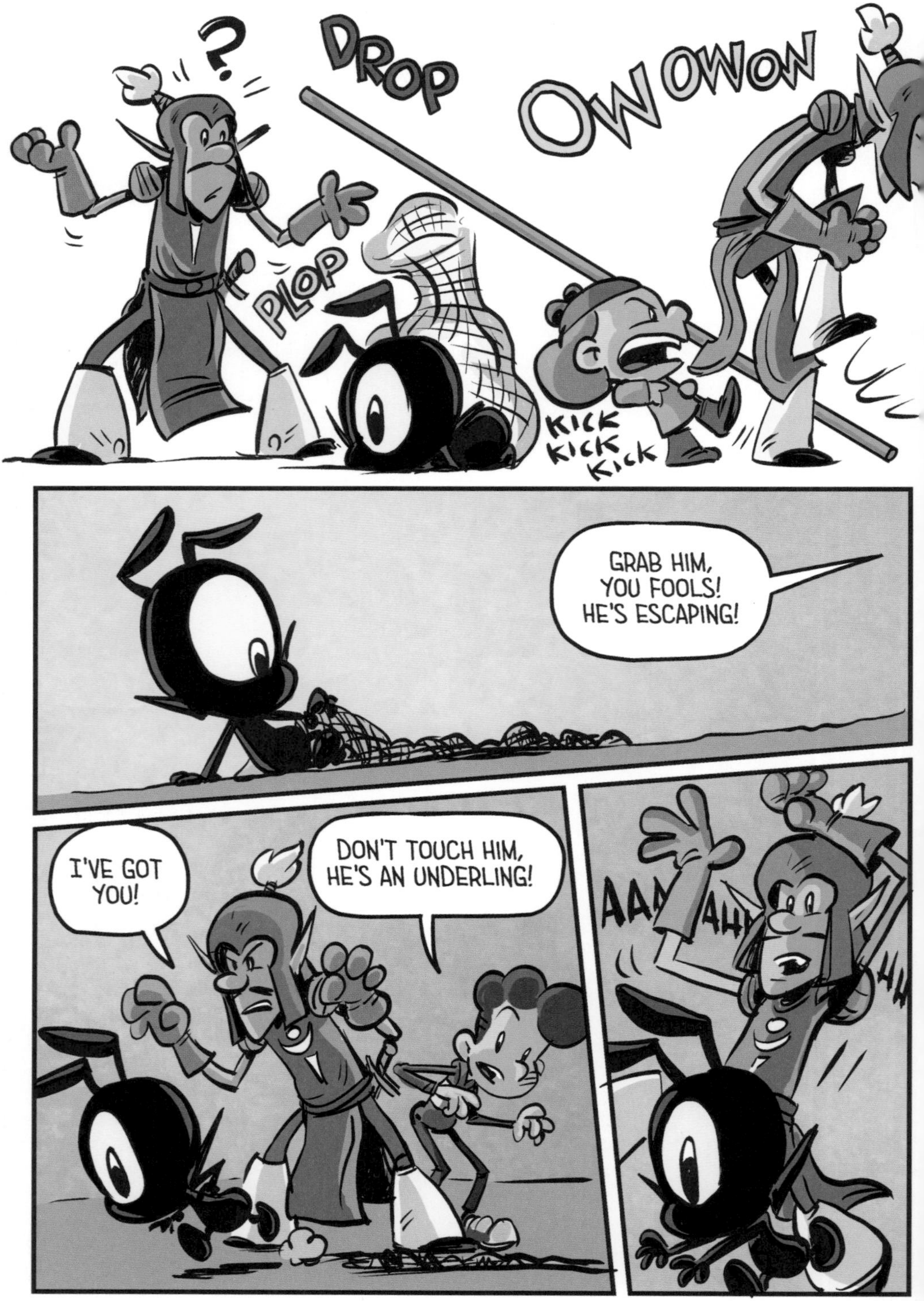
?
DROP
OWOWOW
PLOP
KICK KICK KICK
GRAB HIM, YOU FOOLS! HE'S ESCAPING!
I'VE GOT YOU!
DON'T TOUCH HIM, HE'S AN UNDERLING!

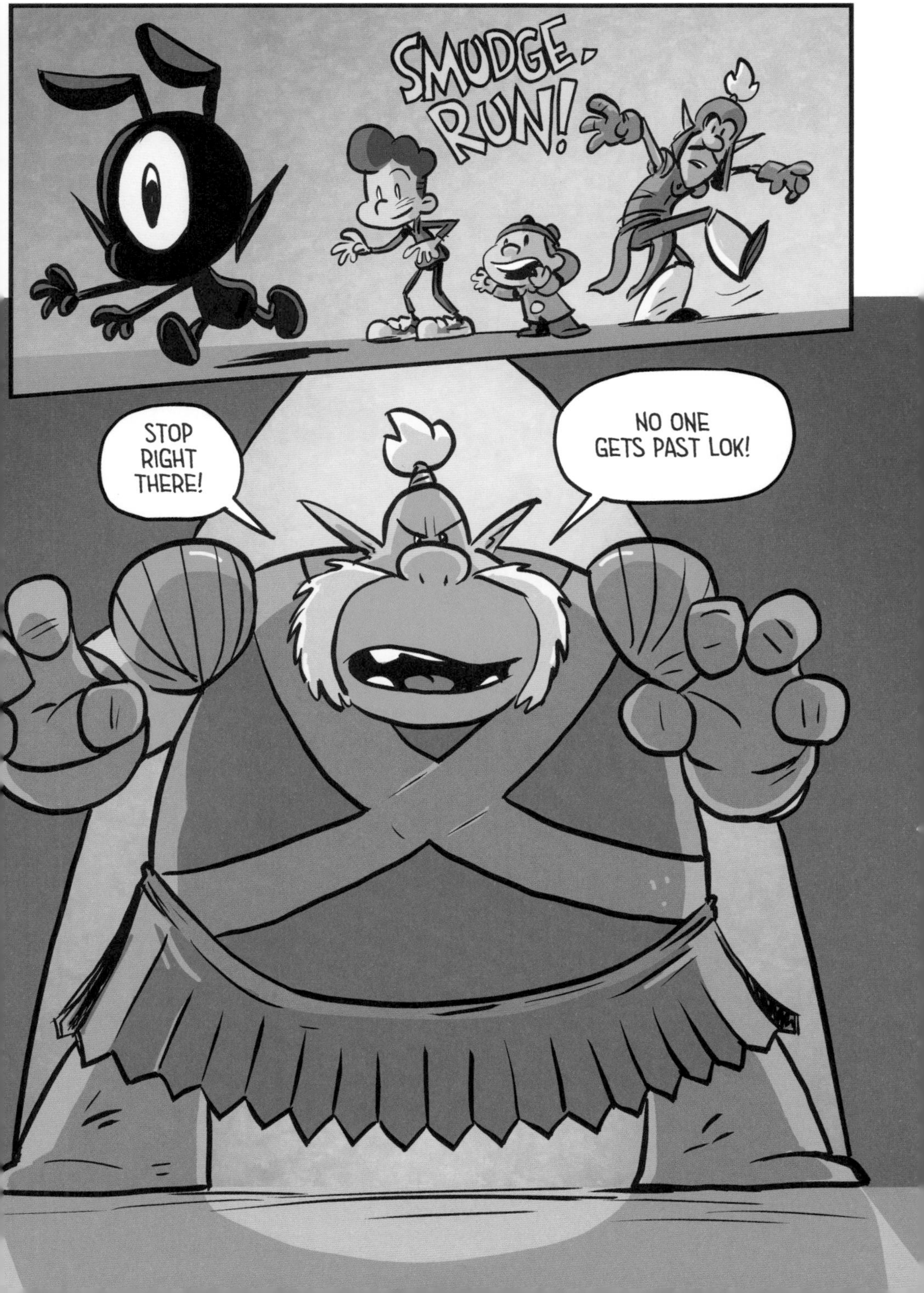
SMUDGE, RUN!
STOP RIGHT THERE!
NO ONE GETS PAST LOK!

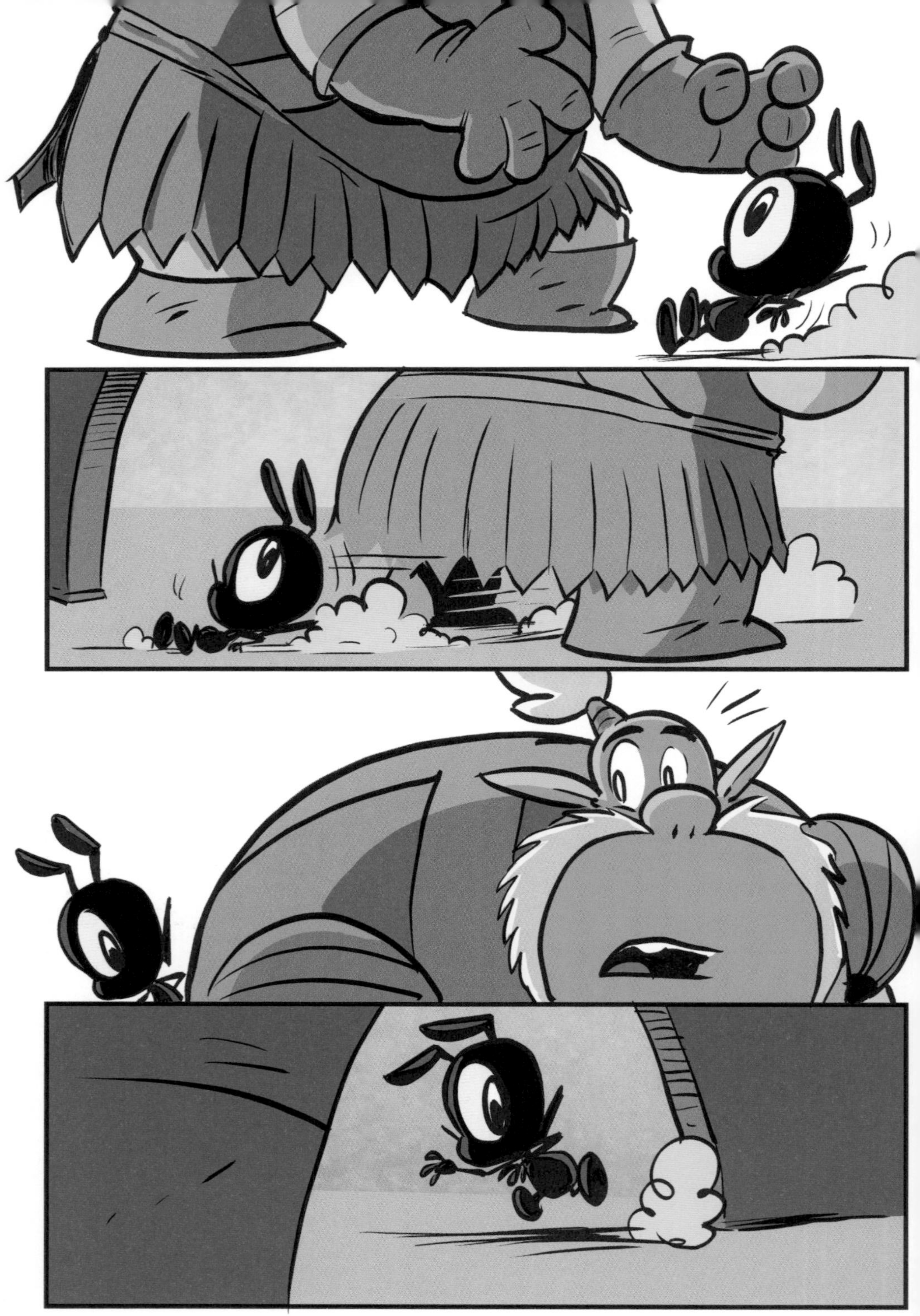

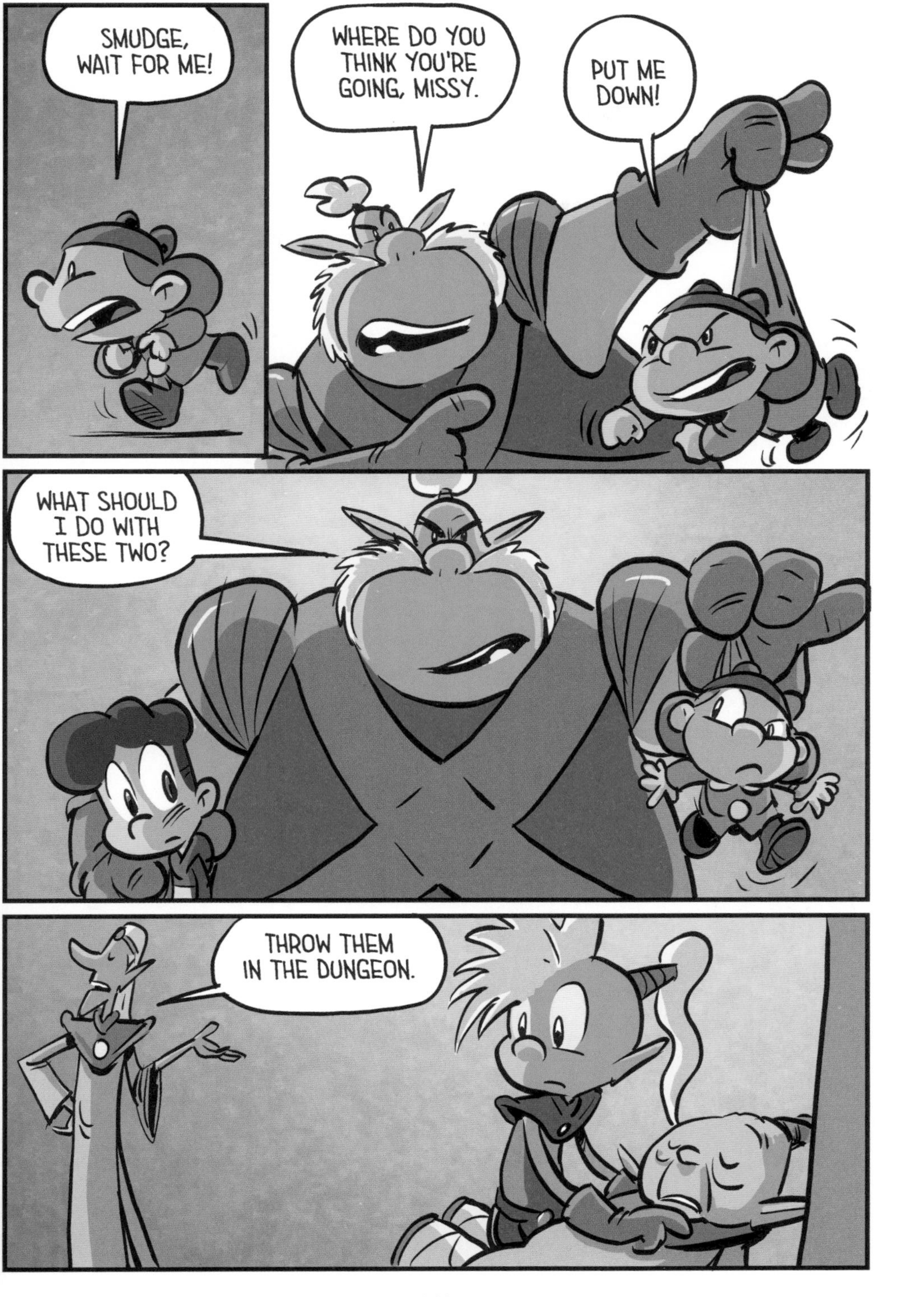
SMUDGE, WAIT FOR ME!
WHERE DO YOU THINK YOU'RE GOING, MISSY.
PUT ME DOWN!
WHAT SHOULD I DO WITH THESE TWO?
THROW THEM IN THE DUNGEON.

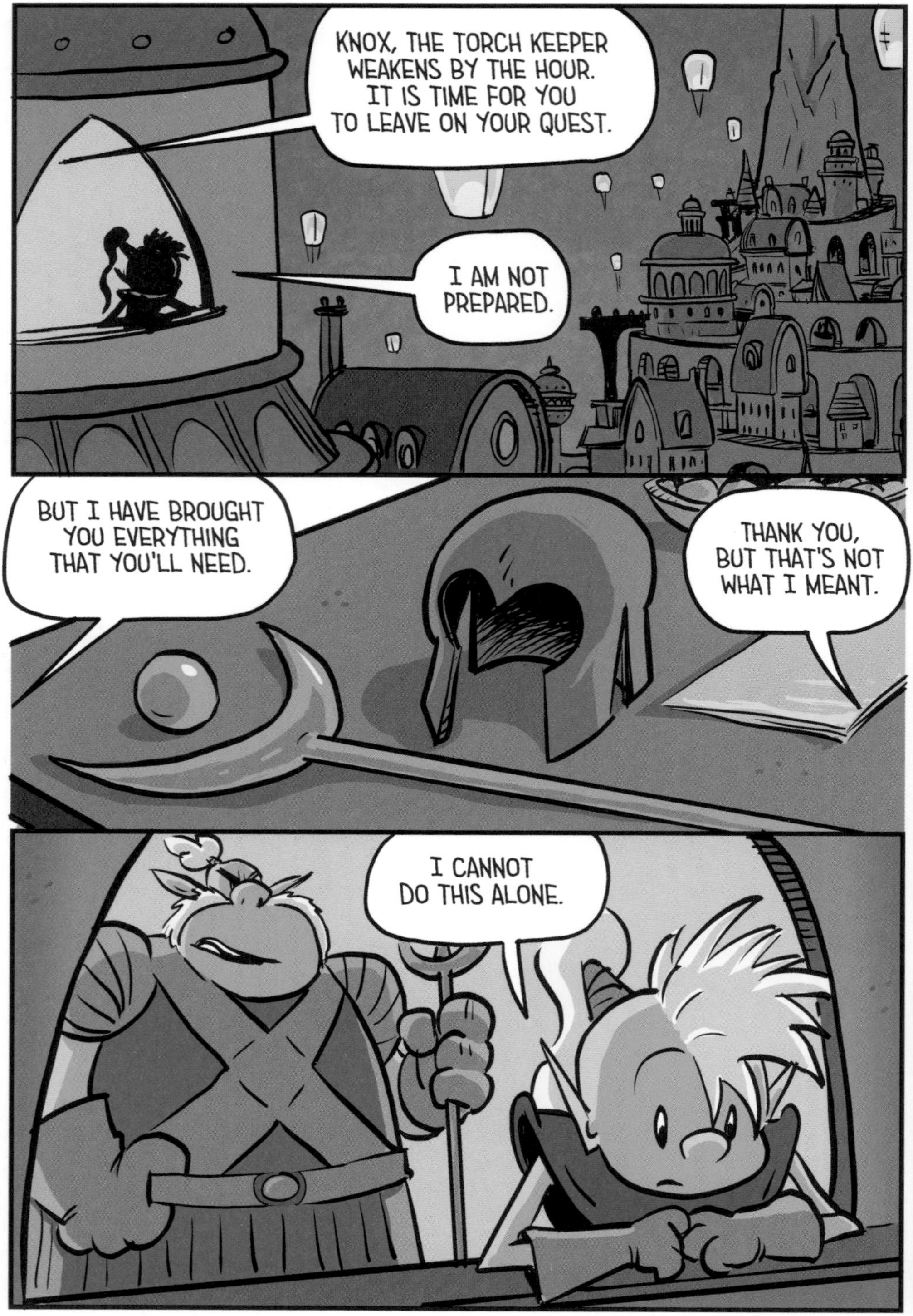
KNOX, THE TORCH KEEPER WEAKENS BY THE HOUR. IT IS TIME FOR YOU TO LEAVE ON YOUR QUEST.
I AM NOT PREPARED.
BUT I HAVE BROUGHT YOU EVERYTHING THAT YOU'LL NEED.
THANK YOU, BUT THAT'S NOT WHAT I MEANT.
I CANNOT DO THIS ALONE.

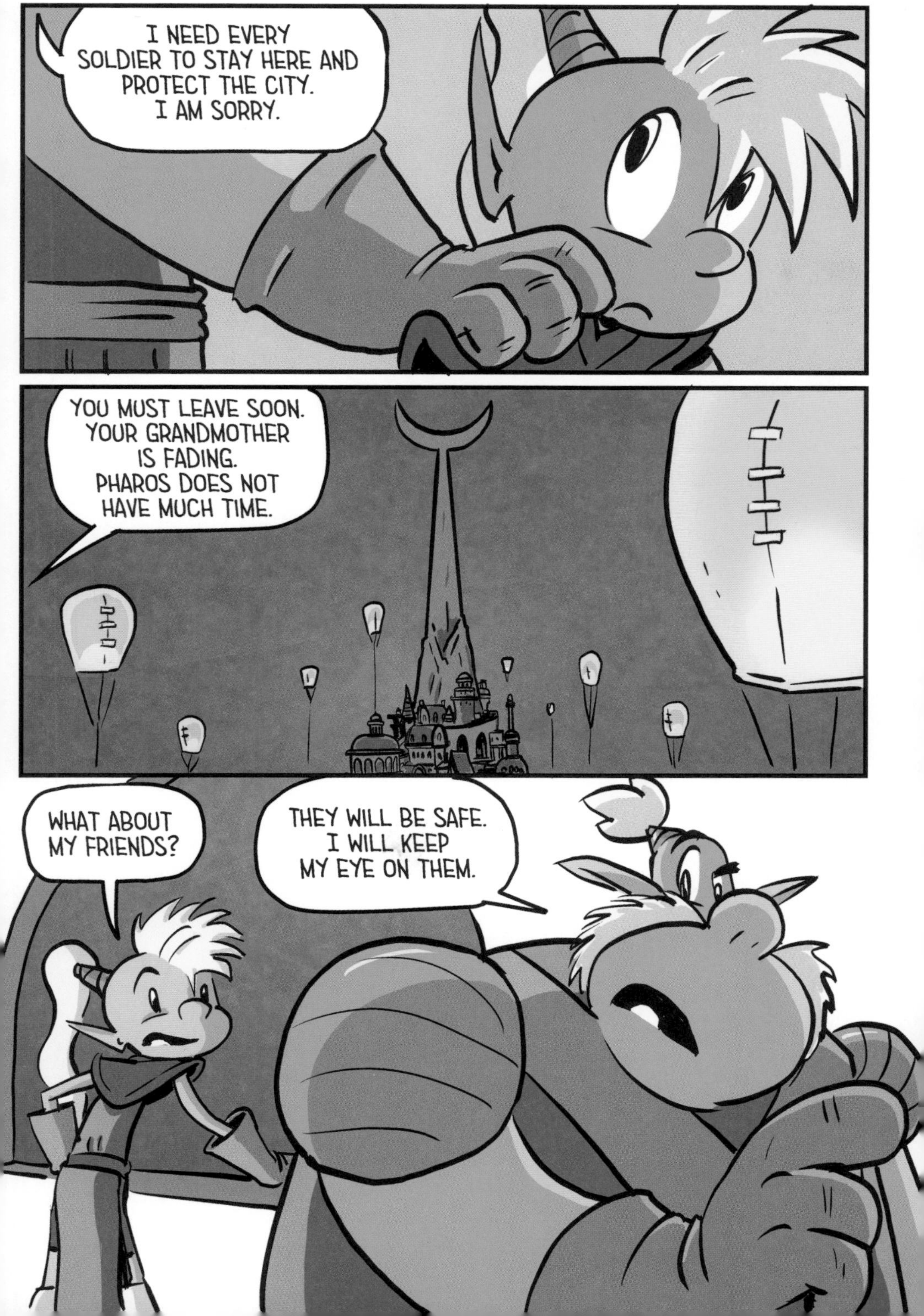
I NEED EVERY SOLDIER TO STAY HERE AND PROTECT THE CITY. I AM SORRY.
YOU MUST LEAVE SOON. YOUR GRANDMOTHER IS FADING. PHAROS DOES NOT HAVE MUCH TIME.
WHAT ABOUT MY FRIENDS?
THEY WILL BE SAFE. I WILL KEEP MY EYE ON THEM.

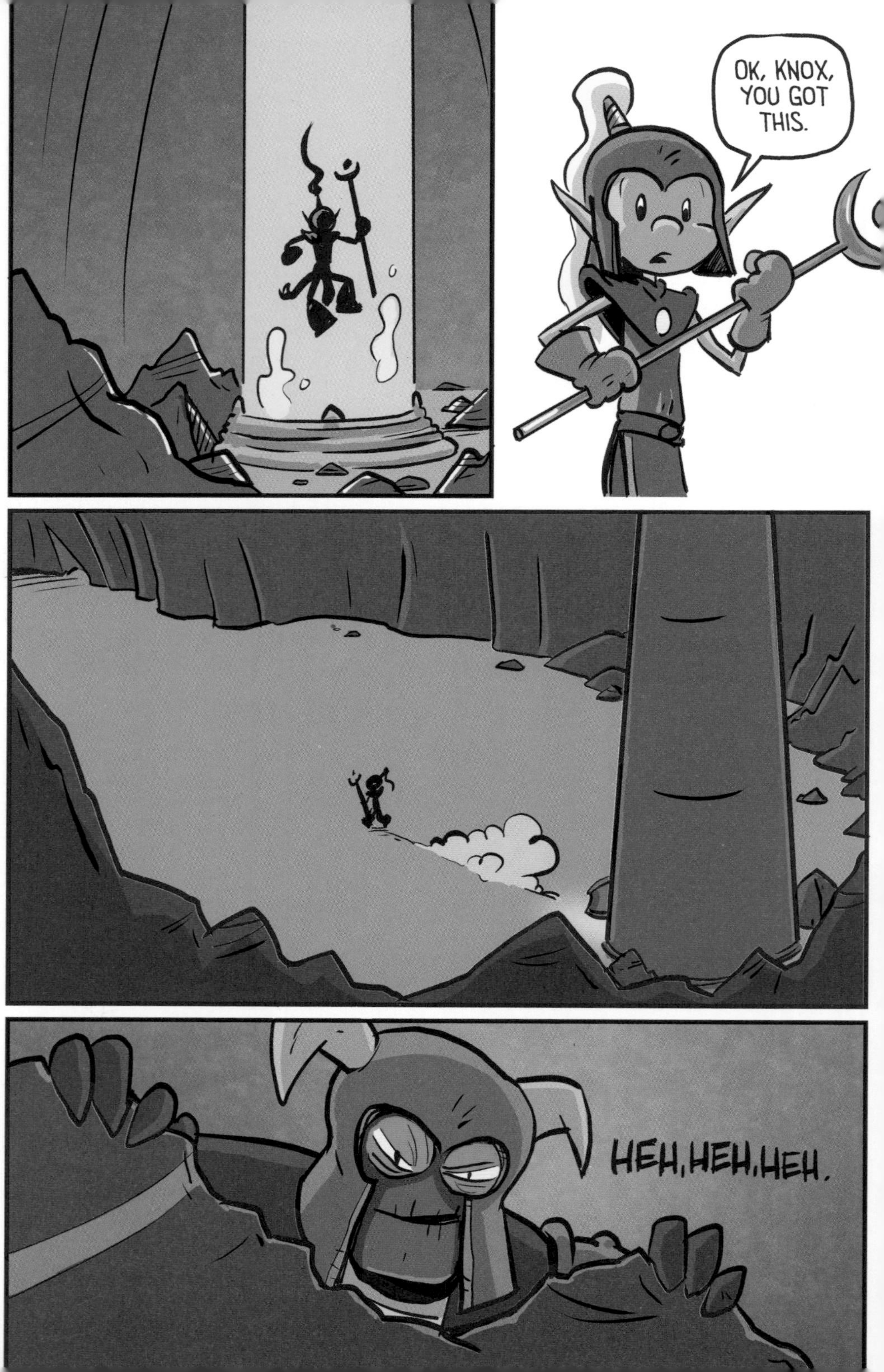
OK, KNOX, YOU GOT THIS.
HEH, HEH, HEH.

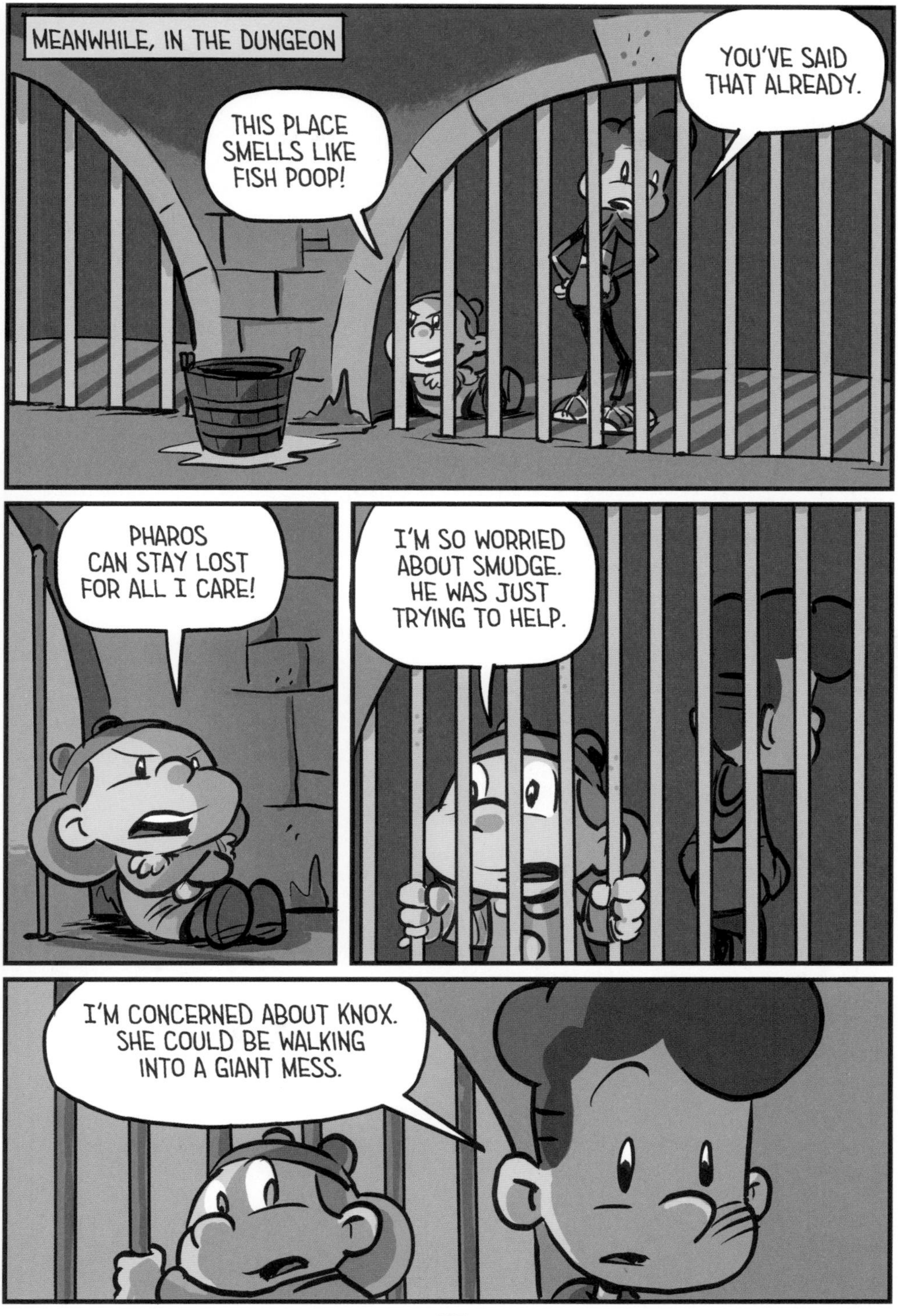
MEANWHILE, IN THE DUNGEON
THIS PLACE SMELLS LIKE FISH POOP!
YOU'VE SAID THAT ALREADY.
PHAROS CAN STAY LOST FOR ALL I CARE!
I'M SO WORRIED ABOUT SMUDGE. HE WAS JUST TRYING TO HELP.
I'M CONCERNED ABOUT KNOX. SHE COULD BE WALKING INTO A GIANT MESS.

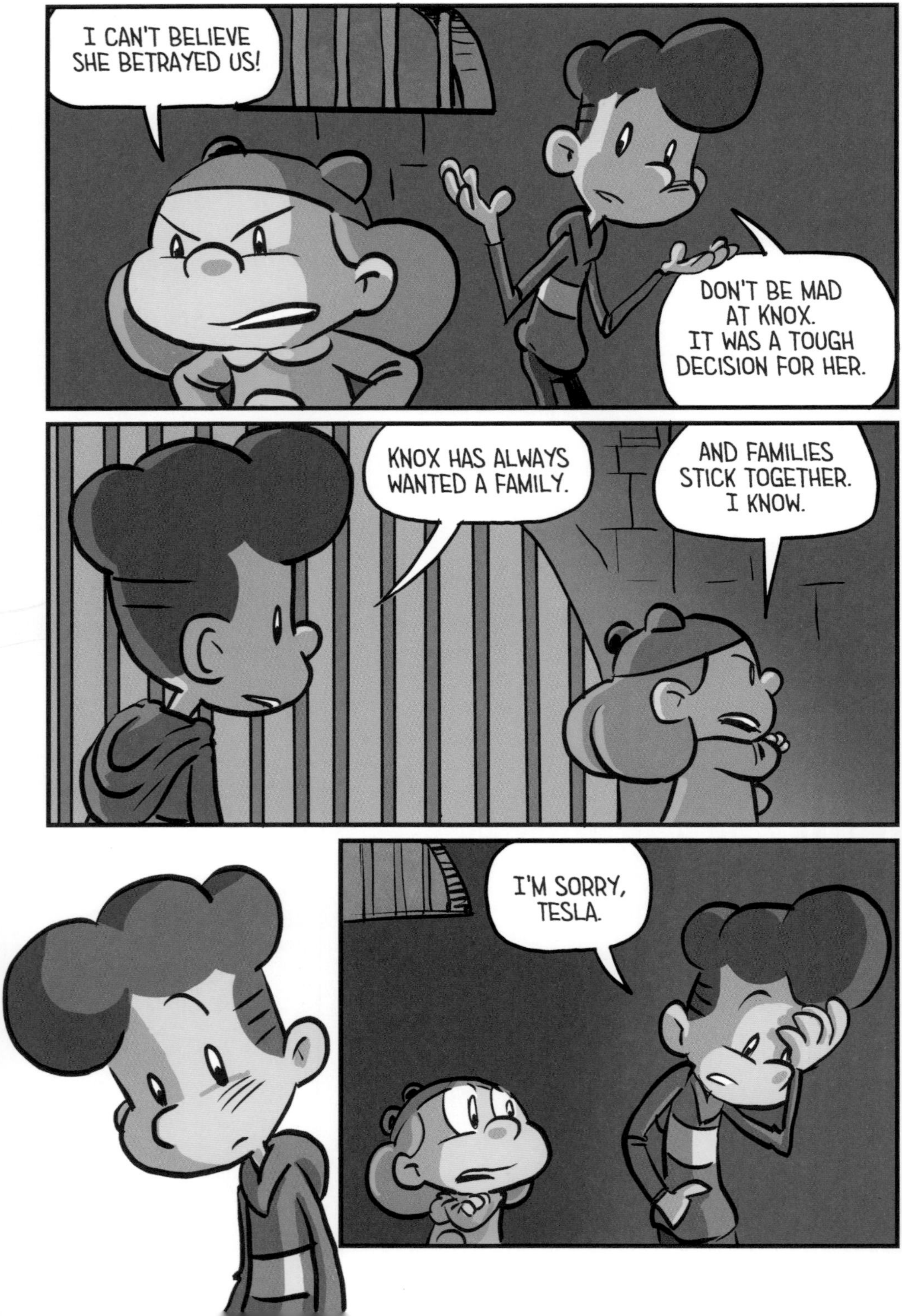
I CAN'T BELIEVE SHE BETRAYED US!
DON'T BE MAD AT KNOX. IT WAS A TOUGH DECISION FOR HER.
KNOX HAS ALWAYS WANTED A FAMILY.
AND FAMILIES STICK TOGETHER. I KNOW.
I'M SORRY, TESLA.

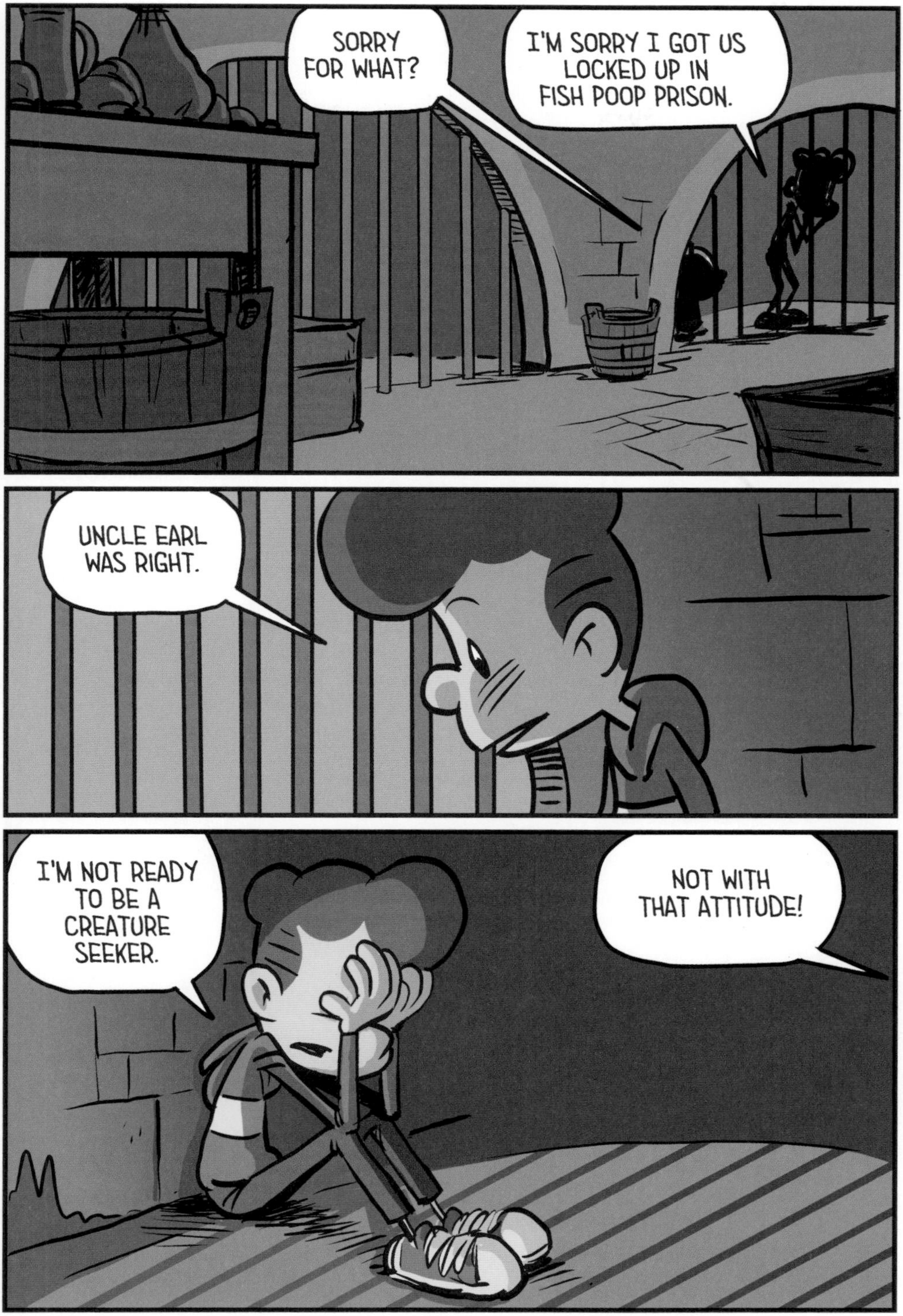
SORRY FOR WHAT?
I'M SORRY I GOT US LOCKED UP IN FISH POOP PRISON.
UNCLE EARL WAS RIGHT.
I'M NOT READY TO BE A CREATURE SEEKER.
NOT WITH THAT ATTITUDE!

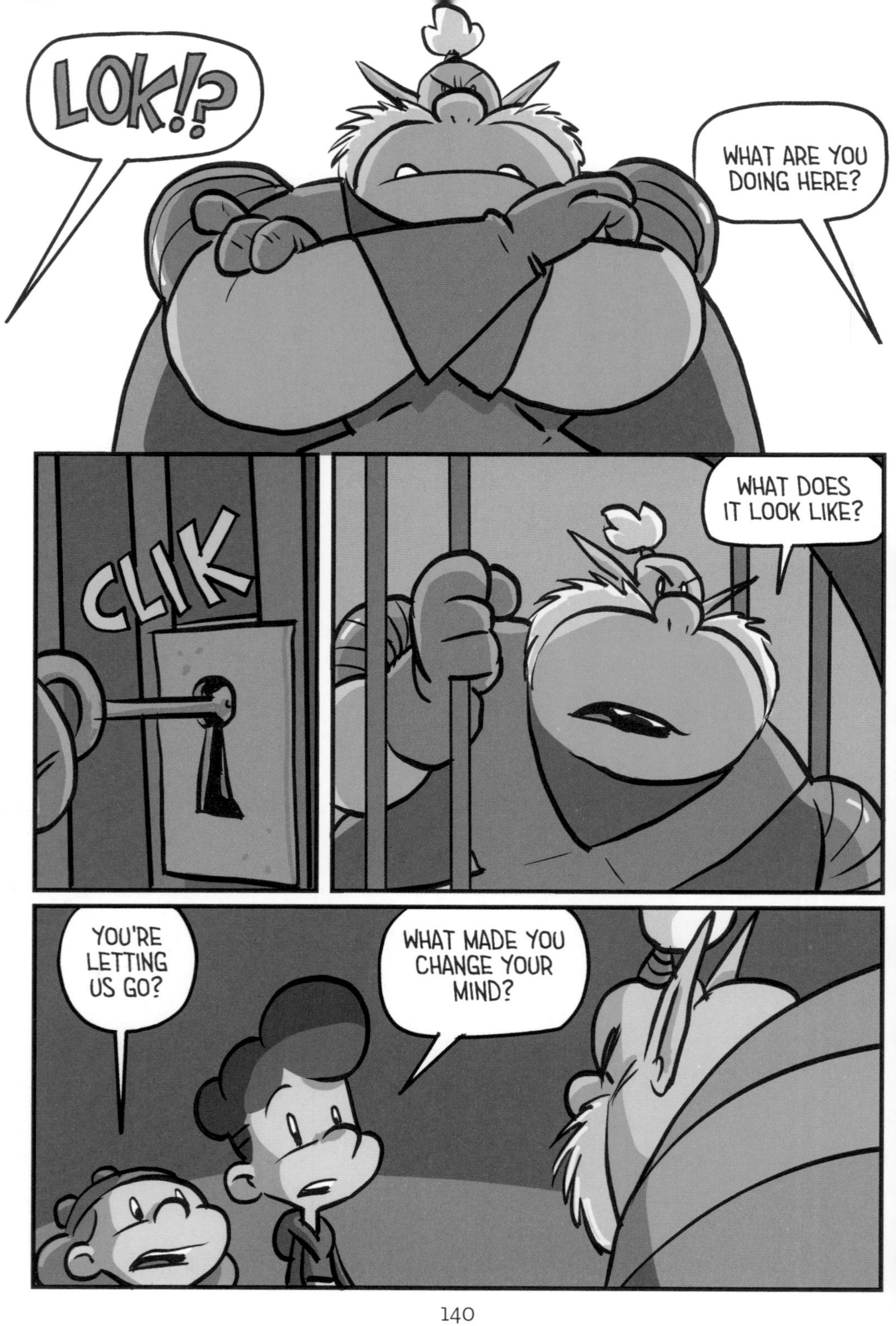
LOK!?
WHAT ARE YOU DOING HERE?
CLIK
WHAT DOES IT LOOK LIKE?
YOU'RE LETTING US GO?
WHAT MADE YOU CHANGE YOUR MIND?

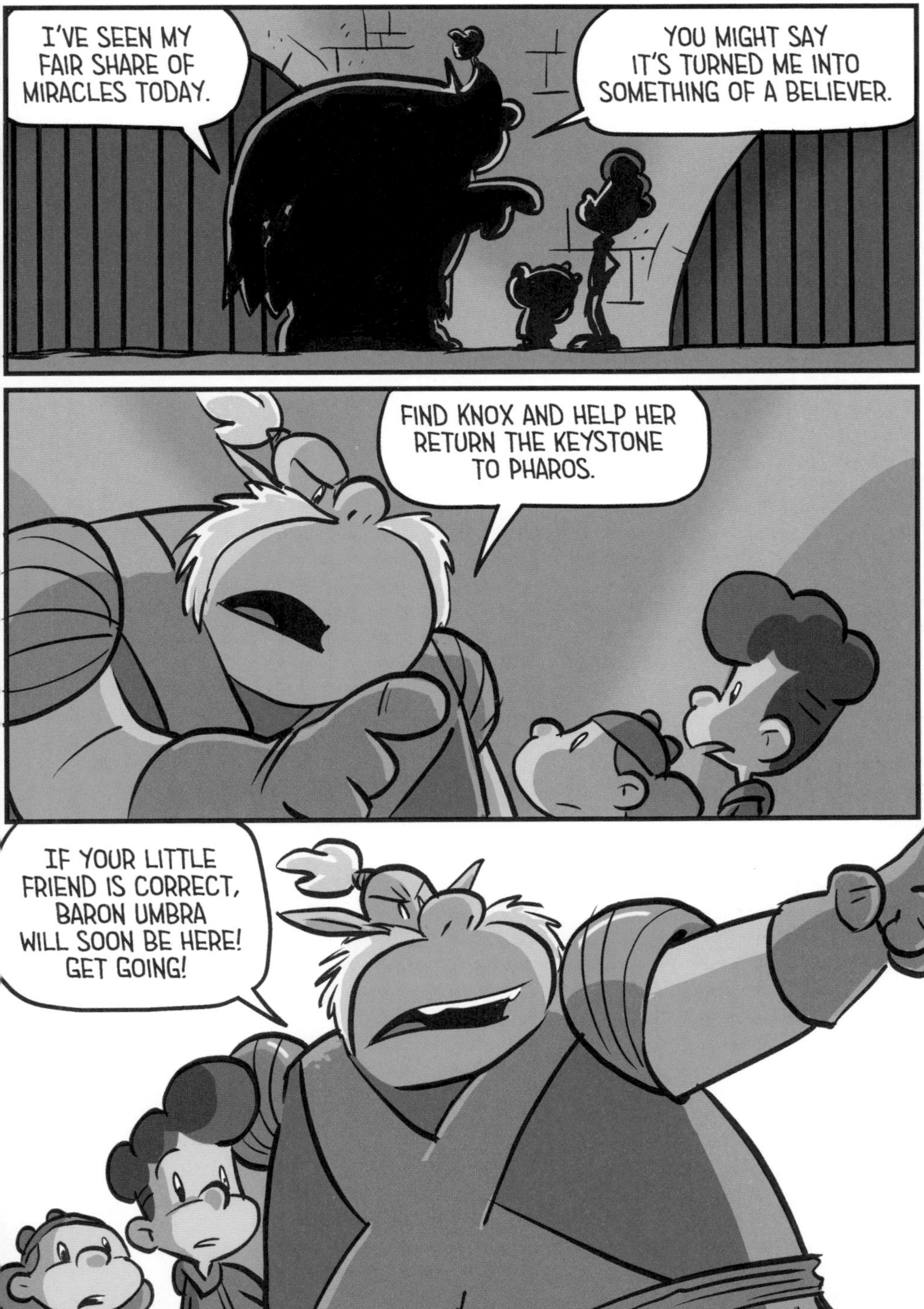
I'VE SEEN MY FAIR SHARE OF MIRACLES TODAY.
YOU MIGHT SAY IT'S TURNED ME INTO SOMETHING OF A BELIEVER.
FIND KNOX AND HELP HER RETURN THE KEYSTONE TO PHAROS.
IF YOUR LITTLE FRIEND IS CORRECT, BARON UMBRA WILL SOON BE HERE! GET GOING!

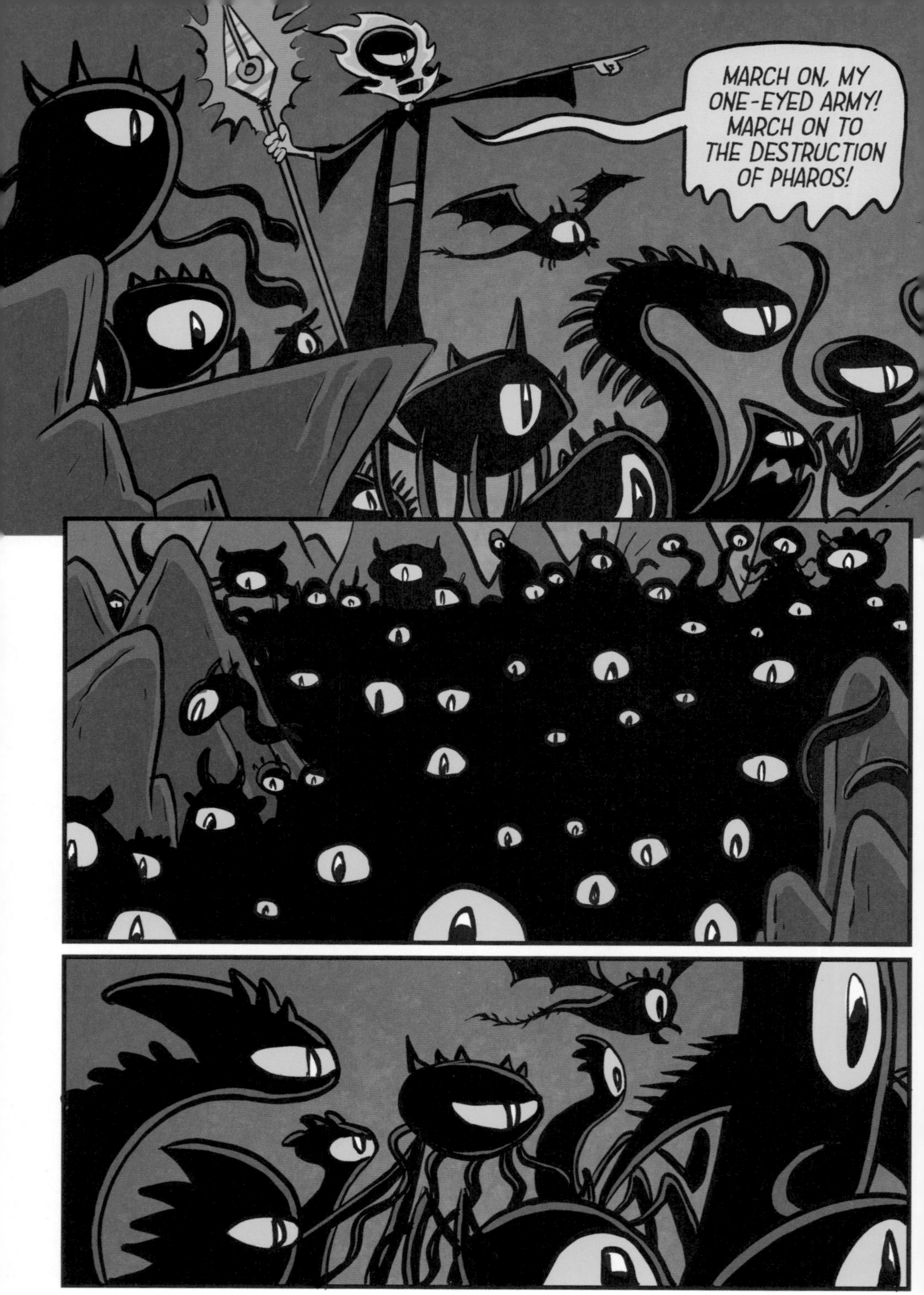
MARCH ON, MY ONE-EYED ARMY! MARCH ON TO THE DESTRUCTION OF PHAROS!

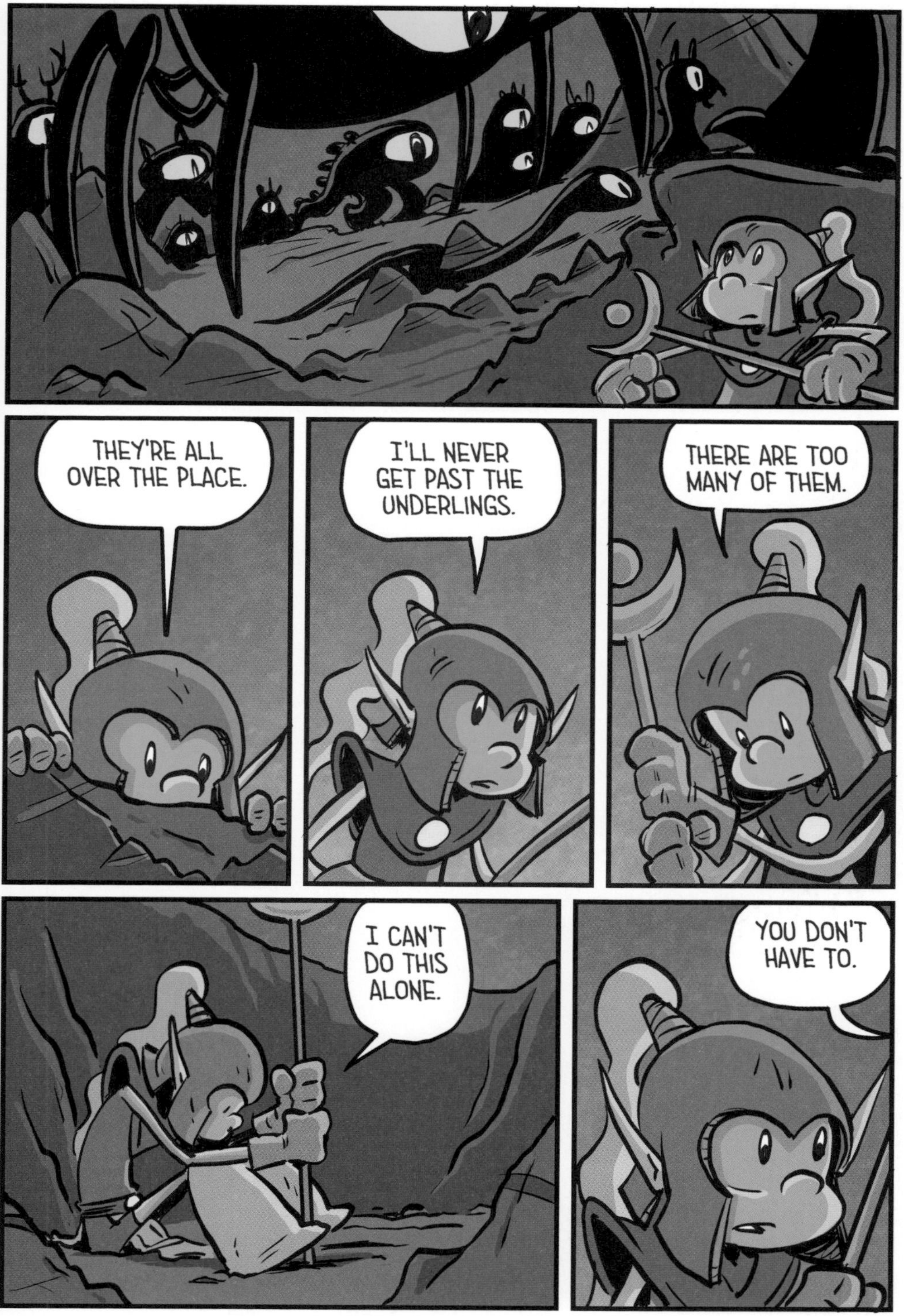
THEY'RE ALL OVER THE PLACE.
I'LL NEVER GET PAST THE UNDERLINGS.
THERE ARE TOO MANY OF THEM.
I CAN'T DO THIS ALONE.
YOU DON'T HAVE TO.

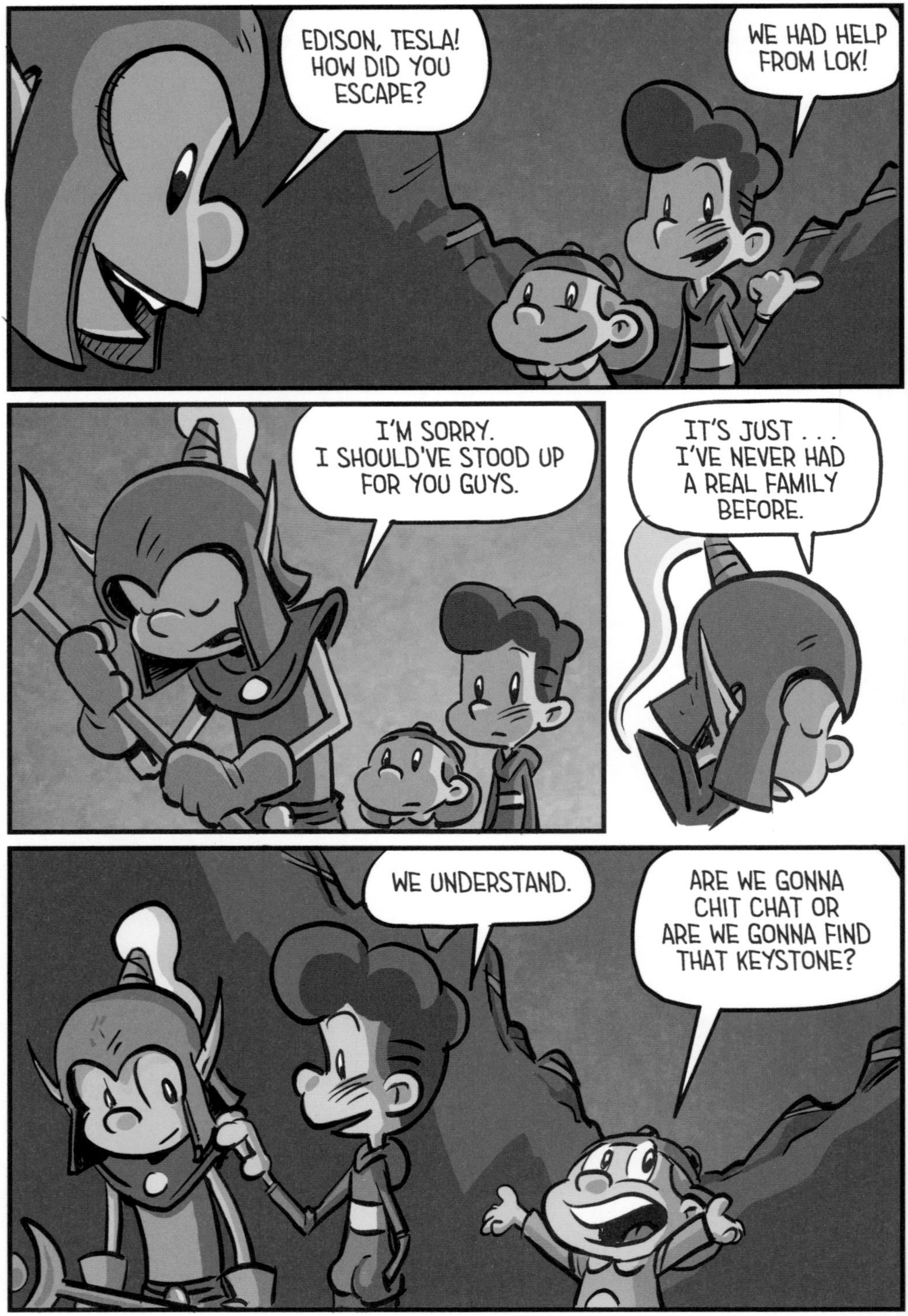
EDISON, TESLA! HOW DID YOU ESCAPE?
WE HAD HELP FROM LOK!
I'M SORRY. I SHOULD'VE STOOD UP FOR YOU GUYS.
IT'S JUST . . . I'VE NEVER HAD A REAL FAMILY BEFORE.
WE UNDERSTAND.
ARE WE GONNA CHIT CHAT OR ARE WE GONNA FIND THAT KEYSTONE?

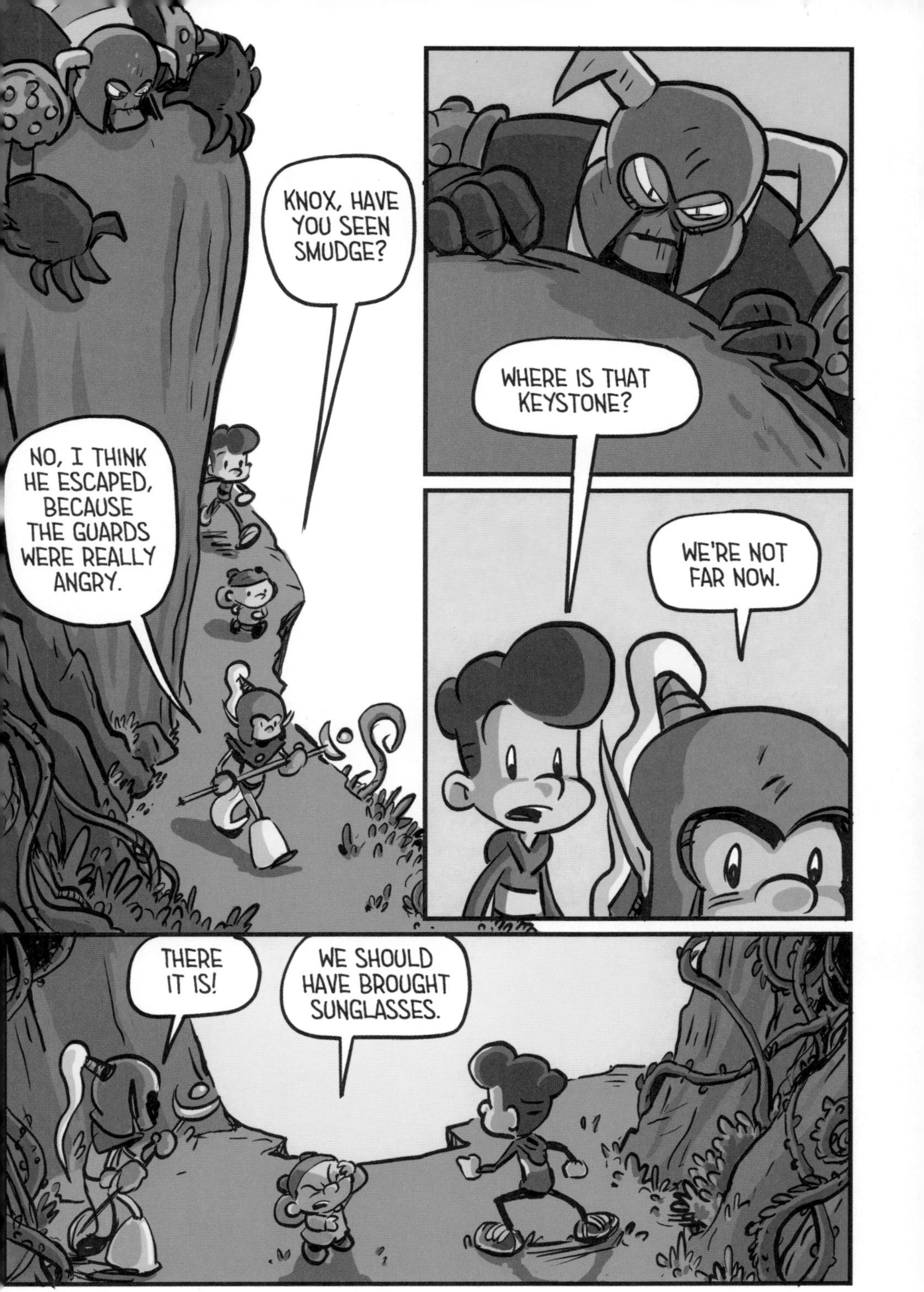
KNOX, HAVE YOU SEEN SMUDGE?
NO, I THINK HE ESCAPED, BECAUSE THE GUARDS WERE REALLY ANGRY.
WHERE IS THAT KEYSTONE?
WE'RE NOT FAR NOW.
THERE IT IS!
WE SHOULD HAVE BROUGHT SUNGLASSES.

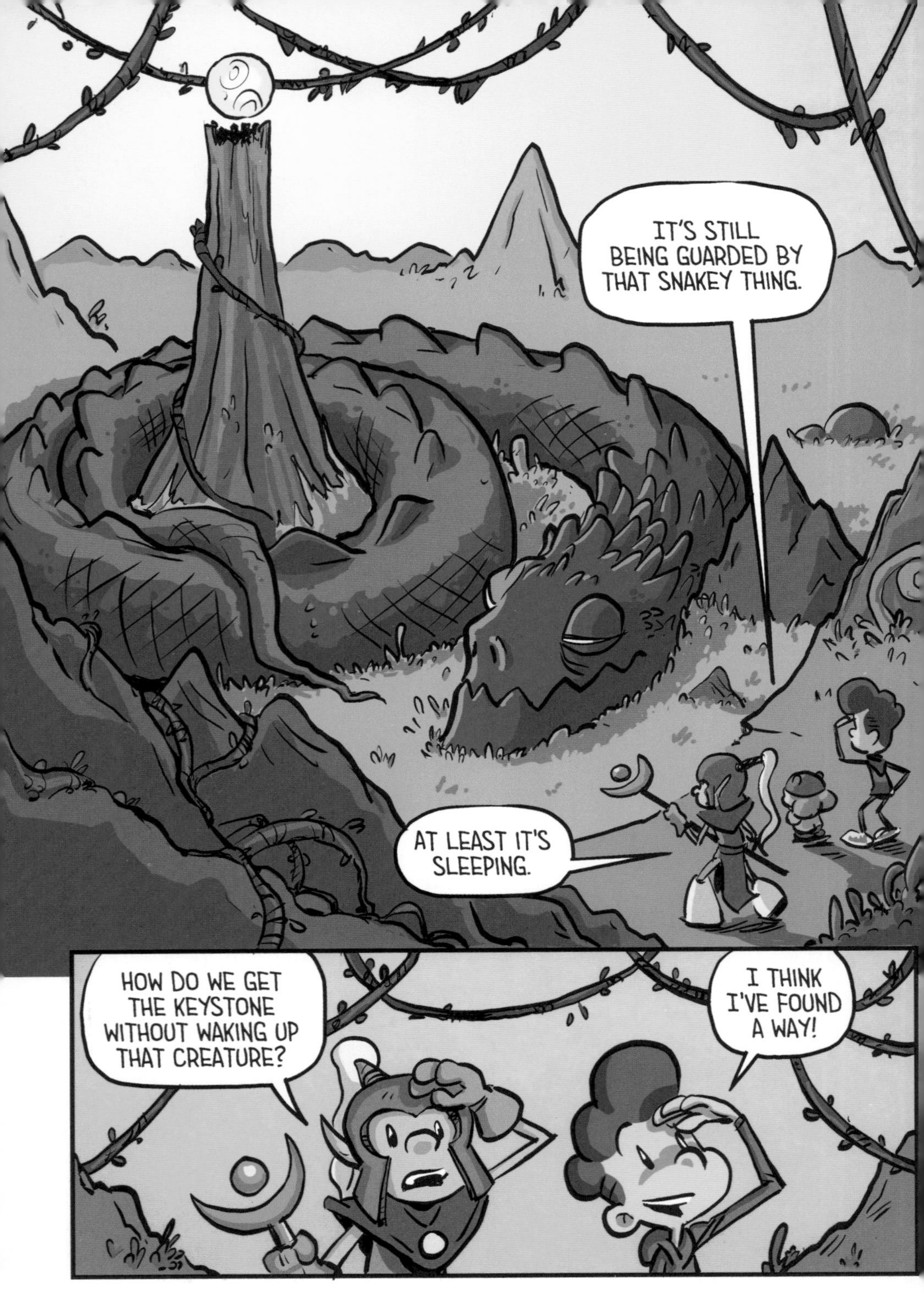
IT'S STILL BEING GUARDED BY THAT SNAKEY THING.
AT LEAST IT'S SLEEPING.
HOW DO WE GET THE KEYSTONE WITHOUT WAKING UP THAT CREATURE?
I THINK I'VE FOUND A WAY!

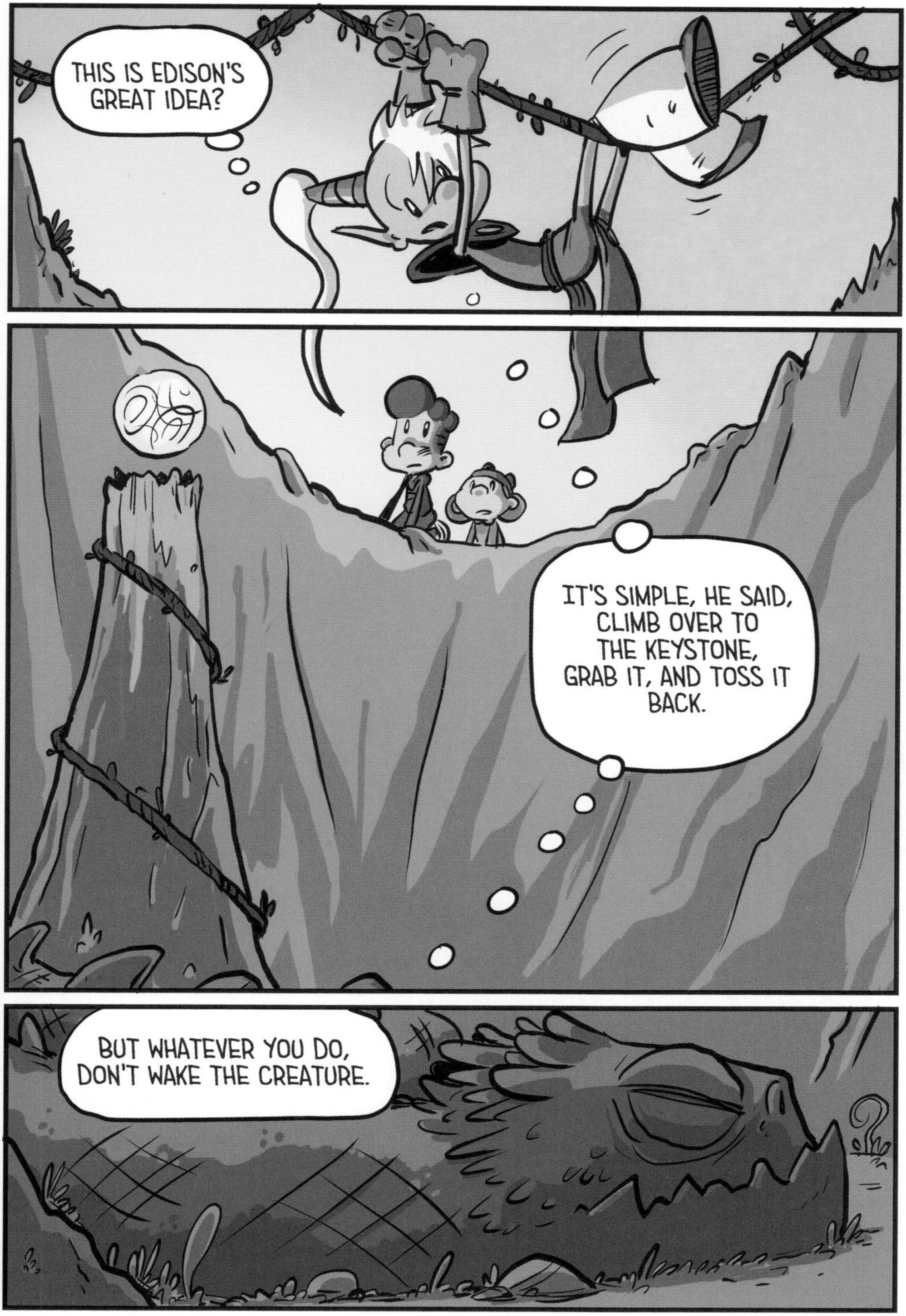
THIS IS EDISON'S GREAT IDEA?
IT'S SIMPLE, HE SAID, CLIMB OVER TO THE KEYSTONE, GRAB IT, AND TOSS IT BACK.
BUT WHATEVER YOU DO, DON'T WAKE THE CREATURE.

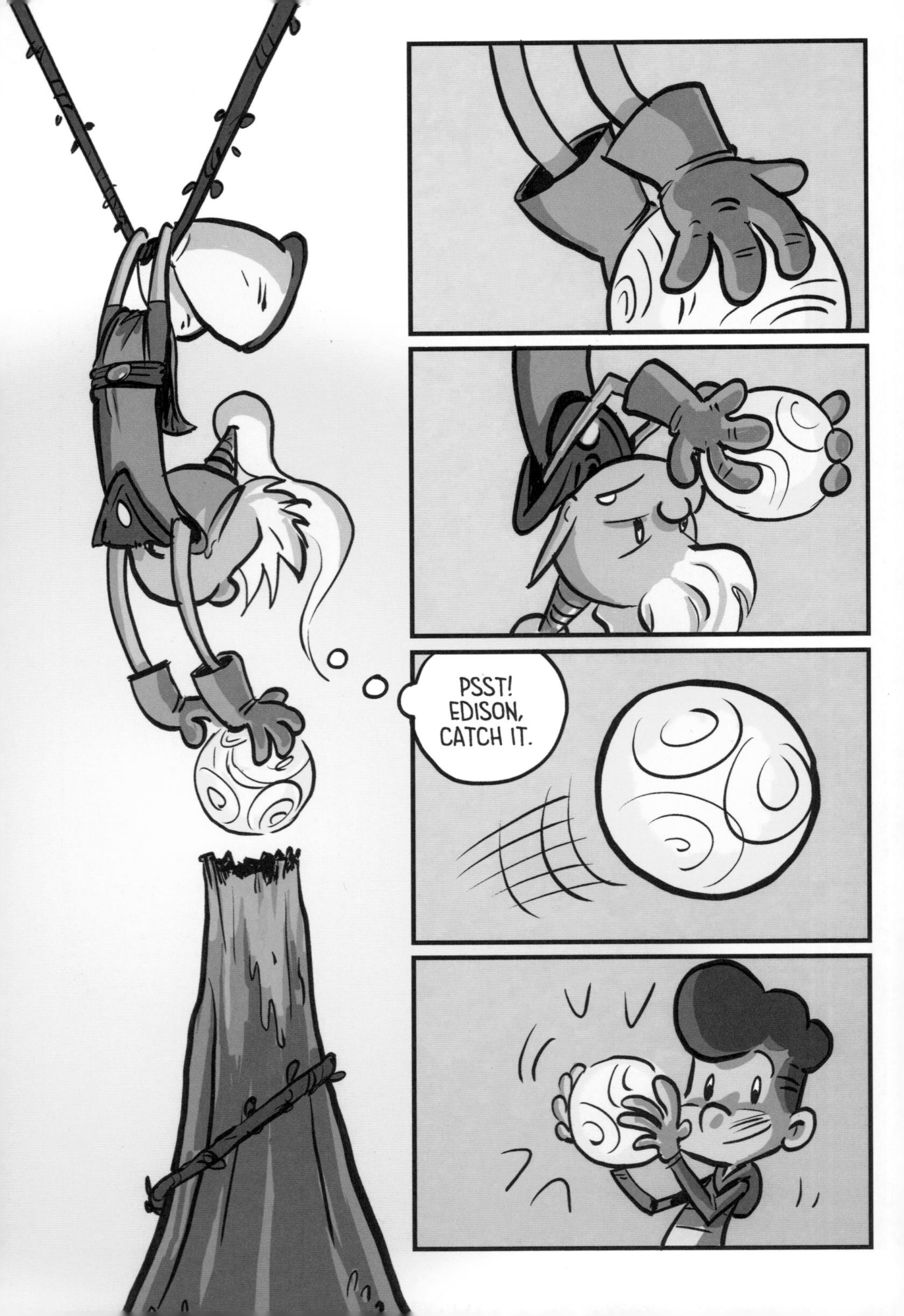
PSST! EDISON, CATCH IT.

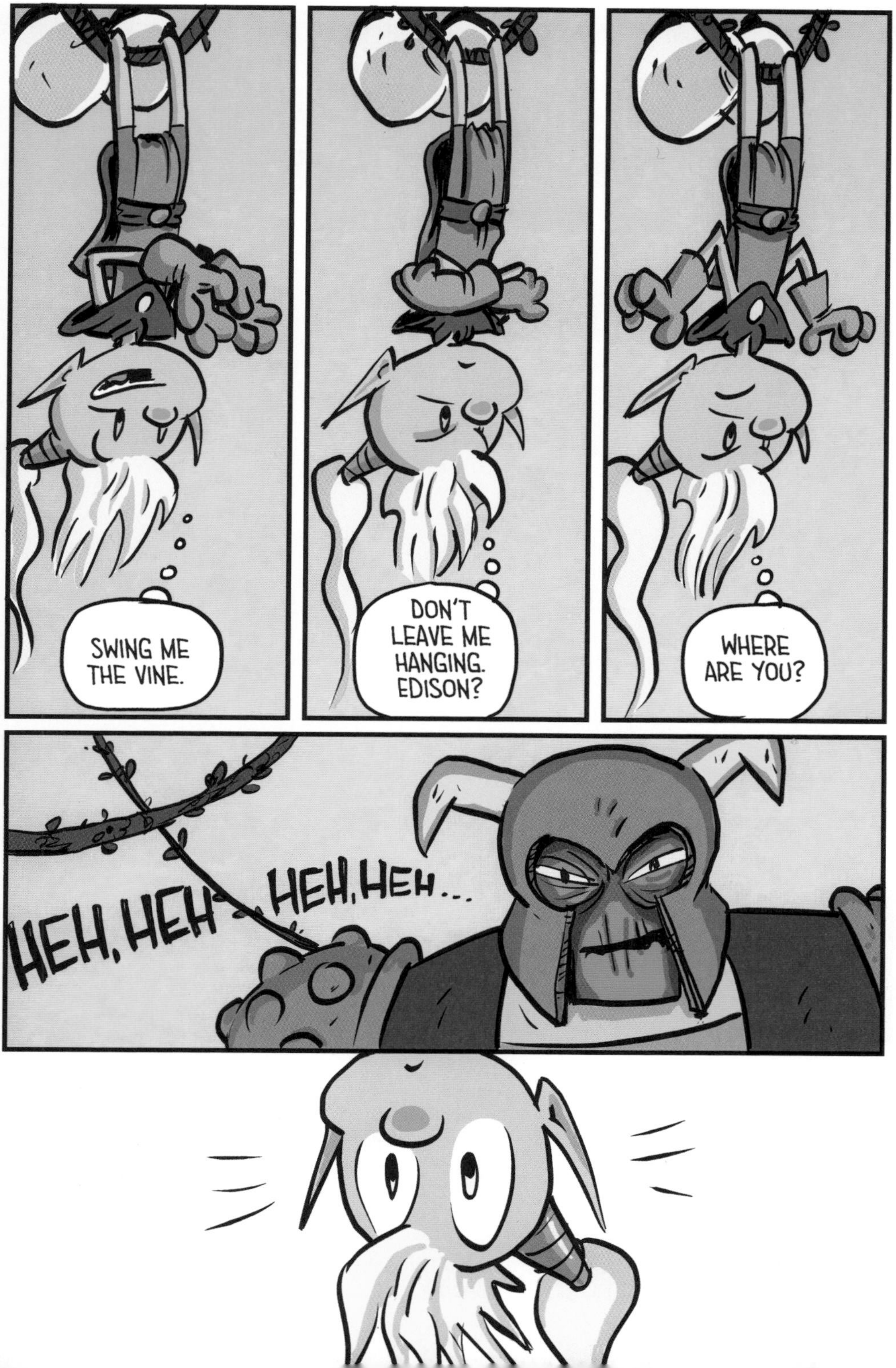
SWING ME THE VINE.
DON'T LEAVE ME HANGING. EDISON?
WHERE ARE YOU?
HEH, HEH
HEH, HEH...

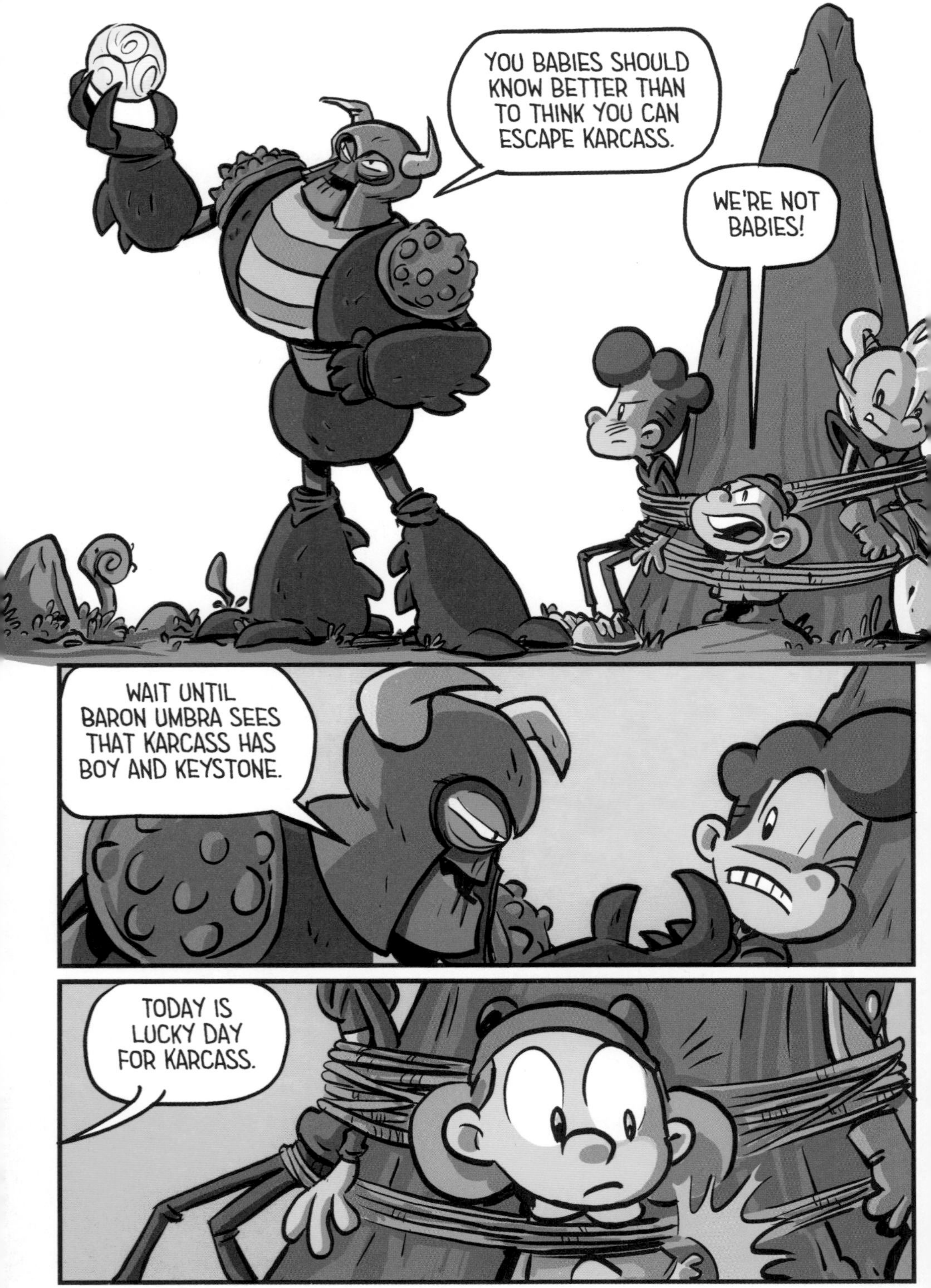
YOU BABIES SHOULD KNOW BETTER THAN TO THINK YOU CAN ESCAPE KARCASS.
WE'RE NOT BABIES!
WAIT UNTIL BARON UMBRA SEES THAT KARCASS HAS BOY AND KEYSTONE.
TODAY IS LUCKY DAY FOR KARCASS.

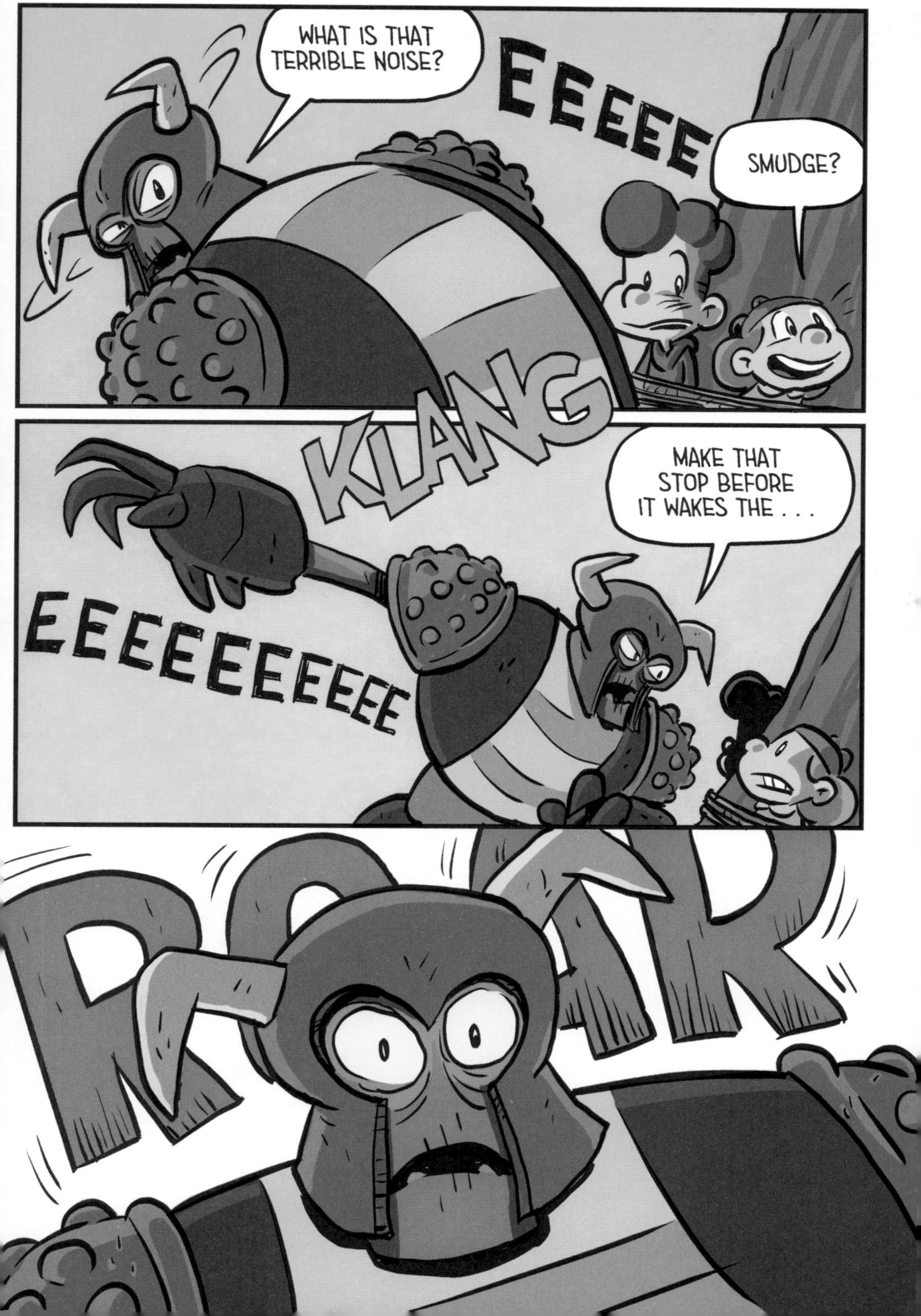
WHAT IS THAT TERRIBLE NOISE?
EEEEE
SMUDGE?
KLANG
MAKE THAT STOP BEFORE IT WAKES THE . . .
EEEEEEEEEEE
ROAR

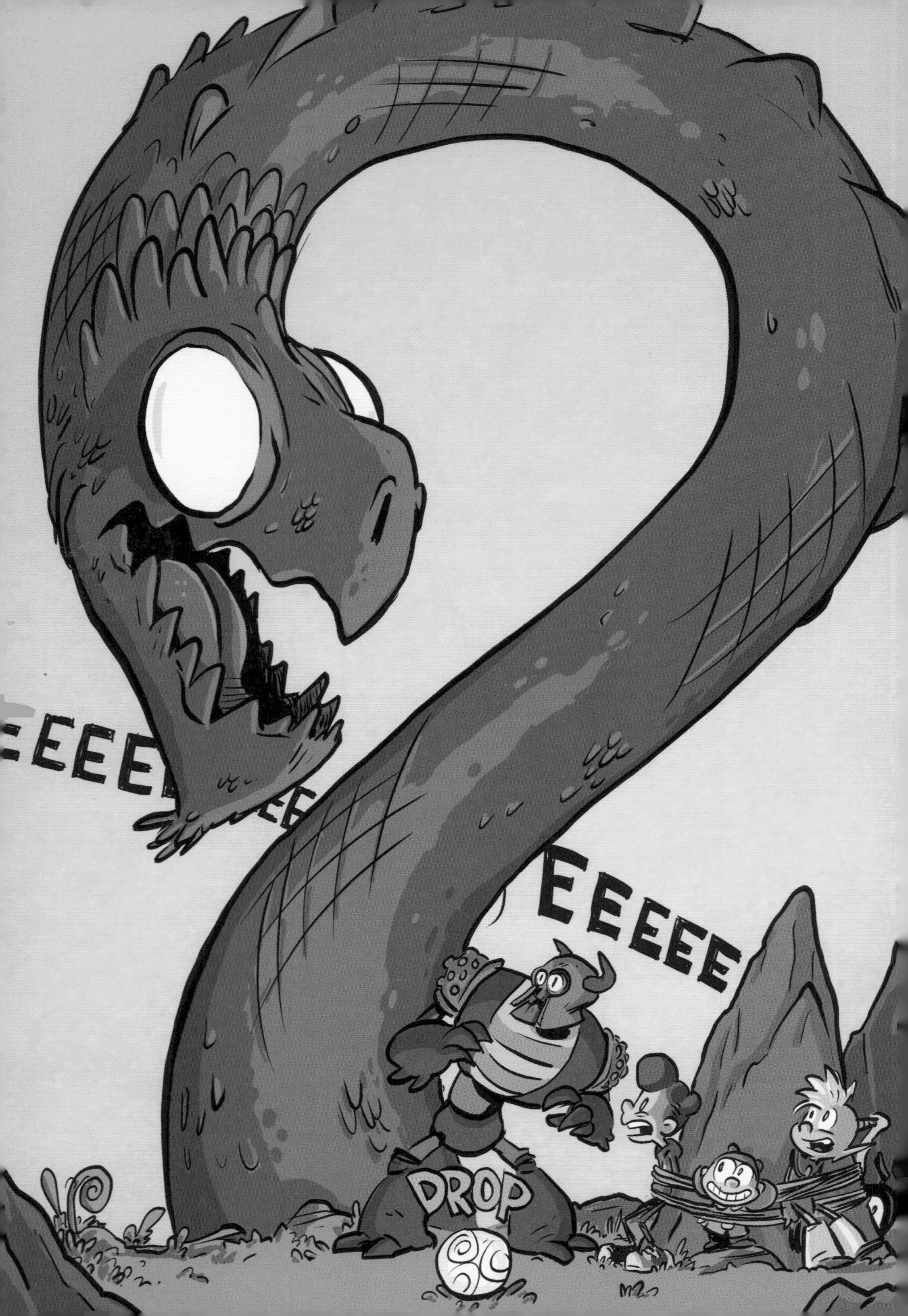
EEEEEEE
EEEEE
DROP

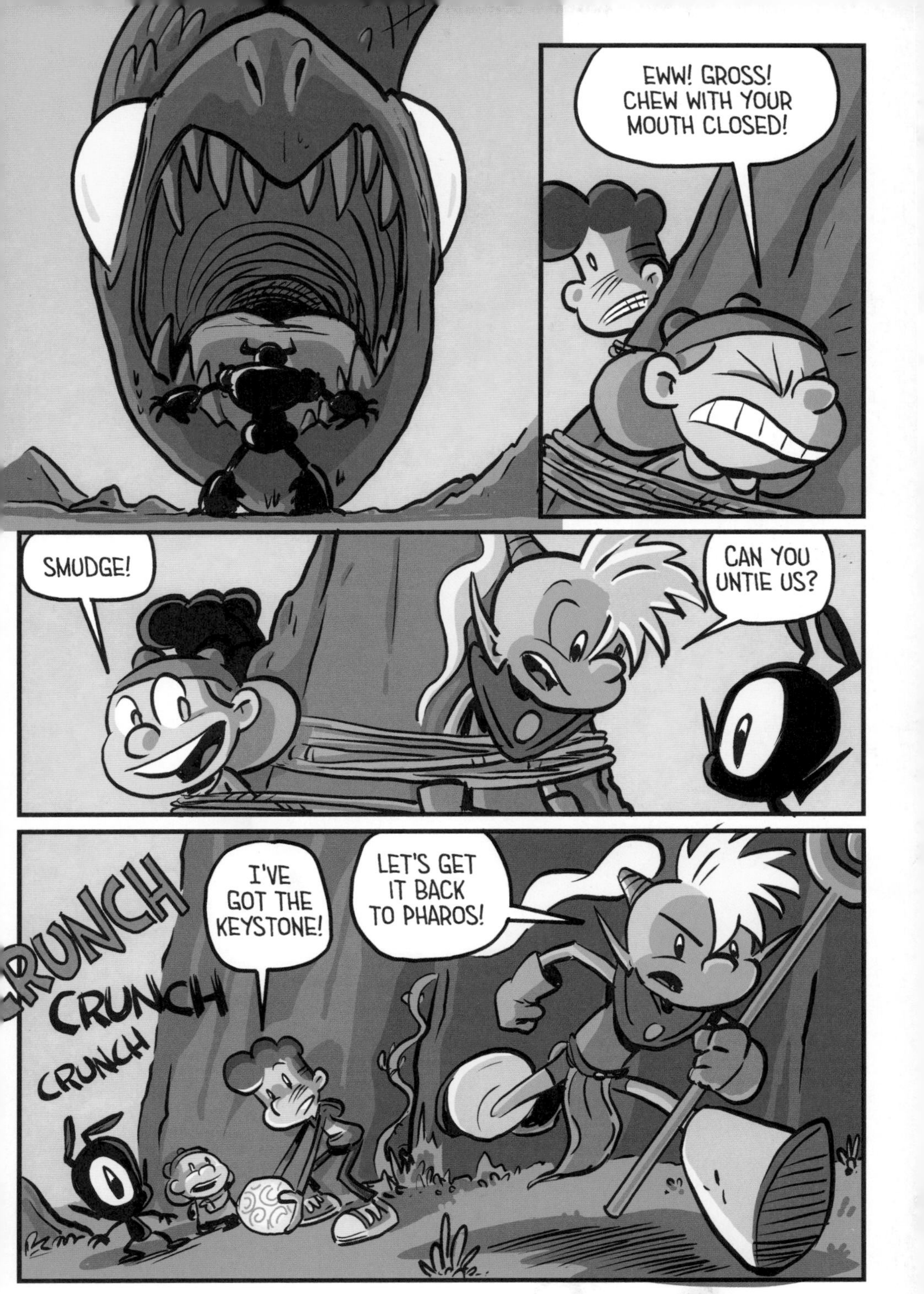
EWW! GROSS! CHEW WITH YOUR MOUTH CLOSED!
SMUDGE!
CAN YOU UNTIE US?
CRUNCH
CRUNCH
CRUNCH
I'VE GOT THE KEYSTONE!
LET'S GET IT BACK TO PHAROS!

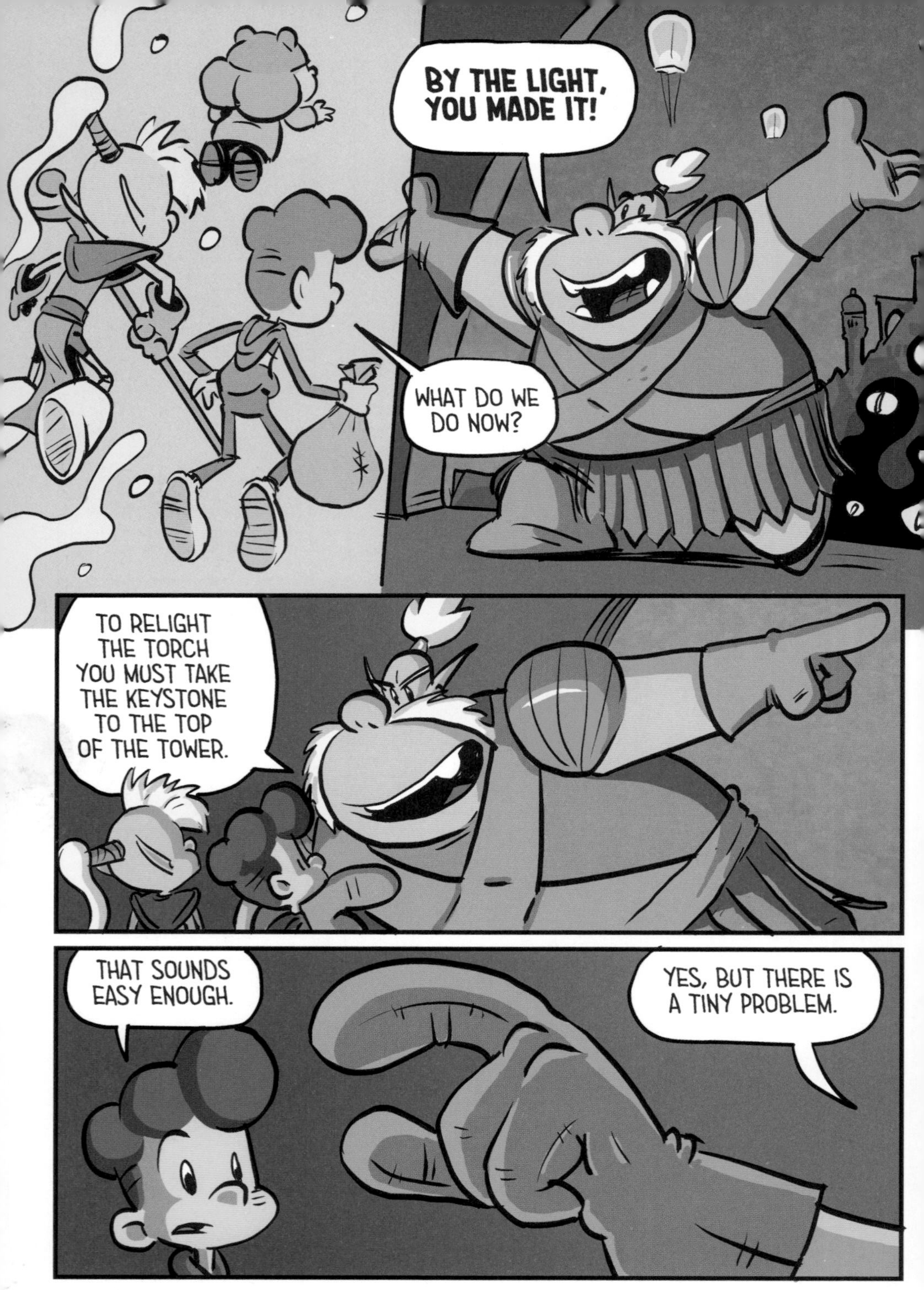
BY THE LIGHT, YOU MADE IT!
WHAT DO WE DO NOW?
TO RELIGHT THE TORCH YOU MUST TAKE THE KEYSTONE TO THE TOP OF THE TOWER.
THAT SOUNDS EASY ENOUGH.
YES, BUT THERE IS A TINY PROBLEM.

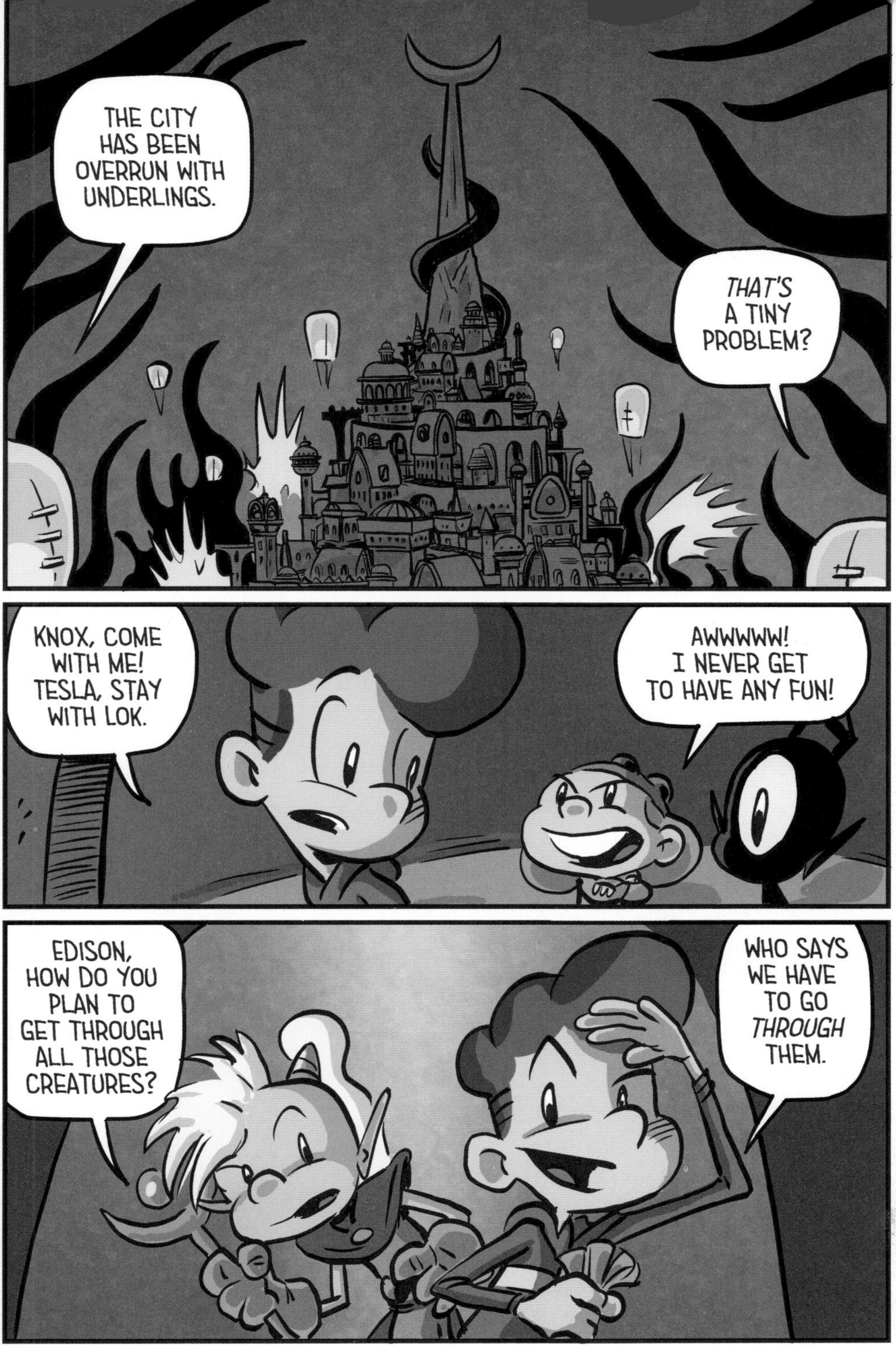
THE CITY HAS BEEN OVERRUN WITH UNDERLINGS.
THAT'S A TINY PROBLEM?
KNOX, COME WITH ME! TESLA, STAY WITH LOK.
AWWWWW! I NEVER GET TO HAVE ANY FUN!
EDISON, HOW DO YOU PLAN TO GET THROUGH ALL THOSE CREATURES?
WHO SAYS WE HAVE TO GO *THROUGH* THEM.

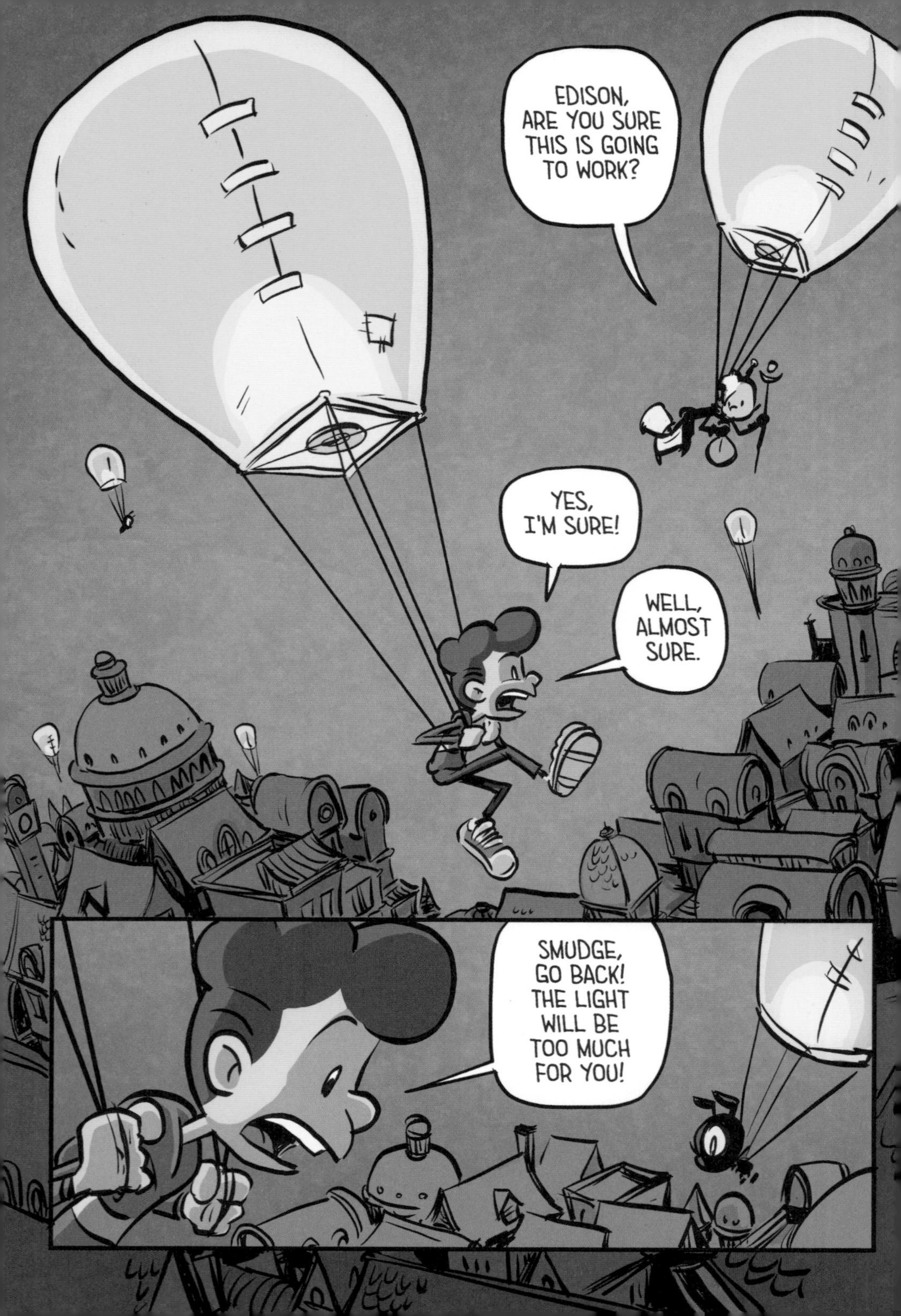
EDISON, ARE YOU SURE THIS IS GOING TO WORK?
YES, I'M SURE!
WELL, ALMOST SURE.
SMUDGE, GO BACK! THE LIGHT WILL BE TOO MUCH FOR YOU!

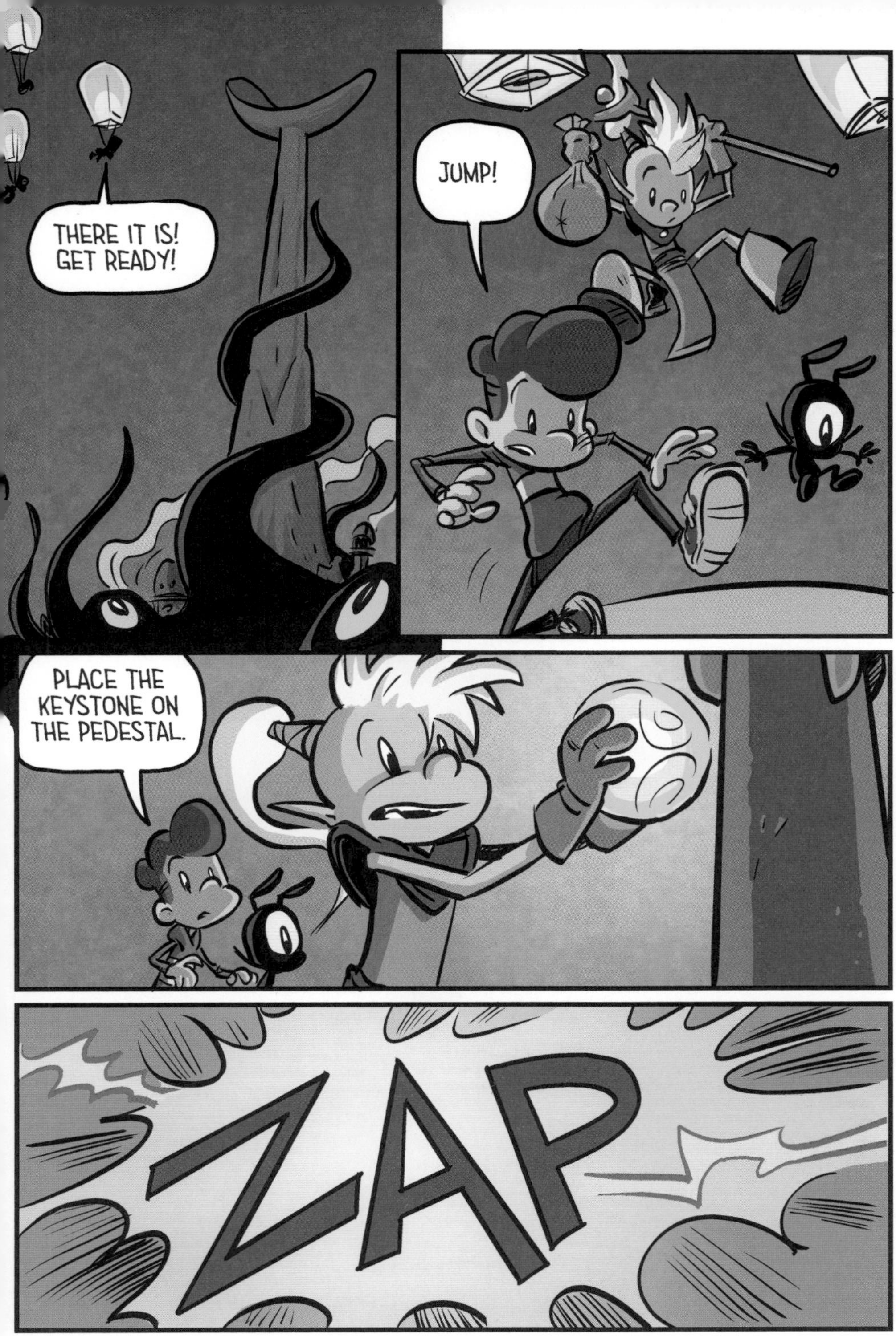
THERE IT IS! GET READY!
JUMP!
PLACE THE KEYSTONE ON THE PEDESTAL.
ZAP

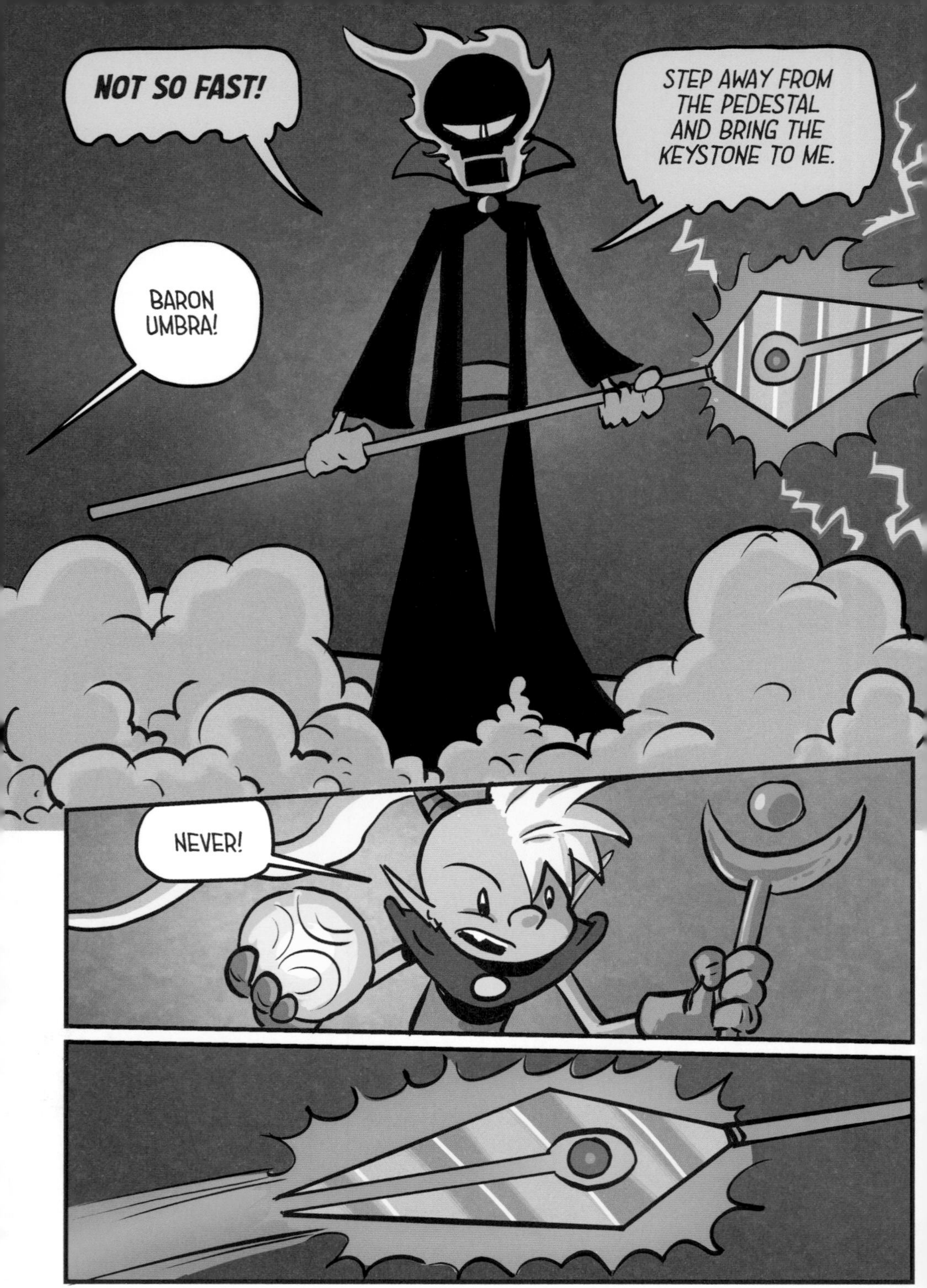
NOT SO FAST!
STEP AWAY FROM THE PEDESTAL AND BRING THE KEYSTONE TO ME.
BARON UMBRA!
NEVER!

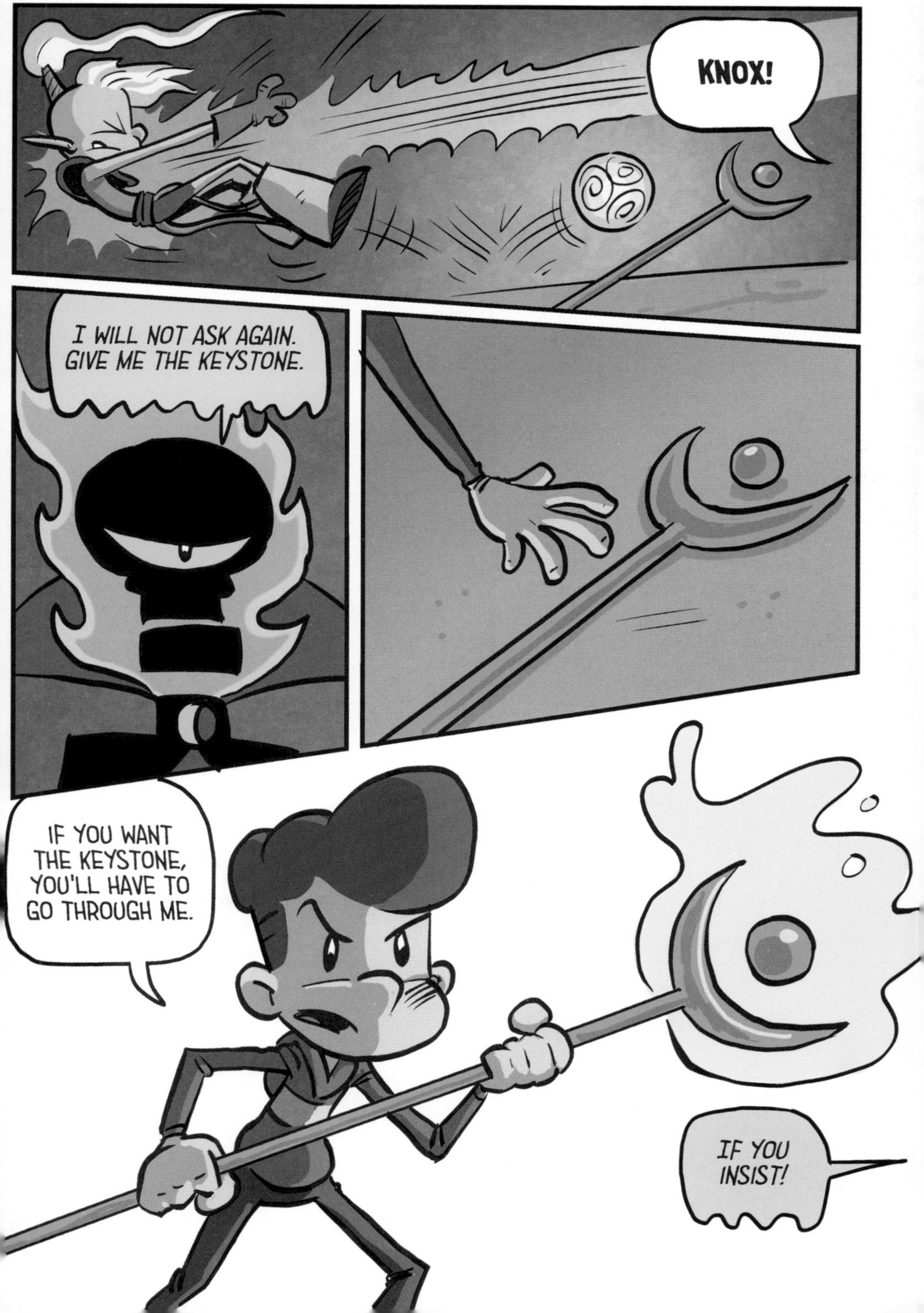
KNOX!
I WILL NOT ASK AGAIN. GIVE ME THE KEYSTONE.
IF YOU WANT THE KEYSTONE, YOU'LL HAVE TO GO THROUGH ME.
IF YOU INSIST!

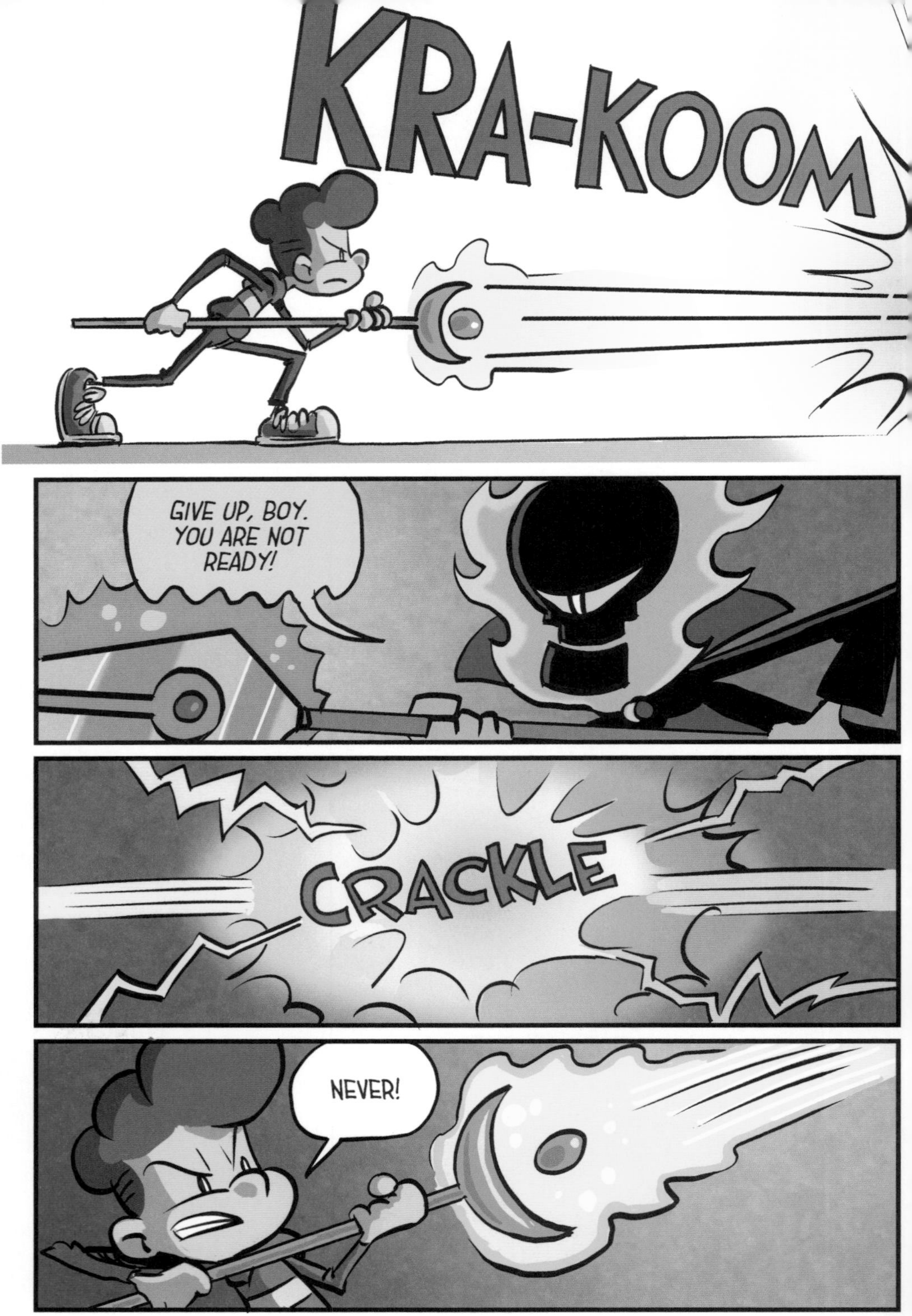
KRA-KOOM
GIVE UP, BOY. YOU ARE NOT READY!
CRACKLE
NEVER!

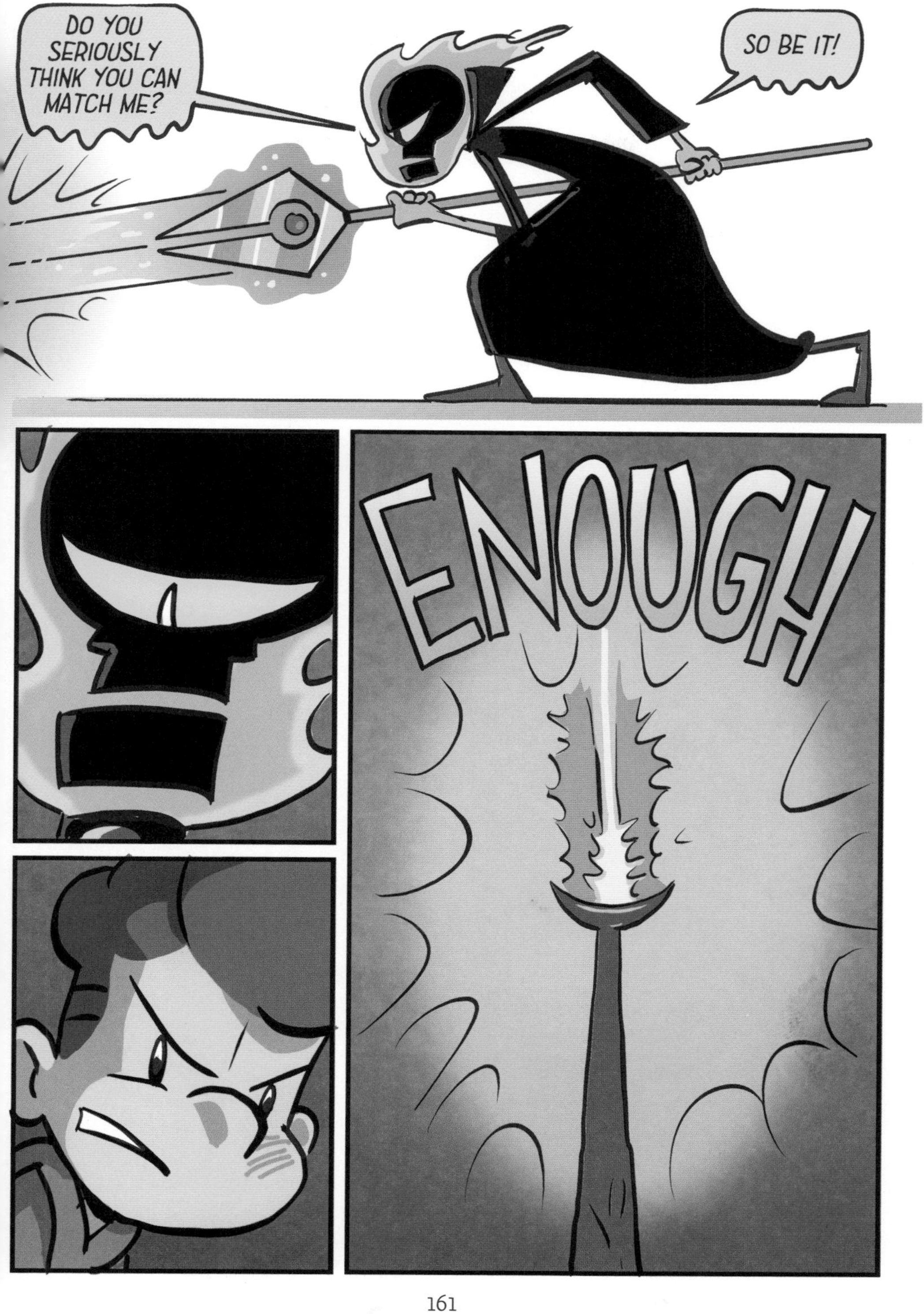
DO YOU SERIOUSLY THINK YOU CAN MATCH ME?
SO BE IT!
ENOUGH

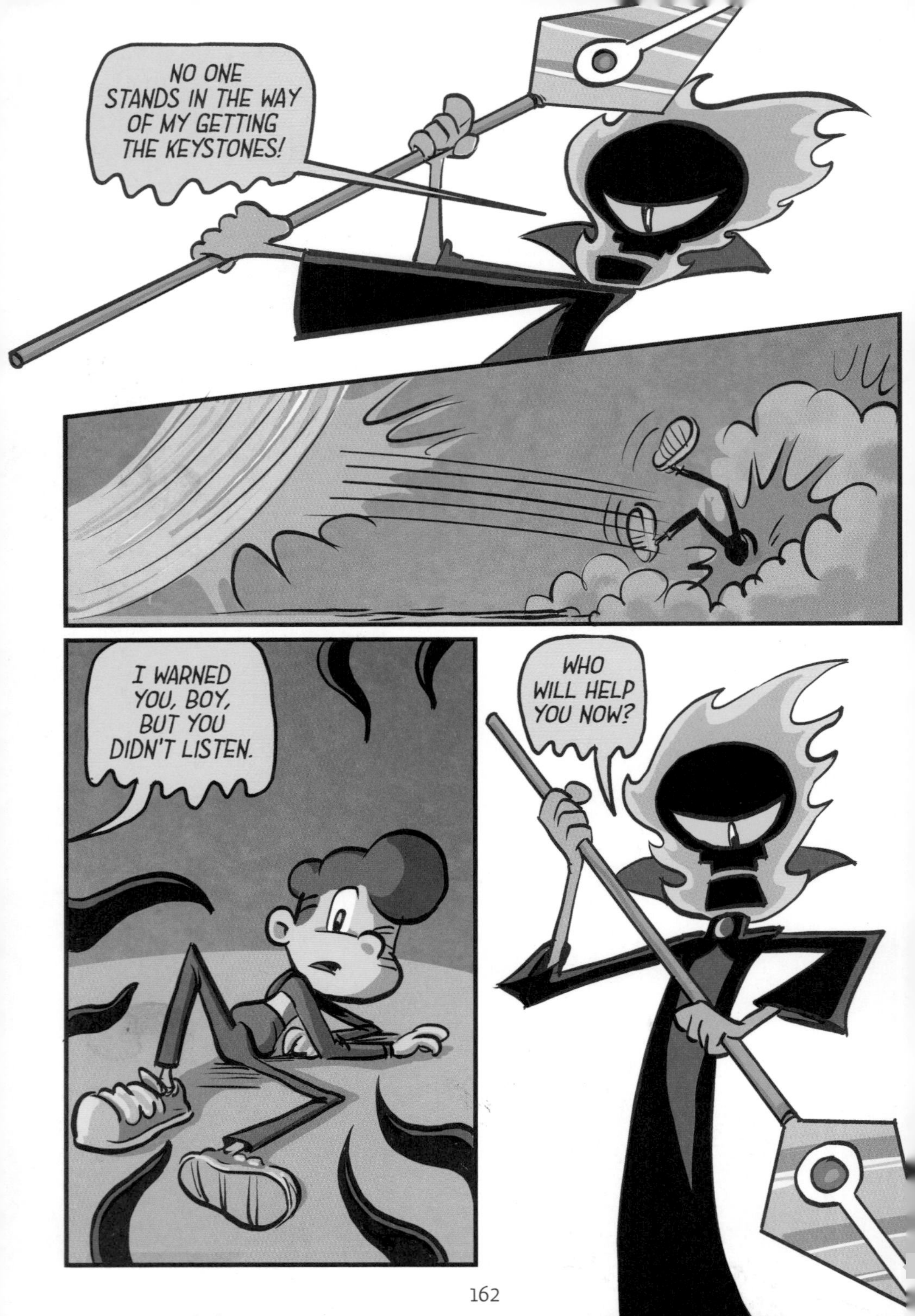
NO ONE STANDS IN THE WAY OF MY GETTING THE KEYSTONES!
I WARNED YOU, BOY, BUT YOU DIDN'T LISTEN.
WHO WILL HELP YOU NOW?

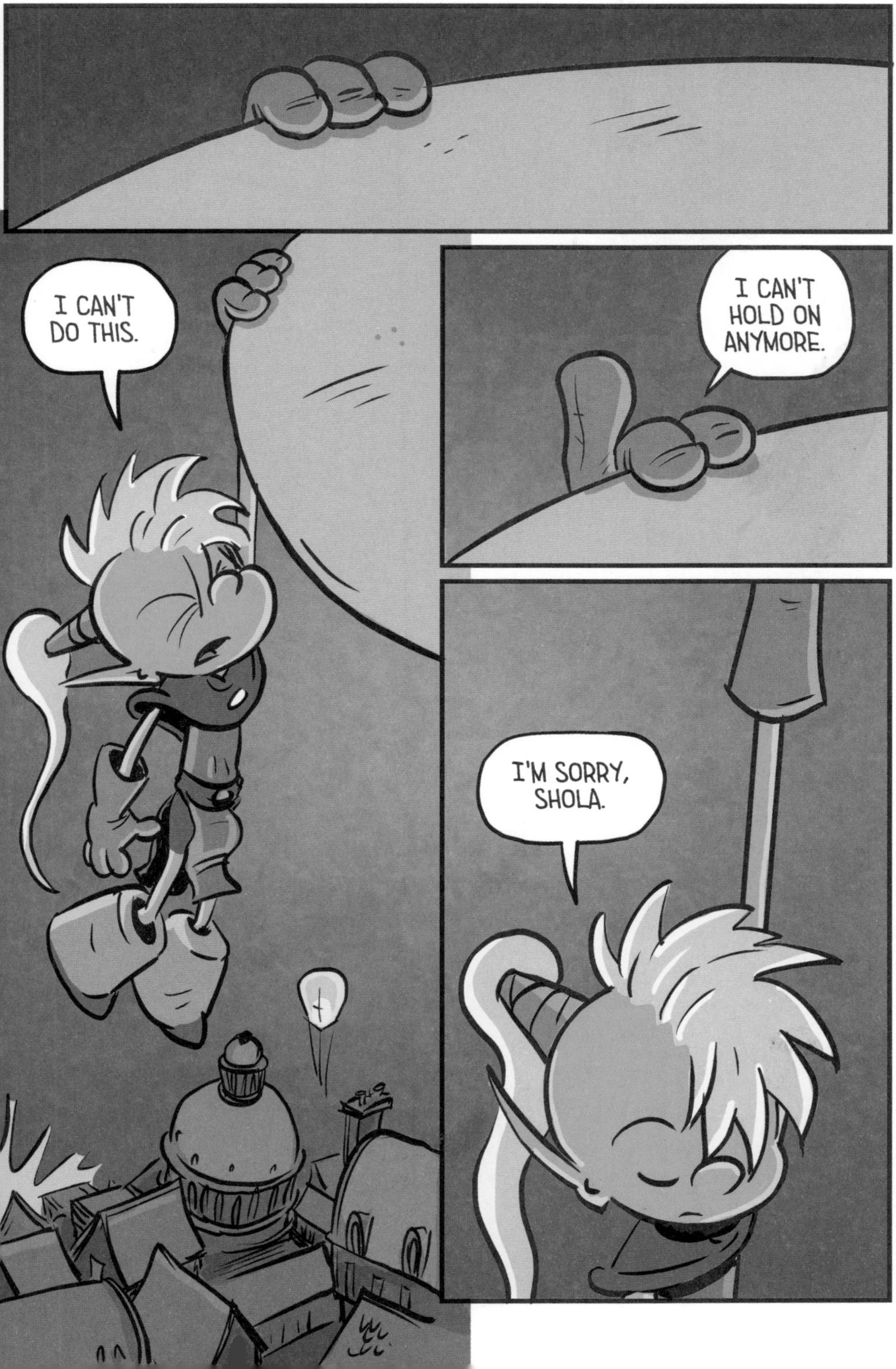
I CAN'T DO THIS.
I CAN'T HOLD ON ANYMORE.
I'M SORRY, SHOLA.

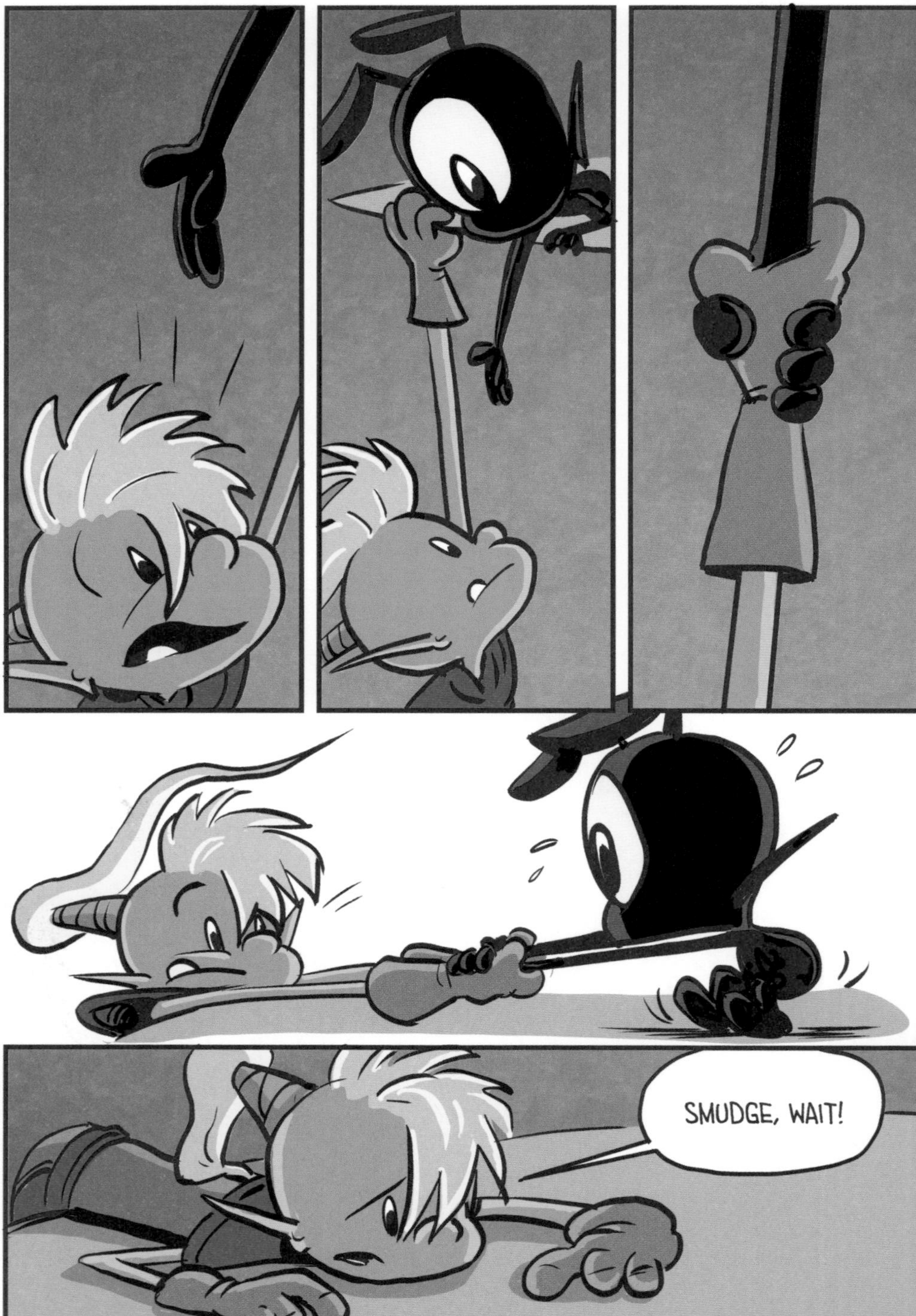
SMUDGE, WAIT!

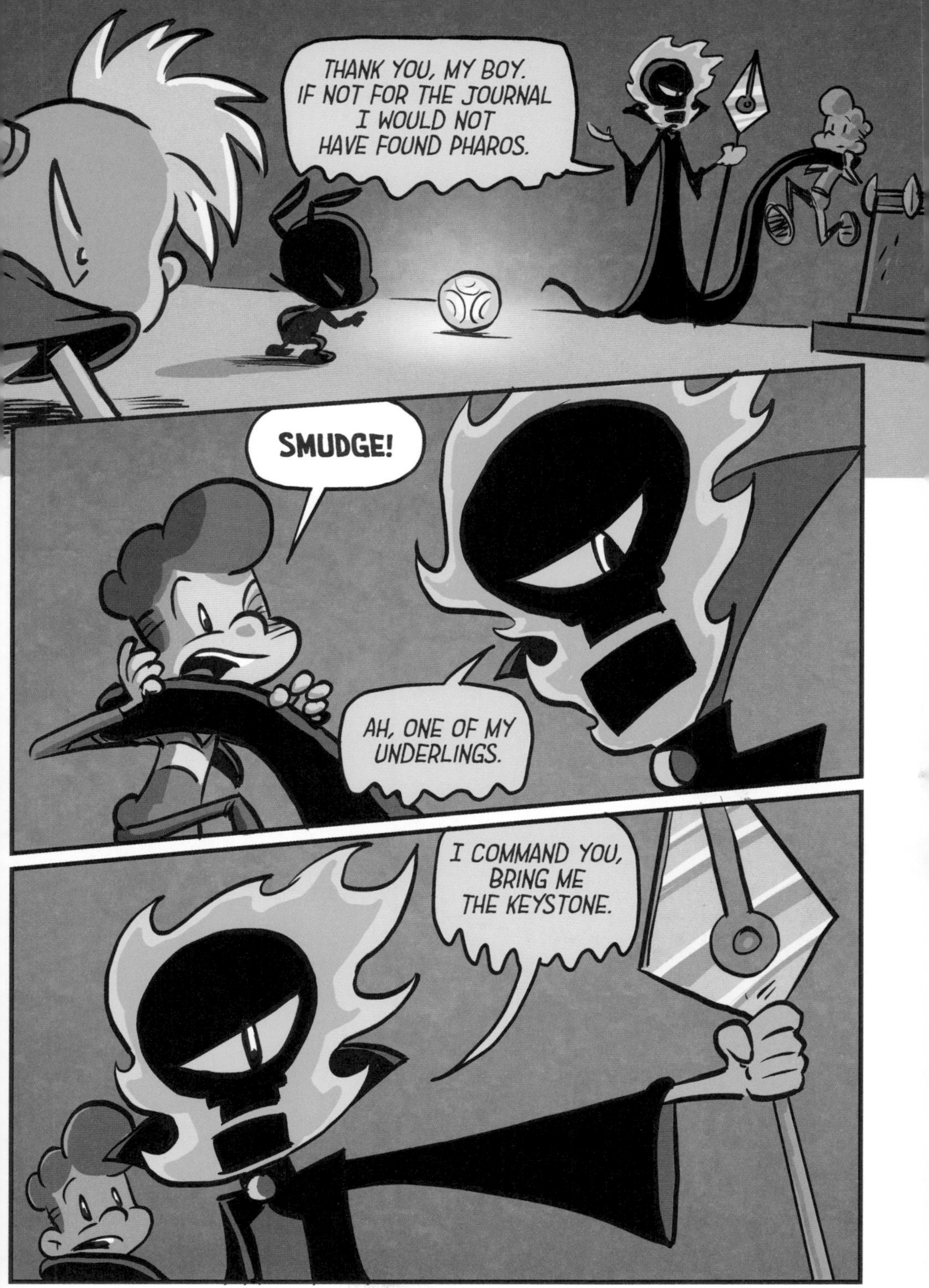
THANK YOU, MY BOY. IF NOT FOR THE JOURNAL I WOULD NOT HAVE FOUND PHAROS.
SMUDGE!
AH, ONE OF MY UNDERLINGS.
I COMMAND YOU, BRING ME THE KEYSTONE.

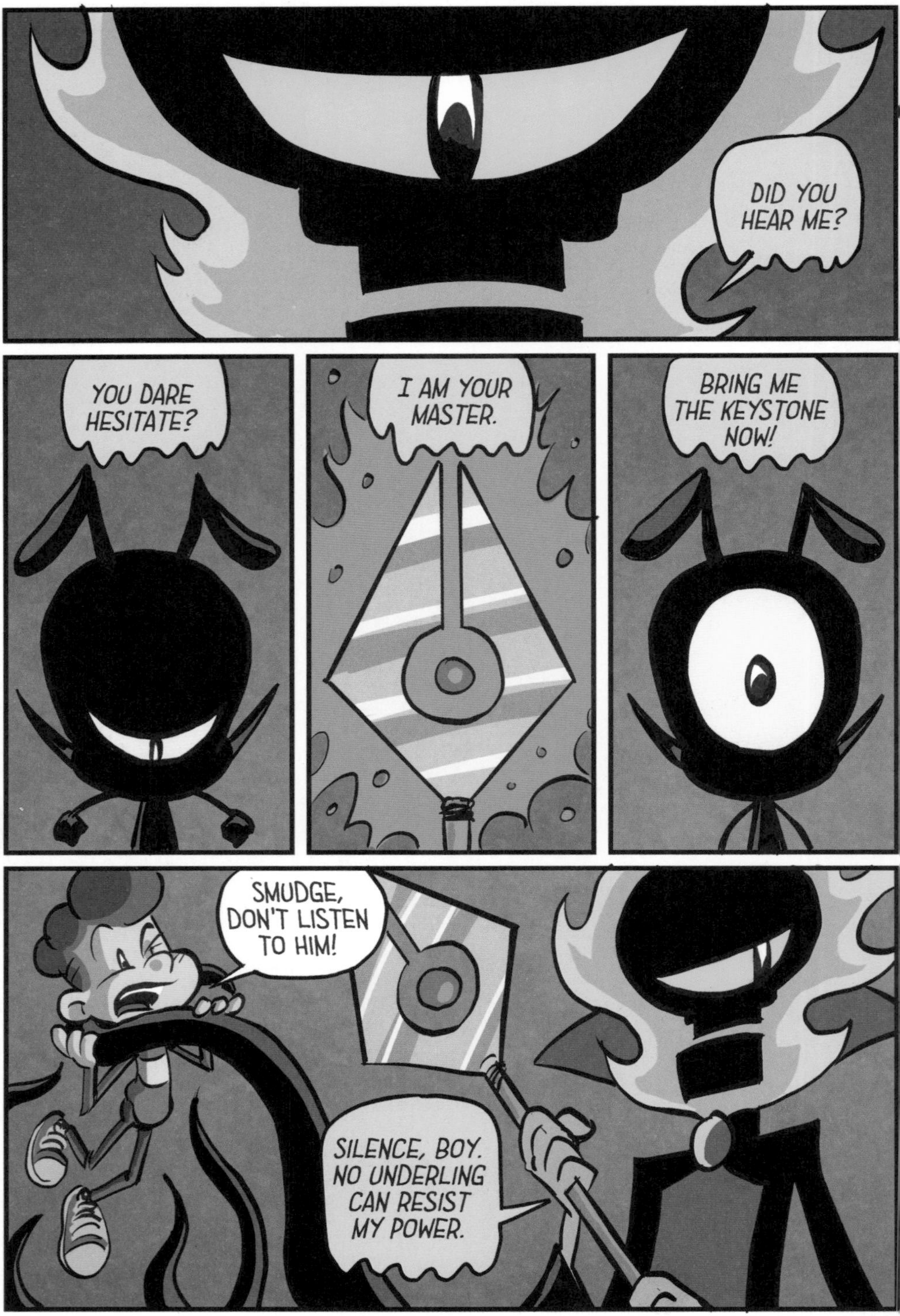
DID YOU HEAR ME?
YOU DARE HESITATE?
I AM YOUR MASTER.
BRING ME THE KEYSTONE NOW!
SMUDGE, DON'T LISTEN TO HIM!
SILENCE, BOY. NO UNDERLING CAN RESIST MY POWER.

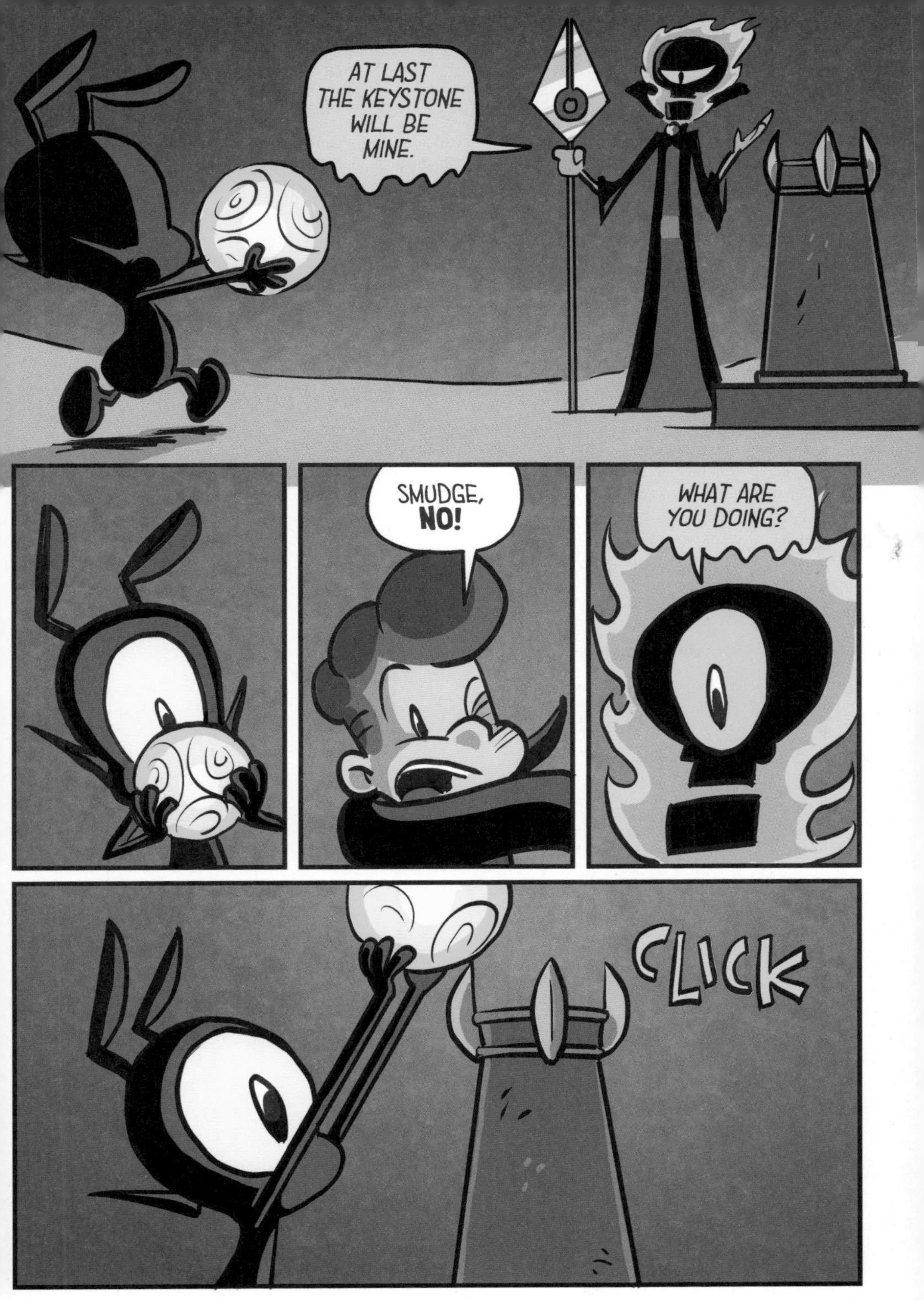
AT LAST THE KEYSTONE WILL BE MINE.
SMUDGE, **NO!**
WHAT ARE YOU DOING?
CLICK

WHOOOOO

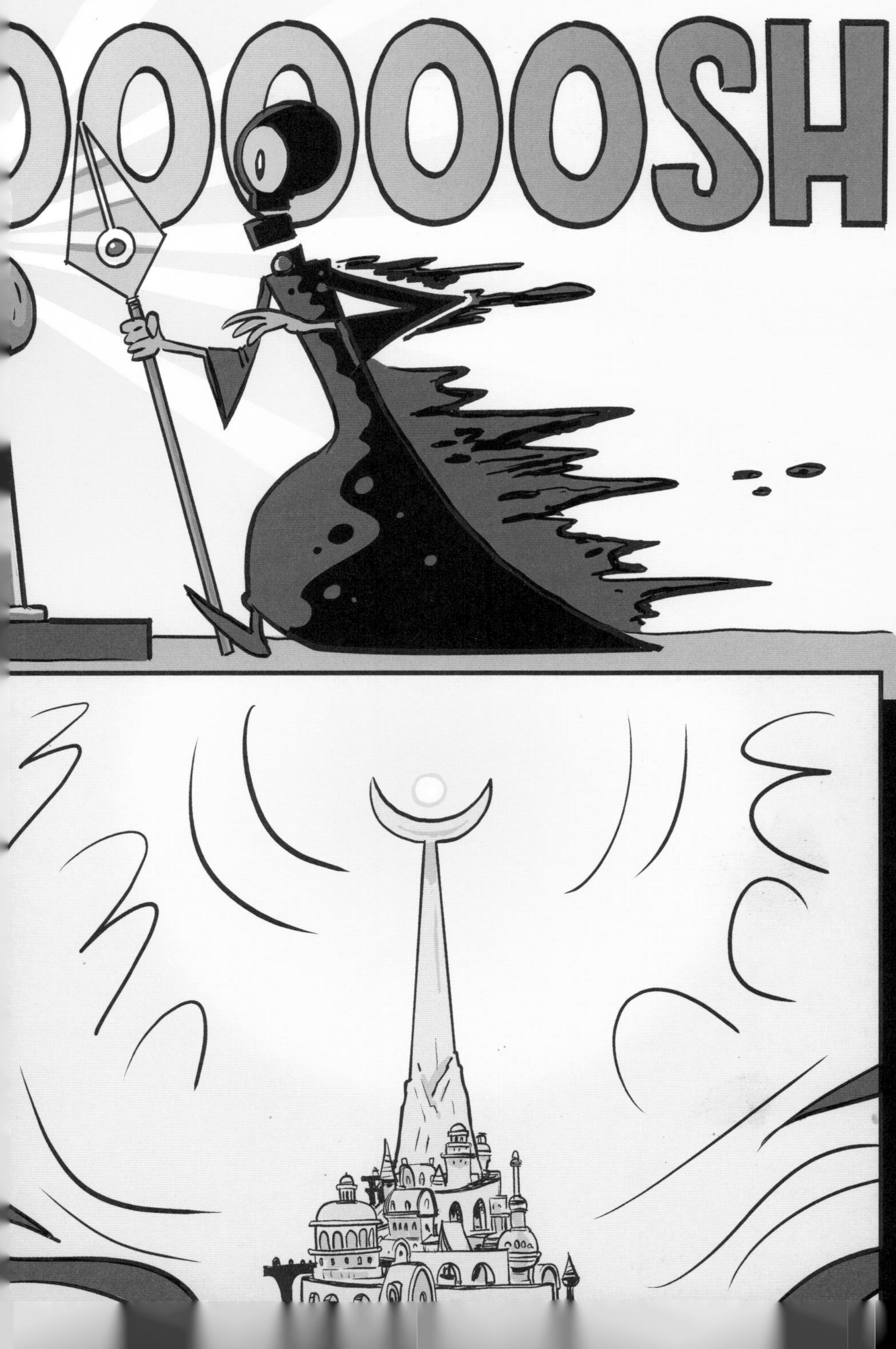
OOOOOSH

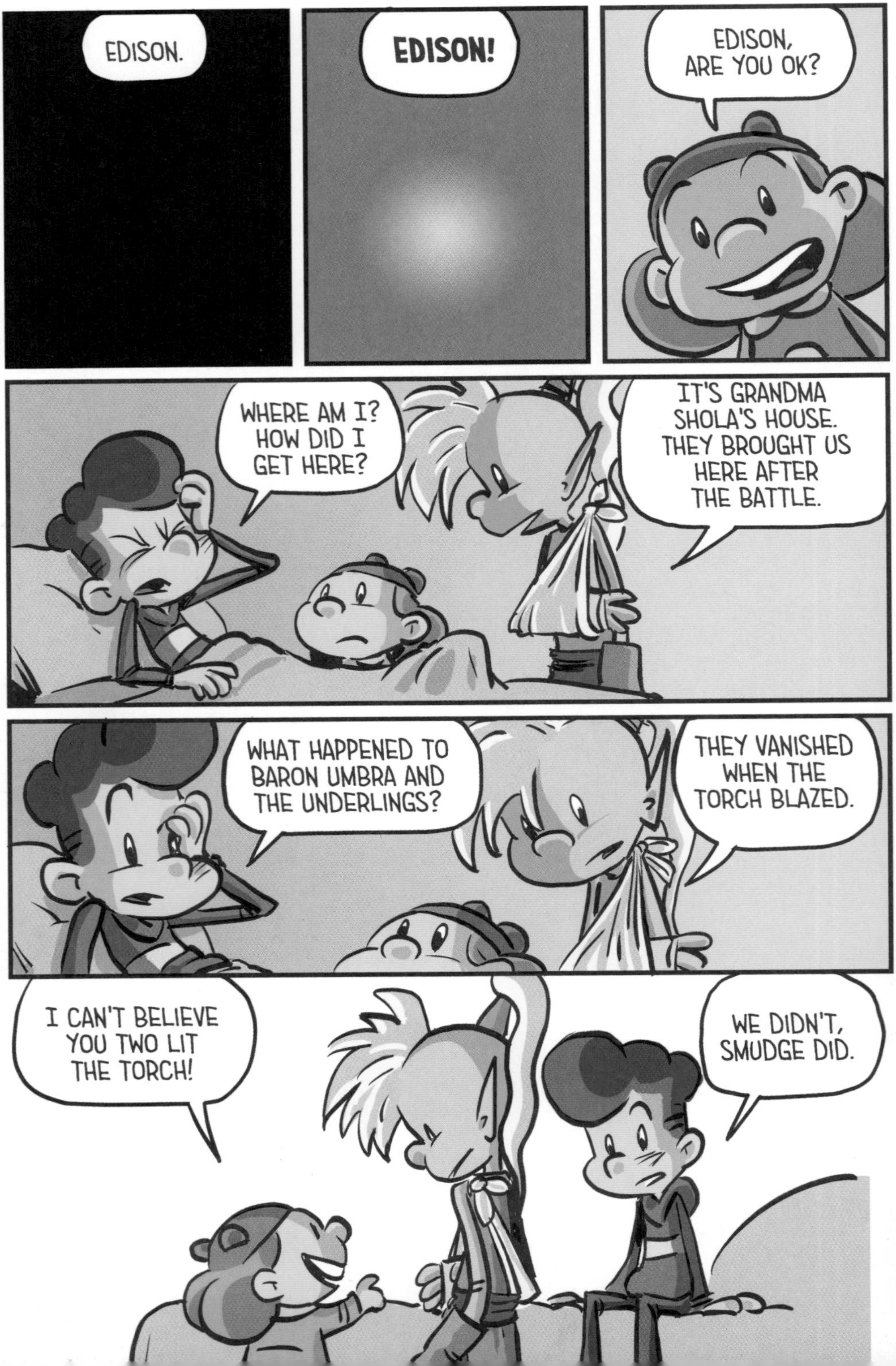
EDISON.
EDISON!
EDISON, ARE YOU OK?
WHERE AM I? HOW DID I GET HERE?
IT'S GRANDMA SHOLA'S HOUSE. THEY BROUGHT US HERE AFTER THE BATTLE.
WHAT HAPPENED TO BARON UMBRA AND THE UNDERLINGS?
THEY VANISHED WHEN THE TORCH BLAZED.
I CAN'T BELIEVE YOU TWO LIT THE TORCH!
WE DIDN'T, SMUDGE DID.

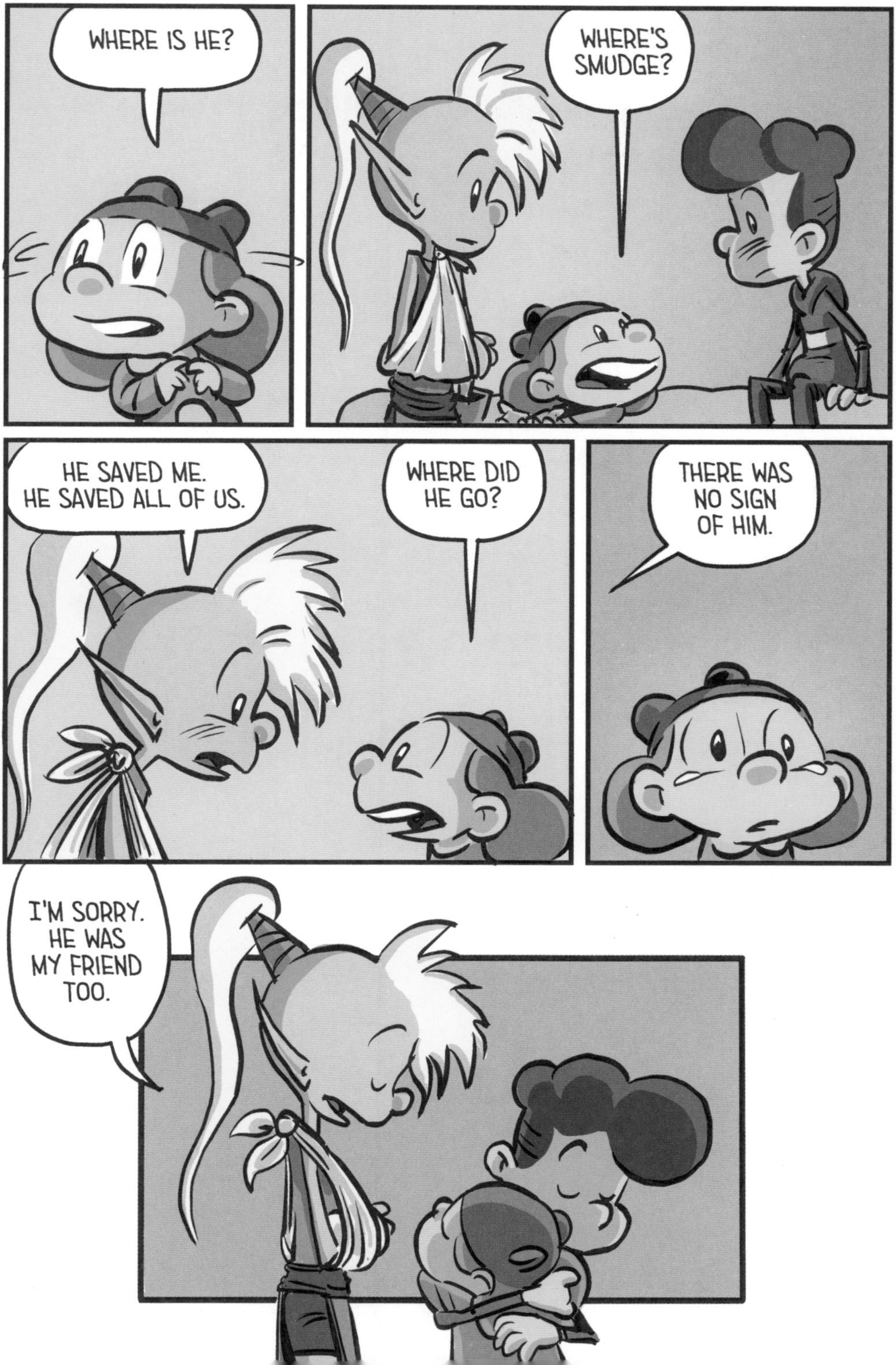
WHERE IS HE?
WHERE'S SMUDGE?
HE SAVED ME. HE SAVED ALL OF US.
WHERE DID HE GO?
THERE WAS NO SIGN OF HIM.
I'M SORRY. HE WAS MY FRIEND TOO.

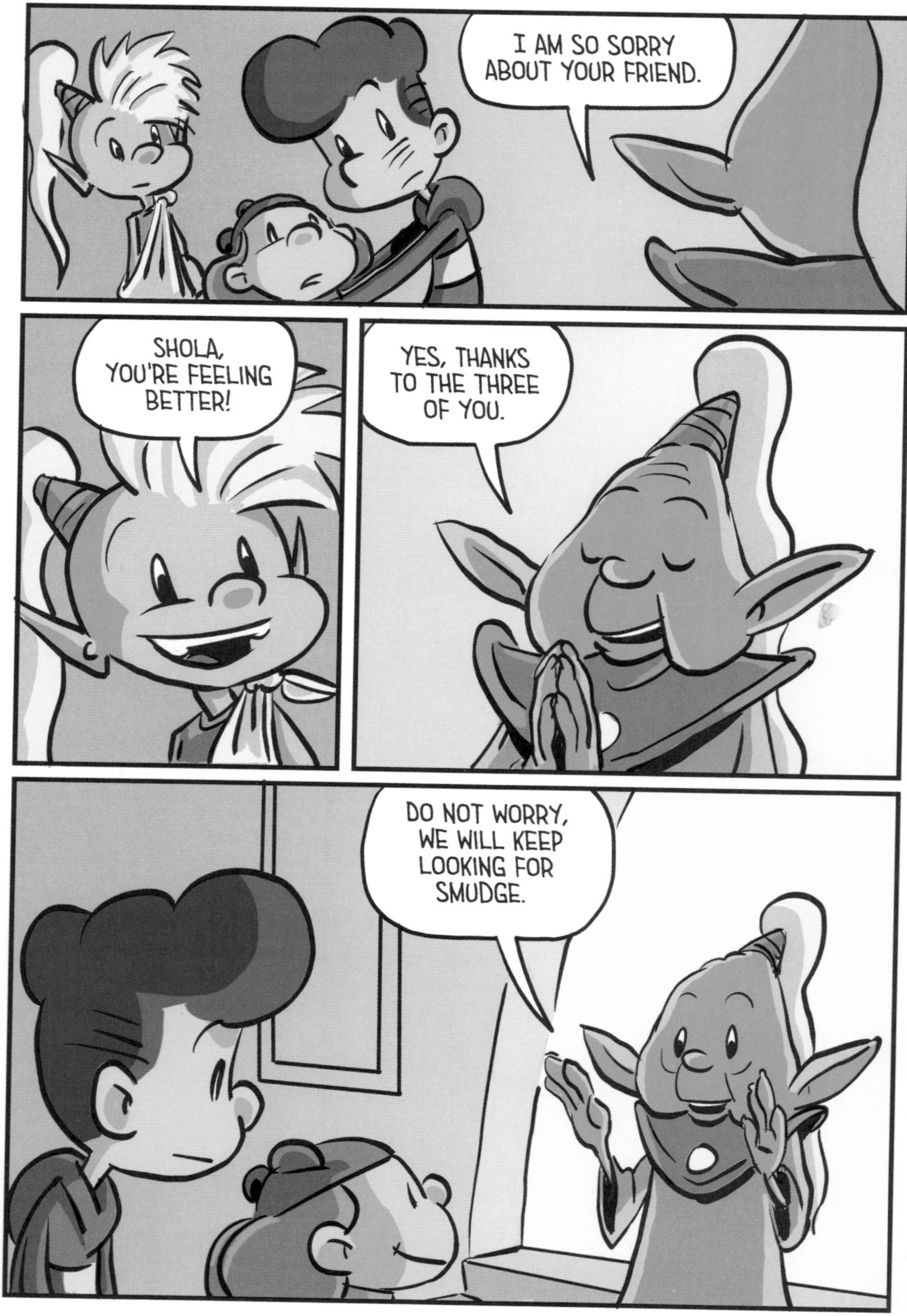
I AM SO SORRY ABOUT YOUR FRIEND.
SHOLA, YOU'RE FEELING BETTER!
YES, THANKS TO THE THREE OF YOU.
DO NOT WORRY, WE WILL KEEP LOOKING FOR SMUDGE.

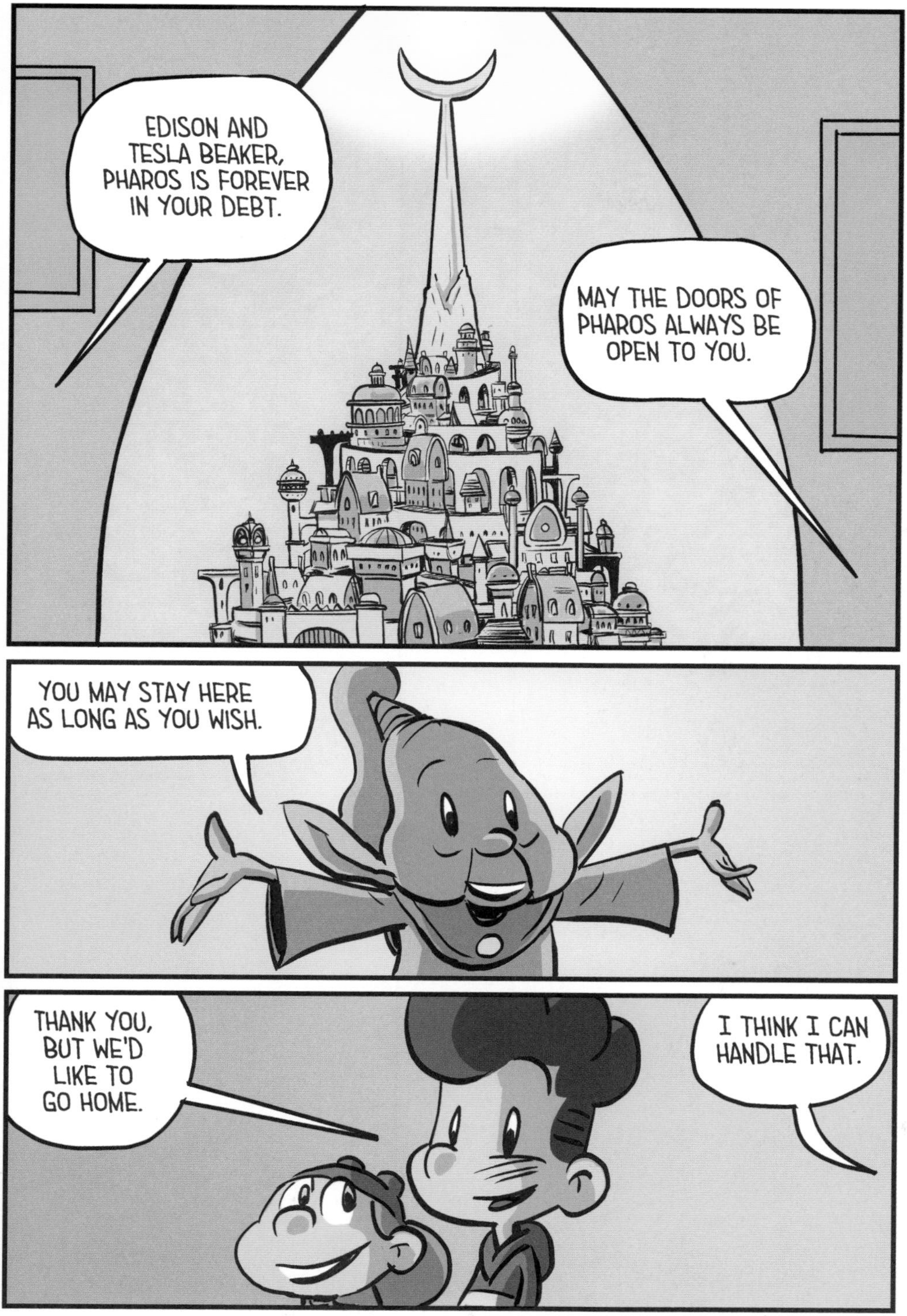
EDISON AND TESLA BEAKER, PHAROS IS FOREVER IN YOUR DEBT.
MAY THE DOORS OF PHAROS ALWAYS BE OPEN TO YOU.
YOU MAY STAY HERE AS LONG AS YOU WISH.
THANK YOU, BUT WE'D LIKE TO GO HOME.
I THINK I CAN HANDLE THAT.

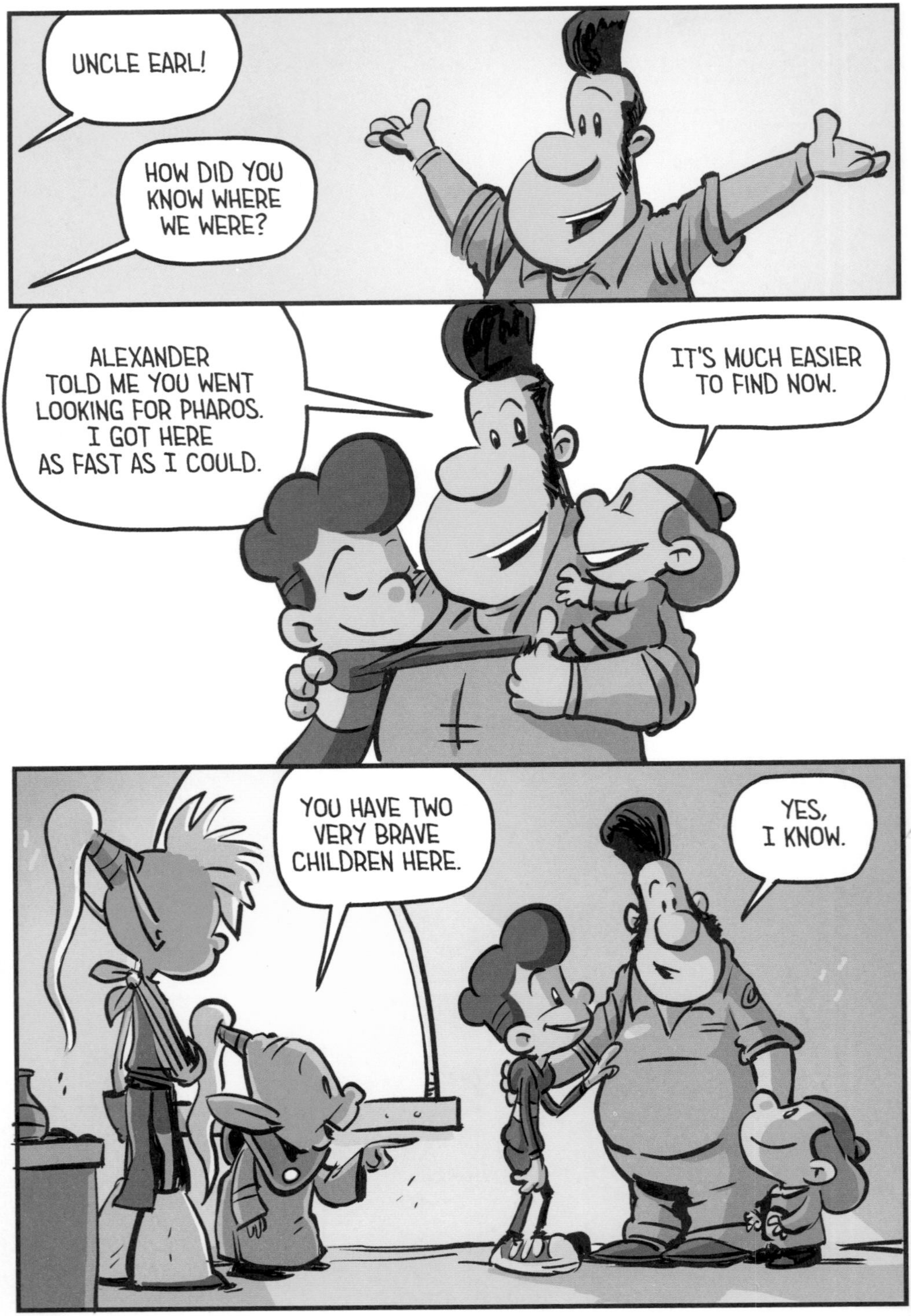
UNCLE EARL!
HOW DID YOU KNOW WHERE WE WERE?
ALEXANDER TOLD ME YOU WENT LOOKING FOR PHAROS. I GOT HERE AS FAST AS I COULD.
IT'S MUCH EASIER TO FIND NOW.
YOU HAVE TWO VERY BRAVE CHILDREN HERE.
YES, I KNOW.

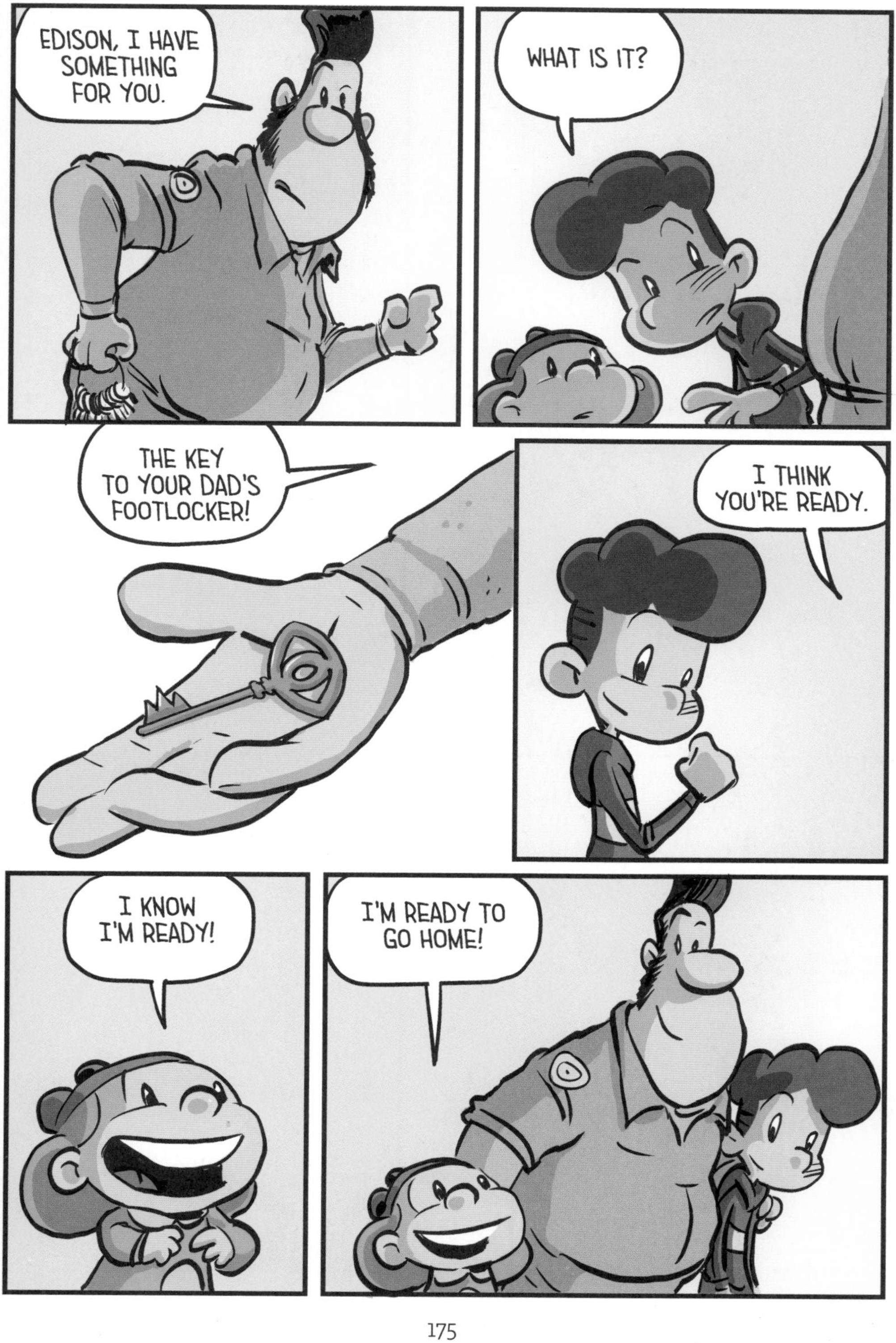
EDISON, I HAVE SOMETHING FOR YOU.
WHAT IS IT?
THE KEY TO YOUR DAD'S FOOTLOCKER!
I THINK YOU'RE READY.
I KNOW I'M READY!
I'M READY TO GO HOME!

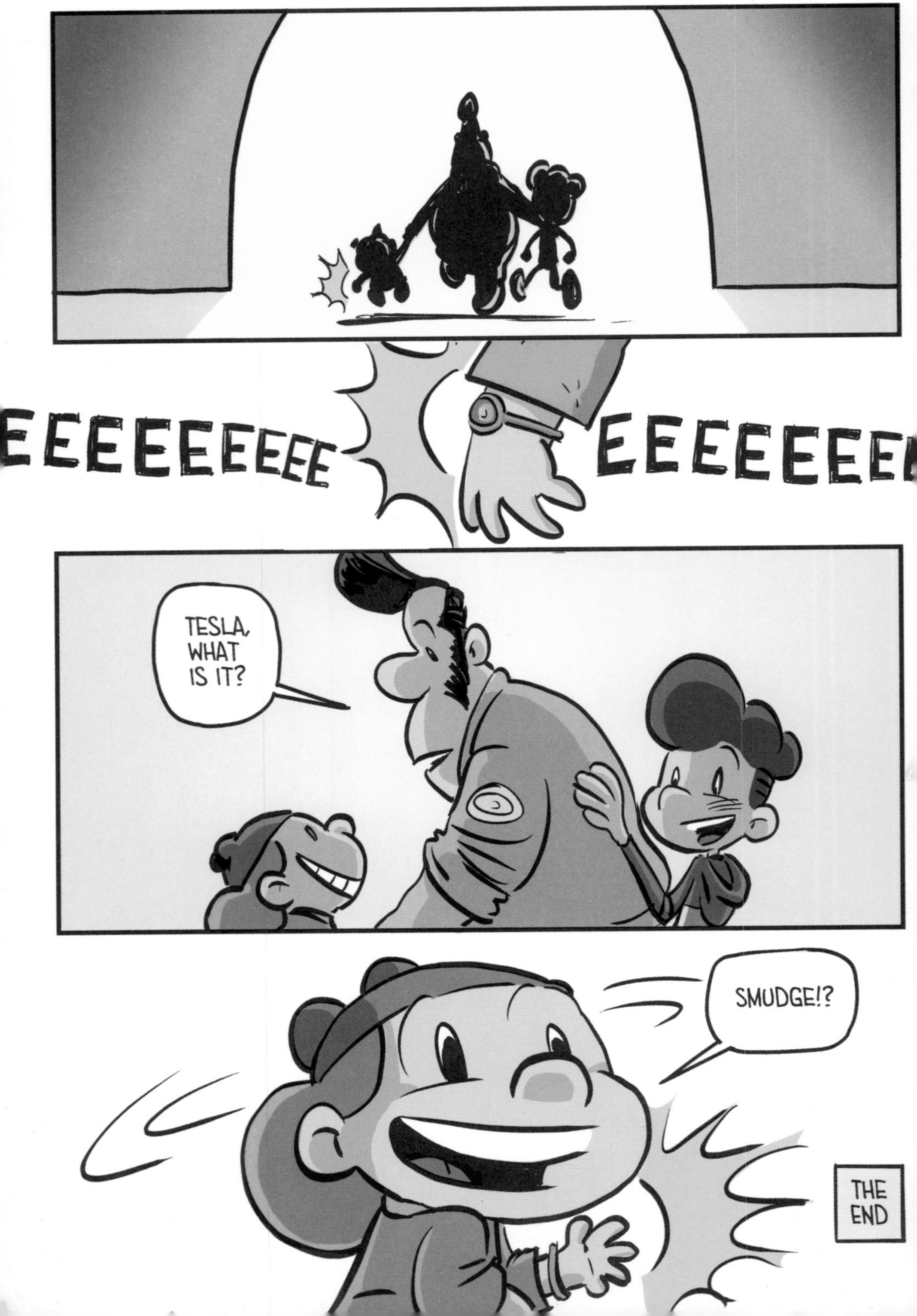
EEEEEEEEEE
EEEEEEEE
TESLA, WHAT IS IT?
SMUDGE!?
THE END